Praise from the UK and Ireland for *Little Constructions*

"[A] brilliant second novel. . . . I can't remember the last time I read prose so profound and so punchy, at once scattergun and forensic. It's like the ink's been made from gunpowder. And every line leaves a darkly sparkling residue that you won't be able to wash off."

—*The Daily Telegraph*

"[Anna Burns] dares to say anything. The writing is energetic, convoluted and courageous. It has a gutsy nervousness that matches the subject matter, as if there is no way to write about violence and violation other than with comedy, digression, wordplay and other peculiarities. . . . Every word matters and the oddities are a joy."

—*The Guardian*

"An exceptionally bold, violent and blackly comic tale. . . . If you give yourself up to Burns's delirious imagination, you'll find much salient wisdom, as well as dark humour." —*Financial Times*

"[A] powerful second novel. . . . Displaying the same dark bite and startling humour as her first, *Little Constructions* explodes into tangents from the opening scene." —*Irish Mail on Sunday*

"At the centre of Anna Burns's novel lies the Doe clan, a closely knit family of criminals and victims whose internal conflicts and convoluted relationships propel this simultaneously funny and terrifying story. Bound by love and loyalty, fear and secrets, the Does make up an unforgettable cast. When unspeakable realities break through, the tale is chilling—and funny." —*Belfast Telegraph*

"Convincingly comic. . . . This is probably the antithesis of the classic holiday novel, which is no bad thing in itself. . . . Bold, funny and unrelenting." —*The Sunday Business Post*

Praise for *Milkman*

"*Milkman* vibrates with the anxieties of our own era, from terrorism to sexual harassment to the blinding divisions that make reconciliation feel impossible. . . . It's as though the intense pressure of this place has compressed the elements of comedy and horror to produce some new alloy."   —*The Washington Post*

"Few works of fiction see as clearly as this one how violence deforms social networks, enhancing people's worst instincts. . . . This book is also bursting with energy, with tiny apertures of kindness, and a youthful kind of joy. . . . *Milkman* is a triumph of resistance."
    —*The Boston Globe*

"Among Burns's singular strengths as a writer is her ability to address the topics of trauma and tyranny with a playfulness that somehow never diminishes the sense of her absolute seriousness. . . . For all the darkness of the world it illuminates, *Milkman* is as strange and variegated and brilliant as a northern sunset."   —*Slate*

"[Burns's] style powerfully evokes the narrator's sense of emotional entrapment. . . . *Milkman* makes a passionate claim for freethinking in a place where monochromatic, us-versus-them ideology prevails."
    —*USA Today*

"Brutally intelligent. . . . At its core, *Milkman* is a wildly good and true novel of how living in fear limits people."   —NPR.org

"Seething with black humor and adolescent anger at the adult world and its brutal absurdities. . . . For a novel about life under multifarious forms of totalitarian control—political, gendered, sectarian, communal—*Milkman* can be charmingly wry."   —*The New Yorker*

"*Milkman* is an explosive novel, very much *of* history but not limited by the names, dates, and places of the official record. It's a more intimate work than that, and an outstanding contribution to the growing canon of nameless girl heroes."   —*The New Republic*

Little Constructions

Also by Anna Burns

Milkman
No Bones
Mostly Hero

Little Constructions

A Novel

ANNA BURNS

Graywolf Press

First published in Great Britain by Fourth Estate in 2007

Permission to quote from The Chambers Dictionary gratefully acknowledged.
The Chambers Dictionary (1993) © Chambers Harrap Publishers Ltd.

This publication is made possible, in part, by the voters of Minnesota through
a Minnesota State Arts Board Operating Support grant, thanks to a legis-
lative appropriation from the arts and cultural heritage fund. Significant
support has also been provided by Target, the McKnight Foundation, the
Lannan Foundation, the Amazon Literary Partnership, and other generous
contributions from foundations, corporations, and individuals. To these or-
ganizations and individuals we offer our heartfelt thanks.

Published by Graywolf Press
250 Third Avenue North, Suite 600
Minneapolis, Minnesota 55401

www.graywolfpress.org

Published in the United States of America

ISBN 978-1-64445-013-0

2 4 6 8 9 7 5 3 1
First Graywolf Paperback, 2020

Library of Congress Control Number: 2019933472

Cover design: Kapo Ng

For Magdalen, in friendship

Chapter One

There are no differences between men and women. No differences. Except one. Men want to know what sort of gun it is. Women just want the gun. The door of the gunshop went ding! on Friday as Jetty Doe burst through it on a mission. This was annoyed Jetty Doe, the one who had knifed her mammy once, and not her less-annoyed cousin called Jotty, who hadn't. Doe headed straight for the gun counter and interrupted a conversation about ufology.

'I'm telling you, Tom,' the man in front of the counter was saying to the owner behind it, 'I'm telling you. Any extra-terrestrial that doesn't look as we look can't have our best interests at—'

'Want a gun!' cried Doe, cutting in across them. 'Gimme a gun! Gimme that gun there!'

The startled owner looked at her. He recognised her too. It was one of those Doe women, the one whose name began with 'J'. He looked along her thrusting finger to the Kalashnikov displayed magnificently in the counter case in front of them.

'This?' he said. 'Well, that's a—'

'Don't care. Gimme it.'

'But don't you want—'

'What?'

'With a weapon—'

'What?'

'You can't just—'

'What? What!'

She stared at him, lip curling, snout forming, snarl gathering. What was this creature? she thought. The owner, meanwhile, decided to mistake the stare, bared teeth and strange little throatie sounds for a settling down to listen, for a quiet and graceful episode of listening. She was now going to listen to what he had to say. He opened his mouth.

'Shut up! Just shut up! Gimme a gun and shut up, will ye?' she said.

Each stared, astonished at the other's rudeness, but she was busy, so she snatched the gun off him as he was taking it carefully out of the case to show it to her. Shoving it under her arm, she then scraped around in her handbag for a bunch of money, threw it, without counting, at the man's face, then turned and the door went ding! as she left. They heard her yell 'Taxi!' from the pavement. Another thing she did before leaving was grab a fistful of bullets that were lined up and being leisurely examined by the other man on the stool beside her. She even reached over and took the ones he had in his hand. She didn't glance at this person, nor did she throw another batch of coins in return for what she'd taken. She gave no inkling either of any further payments to come.

One quick thing to say before I go back to the gunshop is that Jetty Doe was really a Doe, but often others only socially connected with the Doe family also went under that umbrella. It was shorthand – similar to the way crimes happened in war zones. All crimes in such places got connected with the war, lumped together with the war, as if they were a part of it, as if they were because of it, and this happened whether they were because of it or not.

Back to the shop. Gunshop Tom was picking up coins and counting them with shaky fingers but he wasn't taking in what he was counting because he was in shock at the violence of that encounter. Over a year earlier – as long as that, if you count that as long – he had been mugged and stabbed on the way home from work by a bunch of teenagers and anything sudden frightened him ever since. Sneak up behind him and whisper the word 'Friday!' – the day it had happened – and he'll physiologically react for you. Say the words 'Friday night!' and he'll faint.

'Did you see that, Tom?' he said, for it turned out both men were called Tom. 'Did you see? She didn't want to know if it was an AK47 or an AK74. She called it a *gun.*'

Second Tom nodded. He appeared more calm, detached and well-adjusted than First Tom, but who can say what repression people carry around for years?

'I saw, Tommy,' he said, 'but not your problem. You tried to give advice. She batted away your advice. I witnessed it. She said, "Don't want any fucky advice." So, not your fault she's uptight and sore.'

'But did you see the way she grabbed up your pellets from the counter? She even took the ones you had in your hand!'

Customer Tom nodded again, but really he was thinking, ah, holy God, Tom's losing it. His voice is rising and this is exactly the way he was sounding at the hospital. That bloody woman's started him off on to that muggin' thing all over again!

'They're not even modern pellets, never mind bullets!' went on Tom, his voice indeed getting higher and shriekier. 'And she didn't notice! Did you notice that she didn't notice? They're museum pieces as I was telling you. Nobody uses them except as antique ornaments now. How's she's goin' to manage? She's goin' to shoot duck, isn't she? Do you think she's goin' to shoot duck? It would be duck she's after, wouldn't it, Tom? Tom, wouldn't you say she's made a mistake in her choice of weapon? Surely, she wouldn't have chosen the '74 if she'd thought in her heart it wasn't meant for duck?'

Customer Tom shrugged and picked up his egg and onion sandwich. The shop doubled as a café, selling snacks, soft drinks and second-class postage stamps. Tom didn't answer and also he wouldn't look at Tom as he was trying to discourage his old friend from what he knew was really the mugging encounter. He bit into his mid-morning sandwich therefore, still in his re-laxed easy-go manner as Gunshop Tom, now with a pronounced verbal tremor, hurried on.

'Incompatible!' he cried. 'Completely the wrong hardware.' He kept wiping and rewiping his cheek to get the touch of that money – but really, the awful woman it had come from – off. 'The '74 is portable, low-tech and of the utmost efficiency in killing people, but that consignment of pellets was originally meant for shooting duck. Even if she'd rushed off with a light birding piece though, instead of the Kalashnikov, she'd still have to hit the duck first time. If she didn't, she'd have to stand up to reload with the weapon she'd need those pellets for, and of course the duck would see her and have plenty of time to fly off. That's presuming it even appeared, for ducks around here are all dead now. But even if they weren't, she doesn't have a light birding piece. She'd need an eighteenth-century one and I don't sell them. Tom? Hey, Tom – that Kalashnikov – if you were tak-ing a guess, what would you say really, from the bottom of your heart, she's wanting it for?'

'Tommy,' said Tom. 'I think you're working yourself up again. Have a cup of tea. D'you want me to make it? This is nothing.

Just another of them women things. Whatever you do, don't let it link in with anything from your past.'

Tommy, who was now pulling at his cheek where she'd indirectly touched it, and rubbing at his abdomen where they'd purposefully stuck the knife in, showed that it was already too late. The woman thing had linked in very nicely thank you with something from his past. He made an effort, however, just as the doctor at the hospital had instructed him. 'If it comes into your head,' said this doctor who, after all, must have had some experience of what he was on about, 'just pop it back out. *Pop it back out.* Don't let it defy you. Don't let it defeat you. Let it know you're master here now.' So when Tom realised he was slipping back to Friday night, that he wasn't master, that he couldn't do any popping, and that, because of this new shock, his hamstrings and backside were now crawling, he left his abdomen and face alone and tried to get back to where he and Tom had left off. Where had they left off? Oh, yes. Extra-terrestrials.

'When you say—' he began.

'Forget it,' came back Tom.

'But don't at least some—'

'Nope.'

'Aren't they interested—'

'Nope.'

'What about—'

'They don't care about that either.'

Instead of being reassured by these bits of information about women, as any normal man would have been, Tom got more and more agitated. Try as he might, he couldn't get himself back to the ufology at hand. Not only was he feeling frightened and powerless because his nervous system was letting him down again, he was now also getting annoyed and upset at what appeared to be the downplaying of his emotional pain by Tom.

'What's wrong, Tom?' he said. 'Is it that you want me to shut up? Is it that I'm doin' your head in? Is it that I'm not cheerful enough for you? Not my fault, y'know. I didn't ask to be mugged and stabbed.'

Tom sighed and set down his sandwich. 'Seems we're getting off the point here, mate. Don't take it out on me.' He shifted uncomfortably on his stool and wouldn't look at Tom who was directly across the counter from him. 'I'm sorry you got stabbed, okay? We were all sorry. When you were in the hospital we were in the bar being sorry. But that was a year ago. Not our fault. And it's not my fault now that that woman busted into your shop.'

They fell silent. Tom behind the counter looked down at the silver in his hand, but really he was thinking that, although of course, of course, *oh, of course*, it hadn't been his old friends who had mugged and stabbed and hospitalised him, it just kept seeming to some part of his mind that it had. Tom, in front of the counter, stabbed at the crumbs on it which had broken off from his bigger bread, but really, he was thinking that although Tom had always been a decent auld skin, someone he'd known for ages, and a great one once to have a laugh with, it was just that ever since that incident with the teenagers, he'd either been alienating himself from everybody with his verbal splurging, or else brooding himself to death with his thoughts.

The silence was about to come to an end, for Tom, the customer, was tossing a mental coin as whether to ask for another cup of coffee to see if they could get easy footing back between them, or whether to give up, get off the stool and say, 'See you later then, Tom. I'm away.' Instead of either happening, the door went ding!, the men glanced at each other, then, how stupid they'd been ran through both their heads. It stood to reason that if that monster couldn't get the rifle to work, then of course she was going to come back, even more monsterish, in order to get a replacement. Having seen her in such a hurry to get it, they'd fooled themselves into thinking that, once out of the shop, she'd forever and alleluia be gone.

The ding! wasn't Jetty Doe – who was heading east in a temper in a taxi – and it wasn't a female either. It was two females. And the two males in the shop looked at them in consternation. 'We're closed,' Gunshop Tom wanted to say, but he couldn't say anything for he was still coming from trauma and when you're in trauma you can't move. Oh fuck, thought the other Tom. Now Tom'll really get into the muggin'. Please, God. Please, please, God, make them go away without saying anything, make Tom not talk about his hamstrings, about his legs giving way underneath him, about them kicking him, running away, then running back to re-kick him, slipping their hands into his pockets, rifling through his ribcage, turning him over to the back pockets to see what was in there. If he does go into that, God, then please don't make him go further into the unexpectedness of the knife, or the nightmares, or the roughness of them doctors, or the avoidance of us as he saw it – for it wasn't, we didn't, or else he drove us to it, God – or about the dalliance, indifference, interruptions and mockery of them other boyos, those bastards, the police.

'What's wrong with you two?' said one of the newcomers. 'You look like you seen a ghost.' This was Jennifer Doe, who wasn't really a Doe, but best friend of Janet Doe, one of the two people Jetty in the taxi was looking for at that moment. Janet Doe was legitimately a Doe and had been even before she'd gotten married to one. Janet's wedding day had been her

First Great Occasion. Her Second Great Occasion had been the day she was employed to work at the Almost Chemist of the Year. But more of Janet later. She wasn't the other female present at this juncture. The other female was Julie Doe, her daughter. Janet's daughter.

'Hello, Tom. Hello, Tom,' said Julie. Julie was friendly and gentle, and for that the two Toms were grateful. At least there was a fifty per cent chance they weren't going to be shouted at, but they lost by fifty per cent because they were. Jennifer, the elder, having had enough of their imbecilic stupefaction, squashed the butt of her cigarette into the floor and, taking out another pencil-length kingsize, said, 'Leave this to me, Julie love.' Scowling at the men, she exhaled a barrelful of cigarette smoke, cracked her psychotic bubble gum and charged up to the counter to confront.

Before going on, I suggest a quiet contemplation on the thing women. When I say women, I don't know if that's technically correct. We're talking about an older woman and a younger woman here maybe. Or maybe one woman and a teenager. Or is it one woman and a child? For you see, fifteen, what does that mean? Are you grown up when you start menstruating? Are you grown up when you develop breasts and curvy bits about you? Do you become an adult when you have sex willingly or unwillingly for the first time? I don't know. But I would say that the best way to describe Julie Doe would be to forget all that in relation to this person and know that, if 'grown up' is being able to tell the difference between respecting the highest of moral orders and just grabbing, then this fifteen-year-old was older than her mother's thirtysomething friend. Jennifer Doe, in contrast, was pure grabber.

Jennifer banged the counter with the slap of her hand and cracked her bubble gum explosively. She had a habit of making noise – unless around the men in her life, when she could take a back seat and let them make it for her. Making noise is not a bad thing, mind. It depends on the surrounding vibrations. The vibrations in Tom's gunshop these days, however, were a brand new baby, delicate and fragile and very given to shattering. The psychic cords in this gunshop could be destroyed by the lightest of a bad touch.

'Has Jetty, JanineJoshuatine or Janet Doe been in here looking for a gun or something?' Jennifer's voice was sharp, exactly as her ancestral females' had been before her. But it didn't used to be. It used to come from way down in her body, around the area of her toeline, and it would travel up with joy and out her throat on a sweet note. And that was nice. That was very nice. And that was a long time ago. Hearing her question, Customer Tom Cusack, who was on the same side of the counter as she was, jumped off his stool in obvious alarm.

'One of them's been in,' he said. 'One of them women. Are the others meant to be expected in also?'

Jennifer ignored him, for who the fuck was he anyway?

'Look listen you,' she said, finger up and pointing at the other Tom. She was trying to pinpoint him with a stare into looking back. This was proving a fluid situation. Every time she nearly hit home, his eyes slid under hers like liquid doing a runner, he'd be away down the plughole, there'd be a burp, a burst of a bubble, and he'd be gone. Instead of being triumphant, as any bully would be at getting the high ground, Jennifer Doe, in her habitual impatience, was annoyed by it immensely.

'Which of them was it and did you sell a gun to her?' she shouted. 'Well, did you? What's wrong with you? You're like a statue with slidy eyes. Are you sick in the head or what?'

Reality was, she was most disgusted with this person. She'd

9

heard a rumour from a reliability that Gunshop Tom Spaders *was* sick in the head, that something had happened to him once and that he was refusing to get over it. Must have been days ago too, she thought. What age was he anyway? Mid-thirties? More than mid-thirties? That's embarrassing. Only an auld ginny-ann of a man wouldn't be over whatever it was by now.

With everyone staring, Tom tried to say something out of a mouth that could hardly open. It was supposed to be about ducks, but Jennifer jumped, thinking he'd said fucks, and made a move to heave herself over the high counter to get at him. Julie stepped in just in time.

'Aunt Jennie,' she reasoned, her hands on the enraged concrete bolster now being aided back down from the counter. 'If it is Aunt Jetty – as we think it is – we know she'll have been and gone and got a gun, and we know also where it'll be she's heading with it. It couldn't be Mamma, for Mamma never seems to think she's in danger and so will be at work as usual at the Almost Chemist of the Year. If it's Aunt Janine – but isn't she on holiday? – then that would be the worst that could happen, but even then there'd be no point in rushing to prevent it because all the damage, I suppose, would be done.' Aunt Janine, for the record, was JanineJuliaJoshuatine Doe, a very strange and unwomanly woman. People say she'd done or been around that many injurings and killings that she was now looked upon practically as a very man herself. But that's sexist so I don't say it. How shall I put it? It wasn't the murders anyway, or the ruthless amoral aspect of her that worried most people. It was the Saturday afternoon shopping expeditions in town. She'd bump into people and knock them over without seeing them and without apologising to them, and certainly without bending over and helping to pick them back up. She also had a habit of adjusting and readjusting earplugs, and of muttering 'No No No! Get off!' all the time. Thing was, she was embarrassing and odd just in herself. Take her appearance, which in this case was indicative of the inner construct of a disturbed person. Just take a look and you'll see what I mean. A human wearing clothes funny. She was a human wearing clothes funny. Indoor clothes she'd be wearing outside and outdoor clothes she'd be wearing inside. The coat would be on first, right against the skin. Her legs, they said, would be through the armpit sections, with her dress and undergarments arranged about on top. The woman was an example. Of something. Of Not Making It Easy. And if she had been once groomed and beautiful – with husband, home and child, as some said she had been – that was not something you'd be able to tell now. Most people were of the opinion that Janine Doe was too eccentric, that she should be put away – not especially for her crimes, for can't crimes always be accommodated? – but because of all the unnerving back-to-frontness she displayed.

And yes, those crimes. Were they happening or weren't they happening? Well, of course they were happening. Men – and some manly women, mistaken for men – were being found. Janine couldn't have been killing them, though. She hadn't enough awareness of humans as an actual species to go out and kill any of them and, besides, these murders were drawn-out plotted murders and JanineJoshuatine could never sustain the consciousness for that. Jotty Doe was her sister – and you remember Jotty? – the less-annoyed cousin who hadn't stabbed her mammy, in contrast to the very-annoyed cousin, Jetty, now with Kalashnikov, who once had? Jotty worried constantly about her sister for she had witnessed more than anyone the unending torment of her sibling, for both Janine and she lived together in the same house. By the way, Janine's oddities were a source of fascination to John Doe, husband of Janet, father to Julie, and brother to both Janine and Jotty. He was also leader of the town's Community Centre Action Team. Although possessing strange proclivities to his own name, nevertheless he looked forward to hearing the latest of his eldest sister's fads. Lastly, you probably didn't need to know any of that because Janine had, in fact, gone off on holiday. So it's back to Julie, and Jennifer, and the Tomboys in the shop.

Julie's reasoning was top level. There was nothing hidden, subtly layered, or of dry humour underneath this teenager's statement. She was plain-speaking. Aunt Jetty, she said, had most likely got the gun, so hadn't they better leave and hurry off to prevent her? Jennifer heard the girl and, whilst itching to hit that moron who was still standing there like a statue, agreed that yes, time was short and they'd better push on.

'Mental bastard!' she flung at Tom, and honest to God, she thought, who could blame her? Dozy he was. So dozy you could use him as a pillow. And of course he wasn't married, but just imagine if he was. 'It would be awful to be married to him! Can you imagine being married to him?' both Toms could hear as she and Julie made their way out on to the road.

''Bye, Tom. 'Bye, Tom,' shouted back Julie, herding her mother's friend in an easterly direction, the door going ding! as the tender and the enraged disappeared. In the shop one of the Toms continued to stay frozen behind the counter, whilst the other, on automatic reflex, leapt over to put the snib on.

Chapter Two

Not fast enough.

What came after the women was a man, but he might as well have been a woman for all the welcome he got. Tom was a split second from putting on the snib when the door went ding! and a big man's arm shoved itself through. Tom shoved the arm out and then did manage to put the snib on, but the door cracked as the arm, in a thwack, broke the snib through. Tom pushed and the arm pushed and it became a *Wuthering Heights* moment – where the man in a panic in the bed in that book drags the ghost arm back and forth across the windowsill – only here it was a door and not a window, it was daytime and not night-time and it wasn't a dream either and it wasn't about sex. Anyway, Tom pushed and the arm pushed and the door went ding! ding! ding! ding! a few more times. Then the arm paused, took stock of the situation and, with a flick, stumbled Tom to one side. Both Toms watched on helpless then, as the rest of the man pushed himself through. Once in, he shut and barred the door, turned the open sign to closed, pulled down the blind and hauled over a gun cabinet, the weapons rattling and the neat boxes of bullets sliding about inside. When the entrance was blocked, that meant the exit was also. The place was immediately darker, the atmosphere heavier and the stranger, relieved by the transformation, turned in the gloom and walked towards the front.

No nonsense taker.

I think that's how he'd describe himself.

And he wasn't a stranger either, so don't be thinking that.

He went round to the safe side and lifted the giant teapot. That seemed to indicate that perhaps all he'd been after was a nice cup of tea. The Toms were not convinced. There existed in the world a certain taunting territorial taking up of another's teapot, and they were more of the opinion that this was an example of that. They watched as the man lifted Customer Tom's cup, still containing Tom's warm coffee, turned it bottom side up and spilled Tom's contents out on to the ground. Leisurely, he then poured himself a tea, helped himself to milk from the milkbottle, sugar from the sugarbox, then stirred with his fingers, ignoring the tablespoon patently standing in for a teaspoon nearby.

Shocking. Very rude too.

But introductions *please*, no matter how distasteful. Well, okay. This man was Johnjoe Doe, whose real name was Harrison, and although not a Doe *de rigueur,* he was a longstanding member of the John Doe Community Centre Group. He was also an honorary member of the family, and that would be the Doe family, not Gunshop Tom's family. Tom didn't have a family. He'd never wanted one, although there was a time once when he would have loved to have had a wife. He'd forgotten that now. The other Tom did have a wife and one day, when he would get out of hospital, he would tell her of what happened at Tom's gunshop that morning, for he believed it had been that incident that had ricocheted him into his own tragedy later on. But Johnjoe being an honorary member of the Doe family is what I'm talking about here. He knew the children intimately, which was scary, knew the two sisters, Jetty and Janet, impartially, and by the way, I don't think I mentioned – Jetty Doe, the annoyed one, the one with the Kalashnikov and the duck pellets in the taxi – she was Janet Doe's sister and she lived with Janet and Janet's husband John and the two teenage children in the Doe family home as well.

So Johnjoe was John Doe's right-hand man. He was seriously on the staff, being John Doe's lieutenant, and John Doe often delegated jobs to him that he didn't have the time or inclination for himself. He also called upon Johnjoe in any kind of emergency. Like this emergency. But excuse me. I have to butt in to offer a short meditation on the thing men.

The thing men, contrary to appearances, has to be looked at laterally and not linearly. You might cry, 'Rubbish! I know what that is – guns, swamps, crocodiles – a straight line.' But I cry no. Don't be so hasty. I know for a fact there's more to it than that.

You might accept, though with reluctance, if I say that some men don't know the difference between a crocodile and an alligator – even some men living in the crocodile and alligator parts of the world. 'Okay,' you'd say. 'Stretching it, I might believe that.' But if I then said some men don't know the difference between a crocodile and a turtle, 'Oh, now, nonsense, nonsense!' you'd flounce. 'You're just saying that to get me to like them. I may be quiet and unobtrusive and don't like to give bother, but I'm not stupid and I'm not as naive as all that!'

But it's true. It really is true.

Of course we're talking crocodiles here, and not guns, for all men know guns, except the Great Exception and I'll get on to him in a minute. But for now have a look at Gunshop Tom and tell me what you think.

On one level, I agree, he appears the average swamps-crocodiles-big-guns male specimen, but is it not apparent that, since that mugging and stabbing, he's not the man he once was? Time was, he'd rush to open his shop with gusto, whistling tunes, getting in there early, rubbing his hands happily, laying out his hardware, hanging up his 'No licence needed' and 'No children allowed' signs with good heart. But now, since the attack, he was simply going through the motions. There was no longer the purity of the enterprise, no longer the enthusiasm of offering gun assistance. Sickening, he appeared to be, entirely for something else. He had turned from manic gun lover to listless gun indifferent, threatening even to become a full-time milk-tea-bread-and-butter shop man. Come, you'd say, is it really possible for a male to become such a mutually exclusive concept? Ordinarily I would say of course not. And you would say of course not. Even Customer Tom, who was married and settled down but who still liked to keep up with the milder gossip and gun literature, would say of course not. But if you asked Gunshop Tom, he'd become incoherent, stop talking altogether, then turn away. Truth told, it would have been better for Tom to have started falling apart in a manner less obtrusive, for gossip likes a subject and he was becoming it. Naturally, once rumour is up and running, it's only a matter of time before someone wants to cash in on it. The Doe family, for example, had started to hear about this 'antithesis of Tom' as well. 'Won't get over some mugging,' someone said. 'Did a course on losing friends and falling out with people.' 'No longer cares about his stock or hardware.' 'Really?' said John Doe. 'In that case, perhaps he might also be persuaded into no longer caring about running the better of the best gunshops in town.'

So there they were: the Toms silently looking on as Johnjoe drank his tea to the tune of loud slurpy noises. Naturally they were frightened and, energetically, he was aware of that. This made him feel powerful. This made him feel respected. This made him feel like he was a really damn decent person. When he'd finished his tea, he set down his mug, splayed his hands over the sugar, which was splayed over the counter. In his own time, he got to the point.

Johnjoe knew who she was, he said, and he knew she'd been in to get a piece to hunt and shoot John Doe down with. That wasn't a question. Simply, he wanted to know what weapon she'd chosen, what amount of ammunition she'd taken, what o'clock she'd left at and in what o'clock direction did she go? He directed his questions at Gunshop Tom, who now hated it when people directed questions at him. In his numbed-out state he found it hard enough – without all this being questioned – to get himself to attend to anything at all. So, as Johnjoe spoke, Tom tried to do the deep-breathing exercises the man in the training bottoms and Buddy Holly glasses had tried to teach him at the hospital. Even then, though, it had proved impossible, for yer man had kept shouting, 'In and out! In and bloody out! Is this difficult for you?' every time Tom's diaphragm got it wrong. Big Johnjoe Doe, who wouldn't be able to give the appearance of patience even if he'd wanted to, was not at all patient. He lifted the huge teapot once more in his mighty hand.

Now this was a gigantic teapot and aesthetically I would say it belonged in such a large-sized hand as Johnjoe's, but that wasn't meant to be the point of this sentence. The point in that sentence was supposed to be that in the old days this teapot would have been down the back at the bun counter and never up at the gun counter, another sign of Tom's laxity, and – for anyone with an acute eye and a vested interest – a further sign of Tom's weakening gun vigour and of the general despondency that was settling about his life. It was clear this man no longer cared about damage caused by sugar-spatters, or breadcrumbs falling into precious gun oils, or firing mechanisms distorted by careless tealeaves to the tune of point zero zero zero zero one of a degree. Yes, as much as that. Johnjoe noticed though, and his eyes licked their lips as he clocked also that Spaders was increasingly becoming a fatigued and womanish individual – he no longer had drums drumming, no longer had songs singing – and he appeared to be the owner of a body irreversibly falling out with itself. Therefore, according to the famous saying 'Nature hates big holes', Johnjoe began to have an image of Spaders lying dead and buried in one. The shop would be unowned then, wouldn't it, for didn't yer man here have no family? Perhaps – to throw out an idea – the Doe Team could take it over and be the new proprietors instead?

One thing. It's about a situation that can happen – and I know you must know it – where you don't want something for yourself because you view it as a bit of rubbish, but if someone else shows an interest, you don't want that person to have it instead of you. They might end up being absorbed and happy having it, and you might end up being left out and forgotten. So, to keep you in the middle – adored, envied, hated, doesn't matter – you decide to take this thing and you do. You store it, along with all the other things you took and didn't want, and you put them in the attic, in the cupboards, in the corners, in the coalhole, under the floorboards, in huge padlocked boxes under the stairs. They're all around you, covered in dust and increasing atmospheric pressure, and you're in the middle and you're sure to be remembered and, by the way, don't worry if these things rot. There are always more things to be had.

Tom's gunshop was like that.

The team didn't want it. Not really. But not because they saw it as rubbish. It was more that being shopowners and totting accounts and smiling at customers was hardly their inclination. 'Don't open a shop if you can't crack a smile' is a saying the Irish-Chinese have. Besides, the Does knew they could saunter in any time they fancied, take whatever they cared for, and 'See you right about this later, Spaders,' they'd shout, as they waltzed with it back out of his shop. Legally it was Tom's shop. His was the name on the deeds and his was the money that had paid for it. But in real terms – in terms of who can kidnap you and torture you and kill you just for the why-not of it – there was no doubt about it. It was the Doe Family Community Centre shop. They didn't insist on laying claim, just as they didn't insist on laying claim to their other businesses in the town also. As for Spaders, why not let him continue doing the good job for them that up until then he always had?

Because up till then was over. Tom Spaders had lost his nerve. It was said he had drawn into himself and was now tiny in his charisma, so the Does knew that to keep on top of their rivals they'd have to assert themselves and go for the very thing everybody else wanted to have.

For the time being, though, and as instructed, Johnjoe put John Doe's personal life before the Doe Group's business interests. He continued to hold the teapot which, by now, was swinging a lullaby in his arms.

Gunshop Tom saw the sway, then watched it gathering into a momentum. A few momentums on and he fell back against his gunshelves with a cry. His arms flung themselves out, his legs buckled and he knocked off all his handguns. They fell on top of him as he crash-landed on to the ground. Strange thing was, though, even before he hit the ground, Tom knew that neither teapot nor anything else had come anywhere near his body. Oh flip, he thought. It's that Spatial Fragmentation Hallucination Syndrome he'd been reading about at the hospital. It had been in a magazine belonging to the last patient who'd left it behind him because he'd died. Idly, Tom had picked it up and then couldn't set it down again. His eyes boggled. His nerves raced. He one hundred per cent identified with the case study on display.

Do you know this syndrome? Do you have it? I'll tell you. You're having a hard time, say, because something not very nice once happened to you. It was a big thing, and although it's supposed to be over, in your body and in your head and from the way you now look out on the world, it's not bloody over, it's still bloody going on. Or maybe it wasn't a big thing. Maybe it was a series of little things, most of them below the level of police CAD reference number material, but if you add them together, plus feather in the timescale, they amount to one hell of a cumulative assault.

But poor you. It's too late. By now you're infantilised. By now you've lost your language. By now you're no longer capable of speaking about what happened, for didn't you try and try and nobody could hear? You're left swinging to one extreme therefore, which is clutching on to reluctant people, babbling incoherencies, or else sitting alone at your kitchen table, driven into silence, unable to tune in to anything at all.

That's because of evil. That's what evil does.

And it's during this state of stuckness that syndromes like the spatial fragmentation whatjimacallit enter. The main thing to know about the Spatial is that it's the real reason behind people who walk into doors.

To jump sideways for a moment. You can't say you don't know the expression 'I walked into a door' that someone says to you and your mates because they meet you and they've got this big bruise on their face. And you don't believe them and you say, 'Yeah, sure, very sorry to hear it,' and you exchange glances with your mates. 'Liar,' the glances say. 'Yer man, what's-his-name? That man she won't leave? It was him. He hit her.

Does she think we're stupid? Our sweet fannies she walked into a door.' Well, you see, this is where you should just shush your mind and tell it not to be so intransigent. Turns out you don't know everything. Scientific analysis of the Spatial Fragmentation Hallucination Syndrome proves that poor woman was telling the truth. She really did walk into a door.

Which is not to say the husband didn't hit her – poor bastard, I mean him – although he does deserve a good kicking, although don't quote me as I don't like to present myself as vengeful. It's to say that being beaten by the husband is nothing but secondary. How could they not have come into each other's orbit when each other's blueprint called the other forth?

But to jump back to after that thing that wasn't nice that happened to you, or after that huge cumulated assault. You're sitting in silence at your kitchen table because you've no speech left and there's a glass of water in front of you. You pick it up to have a sip. You go to set it down after you've had your sip and you misjudge the height of the table. You bang it down and crash it, thinking the table's lower, or else you let go too soon and again, bang and splash it, thinking the table's higher up than it is. Or you go to walk out a door and you can see clearly the space between the doorframes. How could you miss it? But you walk towards it and you do. You bang one shoulder against one doorframe, step to the side and bang your head against the other and it takes ten whole seconds to get into the next room. Or you're reading a book and from the corner of your eye you see the tail end of an imaginary insect running across the carpet. But not one insect, the tail end of a herd of insects, rustling together as they go vanishing by. Or say you do manage sometimes to walk through the space between the doorframes without banging your body – as you do, someone in black flappy clothes is crashing in from the other side. You

21

jump and yelp and do a double-take, for who is that person, where did that flappy flash come from? It came from nowhere and, seconds from colliding, veers to the side and disappears. You glance around and catch other dark flaps speeding about you also so, to get away from the doorframes and the rapid apparitions, you go outside and walk along the street. You walk along the pavement and, as you're walking, a big bus honks because you're too close to the kerbside. 'One more inch out,' he shouts, 'and I'd've carried your shoulder off.' 'What's wrong with you?' shouts another. 'Are you trying to get yourself killed?' So you move back to the inside of the kerb, which is where you thought you were in the first place. You bump into things that aren't there, then get back home and knock over things that are. Shaken, you decide to go to bed, to get your spatial bearings back during sleeptime. So you turn round to head upstairs but take a step and fall down them instead. When you pick yourself up you find you're in the kitchen when it should have been the hallway and you've got your hand accidentally on the stove. Well, thank goodness it wasn't on, but you hold your hand anyway, just as if you've burned it. And sometimes welts come up that you know shouldn't be there. But you're resilient. You go once more with purpose into the hall. This time you succeed as you head upstairs but, as you turn round on the landing to step safely into your bedroom, you walk slap-bang into a closed door you'd never noticed was there before.

That's what Tom had. The Spatial Fragmentation Hallucination Syndrome. In his hypervigilant state, he didn't see the teapot coming, but he thought he saw something – a big bird, a crow, a rook – and it made a stoop towards him, wings closing, claws opening, lots of flapping. Naturally he jumped back and crashed himself on to the floor. And there he was, still on it. He scrabbled amidst the spilt guns and split bullet boxes whilst Johnjoe, who had been pre-empted from hitting him by this unexpected development, stopped swinging the teapot and looked from it to Spaders in surprise.

'It was an AK47, wasn't it, Tom?' shouted over Customer Tom from the corner. Customer Tom had sensed that his friend – judging from those sudden physical jerks – was going to splurge into 'Did I ever tell you, Johnjoe, I was mugged and stabbed by a bunch of teenagers?' and, fearing the impact upon his friend of any impact upon Johnjoe of being earbashed about the effects of violence, Customer Tom wisely was trying to move the subject on. 'She came in,' he shouted, 'reached over, didn't want any information. We heard her shout "Taxi!" and that's it – except she grabbed up some pellets before she was gone.'

Johnjoe, still holding the teapot, seemed confused at this point.

'A '74 it was,' corrected Gunshop Tom, who was now off the floor and brushing down his trousers. He was pretending nothing had happened, for it would be impossible to explain the likes of ravens to the likes of Johnjoe Doe. He used to be good at imparting gun information, he told himself. So why not pull himself together, do his job and impart gun information? He joined the conversation, kicking bullets from under him, sending them skidding out on to the shop floor.

Johnjoe hardly listened. First he came to the conclusion that yes, absolutely yes, he hadn't struck yer man here with the teapot, for here it was, still being held gently, undented, in his hand. Second, there was something fishy in what those two clowns were telling him. His face hackled as he struggled to comprehend the wrongfulness of their comments, then it de-hackled upon comprehension, then rehackled as he grasped further the implications of what, apparently, had gone on.

'Let me get this straight,' he said.

And that was when it came out. Not only had Jetty Doe bought a Kalashnikov when it was patently obvious a thirty-eight snubnose would have been far better suited to her situation, she also hadn't been given the proper ammunition with which to carry her personal vendetta out. Johnjoe was on a life-and-death mission to stop his Master and Commander's wife's sister shooting his Master and Commander, but it seemed he had an even more desperate compulsion to make sure she had the correct weaponry with which to be prevented from doing just that. That's what I mean about looking at the thing men laterally. You can't understand it by dictionary.

The men got protracted at this point because they fell into a loop.

'I didn't give it, she took it!'

'Were you making fun of her? Couldn't kill a bird with that ammo, and I'm not talking goose here, I'm only talking duck ...'

'Trying to tell you! The door went ding! She shouted for a taxi—'

'... common or garden loading long gun! Man, you need gravity to reload it. Guns follow fashion. Why didn't you tell her that?'

'I just wanted to wipe the counter. Just wipe the counter. That's all I wanted to do, all day.'

'So it was to be huntin' shootin' and fishin' without the huntin' shootin' and fishin' – is that what you're saying? When the duck appears ... that sort of thing?'

'Look, I'll start again – first of all the door went ding!—'

'You expect me to believe that?'

'She wasn't specific. She wasn't scientific. Her ears were blocked to reason. She had us under the table.'

'That's true, Johnjoe. She did have us under the table.'

'Can't get my head around giving that to a person, even to a woman. You'd think the logical, practical, sensible, reasonable, objective, intelligent—'

'But it wasn't done to her! It was all done to me!'

'That's true, Johnjoe. It was all done to us.'

'... a handgun I could understand, but not an ordinary eighteenth-century muzzle-loading—'

'It was a Kalashnikov!'

'Large charge or small charge? Did you premeasure it out?'

'I ended up saying to her, "If you scream at me you don't get my attention." That's what I wanted to say I mean. "Ask me nicely, then you can come and join." That sort of thing.'

'I think you should shut up now,' said Johnjoe. 'I think you were taking the piss because she was a woman. Well, you'll be pishing yourselves on the other side of your sexism when I tell you whose wife's sister that woman who came in here was.'

And that was when the loop ended. Nicely and firmly. No more discussion. If only all loops could end as handsomely as that.

'What way'd she go?' said Big Doe, after he'd imparted the news of the John Doe Community Centre connection. But the Toms were astonished for they already knew about that. What was wrong with Johnjoe? It wasn't as if they didn't live in the same small town as him, and as the Community Centre members. How could they not have noticed this connection? One good thing, though, was that at least with this news, which was supposed to be shocking, they weren't any more shocked than they had been moments before.

'She went east,' they both said, even though they didn't know she'd gone east. They had to give some answer and, luckily for them, Johnjoe accepted it, which didn't mean he didn't do violence to them. But before he did, something else took place in the shop.

Towards the end of the loop session, and before Johnjoe hit them, Tom Spaders began to have a few more sense-perceptor-disturbance disorders. First there was the nosebleed, followed by the crown of thorns.

Some people have it all.

This nosebleed. Now what was that about? And generally speaking, what about that whole connection between physical things and mental things and supernatural things and God? What about them? How do you get the hierarchical order between biochemistry, saints, souls and those tricks to reason called emotions? Which comes first? I don't know. Do you know? 'Cos I don't know.

Tom's nose began to bleed but he didn't accept this as reality. He thought it a simple hallucination complex, based upon his Former Personality Gone and Never Coming Back Disorder and he paid no attention either when four bruises appeared – bang! bang! bang! bang! – upon his forearm. Then his lower lip split, a small squeaky slit, which Johnjoe, who had been altercating over the long gun, even thought he heard happening. This guy's weird, he stepped back and thought. Customer Tom noticed the stepping back and looked up and saw the blood, the cut and the bruises on his friend also, and both Johnjoe and Customer Tom stared, for neither had witnessed Spontaneous Visual Vessel Eruption Disorder before. They had read of such phenomena, of course, in best-selling psychological, psychophysiological, neuromythological, bioneurological and demonic possession books, and had even seen Hollywood movies and real-life documentaries of exorcisms, psychosomatic cures and the biotheological response on the TV. This touches slantingly into God and into the Devil, and into the supernatural, as well as into scientific speculation upon 'the more the crime, the more the ghosts', but we'll have to go into that some time later on.

So, this nosebleed. Some people enjoy nosebleeds although probably they'd never admit to that. As long as they weren't going to lose all of it, they quite liked the idea of some of their blood dripping out. What they wouldn't do, though, would be to deny a nosebleed was happening if, actually, it was happening, and this was something Spaders was doing at the present time. He did nothing about the blood, and this, along with the non-reaction to the split lip, the bruises and that earlier falling up against the gun cabinet, increasingly started to disturb Johnjoe Doe. Was this ghosts? he wondered, for he and the Doe Executive took their belief in ghosts and in demons and in other discarnate essences very deadly seriously. But if it weren't ghosts, was Spaders taking the hand or was it that he was insane as everybody around here was now saying he was? Better be mad, thought Johnjoe, who had heard of the mugging and stabbing and, although he could hardly credit someone getting themselves mugged and stabbed instead of doing the mugging and stabbing, he preferred Tom to be losing it than for any mockery of himself or of his supernatural beliefs to be going on.

So, what was it?

Goodness?

Badness?

Or psychosomatic mad?

This supernatural business, though. Seems I have to return to it immediately. Can't fathom it, for they're very superstitious, them Does. They'd stop for a break, for example, whilst in the middle of killing somebody, and over the boiling kettle and KitKats, they'd begin a round of the latest ghost-talk. They'd scare each other with their tales, to the point of forgetting they had a man tortured and three-quarters dead and tied to a chair just across the room from them. They'd get so edged-out by their ghost mania, they'd even be afraid to go home by themselves. There'd be the wee white woman story of the wee white woman, who was two feet high and who appeared and disappeared and who latched on to the auras of people. She'd shake her head as she walked behind them, making clawing motions and muttering 'No No No No' all the time. She'd follow these people to their homes, and afterwards, those individuals she followed? Well, they'd completely disappear. There'd be no trace of them. Then there'd be the woman on the yard wall crying into her tortoiseshell and the rattling pots in the kitchen and the pictures falling off the walls by themselves. That's not all. There was Lula, half-banshee, half-witch, who came to announce the deaths even before they'd been kidnapped, and also there was the haunted egg factory and don't forget the Ouija. There was the Ouija, which they shouldn't have played but, God forgive them, they did play, and it told them that one of them in that room would be dead before the night was out. That didn't happen, though – unless you counted the tortured man. And isn't it amazing – I mean that little glass tablette thing? It's made in France and you rest the tips of your fingers upon it and do you know you can ask the board anything you want? It can be about the past, present or future and the Ouija has to tell the truth by the third time of asking. It's only allowed to lie to you two times in a row.

'Are you the Devil?'

'No. I'm your Aunty Jacky.'

'You are not. Are you the Devil?'

'No. I'm your father, Senior John.'

'Third time. Are you the Devil?'

'No. I'm your Uncle Joe.'

'Hey, everybody, it's my Uncle Joe. It's Nephew JerryJudges here, Uncle Joe. I'm seventeen now. Which of them was it? Which of them gangs killed you, Uncle Joe?'

Then there's the haunted house on the main road, the one that even made it on to the newstime lunchtime special. The workmen kept running out of it in the mornings for if they left their tools in it overnight, next day when they showed, every tool was buried to its hilt in the newly plastered walls. 'There's a baby voice on the stairway of that house,' said one of the workmen to the TV journalist who was laughing as he interviewed him, and the workman said, 'Fuck you, you weren't there. I was there. It was a baby voice and sometimes it was two baby voices. They were on the stairs and they were shouting out the answers to the radio pop quiz.' Apparently the situation got so bad that the workmen had to turn off the quiz when the voices persisted in shouting out the answers, and when they started singing along to the popsongs, the men had to turn off Radio One as well. It didn't stop there, though. Keith's plasterboard got snapped out of his hands and thrown across the room when he was still in the middle of using it, and Clem's toolkit began to rattle, as then did every small and big thing in the room. In the end, tools were getting hurled and buried whether or not they were left overnight. A ceilingman up a ladders would set his screwdriver down on the top step of these ladders, then turn round to pick it up after only a second. He'd hear a whirr and a crack coming from an inch above him, followed by a flash, then there'd be a 'thunk!' with the screwdriver buried, with inhuman force, again in the wall.

They all swore they didn't do it. Sure, why bury your own screwdriver? Sure, why bury somebody else's? It got to the point where no workman would go into that house and the journalist made jokes about the work never getting done. But the Doe team was wiser. 'What does he know!' they cried. 'Girly lemon-shirt, little pink-tie fruity bastard!' They had nervously watched this light-hearted tail news item, which had followed a 'Body Found! Another Body Found!' murder item, but that tail item – it wasn't light-hearted to them. They knew that particular house, see. It was the Demon House and it wasn't that far away from the Doe Garden Community Centre either. That Demon House – it looked normal but it wasn't normal and it was just up the road.

So the Does would terrify themselves with these tales of the supranormal, or else they'd borrow a stack of horror videos free from that new video-contraption shop and throw up a screen and watch them in the shack one after the other until the cock in the garden up the road told them all was safe at dawn. They'd only venture out then, for the ghost energy would have dissipated. Because of this, they'd be able to joke and bluster and make fun at this point.

'Yeah,' they'd say. 'Yeah, sure. Yeah, right. I'll let you think you scared me. You go ahead. I'll carry on letting you think that.' Then they'd remember.

'Oh flip,' they'd say, and look over to the corner. 'We forgot about him. He's still alive there dying.' 'Check if he's really alive,' said John Doe. 'He's dead,' said Johnjoe. 'Well, throw him away then' – but at least one good thing to say about this is that they didn't believe in vampires. Could you imagine? Grown men believing in the undead who went around taking bites out of people? Then those preyed-upon pursuing the undead back to their coffins in some underground cellar to put stakes through their hearts? Honestly. I mean, honestly. I'm not being flippant but if that were the case, you could understand why that journalist – the girly one the team wouldn't mind killing if only they knew where he lived and could get their hands on him – well, you could understand why such as he might laugh.

But I'm not saying there aren't ghosts either – so don't be putting that about. All I'm saying is that don't you think these people – I mean, *really, these people!* – are off the scale in the number of ghosts they think there are? They weren't all grown up either. Even before they got arrested and it got to the police station and it got to the courthouse and it got to the jail, it turned out the youngest member was thirteen years only. That was the leader's son. That would be John Doe's son – the quiet boy, the disappointing boy, the boy who hadn't found the knack yet. He was the youngest but the rest, bar the second and third youngest, were all in their twenties at least. The third youngest was JerryJudges – he of the Ouija, of the 'Uncle Joe, which of them was it?' question. The second youngest wasn't Julie Doe but, like Julie, she was only fifteen.

So what was going on? Do we have a psychoanalyst or a psychoanalytic psychologist or a psychophysiological profiler or even an unaccredited enthusiast with Jungian leanings in the building who could perhaps do a bit of maturity work for us here? Is this about a state of stuckness? A state of sickness? Did these men perhaps leave school before they'd learnt enough and should have? Or is it that they couldn't get themselves individuated and thus had intermingling mythic mirages, not only in their dreams but in their waking lives as well? I wouldn't know about interpretations, for my expertise lies in being a bystander. But come on – werewolves? Monkey's paw? Murdered youths coming back to get you? And that woman who turns you to stone just because you have a peek at her, and has – if you could credit it – snakes standing in for the auld hair?

Now I know you're wanting, you're busting for me to tell

about God or maybe second best, about whether those ghost noises at the shack later when the group was being arrested were real or if they were imaginary, but I'm not at liberty, so please give up asking and accompany me back to the shop. Tom's nose was still bleeding but now that was because he'd got punched on it. There were also new bruises in the making, given to both Toms by the Doe man.

Now we can't blame Johnjoe for blaming the two Toms for his own psychological constructs. Sure, isn't it natural for everybody to lash out at others when they get into the fear state? Johnjoe became convinced that Spaders's face was starting to turn into an old woman's and not only that – that it was turning into the face of Johnjoe's maternal grandmamma. So he punched it. As he was doing so he had the perspicacity – which you can only get in situations when you start meeting your dead relatives – to turn quickly and check out the person behind. Guess what – Customer Tom's face had turned into dead grandmother on Papa's side. Naturally, Johnjoe had a go at her as well. Then he repunched the maternal for she was back on her feet, adjusting her headscarf and her gingham housecoat, then he took out his gun and jabbed it into Auld Ma Harrison's side. The old lady squeaked, which had Johnjoe squeaking himself and jumping away, for it was too real, that squeak. It really did sound like his old granny, whereas he had been hoping that if he only half-believed it, she wouldn't have taken on the three dimensions that she had. He kept re-hearing too, that slitty sound, that slit-slit-slitty sound of the split lip, of the skin ripping, of something tearing, that had been done by invisible forces upon Tom Spaders. It kept repeating itself, over and over, in Johnjoe's by now fraught mind.

'Get away from me! I mean it!' he screeched, swinging his gun, his body drenched in sweat, fear and revulsion. 'Get away from me!' and then he took a shot at the paternal, but she ended up unshot for, in panic, he fired very wide. 'Okay, dear, all right, dear!' it seemed the wee granny was cooing, even though in reality, this woman never had cooed. She had smacked heads and jabbed people and snarled, 'Stupid boy! Get out of the way. I said out of the way, stupid boy!' – crack! That had been more Granny Harrison's style. She was worse in her prime and her prime lasted all the eighty-five years of her life and appeared still to be lasting, and it didn't matter that Customer Tom Cusack, in reality, was yelling, 'Johnjoe! What did I do? I didn't do anything!' as he jumped behind the counter to be beside the other Tom. Both Toms were now standing with their hands up. Keeping his gun on them – for, between us, this was not the first time his grannies had appeared and disappeared and reappeared out of nowhere – Johnjoe backed into a glass cabinet, which some idjit had pulled over to block his exit from the shop. He was calming down, however, for he knew from experience that putting even a few feet between himself and his old caregivers would bring about their reduction, eventually their dissolution. Indeed, already they appeared to be turning back into the men they once were. Wait till he told the others, though. Two emanations appearing simultaneously – *and* walking, *and* talking – not silently hovering, as in 'Stage One Phenomena'. As long as he didn't reveal it was the grannies, he'd be quids up with the others on the ghost front.

Now it was the Tomboys' turn to stare as the big man yanked, shoved and in the end pushed the tall cabinet away from the exit. He did it with such ferocity that it carried on moving and he emptied his gun into it as it started to fall. It fell, toppled, its glass doors smashing on to the glass countercase in front of it, but neither Tom retaliated, except in so far as to get out of the way.

Johnjoe was out the door – or almost. First he experienced some doorframe moments. He banged his body against one side, stubbed his toe against the other, paused, thinking, there is the door, there is the opening, just go through it, why can't I go through it?, but he couldn't, not until he'd knocked his head and torso about four times. Eventually he was through, after successfully ducking out of the way of four flashes of flappy people, then he managed to get over the threshold, screaming, 'Can't stand hysterical women!' as he ran away.

Chapter Three

The meaning of 'lull' is to soothe, to compose, to quiet, an interval of calm, a calming influence. But that didn't happen when Johnjoe left the gunshop. Neither of these Tomses was going to feel lulled and even the one with the wife wouldn't have a good sleep that night.

I don't remember what Customer Tom said first. I was taken up with him, wedged in between the top of the fallen gun cabinet, which had been thrust up against the side of another gun cabinet, and with him lowering his hands – which were still up in surrender – to shift one of them out of the way. Glass crashed and a thick shard fell from the counter on to the top of the left boot of Tom Spaders. Spaders didn't notice or else he didn't care. I think Customer Tom Cusack was annoyed and said, 'Were you messin' about there, Tommy? Were you actin' the goat, pretending all them cuts and bruises were from God or the Devil or something? 'Cos if you were, and yer man goes away and decides you were making fun of him, he'll be back, and guess who'll be included in his revenge as a grudge of association? Seems you didn't give any thought to my wellbeing there.' But maybe that's not what happened for, you know, things can get muddled during the happening and during the after-happening – even for us bystanders – so, upon reflection, I'm now thinking Cusack might have said something that sounded less annoyed, and more that he thought it was funny, that he should escape with only a bit of a punch, and only a bit of a kick, and a gun shoved into only a bit of his abdomen. So maybe it was Gunshop Tom who got annoyed and upset instead.

'Just like you, Cusie,' he said, coming back into his body from wherever he had disappeared to out of it. His nose felt cracked, his teeth numb, his head jerked back as if someone were hauling on it, and he had the momentary sensation that Cusack was covered in black and white fur. Bits of loaves covered in pigeon feathers, cigarette packets, cigarette butts, auld chewing gum wrappers, auld chewing gum too, all seemed to be stuck on the floor and on the counter and on top of Cusack also, when really, after Spaders squeezed his eyes, those things were guns, bullets, cartridges and sugar – none of them on Cusack – and not bread, litter, hair or any type of fur at all. He felt sick and opened his mouth to breathe better.

'You never want to face anything,' he said. 'It's not funny, Cusie. Maybe the only way you'll stop finding awful things funny is if you go out and get mugged and stabbed by a mob of teenagers yourself.'

It slipped out, the way those things do slip out during periods of associated damage. One thing's smashed? Hell, why not dive in and smash everything else up as well?

During Spaders's mini-breakdown in his twenties – I did mention he had a breakdown fifteen years earlier, didn't I? Apparently every normal person's supposed to have one every seven years. The sums don't compute, though. It's supposed to take ten years to get over the average breakdown, so that means you'd be in arrears with no respite in between. I don't know who you could write to about that. Anyway, during the time

Spaders had his mini, he kept experiencing funny things around his friendships. By funny I mean dreadful. He started falling out with all of his friends. Except Cusack. Cusack wouldn't let himself be fallen out with. He'd turn up, hang around and initially Spaders would feel annoyed because he was continuing to show himself and asking if he, Spaders, wanted to go to the bar or something. So Spaders would resolve, next time Cusack showed his face he'd pick a big fight and get rid of him as well. Whenever Cusack did show, though, and asked Tom if he wanted to go to the bar or something, Spaders's paranoia would melt and he'd feel nothing but unspeakable gratitude towards his old friend. This time, however, in Spaders's latest breakdown – and aren't breakdowns amazing in their versatility? – the thing about the friendships was the other way around.

This time Spaders kept wanting the contact with his mates to stay the way it used to be before the mugging and stabbing, so he'd long for Tom and the others to call and keep everything on the light and breezy front. But whenever they did, and were sitting around, having tea, playing with guns, chatting away, looking at postage stamps with gun pictures on them, Tom would get annoyed, for it seemed their lively cheer equalled a huge discounting of himself. How could they act as if nothing had happened, he'd think, sitting there, joking and patronising? So he'd feel as if it were those bastards, rather than the teenagers, who had ganged up on him themselves. Of course, at the same time, he knew what rubbish this was, that these were his mates. Still, though, the continual spurt of grudges – murderous grudges – kept coming on. 'Kill them!' something would whisper. It would prompt him, almost physically push him, nudge him in the shoulder. 'Why don't you just point that gun you're holding and shoot them all now?' But the moment would pass and thank goodness he hadn't done what this persistent insane part was urging him on to. 'Ach! You could have killed them,' it said. It was disgusted. 'If only you'd shot them when I told you. Make sure you shoot them next time they come around.'

So them coming, and them leaving, and what would happen inside Tom about shooting or not shooting became a routine – twenty or thirty times they all had to go through it, until the friends, even the thickest-skinned, felt something was wrong. They couldn't put their finger on it, but after each short time of visiting, they themselves were becoming nervous – something to do with Tom not playing with his guns in the normal way he used to play with them before. Eventually, they stopped calling. No harm to Tom, they said, but it was gentler on themselves to go for tea and buns and guns in one of the other gunshops. So they did, urging Cusack to come as well. He wouldn't. He continued to stick around and Spaders, in his trusting phase, in his grateful phase, would notice this loyalty and, in a softer mood, would rehearse trying to tell Cusack a few things he hadn't quite told the truth about on the subject of that mugging, but in case he messes up, I'll tell you it myself.

Three things important. First, how many teenagers were there really? Second, what age were these teenagers? Third and most important, when something awful happens to you, how long are you allowed before you're supposed to be over it, and what happens if you're not over it and take longer than the officially allotted time?

Big questions, except to people with disintegrated personalities. But we're not them so let's take the first one first.

How many attackers? Well, Spaders managed to tell the ambulance people when they were taking him to the hospital that there were 'about ten teenagers who attacked me'. At the hospital he told the doctors before falling unconscious that 'there were fifteen, Doctor, fifteen, maybe more'. To the police when they showed eventually – for, you know, those boys are understaffed and overstretched even if they do get the best pensions – he said there were twenty young adults. And every so often afterwards, whilst doing an involuntary splurge on the subject, an extra two or three seemed always to get added on. So, what's the crack? I'll tell you. The teenagers numbered three. One, two and three. That's all.

This is not to say three teenagers can't do a lot of damage.

They did do a lot of damage. Next question, what were their ages specifically once and for all?

This is shocking so prepare yourselves.

Those teenagers, the ones who stabbed and mugged Spaders and whom Spaders maintains were variations on vast groups of people? Over the course of splurging he said they looked to be crowds of about eighteen-, nineteen- and perhaps twenty-year-olds. Well, no. They were a batch of children – an eleven-, a ten- and a tag-along eight-year-old.

And lastly, how long ago did the mugging happen, or how long are you allowed to suffer and be in struggle before all around you get angry, shun you, or moan?

Oh dear.

Feel sad here, but I can't protect him forever. Four years, that's how long ago it was.

People here have their own version of time and it's called the Jumbled Time Syndrome and it is contagious and everybody who suffers from Jumbled Time can't help but suffer from Imprecision and Indiscretion too. Simply put: if you can't countenance the concept of someone not being able to let go of something after four years and counting, you have to condense that figure to a number that would represent your personal version of the time spent on it as having been enough. That's what everybody did in Tiptoe Floorboard. Tiptoe Floorboard, by the way, was the nickname for the town. Its real name was Tiptoe Under Greystone Cliff. People who could take the town or leave the town called it 'that auld shitehole' and those who really adored the place, and who liked their diminutives also, strung out their intimacy with 'Tippy-Toe-Under-Tippy-Toe-Ette'. They're deranged those last people, though. I wouldn't recommend hanging about with any of them.

Customer Tom decided the mugging had taken place as long as a year ago and initially that's what I heard, which is why, innocently, I passed that on to you. Jennifer Doe decided it happened as far away as days ago, so what was wrong with yer man, she said, that he was still so dozy yet? Johnjoe decided it was yesterday, so why wasn't Spaders out and about, spinning deals and getting on with things? And Spaders? Well, if reality were down to Spaders, he'd tell you right now that it happened to him a second ago. If you asked tomorrow he'd say, 'It's taking place simultaneously as we speak.' It was so huge and terrible a thing to him, you see, that he needed to narrow the gap continuously in order for it to be remembered – the way people who go to the doctor's always multiply up their ailments because they know the first thing the doctor's going to do is to divide them back down. But it was four years ago, and it involved three children with one sharp knife between them. Tom decided this was shameful and, shame being terrible, how terribly shameful was that?

And that was why Tom knew he needed to tell his friend – tell another human being – the truth and the whole truth about the number, the age and the how long ago. He knew it would appear trivial, especially after how he'd been presenting it, but he sensed also there was a horror and a darkness underneath the triviality, and that this horror and darkness, so far, he'd been unable to haul up and put out. The versions he'd told so far were his way of trying, and they had helped him initially, but he sensed that if the truth didn't start emerging, those lies he told would turn against him and eat him up.

So, standing in his damaged shop, to which he appeared oblivious, Tom attempted something along the lines of telling the other Tom that he had read something in some paper once.

'Eh?' said Customer Tom, looking round.

'It was about a group of children in a different country from ours, and ridiculous that it should be children, Tom. Not the sort of thing you'd imagine anyone ever being frightened of'

'Eh?' said Tom again. He was staring at Spaders, truly puzzled and lost.

'Well, these children, see, these children – let's say, for instance, there were six of them. No, let's be truthful. Let's say five. No, three, and they're young, remember, Tom, about twelve, twelve and twelve.

'Wait! Hear me out! They go on the rampage, see, and they have no sense of social order. They have been shown by no example from adults the meaning of the expression, "*Just a moment, I don't think morally we should be doing that.*"

'Between bricking cars and bricking buses, what they like to do, these children, is to attack adults, and the adults they attack, Tom – say, one adult – well, he, no, she ends up running away and not talking about it to anyone. She tried to talk to the police at the start of her terrorisation, but the police, you see, Tom, the police, oh God, the police, she discovered, were nothing but bigger versions of the small children themselves. These police children in their adult bodies said the right words that they had been taught to say at the police factory, but looking in their eyes, she knew they didn't have a clue as to what any of those words they'd learnt by heart meant.

'At first when she'd go to see them they'd present themselves in their uniforms, with their shiny guns and holsters and say not to worry, oh, not to worry, that they were on the case. They promised to do something about it, they said, and they said they would help her, but when she kept going back to find out what they'd done to help her, these gatherers of information would say they didn't know who she was. They wouldn't re-member anything, either, of what she said she reported to them. There was no record, they said, of her complaint. Or of any dead body. Did she say she filed a complaint about a dead body? No, she said, I wasn't complaining about that. Besides, they said, interrupting, no one else had complained about a dead body, and then they'd pause and take a look at her. They'd take a long, hard look at her. And that was when she realised that if she kept going back she'd end up being arrested and made the enemy herself.

'So that adult who was terrorised, Tom, she lost her speech, see, through writing the official reports for years for those huge child police officers. And she lost her wits also, through reading the police's official responding reports. Those reports, Tom. Oh, Tom. They were unsigned and undated, and before they became threatening, all they ever said was, "Thank you for your instant letter. After examination. You need to appreciate. At the present time. Allowances for holidays, time off and reallocation plus National Response Times and the odd sickness paper get-ting lost" – then finally, and always, "If there's any problem please don't worry about hesitating to call."

'So this woman, Tom, the children got, she got away from the children, and he, no, she, got away from the police also. But she stayed afraid even though she got away because she hadn't been able to expel her experience from deep inside herself yet. She learned, too, that her wits can be taken away from her, in the middle of a conversation, in the middle of speaking to anybody – *whoosh!* – speech, wits, energy, taken away from her, all in a second, just like that. When she tries to say anything now, absolutely anything, she remembers that people interrupt, ask questions, then interrupt the answering of these questions to ask more questions, and so she stops herself with "Best, most safest, not to bother speaking. They mean well, in that ignorant way they mean well, but they'll grab it off me and – laughing or commiserating – turn it into some light, cheery, forgettable coffee-table talk."

'So that's my point,' concluded Tom. 'And do you get it, Tom? That the children don't come only in child packages, and that I know it's been five years—'

Five years! Did he say *five years?* Not four then?

'—but five years, Tom, is the tiniest of getting betters. I hope you get this? Do you get it? Don't you get it, Tom?'

Well, of course Tom didn't get it. He gave a smallish laugh at the delivery of this nonsense, and made a joke along the lines of 'Doesn't she know she can get a prescription from her doctor's for the likes of that?' It wasn't a real joke or a genuine laugh of connection either, but it was a response that hid Customer Tom's confirmation of the real reason he thought his friend was talking rubbish to him like that.

And here I need to tell you what Customer Tom gets up to in bed before he goes to sleep at night. He reads his wife's dictionary. And it was the consequences of the reading of this dictionary that brought about the Tomses' falling-out.

Two things: Schizophrenia and Blueprint. First, Schizophrenia. I think some people should leave well alone – I myself would and I bet you would – but Customer Tom considered himself not one of us people. He had read in his wife's favourite medical dictionary, which she had stolen from a library accidentally and had meant to, but so far had been too tired ever to bring back, about the type of schizophrenia – the other type, not the one where you hear voices and they start off friendly and sing to you and quote you poetry, then take you hostage, urging you to ransack your house for bugging devices and hidden surveillance equipment, then to write advisory letters on the use of shadows, artificial foliage and disguised local garnish to Heads of State at the Town Hall. Oh boy, no. Not that one. That one has you fragmented and terrified and talking about something or nothing to somebody or to nobody, and if there really is somebody, they've become nervous or aggressive around you and have no idea either what you're on about. Tom apparently meant some other schizophrenia, one where you don't hear voices and you don't become fragmented, but you find anyway that you start to distrust your nearest and your dearest, those who were your friends, those you thought you loved. You shut off intimacies, and you go away and isolate, and that's the condition Cusack on the whole tended to think Spaders was suffering from. Every so often though, like now – with Tom muttering those 'kiddie on the rampage' stories – Tom would wonder if perhaps it was the first schizophrenia that his friend had after all. Of course he wasn't qualified to diagnose, but most nights now he had been going systematically through the mental part of the medical dictionary, pulling out different conditions and complexes, wondering if it could be 'this' or 'this' that poor Tom had. For a second opinion he ran possibles by his wife, who was in bed beside him and, as Tom's condition had been going on for 'a year' now, they were one hundred and fourteenth time round to the 'esses', which was what brought up this schizophrenic talk.

'Well, I don't know, Tom,' said the wife, who was called An-gelus. She put on her reading glasses and took the heavy dictionary plus notepad off his lap. 'You've an awful lot of sensation perceptions on the jotter here already. Are you still walking on eggshells, or have you got up the courage to speak to the man himself about it yet?

'Also,' she went on, 'I see once again you're misreading that definition of schizophrenia. There aren't two types. It's just that the symptoms of the one type have been divided up.

'I wish you wouldn't mumble, Tom,' she then said, for Tom had reached over and mumbled what was supposed to be 'Where? Let me reread that definition!' and it was true, Tom did have a mumble problem. It manifested mainly when he was in a prolonged state of being upset or annoyed. A difficulty in enunciating would come upon him and he would start eliding and ellipsing, leaving vowels, then syllables, then words, then whole necessary sentences out. If he didn't leave them out, he condensed them, abridged them, according to some highly private, regulated system, trusting to the listener to be on the same wavelength as himself. The listener rarely was. Sometimes this listener understood intuitively and sometimes he didn't and sometimes he cried, 'Stop, Tom! For the love of God, stop!' Tom, feeling hurt, would then feel obliged to muster huge amounts of energy in order to re-mumble his initial condensed statements, but he could never do the second mumble as clearly as he did the first. If the listener chose to be polite at this point rather than honest, he could pretend to have understood and hopefully that would be the end of it. But if this person was having a day of authenticity – and Angelus was always having days of authenticity – they could be at the same point in the exchange for well over an hour. When Tom was especially upset or annoyed, which he had been of late because of this mental breaking-down process of his old pal Tom Spaders, he could hardly regulate any thought patterns, and this might account for why the mistaken definition of schizophrenia had come about.

By the way, I must talk about this 'upset and annoyed' business. You may have noticed that people in Tiptoe Floorboard only ever spoke about being 'upset' or 'annoyed'. It seemed that all emotions, even positive ones, had to be couched in terms of whether a person was in a state of annoyance or not. And if not, why not? What about upset? Was it that they were upset then, instead? If not upset either, which could imply that they were perhaps happy, that would have to be expressed in terms of them not being upset or annoyed as well. They might be 'Not too bad, thanks'. Or even better, 'Not too bad but I was annoyed and upset earlier, and I'm due to be upset and annoyed again later on'. Best of all, they might say, 'I'm warm I'm hot I'm cold I'm tired I'm hungry' – in response to a question as to how they were feeling emotionally – 'I'm warm I'm hot I'm cold I'm tired I'm hungry.' That was allowed. That could be said in this town. If someone was in grief – owing to some murder or to some disappearance of some loved one – that still shouldn't call for any spilling out of the 'upset and annoyed' position. They couldn't say, 'Distraught, distressed, maddened raw – what else do you think I'm feeling?' in response to a question as to how they were bearing up emotionally. 'How do you think I'm feeling,' they can't cry, 'when "Regretfully informs you ..." the policeman has just called to say?' All that 'Want to make him alive. Can't believe he's dead. Can't make him alive and I want to make him alive!' talk would be an intense, embarrassing thing to come out with in Tiptoe Floorboard, but you know, sometimes those words actually managed to break through. Such have been used by a few eccentrically suffering people, but in those cases, it's really up to the town's discretion whether to overlook them or not. But hey, I don't want to make a big thing out of a small thing, for every town has its idiosyncrasies. It's not as if nobody could express anything. It's simply that, in this town, regarding emotions, two words were enough.

'Anyways,' went on Angelus, her right big toe now unconsciously tickling the left calf of her husband, 'if the bruises are there but have come about by supernatural forces, what's the point in consulting a scientific medical dictionary about them? And – don't interrupt, Tom, let me finish, I said let me finish – if they're visual hallucinations and you and Johnjoe are the only ones seeing them, wouldn't that mean you two were having the problem and not poor Tom after all?'

At this point Tom thought that sometimes there was too much criticism, speculation and too many intellectual games in the world and not enough focus on what was working. Angelus had a semi-point, he would concede that, but what she wasn't reflective enough to realise was that this could be a case of Tom Spaders having an Inverse Hallucination and not he and Johnjoe having Standard Hallucinations Grade One. He didn't point this out, however, for she would only comment on his comment, the way she seemed to be addicted to commenting on everything that was commented. She might not interrupt people the way he interrupted people but hey, this constant commenting was to him just as bad. Why couldn't she just listen? he thought. Why couldn't she be quiet and just listen and remain quiet even after she'd listened? Why did she have to jump in, question, sum up and pass judgement all the time? That was why, every so often, Tom defended himself by not running things by his beloved wife but instead would suggest they retook the self-help stress test they took together periodically, to see whether they'd regressed or progressed in their mental health since taking it last time.

But here, right now, in the gunshop, thinking this might be the ideal time to run various mental illnesses by his friend Tom Spaders, Tom Cusack was wondering how to broach the subject, given Tom had become touchy in the matter of advice these days.

That's unasked-for advice, by the way. And you know how it is with unasked-for advice.

The great thing since the discovery of Recovery is not to be seen to be giving it. It's no longer appropriate to interrupt people while they're listing their problems and say, 'You should' or 'If I were you' or 'If I was you'. Apparently if you do this, you show yourself up as ignorant, anxious, controlling and old-fashioned. Only in the long ago did people behave like that. However, none of us likes to be told we can't interfere and organise another person's life for them, no matter how evolved into psychological modernity we are. Even whilst standing back with our calm bodies and our meditative breaths during, let's say, Tom Spaders's little spews of messiness, we always want to burst out and let him know what we would've done had we been involved in a mugging and stabbing affair.

What's required now, in order to get in there and manage people without them wising up to it, is to use language in such a way as to make it appear we are not the ones running the show. Now we have to listen to them – yes, that means without once interrupting – but as soon as they've finished, we nip in quick with our alternatives to 'you should' and 'you must'. There are many variations. You could say, for example, 'Some people say, Tom ...' or 'Have you considered such and such, Tom?' or 'Can I make a suggestion?' or 'Shouldn't we ...?' or 'Tom, I remember someone once ...'. In this way we manage to let Tom know what we would have done if it had been us instead of him in that mugging and stabbing incident, and if we do it properly, Tom will never know his mind has been fucked with or that, although he hasn't been interrupted, he hasn't been listened to as well.

Customer Tom, though. What a mess. Of all the people I know, he's the one who's just too messily human. Just too human. Didn't manage, couldn't manage, to stick to the 'you should' variations, which are a must for thrusting advice on to people these days. For his part too, Tom Spaders wasn't proving to be all that compliant and complaisant, which shows I suppose, that just because you're having a breakdown doesn't mean you've become stupid, or that you're not vigilant of others' reactions, or that, through fear, you're now socially and ineptly unaware. Clearly, Spaders was annoyed and upset that Cusack here had given that little laugh and made that insensitive 'prescription' joke after he himself had tried his best to tell the truth about what had happened to him, even if he didn't get round to admitting that the woman he was referring to was himself. Second, there was something so primevally annoying and upsetting anyway about the Ordinary Decent Folk trying to delude you into thinking you are being heard by them, whilst all the time it's obvious they can't stand what you're saying and are waiting for you to draw breath so they can shut you up. They think they've fooled you, he thought. Might even think they've helped you. Well, he wasn't going to stand around listening to 'transparent and good-natured' – which in Tiptoe meant 'stupid' – Tom trying out a disguised advice number on him. Instead he wished he could take and shake Tom and make him into quality audience – which meant 'Sit down, Tom.' 'Listen, Tom.' 'Tom, shut up.'

But he didn't take and shake Tom into quality audience and

49

Tom didn't try some new-fangled advice number on him. Instead what Tom Cusack did was much worse.

Before I go into what Cusack did and start a discussion on the Blueprint and the Anti-Blueprint, I have to go first with Spaders. He had opened some door and stepped back through seven years of time. We're going too. So now here he was, having forgotten Cusack, having forgotten the state of his shop also. Instead he was muttering, 'Didn't think she was right but seems she was right. Maybe I should have done what she said years ago and chucked this bloody shop.'

Him and her. And too long ago. But he had wanted her. Then he hadn't wanted her. But even when he had wanted her, it was that too much seemed to be getting called forth from him to be able to keep up with wanting her. Then he couldn't believe he'd wanted her. Then he didn't think of her. But now, strangely, unpredictably, since the mugging, she just kept coming up.

He had thought she was just being woman – 'Wash your own dishes.' 'Iron your own shirts.' 'Sew your own trousers.' 'Pack your own lunch.' 'Get rid of the guns. Stop having dealings with that Doe gang' – that sort of woman, that type of thing. And it wasn't even that they were together, never mind living together. And it wasn't dealings either. 'Not *criminal* dealings,' was what he had protested. All he was doing was running a shop. 'Besides,' he went on, 'you're a Doe yourself' 'Ah no,' she said. 'That's different. That's blood.'

'But it's legit!'

He tried to reason. He tried to persuade. He tried to apply his intellect into intellectualising her into a corner. He tried to get her round to his sensible way of thinking on that dark early morning of that particular day. Turned out to be their last.

'I'm doing nothing wrong,' he said. 'And I'm not blaming

my guns just because you don't like them. This is what I do and it's legal, and it's entirely because you're a woman you're thinking this. I could walk into any police factory in any city and show my papers without an eye being batted any day.'

Cough. Splutter. Sneeze sneeze. Attention attention.

I had to cough and splutter there to indicate these two people weren't telling the truth about the subject of their bickering. They were pretending the whole subject was whether guns were good or not. As if that mattered. As if, in the name of God, such a thing as that mattered. I think by now you must know what it is I'm really talking about.

That's right. This was the morning after the night before, and it had been a difficult night before and it was her fault and he couldn't leave because they were in his bedroom. She had invited herself to his bedroom, to his home, and there they were, still in it, in his bed. They were on their backs, side by side in that early-morning darkness, both definitely not touching, hardly speaking. So, do they think we're stupid? As if guns could ever be the point here. Like murder and torture and victims and cold-blooded killers and cold-blooded justice-seekers, guns, too, are incredibly easy of facilitation during an emergency. We dive upon them as subjects earnestly to argue about – all so we don't have to venture into that other, most tender, most delicate, most volatile of areas knowing that, once the guard was down, one of us, at any moment, might be invaded and taken over by the other or, at any moment, one of us, by the other, might be annihilated and destroyed.

So Tom had no idea he was on the defensive – I mean against desire, I mean against vulnerability. He really and truly thought the subject was guns. That was why he said,

'You snore. I can tell you now, so you know, you definitely, most definitely, snore.'

51

What a shitty thing to say. And I would say, had it not been for rejection and threat, and by threat I mean from that vulnerability, I mean from that desire – desire that had the power to take him and shake him, and open him up like he was a caught rat by the neck that was about to have its spine squished up and out of it, before being let go and dropped quivering on to the flagstones, only to be picked up just when it thought it could at last get back to theorising, and instead, being shook by the neck, this time by vulnerability, all over again – well, if it hadn't been for that, it wouldn't have been in Tom's character, consciously or unconsciously, to shame in the accoutrements of being female to any woman. But what can one do? Such things as women exist. I know you're thinking, oh, if only we could get our erections and total sexual, emotional, spiritual and intellectual satisfactions from guns, bullets, postage stamps and suchlike controllable essences. Wouldn't that be easy? Why can't we? After all, some men do. Why can't women be gun-shops? That would be even easier. How much safer, how much simpler, how much more predictable going into them then, might be.

But life isn't and we can't and women aren't, so Tom made that remark and it was out in one of those bursts of retaliation before he could stop himself. We're at the sexual level of him saying this and it was that basic because what else in that moment could it be? Angry, because she hadn't wanted him. Angry, because of rejection when he'd exposed his desire for her body. Angry, because she made it clear, after them starting, that he was to stop, that that was that, that he was to 'Stop', that he was to 'Don't', that he was to 'No, don't. Stop, Tom!' – that he was to get the message she no longer wanted him to proceed.

And she wouldn't look at him, wouldn't look at his body,

wouldn't *see* him. He gave to her and, although he said it was all right, that he wanted to give to her, it wasn't all right. He wanted something more than the pleasure of giving to her back. Even appreciation. She could at least have appreciated. But she didn't and all the time she wouldn't look at him, except for that once she looked at his face. She touched his face. Would she get on top of him? 'Will you get on top of me?' And she did, and then, after a second, all wooden, she slid off. Then the row – started by her – over something he couldn't remember. Well, he could remember, but he didn't want to remember, and anyway, it was her fault, that row, as well. Twisted it. Twisted his words. In the domain of sex – *'fuck'*, and just *'fuck'*, and *'When I fuck you ...'* – was an acceptable turn-on and she'd been childish in being the opposite of being turned on by it. Indeed, he had told her she was childish. Inexperienced. My God, he thought. Definitely inexperienced. Not sophisticated. She got dressed, damn her, partly dressed, then she disappeared into the bathroom. Then she came back, got into bed, then out of bed, then into bed, then back out of bed, rustling bags in her bag at the bottom of the bed, over and over – all during the goddamn hours of the night.

So, not surprisingly, he got her in the belly – intuitively rather than calculatedly. And he did it with that snore remark. I'll tell you now, though more of her later, she was got by that snore remark more than she was got by the *'Fuck you'* remark, though not as much as she was got by the *'Have you any idea how childish you are?'* So now it was next morning, and there she was, and it seemed as if an unexpected slap had come out of the darkness and landed itself upon her. It wasn't so much she did snore that it hurt her. It was that she understood – even if he didn't – the exact meaning back of his words.

Undermining bastard! was what she thought she should

have said. At the time, though, given she was still in his bed, still in his teeshirt, still in confusion, still in his territory, still attracted to him, still fighting her past, still holding her face as if that slap really had happened to her,

'You snore too,' was what, ineffectually, she did say.

Ineffectual, of course, because men are allowed to snore. It's part of the psychological mechanicals of being male. Women won't be astonished and think, God, how shameful! How ungenderlike! How destructive of his masculinity! A snoring man! I must ring up and dissect this with my friends.

So he got in there, to her vulnerable area, because she got in, the night previously, to his vulnerable area. In both their opinions they couldn't help but feel justified in reaching out and kicking as many vulnerable areas as they could.

Neither of them was admitting it. Hence the guns. Good auld guns. What a standby. 'Get rid of them,' she said.

'No,' he said.

'Get rid of them,' she said.

'No,' he said.

'I mean it. Get rid of them, Tom,' she said.

'I mean it too and I won't,' he said. Then she said,

'Tom, why is it you've never said my name, not once?'

And it was true. He had never said her name. Indeed, he couldn't say it. Not because he'd forgotten it. Most certainly he hadn't forgotten it. It was the dread of the capitulation of it, of the handing over to her of himself in it, of what it might take from him to pay her the compliment of letting her know he really knew her name.

You know how it is. Once you've said the name you've stepped over. And I mean the name of someone you want, someone you really want. I don't mean someone you don't want but are deciding to marry anyway to teach the person you do want a lesson. Someone you don't want, *you think,* doesn't take from you. So you say *that* name over and over, but not so the desired one's. To say *her* name means you're acknowledging, means you're at the mercy – for might she not kill you, just when you've decided you're happy, you're safe, you're totally at peace with this person? That's why you won't concede. That's why you'll say a version of it. That's why you'll say a nickname instead of it. You won't ever, consciously or unconsciously, get that name right.

Tom didn't have to answer the name question because Jotty Doe – not her Cousin Jetty, if you remember, with the Kalashnikov – now completely horrified at weakening her own defences by asking it, quickly rushed them on to their definitive falling-out. It was over the Fourth Dimension. Oh no, thought Tom. Not that Fourth Dimension. Yes. Fourth Dimension. Like the guns, Jotty brought it up.

You know how it is when you can't put your finger on something, I mean because it isn't physical, because it isn't material, isn't tangible? Tom said he was running a legal gunshop. Jotty derided with 'A concrete fact, Tom, that's all.

'And nothing's ever just about the concrete facts of a situation,' she continued. 'There are spiritual unspokens, non-verbal communications, invisible energies and a sense world beyond the material. And, Tommy, they're the bigger part of anything that happens to us here.' Now, this is not rubbish, but in the context of cover-up, *which this was,* it was rubbish. The perfect plane of non-temporal phenomena, in this context, delivered by Jotty, was identical, absolutely identical, to guns.

And here it started to get super-frustrating for Tom, a man who prided himself on his fairly good switch for picking up mentalness. He knew she was a Doe, of course – which meant a family of neuroses, psychoses and Edgar Allan Poe horror stories. So even if she seemed normal on the surface, there were probably enormous murderous tendencies underneath. Of course, when it came to dating, there was always that little problem Tom himself seemed to experience, but he didn't much like to dwell upon that. They can't all be mad, can they? he'd think instead, meaning women, and this would be whenever his switch for mentalness became heightened, which it would do any time an attraction to a woman threatened to go beyond the physical stage. She would start to appear not so attractive, not so safe, indeed rather startling and sinister – and, strangely, this would be whether she came from a psychopathic murderous family or not. So he'd ditch her, whoever she was, usually by forgetting she'd ever had an existence. Then he'd be free to look for the right one all over again. He'd wanted the right one, see – one he could click with, one he could be happy with, one he could acknowledge and recognise, for he'd really wanted to click and be happy and recognise, but with women it was as if you got to the top of the mountain thinking it was all over but instead it was 'Oh no! There's more mountain!' All the women he'd met so far had been exactly like that.

But in this case he could hardly believe that here was Jotty, sister to the Main Doe Man – a gang leader who, after all, was an unmistakable dangerous concrete fact if ever there was one – having the cheek to go on at him in a moral fashion about things you couldn't see, hear, taste, touch or smell. If only she could be like her sisters, he thought. Indeed, he couldn't help thinking, but I'll tell you about Jotty's five married, mothering, glamorous yardsticks of sisters by which Jotty – not married, mothering or glamorous – was constantly measured, when I get on to beautiful women with blood on their hands later on.

So that was what he was thinking. If any women could be

described as totally perfect, those Doe sisters, he thought, were it. But oops. Jotty could read minds. She was finely tuned, highly strung and her brain was never in neutral. She accused him of accusing her of not being like her sisters. This startled him. How in the name of God, he thought, did she know that?

He denied it. He said she was being ridiculous. But she reminded him again of how things – 'which include thoughts, Tom' – could be transmitted without the conscious material expression of them. Then she told him to get rid of the guns – a last-ditch default sentence that automatically came out of her. As his automatic default sentence, he said no, he would not. Then he said,

'I can't take responsibility for the actions of other people. I sell guns, but I've no control over what goes on with them when people take them from my shop.'

Spaders was glad he'd said that, for it sounded as if he could spout words of wisdom just as much as she could spout words of wisdom. But he looked at her and she was so into her authenticity, and he was so into wanting to be comfortable, and his guns made him comfortable. Jotty Doe rarely made him comfortable. So he ended up keeping them and giving her up instead.

That was the short version. The long version involved him buying lots of new, expensive gun literature, which was okay because he could claim them as tax expenses, and going to gun conferences, also tax expendable, and to those week-long, intensely involved gun lectures in many different towns and cities, where every member was entitled, drunk or sober, to stand up and give an hour's rambling speech-worth. He threw himself into these activities, and what with them, and dates – with women other than Jotty – interspersed between the gun adventures, his mind was taken off everything difficult, and that had been the procedure until those teenagers – he had reverted back to teenagers – happened to him six whole years ago.

Six!

Surely not.

Did he say 'six'?

That's what I was thinking and I was surprised at it being six – and I don't think that could be true, you know, for if any more years get added on to this mugging and stabbing, we'll be back to that early-teenage-angst breakdown he had in his twenties all those years ago.

While we were with Tom and Jotty, in Tom's past, with him dwelling on the impossibility of it ever having worked out between them, the Psycho Spatial part of him I had been telling you about earlier, that wanted him to go out and kill everybody, was fuming at just how easy a life, how settled and comfortable a life, yer man Cusack – who had never been mugged and stabbed and who had a wife – had. This part of Tom was still in the shop, with Cusack unwittingly preaching to it some rubbish called Blueprinting. 'No, Tom. No, Tom,' corrected Cusack, as he pointed to a section on a printed page torn out of a medical dictionary. He had spread it out on the counter between them. '*Anti*-Blueprinting! *Anti*-Blueprinting!' – point! went the finger. Point! – 'That's what I'm talking about here.'

Now, don't you think that when something happens, when you have a new experience, a little electrical pulse gets wired up around you? Your psyche says, 'Okay. New experience. Let's cut out the pattern and put it in the pattern box.'

That's Blueprint. The psyche makes preparations, believing this new experience will reoccur some day. Anti-Blueprint's different. Have you ever come across this:

The Well-Meaning stand in front of you – perhaps with a superabundance of confidence. They might take a hold of your hand – without permission. They might touch your cheek – again without permission. They think you welcome their gentle, unattacking touch. With these hands upon you – and I have no sense of humour here – they say, 'My dear So-and-So, believe me, it was terrible that thing that happened to you. But you know – here's the good news – if it's happened to you once, it won't happen to you again.'

That's Anti-Blueprint. It died a death many years ago because of its sheer utter ridiculousness. So what was Cusack thinking to bring it up with his old friend Spaders now?

Nervousness. Idjitness. A feeling of he'd torn the page out and therefore had to finish, but before he got going properly he had a clairvoyant moment which, believe me, was unusual for him.

Spaders was pointing a gun at him. And now, you always get a foreshadow, don't you, some little adumbration, when you're in that position of 'Watch out! Be careful! Don't do it!' because you're in the mood when you just might kill somebody? Equally, you get a foreshadow, don't you, when you're on the receiving end of someone in that mood?

Incredibly, Cusack refused to accept the message the universe, patiently, over time, had been handing him. First his friends had said, 'Tom's gone funny, Cusie. We're keeping away. We think you should too.' Even Spaders implied he was sick and tired of Cusack turning up and hanging around as if he were his nurse or something. And Angelus had said, 'Invite him for dinner, Tom, but don't go to his shop any more.' Even Johnjoe wrecking the place and shooting at them that day could be taken as a premonition of some sort. So warnings were running out. But still Cusack was determined. He had to get himself back to Anti-Blueprinting. 'Honestly, Tom,' he'd say. 'You've been mugged and stabbed already by hundreds of bunches of teenagers. That means you can never be mugged and stabbed by hundreds of bunches again.' Spaders, though, with the gun still in his hand, actually fired at Cusack – and all the white feathers and pieces of rubbish that Cusack did indeed, at that moment, seem to be covered in, rose sky-high, along with the sound of the gunshot, into the air.

But did that really happen? Looks like it, for the next thing I saw was that Spaders was back in the shop, coming to and, as he did so, finding himself behind one of his counters and apparently alone in the gloom of his premises. Where was Cusack? he wondered, setting a gun he happened to be holding down. Didn't have the decency, he then thought, to offer to help clear up after what had happened with Johnjoe. 'Well, that's friends for you!' And it was only later, when Spaders was in prison, that he began to appreciate the kind and quietly noble nature of his friend, Tom Cusack, but before we leave him to it, I'll just say that that crown of thorns I mentioned earlier that had broken out upon the head of Tom Spaders after he'd had his nosebleed with Johnjoe – I was only joking. There was no crown of thorns.

Chapter Four

At last. At long last. We can get back to Jetty in the taxi. I didn't want to alarm you but I was becoming worried we wouldn't get back to her at all. First, let's discuss what she was doing with that non-birding piece, and while we're about it, let's have a discussion also as to what sort of person she was.

Jetty was the older sister of Janet Doe, and Janet was married to John Doe. John Doe, as well as being other things, most of them not legal, was also very fond of women. Oh, and of girls. *His* girls. This means you're probably thinking Jetty – God love her – in devoted loyalty to her sister, as well as out of a sense of protectiveness towards her niece, had discovered that John was cheating on his wife and interfering with his daughter and so was on her way to the garden shed to shoot and sort him out.

You can think that if you like.

Here's what happened after she hailed her taxi. 'Taxi!' you'll remember she rushed out with her purchase and yelled. A taxi stopped and she got in. At this point I have to own up and admit that I was wrong, for I thought she was going to two places. I thought she was going to John Doe first, to shoot him at his headquarters, then was going to the Almost Chemist of the Year to shoot Janet, the sister, the wife. The Almost Chemist of the Year was at the top of the road, and Janet worked there, and Jetty worked there also. It was Jetty's day off that day, though. The reason I thought she was going to shoot Janet was because Janet was sleeping with Jetty's lover, and it was that way round, yes, that way round, as Jetty saw it, and not Jetty who had come in and grabbed the husband from without. I'm reporting this faithfully and that's why it's complicated, but I know you wouldn't want me to be making these things up. As far as the daughter and incest were concerned, Jetty wasn't capable of incorporating child sexual carnage. 'Child what what?' she'd say, if you were to put it to her for, you see, she could incorporate the strife of Two Women wanting the One Man, and she could incorporate the strife of Two Men after the One Woman. She could even incorporate murder, torture and social mayhem if she had to. But sorry. I said sorry. Jetty, along with everyone in Tiptoe Floorboard, was incapable of grasping inside sex. 'Why?' they'd ask. 'What for?', but they wouldn't really want the answer. Instead they'd retreat into incomprehension, thinking, how can anybody get their head around something like that? If further proof of this lack of grasp were needed, you'd only have to look at the later court proceedings. At many points during Janet Doe's trial, the gallery was seen to nod in complete accordance with the defendant who, when knowledge of her husband's perpetration of incest had been put to her, shrugged and declared in bewilderment that she didn't understand the question, that she worked at the Almost Chemist of the Year, and that shouldn't that answer questions enough?

So Jetty left the daughter, forgot her, and hurried back to Mary of the House Slippers, to the Girl Who Couldn't Wait To Get Married. In fact, 'The Girl Who Couldn't Wait To Get Married', thought Jetty, could be the exact thing they could put on her sister's grave. As far as Jetty was concerned she, and not Janet, ought to be coming first. She was the original, the legitimate, the first one and only, she'd been the girlfriend way before the wife had been the girlfriend, but John had told her the night before that he was never, not ever, going to leave Janet – 'Sorry, Jet, old mate. I sort of love her, she's the wife and the mother of my children' – but if it was any consolation he was not going to leave Janet for anybody, and not just not for her.

Jetty couldn't believe it. She tried to pull the curtains over in her brain to stop the harshness of the reality, but sometimes there aren't enough curtains – what with them being used up on incest, child molestation and suchlike.

Bastard.

John Doe, I mean.

That's what Jetty was thinking as he said those words to her. He went on explaining and excusing and still she couldn't take in that he was saying that, after another three or four or five or six or seven or eight or nine or ten more times of sex, they'd have to part and not be lovers any more.

She would not accept it. She could not take a back seat and hand the true husband of her heart over to that sister. That's why she was in the back seat of a taxi holding the Kalashnikov, with Bob Marley being played on a cassette tape up front.

Men.

That's what went through her head.

Then,

Fuckers! Then,

Men. Then,

Fuckers! Then,

Never mind them. What about her?

She switched to Janet. The total magpie of the woman was enormous. And you'd never think to look at her. You'd think

she knitted baby charity cardigans and made chocolate dona-
tion cakes all day. And after all Jetty had done for her. After all
that discount she'd given her at the chemist, before actually getting her a job at the chemist so she could then give extra-special
staff discount to herself. After all those crisp twenty-pound
notes from the till – the crisp ones, mind – she'd given her sister
in the olden days as change in advance for the things Janet
might one day purchase. It would break your heart, the grabbi-
ness of blood.

Bob Marley was being played loud for the taxi man had
turned it up. He kept trying to turn it up every so often, but
how could he, when it was already at the top? He tried anyway.
He wouldn't settle in his seat and be at peace and listen to the
song at its present very loud volume. If only he could put it
up, he thought. 'Don't worry about a thing,' said the song. But,
you see, the problem was it wasn't sung loud enough. He wanted
to hear it sung louder. He twisted the knob and twisted it but
all that would happen in this situation was that after a certain
amount of twisting the knob would come off. He stuck the
knob back on and twisted it again, and again it came off. And
loud. Very loud. It was really dreadfully loud. 'Mammy!'
screamed children, pointing with their toes, because their
fingers were in their ears, their eyes, in agony, scrunched up.
Other people on the street stood and stared or expressed horror
at this phenomenon, or else laughed at the rocking vibrating
madness of the car and of the driver who, at that minute, was
looking back at Jetty whilst driving forward, shouting, 'That
Bob Marley – is he annoying you? If you want, I can turn
him up.'

Jetty had dropped Janet and had gone back to men and
fuckers and that's why I was getting confused and even suspicious as to her plans. Was it to be the one, or was it to be the

other of them? Who was to be shot with the Kalashnikov? It was starting to seem she had no clear idea of this herself. Her memory kept drifting back to a stern and solemn judge who had looked down upon her once from the court's high altar. He had said something like 'Taking the law into your own hands is ...' but after that she couldn't remember any more. And when had that been? Twenty years ago? Twenty-five? Must have been a teenager. She remembered he'd addressed her constantly as 'young lady' and had said, 'The worship concludes the defendant suffers from wrong-rootedness.' What a thing to remember, but apart from it having something to do with her mother, or her aunt, and her cousins, and some mistaken-identity information, she couldn't remember anything about it any more.

Memory and selection. Those women pages always said don't get into triangular relationships. And although she would have said that she agreed, absolutely, and that she hadn't, that it was the wife who had interrupted into this one, a part of her suspected she had a bad track record when it came to her and men. She worked out once on a self-help chart why she'd chosen the men she had. First reason was because they were angry. That was thirty-two times. Second reason, unreliable – different men – also thirty-two times. Third, dishonest, dishonourable, vastly criminogenic, but seeing themselves as noble – Good Guy With Gun. That was twenty-eight times. Then weak. Oh, dreadfully weak. She went out with twenty-three weak men thinking they were strong but because they were weak. She went out with twenty-two men because they had boastful complexes when in public, which became self-hating complexes later on when it was them on their own. Does this seem a lot of men to you? It seems a lot of men to me. Then again, if you do the math – as those Americans say – and assume the dating had been taking place over a period of twenty-five years unless she'd started in childhood, Jetty so far would only have been with a man every 34.43 days. That's not much. But that's not all. There were twenty cruelly gorgeous men – who didn't want her, the number of loners she couldn't remember for in the end they were boring, and then there was a forgettable number of the depressed who went through the roof. The sex addicts, romance addicts and anorectic deprivers would each number about nineteen, she'd reckon. The ones intellectually beneath her – *but wouldn't that have been all of them?* By now, the chart's negative characteristics had put her seriously into the red. Finally she desisted from the exercise when it said, 'Well done, very brave, first part over, and now I want you to be braver and draw up a list of the negative traits *you yourself* brought to these entangles.' 'Fuck off!' she said, and ripped the chart up.

What Jetty had purposefully left out of this self-exploration, which turned out to be not that self-exploratory, was the murdering aspect. That was because a murderer who wasn't murdering her didn't count. Same with violence. And here I feel called upon to talk further about memory and selection, and especially as to how people think they don't know a particular thing when, deep down, they do. They live in this not-knowing yet knowing land, the land of the unconscious register, and one day something occurs that makes the penny drop. Unless you come from a mad family *and* have had extensive therapy *plus* experienced this penny-dropping phenomenon, I can see you'll have trouble understanding the concept. So let's have a gentle little supposing to clear the matter up.

Supposing you're fifteen. You've just come home on your lunchbreak from the Almost Chemist of the Year. The Almost Chemist of the Year is up the road and you got this part-time job as a store detective because the owner had started to notice most of his stock had disappeared. Jetty Doe, a staff member, had helped. She advised him to employ one of her relatives. 'My niece, Mr McSomebody. She's never done any store-detecting, and she's only fifteen, but at school our Julie is known as a bright button. She'll find out, so she will, who's doing all this knocking-off.'

So, you're on your lunchbreak from this, your first job, which you didn't want and which you hate because you know it's your own relatives – the Does by affinity and the Does by consanguinity – who are doing all the thieving, and say you walk in the door and you come across a dead body. Again. In your parents' house, in the house you live in. Again. And the house is empty of perpetrators. It's empty of everybody except you and him, and he's sitting there dead on the other side of the room. Say you do that. You walk in, and you don't want to drop dead yourself from the up-close reality of it, so either you play a ruse upon yourself and say the dead body's not there really, or else you take an aspect of the dead body that strikes you as normal and pretend to yourself that, because of this normality, everything else is the same as before. 'Uncle Joe always goes to sleep around this time in our house with his head resting on the cushion, with the cushion resting on the table,' you tell yourself. 'And look – cushion's resting on table, Uncle Joe's having his doze, head resting as usual on top.'

Head resting. Head resting, your mind tells you to focus on – and not head crushed. Head crushed. What tells you he's not dead, even though you know he is, is the resting of this head upon this cushion. And I don't mean it's decapitated. Don't be silly. I mean Uncle Joe's head is turned to the right, left cheek gently supported, arms below the table, limp and loose, relaxed, on his thighs, as always before. Uncle Joe's sloping over from the kitchen chair too, in just that fashion he's always sloping over in. He gets sick a lot now, because of his ulcers, you see.

So Uncle Joe gets ulcers and, of course, he's not really your uncle. He's your father's friend and a member of your father's Community Centre Teamwork Executive. He's the left-hand man as opposed to your Uncle Johnjoe Doe's right-hand man status and he and Uncle Johnjoe don't like each other much. Joe once said to JesseJudges, his seventeen-year-old nephew, 'If anything ever happens to me JayJay, I'll tell you what you do for reprisal. You hunt out yer man Johnjoe – for don't be fooled by what they'll say, it'll have been him that'll have killed me – so you kill him, that big fat ugly pig of a cunt.'

Anyway, his ulcers are the reason he has his sleeps in the afternoons although he won't go home to his own house to have them because he's afraid he might miss something. So he always naps at the Chief's kitchen table and little Julie – that's you, by the way – is expected to make him tea at lunchtime, leaving it, along with the German seltzer water and the biscuits, on the table by his side. You're expected to wake him before going back to work for your afternoon shift, for this is what you always do for your uncle on your store-detecting lunch-break. Today shouldn't be different, so why are you stalling this time?

You decide you'll leave Uncle Joe his tea and water and lemonpuffs as usual, but – unlike other times – this time you'll leave him to wake up by himself. You take a tray, as usual, up the stairs to your bedroom, but when you're finished, you leave your bedroom, wash your hands in the bathroom and shampoo the dishes in the bathroom sink. You leave them in the sink, clean and drippy, for you won't be bringing them back down to the kitchen. You'll fetch them and put them away when you come back from work later on. For now, you lean over the bath-tub and again give your hands a good scrubbing, then you're downstairs and ready to go out once more. You stay out of the kitchen and, closing the big door with a click, you head away from that house you live in. You go up the road quickly to the Almost Chemist of the Year. Your boss looks at you as you enter but you don't acknowledge him. He's a nice man and you know he's thinking, things are still being stole and she hasn't caught anybody yet.

So that's the knowing and the not-knowing, but without the penny-dropping incident. Unfortunately, I heard a rumour that poor Julie might not make it to the penny-dropping stage.

Preposterous! you might cry at the end of this supposing. Absolutely far-fetched! Well, okay. Don't boil your little blood. Don't bust those little body vessels. How about another gentle supposing on an even more normal scale?

You might prefer to be Julie's mother whose sister, Jetty, works at the local chemist and you go up there to get things cheap. You pick up hairspray, bubblebath, bathcubes, salts, tooth stuff, creams for the body and creams for the face. Wet tissues also, and dry tissues, and soaps-on-ropes and shampoo – a big bottle of the cheap stuff because that's what you're used to, but hey!, a bottle too of the most expensive in the shop. A lot of other things you wouldn't normally waste your money on you buy also, and you grab these things quickly – not because you've no intention of paying, for excuse me, you most certain-ly have. You'll get discount too, because you're related to a staff member. But that doesn't mean you're not righteous about your purchasing. You're moral and intentional and very upfront.

'Here you are,' you say loudly, handing over your one-pound note to your sister and getting your fifty-pee coin back in ex-change for it. You also get back a few lipstick samples, plus twenty boxes of French earplugs, and not having that same pound note coming out than when you went in proves you really did buy something in the shop. That fifty pee, you see, is called your change. Also, though, you're handed two nice and new twenty-pound notes from the till, which is called an advance on changes that you would get in the future should you buy things regularly from this chemist. This is not stealing. It's simply getting your changes, as I say, in advance. You get your purchases put in plastic bags, which further proves you couldn't have stolen them, and you have the door held open for you by a distressed-looking store detective as you leave. You struggle through and you smile at everybody and your smile says, 'Oh, me and my shopping!' An excellent day's chemistshopping, and you thank your sister who served you and you go to your house, which is just down the road. You go into your kitchen and you shoo that raven off that block, the block that has the axe stuck in that your husband brought back as a souvenir that time he went to the Big London, and you wave to your husband through the back window for he's out there in the garden with his mates. They're in a huddle and there's something lying between them in a hump on the ground. They're looking down at this hump but you yourself don't have time to look. You give John, your husband, a smile and he gives you a distracted handwave back. Then he shouts – as if he's just remembered – that he'll be in in a minute, that he wants to have a word with you. You're not to go out till he speaks to you. So wait there. Do you understand?

You turn round and this time you see one of the trapdoors is open that leads down to the tunnels. You didn't see that when you came in first time. So now you've got a headache – an instant dreadfully rotten bad-luck headache – so you drop the shopping on a corner of the kitchen table, ignoring a stained cushion, a mug of cold tea, German water and some biscuits going air-ridden in their open packet by the side. Instead you go to your room to tie a belt round your head and to have a lie-down to help this rotten headache. On the way up you notice somebody's left dishes in the bathroom sink again.

And now you don't care. Not just about your shopping, even though the whole happy business of it has been ruined for you. You don't care for anything, because all you know is this headache, and this annoyance at your daughter. Why oh why does Julie keep leaving dishes like that? And at Jetty, too, you're annoyed. So what if she gave you discount? Instead you're of the opinion that Janet and John – that's you and your husband – are the ones who have been more than generous to her. And for how long are you both meant to be so generous? She was thirty-seven. So why wasn't she married? And if she wasn't getting married, why wasn't she one of them modern women getting a house of her own and a little car to bootle about in, instead of cadging lifts from your Johnny all the time?

John comes up the stairs into the bedroom and he lies on the eiderdown beside you. He places his hand on the middle of your abdomen where you don't like anyone, ever, putting their hand. He says,

'We've been lying in this bed, Janey, together. You and me. All day without exception.' Then he makes you repeat and you say, 'We've been lying here together all day, John.'

Then he says,

'Good, very good – and we never separated, not once, and it's all right to be ashamed, honey, if anybody tries to fluster you by asking if you and me were having sex – don't worry about hitting a reddener, but make sure you say yes and that they hear it loud and clear.' And he makes you repeat that as well. You feel embarrassed but look – I've gone and done it again and given another inconclusive example. As with Julie, so with Janet. I heard a rumour the penny isn't going to drop in this quarter as well. But you know, maybe penny-dropping anyway, isn't easy of accomplishment. Perhaps it's normal to live with the curtains pulled over, practising knowing and not-knowing simultaneously all your life.

Of course Jetty Doe in the taxi knew, and at the same time didn't know, that her lover was a killer, but if pushed to define him in court, or indeed to God when she should go to Heaven, all she'd be able to say would be 'He's mine!' Like incest, murder was an accusation taken out of context, taken out of a dictionary. It was a matter of opinion. *This is what murder means because we say it's so.* If Heathcliff were to dig Cathy up and keep her, she thought, I suppose *they* would jump to hysterics and think that was wrong also. *And why didn't he keep her?* That was something Jetty, regarding her favourite love movie of all time, could never understand. So, if we're talking Johnny Doe and perpetration against others, she would shrug and suppose that, yes, if you're gonna put it like that, John could get a bit intense and into fierce discussion with other males sometimes. That was normal. That was attractive. But if you're talking Jetty and him and any violence towards her, then forget it. Johnny would never lay a hand in that way upon her.

They were a normal couple, see – apart from the Janet thing – and Jetty was a normal woman and, like any normal woman, the things that got to Jetty were normal also. Him throwing his sweet wrappers on the floor, for instance, instead of throwing them out the window like other people. Or him watching her painstakingly sew sequins on to a dress that he knew she was going to wear on a date with him that evening, yet saying, 'I don't know how you could be bothered doing that.' Or that he'd bring out his wife from behind the curtains any time he needed bolstering. Or bring up his daughter to cushion himself from her. Or haul out his biggest parental responsibility of all. She'd be saying, 'I need to protect our relationship because we are relating,' and he'd say any relating was out of the question because of the problem he was having with his maladjusted son. So then she'd say, 'When are we meeting?' And he'd say he couldn't see her Thursday Friday Saturday and Sunday because he was busy. So she'd say, well, wasn't that a pity, for she wouldn't be able to see him Monday Tuesday Wednesday and Monday.

Ragetime.

They'd have a fight then, and in that fight he'd manipulate her into declaring that that was that, that she'd had enough of him. But ha! – what he hadn't counted on her also saying was that someone not grown up enough to answer decent wee notes she'd taken the trouble to write him didn't deserve any more either to have those false murder alibis. He'd have to go back to Janet then, she said, to get her, the wife, to back him up in his whereabouts. And we all knew how Janet was under questioning. '*Almost Chemist of the Year! Almost Chemist of the Year!*' Lord! The woman was a bafflement – total world of her own.

And yet.

Oh, and yet.

Yet, my darling. Yet …

She'd get so charged, so bursting, never so connected as when, after their every romantic row, he'd grab her wrist sharply and say, 'My Jet, and this you'll like,' and she would soar with the danger and the charisma of him and it would be perfect, everlastingly perfect. And then. And then. Oh, well, and then …

It would be back to where he'd say he'd call but he wouldn't, even though he lived in the same house as her. He'd ignore her

73

and her reasonable notes that she'd write not quite insistently – just a decent letter every now and then to find out why. She knew he'd get them for under the breakfast table she'd be sneaking them and yet, whether or not he read them, he still, still, still – would not. A rumour would come by her about another woman – not Janet, forget Janet – and she would listen to it, and then write him another note enquiring about it. And all the time, behind her, without telling her, his secret fomenting was to stay with his wife. So you see, you didn't, you couldn't – how could you? – know the minds you're dealing with in this dreadful abyss of brokenness, this dead valley of hopelessness, this nethermost pit of faithlessness. Oh dear. Jetty Doe was in love and not having a good day.

The taxi man, though, who was nearly all right, in fact, he was all right, I liked him – in spite of the police and court much later getting it wrong about him – wasn't offended after speaking to his customer about turning Bob Marley up when he meant to say down and not getting any reply. Normally he didn't get replies when he spoke to his customers and, besides, he could see she was busy, that she was having some sort of inner conflict with herself. She kept muttering and twisting the strap of her machine-gun and, of course, he would call it a machine-gun for, you see, here was the Great Exception, the unique man, the man who could have been famous for his ignorance if only he hadn't been ignorant of his ignorance. Here was the only man in the world who didn't know guns.

'Rifle!' is what he guessed later in court when the authorities bullied him for a proper definition. 'Or maybe a shotgun,' he added. 'What's the difference? Is there a difference?' He admitted under oath also that he had a vague idea only that a rifle was a rifle because it had – 'Oh my goodness yes, rifling!' Normally he was happy, he said, to call guns guns. Also in his defence and in answer to a nasty question put to him by Prosecution, he said that although of course he'd seen this machine-gun in the possession of this woman, why did this man questioning him think he should be penetrated by any significance about that?'

'So what did you do?' Prosecution asked, and he said that he went on up the road to that wasteland. 'Ach, you know,' he said, 'that space on the junction where men beat up their wives and girlfriends?' He said that was where she instructed him to take her, and when the last track of his cassette ended, he took it out, flipped it over, adjusted the volume, stuck the knob back on and played Bob Marley again on the other side.

So the car wailed its way up the busy shopping road on this particular Friday, driven by the man who didn't know guns. In the middle of the back seat sat Jetty Doe holding the Kalashnikov, running over in her head what I took to be a distinct revenge plan. Right then! I thought she was thinking. I'm psyched-up! I'm ready! I'm gonna show that rat! I'm gonna bust in bangin'! I'm gonna blast that lyin' cheatin' two-timin—'

Just a minute. What's happening now?

If you're a woman with a gun, and you're getting into a conversation with a man you're attracted to, for example, at a party, it's always best to say, should he look quizzically at your weapon, 'My father taught me. I'm rather a good shot.' What you don't say is, 'My mother taught me' or – even worse – 'My ma taught me and I'm an expert crack shot.' This last has an aura of defiance and impropriety about it. Not the thing to express if you're intent on demureness. In fact, if 'demure' is your intention, I'd suggest leaving all weapons down the settee at home. If you must bring one, remember, don't scowl, and don't say, 'My ma taught me,' for if you say it, this fellow will think, goodness! What sort of household was it? She's attractive, but are the genes abnormal? Will our progeny be tainted? Will she try to kill me some bright afternoon day? Thus, the high-standing 'My father taught me', with the noble father now dead even if he isn't, always sounds better – tomboyish yet playful, teasing yet submissive – no matter that it's nothing but a huge disgraceful lie. Good sport, he'll think. And yet look! Isn't she bashful? I hadn't noticed but, really, she's decidedly rather bashful. Charming. Not one of those lesbians. Also, not one of those women who don't like men but who aren't lesbians either. She was obedient to Daddy. She took instructions from Daddy. That means she'll be obedient and take instructions from me too.

So there you go. Advice on how to get a certain type of man without jeopardising any of your weapons. But remember, that's only if you want that certain type of man. There are other men, but they will be way out of your category. That type won't pursue you. That type might talk to you because they can't help it, because you're beautiful and because you're standing beside them at the party, but they'll leave, and they'll not take you with them when they go. Before they go, they'll drop your hand, perhaps even regretfully. They'll say, 'Sorry. Can't do this. Life's too short to date a person with a gun.'

But chin up, never mind him, don't run after him, shouting, 'Wait! Come back! I'll get rid of the gun! I'll get rid of all the guns!' for he'd always be at you, hectoring, nit-picking, wanting you to give up all your chaos. Chances are, you'd have to get another gun anyway, to shoot him with in the end.

But back to Jetty. Back to Jetty, who defied all the odds that I might have placed upon her. Back to Jetty who shocked me by opting for 'My father taught me' when I never in the world thought she would. It wasn't that she'd gotten soft on Doe, her lover, during the length of that taxi journey. Incredibly, astonishingly, she'd never had any intention of shooting him all along.

I am too trusting and untutored in matters of twisty-turny sexualness. I am not stupid but I do not understand this world. Someone says something's going to go one way and I think, rightie-o! If you say so, and I believe them. What I don't realise is that, with some people, the opposite is true. With them it's the drama, it's the crisis, it's the delicious world of the fiction catastrophe. 'Gonna kill him!' 'Watch me kill her!' These are leadups to scenes that are never intended to be.

So, at the end of the tender 'soft as shit' milkbottle fantasy – oh, but I haven't told you about that yet – Jetty picked up the Kalashnikov and was nursing it. She was fantasising it was John, lying bloodied in her arms. By not killing him, but instead lowering the punishment so that she didn't have to deprive herself permanently of him, she could carry on enjoying him, whilst taking her revenge in never-ending pickings and scratchings later on.

So Jetty was imagining she'd arrive at the hut and he'd be alone, lying on that settee of his. He'd be sleeping, breathing deeply, in some private dreamland of his own. She'd tiptoe over to the Martini fridge and take out one of those chilling milkbottles, then tiptoe back, and break the bottle over his head. She'd take one long lingering look first – for soft as shit she was really. And, yeah, I know. The Martini fridge. How does one figure that?

You know how, in the olden days, if two men were in the bar and one said to the other, 'So I hear your wife hasn't produced any sons yet?' and he smirks and the man who hasn't any sons yet puts his glass down and legitimately punches the other man in the face? Then a fight breaks out and everybody in the bar wants yer man with the no sons to win because he's the poor bloke who's been hard done by already. He's been married ten years and has ten girls and that's all. So things are bad enough. So go on, God, let him win this battle. Let him take yer man and pull his head off. Do you remember how it used to be like that? And how, now, in these days, all these years on – in the days of therapy and of sitting in-group saying, 'Thank you for relating to me your anger response, I am delighted you were able to tell me you were angry' – you'd laugh at such behaviour? You'd think the smirker was an idjit and, if you were the man with the no sons, you wouldn't bother getting all Henry the Eighth about it at all.

In the same way as in those days, John Doe was a bit touchy and could still smart easily at any perceived threat to his manhood. That was the reason he kept the Martini fridge on the premises. You might think, ah! Aversion Therapy – pretty lilac feminine fridge, very female, therefore make himself get used to it. But no. Not that. It was a pre-emptive taunt in the face of other men, in case they were thinking of taunting him in the face, to let them know that he was so a man of male eccentricity that he could include pretty fridges or indeed anything pretty in his repertoire anytime he liked. Some said this was far-reaching of Doe and others said no, he was just a madman. Who would taunt him anyway? Not his team, they said, even though palpably these men were of the type who experienced problems with even minor splashes of colour. And not his rivals or random victims, for they didn't come into the shack unless they were being forced in to be murdered. Once inside, these men would then have concerns other than pastel fridges or whether John Doe was really a woman or not on their minds.

So it was seen as a bit of an unmale thing, the colour, the

dainty size, and what it was I mean – a Martini fridge I mean. Nobody used it for Martinis, because none of these men drank Martinis, and not often were any Martini-drinking, or indeed any women, allowed in the Doe Community Centre Hut. Two females only. One was Jetty, the consort. The other was that fifteen-year-old mascot. Neither of them drank Martinis, but Doe was adamant. Teabreaks were essential, especially at the end of all-night sessions. So, for practical reasons, they needed somewhere to keep their milk cold.

So Jetty was in her 'soft as shit' fantasy as the taxi approached the junction where men beat up their wives and girlfriends. The car stopped and Jetty climbed out. Kalashnikov under arm, she scrabbled in her handbag, threw some lipstick samples, duck pellets, toe clippings – yes, toe clippings – a handful of old eighteenth-century pistol balls she'd had in her bag, which had been taken off Napoleon by the English that time he'd been arrested, and 'Keep the change!' she screamed before making her way towards the Action Centre Hut. The taxi man hesitated, wondering if he should go after, then he decided against it. He shrugged. He was easygoing, so easygoing all his friends chided him because all his fares diddled him. But you know something? He believed monies due to him in the universe would come to him from somewhere. And something else. One way or another, they always, always did.

But back, back to Jetty and John and Janet and the Kalashnikov. Back to the police, who weren't supposed to be there arresting everybody. And back to what was contained in the garden and in the tunnels below the garden, and to the Community Centre Team itself.

The Community Centre, the team's headquarters, was a tinshack lumber room, a romper room, a ructions room, a room of noisy disturbances taking up the Doe back garden.

But this was only the iceberg tip. Originally the Centre had been the little garden tool shed down the back in the corner, but even in those days, if a cat had gone in exploring, it would have cried, '*Feng shui* miaow! *Feng shui* miaow!' and turned and run out. Now, it was the tool shed multiplied by a hundred, with most of the multiplications taking place underground. Of course there were no windows, and the structure in reality wasn't tin-fabricated. It was a building of the steel-reinforced-brick-iron-cage-concrete-fortified-with something-breezeblock type. You needed a password to get in and permission to get out, and once inside, you were expected to speak in a code language that was changed every week. Every so often a certain number of the uninitiated were brought in, and this would be at night-time. They never left in the same condition, and sometimes their bodies never left at all. First thing on entering was a makeshift bar, then, right beside it, a little stage or platform, then a stereo in one corner with records, cassette tapes and a few of those compact-disc things scattered around on top. A perennial smell of something hovered painfully over everything, the lighting was dim, a three-seater settee could be made out against the far wall. There was also an assortment of tables and other seating arrangements, with a further round table at the back, used for consulting the Ouija, and a pretty little fridge was just opposite across the dancefloor. If this place had originally been used for the Does to keep their innocent garden bits and pieces in, quite clearly it was no longer being used for that now. It still had bits and pieces – apparent junk – as well as some actual garden shed implements. At that moment these, and everything else, were being bagged and tagged by the police.

Huh.

Women and their fantasies.

You've got to laugh.

I mean – at women and their fantasies.

There was Jetty, entering the shack, and there wasn't John Doe, by himself, lying on the settee, eyes closed, all ready to have glass broken over him. And there wasn't the Martini fridge full of nicely chilling bottles of sharp milk. The milkman had arrived as usual, but he'd been unable to get up the path to deliver because he'd been prevented by millions of police people. Only reason Jetty'd been allowed up was because she was also going to be arrested and it seemed feasible for the police to blend themselves into walls and behind the nettles, tall weeds and grasses that made up the Doe front garden, and to let her come to them, rather than have them burst into sprints to try to catch her up. Turned out, therefore, that Doe wouldn't have been able to have had his head split open even if he'd been begging and whining to. By the time she arrived, he'd already been arrested and was in the van along with the rest of the handcuffed gang.

You've got to chuckle. They're so romantic, and again, I mean women. They think something's going to go a certain way and their energy spins and spangles and they get out their ribbons of detailed thought and their painstakingly hand-made heart tinsel. By now, everything's painted, borders festooned, all in sentimental, joyous anticipation. Well, all I can say is, disappointment is an extremely downplayed word. First thing that happened when Jetty walked into the shack was a mass of policemen immediately surrounded her. One tried to take the Kalashnikov while another said, 'Please hand it over. It's fruitless not to hand it over. And you too. There are instructions to take you also, I'm sorry to say, Miss.'

Chapter Five

John Doe had known that Jetty was coming after him with a weapon of some sort. He wasn't taking it seriously, although naturally he was flattered when rumour reached him of this affair. He and the gang were at Ouija, so all their valuable solemnity and concentration had to be saved for consulting. They were trying to discover who was the informer of the Community Centre Shack Action Team. It wasn't that he didn't rank her. I don't mean as informer. I mean as important. It was just that she was starting to take upon herself too much of the wooing in their love affair. He was annoyed by this, although naturally, whenever he pictured her holding all those male weapons, he'd forget his annoyance and a braggy boastfulness would come upon him and burst inside his heart.

That's my girl, he thought. 'That's my woman,' he'd say to people. 'That's my Jet. She takes no prisoners and, God, isn't she sexy? And look – even though she falls down by not taking an interest in the type and model of the piece she's currently handling, see how she's not afraid anyway to click one up the spout like that?' She had told him it had been her long-dead father who had started her in the bang-bang-you're-dead business. This was a lie, of course, based on the 'My Father Taught Me' premise, and John Doe should have known this, based on the 'I Know My Father-In-Law' – if yer man who was supposed to be Doe's father-in-law *was* his father-in-law – 'And He Isn't Dead And That Doesn't Sound Like The Dozy Auld Bastard' premise – but he did believe her, though not without the addition that it had been himself, and not Daddy, who'd got her into finishing school and finished her off. It was just this ballcrushing part of her that he was uncomfortable with. How could a daughter of such a dead, apparently noble, honourable man's man be so determinedly emasculating? It seemed these days one of his balls was continuously being grasped by her, whilst he was scrabbling to protect his dick and other ball with both hands. Unless you grow more hands here you don't have any hands left for manoeuvring. And also, you can become witless – what with guarding your privates, keeping an eye on the woman, being a husband to a wife, and a father to two off-spring, as well as heading up and keeping a tight rein on a serious Community Centre Shack Team.

It was always the same. And contrary to what she was implying, it wasn't his promise of ten, fifteen, twenty, twenty-five, thirty, thirty-five, forty, forty-five or fifty more times of sex before he finished with her that had annoyed her and started her off into that rowing. It was this giving and receiving business – for what on earth was wrong with Jetty there? In the bar, and just like his wife, she'd properly say, 'Yes, I want a drink, John.' But unlike his wife, she'd then say, 'But I'm not helpless. I'm perfectly capable of going up to the bar and getting it.' 'But I'll get it, Jet,' he'd say. 'No. I'll get it, Johnny, and while I'm about it, what would you like to drink yourself?' 'I'll get for both of us,' he'd say. 'And, Jet, let's not always be doing this. I'll get us taty-crips, and scampi-champ if you're hungry, but how about you drop this and we call it a male thing for today?' 'No,' she'd say. 'I said I'll get them. You stay here and hold your dick and ball and I'll be back in a minute. So. Drinks, taty-crips, cigarettes, scampi-champ, chewing gum. Anything else and any flavours in particular you fancy having there?'

See. See.

She was taking on the wooing. And although she wouldn't have actually said that ball and dick part, he knew she would be saying it really, behind the scenes of her utterances. And he'd feel that ball – the one she still had, up there at the bar with her – becoming more and more shrivelled, and he would sense he was handing over some elusive but enormous victory to herself. The strange thing was, he knew instinctively that if he were to stop the dance and cross his arms and lean back in his chair and smirk and say, 'Thanks very much, Jet,' and let her pay for everything hereafter, she'd soon stop all that crap and get properly femalely upset. But then it would be out in the open and did he really want to have it out in the open? He wasn't sure what 'it' was, but it seemed to involve him losing perhaps more of his anatomy, and her refusing to sew feminine sparkles on to pretty dresses to wear on dates with him any more.

But on a non-genital level it was all very annoying too because this had snuck up on him just when he hadn't time for it. It was distracting him from meditation upon the occult powers needed for the job at hand. A few of his policemen relatives had tipped him off, saying that ever since the arrival of that Interfering Outside Policeman, the town's police themselves had been shaken thoroughly as well as officially divided up. They were now operating from within secret inner circles within other, smaller, even more secret inner circles, each issued with new camouflage cryptography symbolism, and that they were being forced, the cousins said, because of all the extra murders, to step up investigative activity into the Community Centre Action Team. So Doe brought his attention back to the round table, for obviously there was an informer amongst them. And look, already the Ouija was spelling out some words.

They all leaned forward. It was saying the betrayer was the one putting his fingers into the sugarbowl right now. 'N-O-W,' it finished spelling and then it whipped out 'KNIFE IN BACK! HE'S BEHIND YOU! OH LOOK BEHIND YOU!' and he looked round quickly. They all whizzed round and guess what? There was the son, John Doe's son, his own bloody son, unaware they were looking at him, muttering 'habitable-uninhabitable-inhabitable' in the corner, whilst absently dipping his shovel into the sugarjug.

'J! J! J!' screeched the Ouija, now hysterical and all of a stutter, but no one was paying any more attention. Everybody had got the message and, God! the gang was thinking. Who would have thought it would have been Judas, that it would have been John Doe's own son? What was John going to do? they wondered. And what about JesseJudges? Would he finish JayJay off because he'd started and therefore wouldn't want any testifying witnesses, or would he bestow forgiveness upon the boy and take him back as a reinstated member of the Doe Garden Shed Shack?

JayJay, or more formally, JesseJudges – a half-solemn name for such a seventeen-year-old youngster – was the latest to be half-dead and tied to the torture chair. 'Cept he'd fallen over, this one, along with the chair, and was now lying on his side breathing hoarsely. He had some doubled-over brown thick postal paper sewn into a hood over his head. That teenage mascot was on the floor beside him, and I don't understand but she seemed to be giggling. She was biting her nails and tittering, splayed on her bottom, splat on the floor. Her legs were sprawled out one minute from under her miniskirt. Seconds later they were drawn in primly. Then, after another giggle, out they'd be, sprawled over the floor once more. She kept touching, ever so lightly, this boy's hood-bag, leaning her ear, so slowly, so rhythmically, towards him but I think it must be that JesseJudges was the latest to get the blame for betraying Doe to the authorities. It had only been days since his Uncle Joe had been secretly tortured, tried and executed for the same offence.

So yer man Johnny was going a bit J Edgar Hoover. He got it fixed into his head that somebody was doing the betraying, so he postponed business as usual to carry out interrogations on various members of the team. With JesseJudges, though, it had been different.

If we're going to be mentally healthy, you and me, and have days of authenticity going on between us, you'll need to know 'The Great Betrayer' was just one of those herrings – one of the red kind. It was an issue certainly, and the team did need to deal with it, but the real reason JesseJudges was being murdered was because of John Doe and his woman code. He had this code that was all to do with him and his dating of the females. When it came to enforcing it, he took no prisoners himself.

He had these romances, Doe, and after he'd had them, the women he had them with, they became his ladies. That meant there was no way he'd let anybody put a finger on any of his girls. His ladies included not only his wife, his daughter, and most certainly Jetty, but also anybody he currently happened to be having, or whom he hadn't had, but who was in his savings account and waiting for him there. His ladies were his ladies, said his code. That meant you kept your hands off. Apparently, you kept your eyes off as well.

So that was why he was upset when he came down the stairs one lunchtime, during a pause with Jetty, and heard a low sound of murmuring coming from the porch. He was in the front parlour, having come in to fetch his souvenirs, which he kept in a box beside the museum suit of sixteenth-century Flemish body armour, next to the broken Versailles clock that held the three samurai swords and the Glock No 9. He wanted to go through these mementos in their transparent pouches in order to gear himself before returning to Jetty – just a little idiosyncratic thing he did now and then. The pouches were full of men things, and I mean things that had belonged to certain men who were no longer living. These personal effects appeared to belong exclusively to Mr John Doe now.

But this bloody murmuring! He glanced up from his trophies. Who the hell was making it? *Murmur-murmur.* What was it? *Murmur-murmur.* Oh, stop it, stop that murmuring! But was it murmuring? Where was it coming from?

He moved to the bay window and juked out from behind the curtains. His daughter Julie and JesseJudges were sitting on the windowsill. They were side by side, their shoulders almost touching, their backs turned towards him and the awful cheek, for they were only inches from himself behind the glass.

First thing he did was check out their hands.

This took manoeuvring, but he managed to get his body into a pose of imaginative detecting, and could see clearly JesseJudges's left hand on his own left thigh. The boy was gesticulating with his right and good, that was good, just as well he wasn't touching my daughter, thought Doe. Though I'm still going to get him. Concerning daughter Julie, Concerned Father could see clearly that she had her right hand up, pulling nervously on her right earlobe. As to what that left hand was doing – damn and blast – he simply could not see.

He tried to listen. He really tried to listen. Mostly it was drones and murmurs, except for the odd unrevealing phrase. 'Yeah, I know what you mean,' he heard Julie say. She laughed a little nervously, a little panicked, tugged her ear again, and now twirled a twine of hair as well. JesseJudges laughed quietly and went on murmuring – *God, that murmuring!* – and their shoulders touched and Doe flinched as if he'd been manhandled himself. With great reflex he jumped over and grabbed up the Glock No 5. This Glock was loaded, as were the other Glocks, but he kept Five balanced precariously on top of his wife's empty pincushion. This was for emergencies. Male and female was the emergency now. He knew males and females only murmured together after they'd done lots of interacting previously. And what about that shoulder-to-shoulder? And what about that left hand?

'*Well*,' said someone. *Jesus himself said, "These things that I do, you can do also"* ' – '*Ach, yeah*,' said someone else. '*But that was just Jesus. He didn't mean that. He was only saying that to be nice.*' I thought you might want to know that that's what was on the TV in the back room when John Doe had his fit. He didn't have the fit in the front parlour and he didn't have it because of this mention of Jesus. He didn't hear Jesus and, also, there was no bursting out on to porch naked and shooting Glock at JayJay and perhaps at Daughter Julie also. Instead, he withdrew from the window and replaced his weapon slantingly. Quietly, he went back upstairs and got dressed.

'Yeah, see ya, Jetty,' he said, though distractedly. His lover, now also dressed, was going back to her afternoon shift at the chemist. His wife was out somewhere, and Julie too and JesseJudges too were no longer on the porch when he came back down. Brooding, and now plotting, he went into the rear living room and, along with the TV, switched on radios on competing channels. He had these radios and TVs blasting and it didn't matter what was on for, given his mental state, nothing was going to get through.

So we had doubters and believers on that faith programme on the TV in one corner, and we had a radio book programme – *'It's always best to reread a second time in order to be more critical and in that way we can really train ourselves not to like it'* – in another corner, and we had a social commentary radio drama – ' *"Put more fuckin' curry in it!" snapped the lowlife to the Indian. So the Indian in the takeaway – did'* in a third and still that wasn't enough. Doe had a fit of the headstaggers, but before we go further – where I describe Judas, the son, describing John Doe, the father, trying to kill Julie, the daughter – we'd better go back for me to give the whole contextual picture as to why.

It wasn't just JesseJudges, you see.

It wasn't just other boys who might appear or who might have already appeared upon the horizon.

It wasn't just that cunning over-active left hand.

It was also 'Noises' – a condition that used to afflict Doe as a child and that he'd forgotten he used to be afflicted by. It had made a return – *'Hello! Guess what! Guess who! Guess what!'* – to torment him again, mysteriously, after all this time.

Here's the thing.

This condition was termed 'Noises' by the original Doe children, but I don't know what an expert psychoperson writing a thesis on them would call them today. In John Doe's generation, Benedict got them first. He was John's brother and he was the eldest and he was thirteen. Then a day, or maybe even less than a day later, he infected JanineJoshuatine, who was his sister. Some of the younger children could structurally remember this happening, for it seemed as if an invasion of the Noises travelled across the very air. JanineJoshuatine, who was twelve, then passed them to their sister, Unity, or else Unity caught them, again like an infection, and again, which way round has never been clear. It took a week, or maybe five days, for Unity, who was ten, to get them but she got them, and she gave them to Jotty. Against her will, Jotty took them. It happened in twenty minutes. Jotty was nine. Two weeks later, Samuel, who was eight, got psychologically infected by Jotty. A month later he gave them to John. John Doe was seven. He was seven. The two twins, Abel and Abel, who were five and five, caught them simultaneously from John, then thrust them on to little Gussie. Gussie was four. Hale, who was two, had them from Gussie and eighteen years later – and isn't that strange? – Hesit, who was a one-year-old when the Noises spread amongst her siblings, got them herself when she was nineteen. She killed herself and three other people during a séance when she was twenty-two. It is not known from which sibling she caught the Noises or why it took her so long. So, the Doe batch got the Noises, but nobody paid attention to batches. Their parents, when they thought of it, were of the opinion that 'the kids' were exhibiting some quaint, quirky, diverting little phenomenon – and before anyone realised that this was an affliction and not an amusement the Noises had multiplied and got a great hold.

Off record, I can tell you that, bar John and one and a half of his sisters, those initial children were now dead, or in jail, or had been removed long ago to join older-generation mad relatives in the Tiptoe Under Greystone Cliff's Peninsula Mental Asylum. Jotty was the one sister who was still up and running and JanineJoshuatine constituted the half. Janine was required to go into the mental hospital every so often to get some sort of top-up. Apparently, when they said she was going on holiday, she wasn't going on holiday after all. In a nutshell, that was how the Noises began. As soon as you've taken in this information, let me know and I'll have this evidence destroyed immediately. This is top secret. Don't repeat what I'm about to tell you, or I'll be in trouble with everyone for sure.

There grew to be about eighty of these Noises, so I'm not going to list all of them. From the outside they do seem funny, but just from the outside. So remember that and please don't laugh.

First, eating and drinking. Those munching sloppy and slurpy sounds, with the food white and mushy in the mouth and going round and round like a washing machine because the eater doesn't know how to eat with his or her mouth closed and doesn't realise that a lot of people in the world can partake of meals without huge torrential splats and snorts. John Doe and his siblings got disturbed first by that. And by the blowing- on of food – even if it was cold, even if it was ice-cream – this blow-blow, spit-spit, blow-blow, lick-lick – ultimately to exert posses-sion, ostensibly to test and cool the food down. It was their big parents doing it, their huge angry frightened distorted big mamma, and their even huger angry frightened distorted big papa. Then Mamma and Papa's angry frightened friends did the smacking and sucking and blowing and licking, whenever they, too, came to call.

The children, acting as one, would try to leave the room whenever these Noises started – upstairs, out the back, straight out into the street, on to the path of horses, stagecoaches, carriages, trams and oncoming locomotives – anything, just to get away from those adult menacing sounds. If they couldn't get away, it would be rolling up into balls on armchairs and settees and behind pieces of furniture, fingers in ears, faces screwed up. It would be shoulders scrunched up to and including their very earlobes. It would be eyes closed tight, for the sight of those mouths and that relentless devouring jawing became, in no time, a visual Noise as well. And counting. They'd count, over and over, in their heads, 'One Two Three Four' and right up to the numbers they'd learnt at school that morning. They'd count and count because that was preferable to having an attack of the Noises coming on.

Or they'd copy. But that was dangerous. But they couldn't help it. The Noises urged them on. Papa would belch, a giant explosive unconscious 'fuck-you-world' belch, and they would all belch 'fuck-you' after him. They wouldn't dare look at him as they did this. They wouldn't dare look at each other. And when Mamma farted spectacularly into the living room, they'd all make their pretend farts as well.

It helped to copy, to imitate, to have a bit of power, in order to cancel out the ghostly mental repetition of the Noises. Otherwise these Noises would reverberate, sometimes for hours, inside the children's delicate little heads. But now and then Mamma or Papa would realise and say, 'Are you copying us? Are you fucking copying Mr McCotter over there, sucking his teeth and scratching his head and swinging his leg and playing with his crotch in that armchair?'And John Doe and his siblings would be hit hard and thrown in a heap-of-puppies movement up to bed. Sometimes it didn't stop there, for through blocked-up ears, through pillows they'd pile on top of their own heads, through their crying, they'd continue to hear Mamma, and the echo of Mamma, who was addicted to eight-in-a-packet penny gums beechnut bubble gum, cracking away hard and triumphantly, as many bubbles as she could on one breath. 'Cheeky bastards,' she'd say to Papa. 'A bloody good hiding.' And she'd glock and clack and crack, doing it for badness, knowing that they knew that she wanted them to know that she'd forgotten them, that she hoped they didn't seriously think a pack of kids could interrupt her in her life.

Soon the Noises spread and it wasn't just adults who tortured them. They'd punch a child at school who had sniffed and sneezed and blown into her handkerchief, or they'd get punched at school themselves for copying some other happy child playing his imaginary guitar. 'He started it!' they'd wail to the bewildered teachers, and they'd believe this, and they'd try to explain and convince the teachers that he'd attacked them with the sight of his moving fingers. He assaulted their bodies between their legs by the sight of those spidery fingers moving in the air by themselves. So, you see, after their eating success, the Noises gained power and eminence and spread forth their kingdom. They had introduced sniffing and sneezing and coughing and fingers and found localised body parts inside the children in which to experiment as well. Fingers did damage. Tiny movements. Little movements. They twirled, they tapped, they pointed, they picked, they pressed, they placed themselves in mouths and touched tongues and pulled at loose cuticles. They even employed other fingers to crack knuckles and prise at thick and thin finger- and toenail ends.

The siblings made their own Noises too, of course, and they bothered each other with them but, knowing it was to their mutual benefit not to torment, they formed a pact against accidental slippage by allowing any of them to shove any other any time a Noise was made by one that might set the other nine off. So they did. They shoved and hit and thumped and shouted, 'Stop that! Stop that! If you do that again! Say you're sorry till I tell you to stop!' This had worked and had kept an empathic peace amongst the children until one day something new happened. The Noises, for some reason, for some of the children, stopped.

Through natural immaturity, the apparently cured Doe children had in reality unconsciously swapped their Noises for something more manageable. Violence – and by the bucket-load – kept the Noises away. The more they learned to put it out in any situation or circumstance, the more their particular brand of Noises disappeared.

John Doe was the luckiest of these lucky chappies. As a boy, he started doing as much damage to others any time he got the opportunity, and within a day of his new addiction to violence being set up and running, he forgot he'd ever had the Noises. He even forgot the term 'Noises', and as an added bonus he found there was something else. If he was to breathe loudly, or rub his hands, or pick a knot on his face, even if it was imaginary, or whistle, or pretend to be kissing, all in sight or sound of most of his siblings, they would writhe and contort as if they were his puppets and he their puppet master. They'd go berserk as he increased the pressure and drove them in torment up the wall.

So Doe was cured. Only now he wasn't. The Noises had returned – *'Hello! Guess what! Guess who! Guess what!'* – to make his life a misery. But why, after almost thirty years? It wasn't as if he'd tailed off in the doing of his violence. It wasn't as if he wasn't at his top-notch capacity for the infliction of his violence. Could it be that the amount of violence needed to control such a phenomenon was no longer proving adequate, was no longer enough?

At first tiny irritating sounds had started to creep in and prod at him, and again, at first without him being fully aware. Jetty would be eating her chewing gum and he'd want her to stop eating that chewing gum. If he looked at her in annoyance, she'd laugh and chew and crack it even more. His wife would be examining her bitten fingers to see if there were any other ragged stumpy bits she could chew off and spit away from her, and he'd want to lift his arm and whack her in one hard whack right out of and across the room from that chair. His son would brush at his nose as if he were doing drugs when he wasn't doing drugs but instead wiping at a blackhead. 'Fucksake!' Doe would shove him and say. And it went on – daughter pulling at earlobes, daughter fiddling with hair – then, of course, fingers, fingers, more fingers and murmuring. Then neighbours with their TVs, their radios, their chatting, their laughter. Even his gang's juddering footsteps as they walked or dragged things back and forth across the shack's floorboards. Those men in the chair too. *Those men.* Every single one of them seemed now to exert power over Doe and that shouldn't be, given he was the one killing them. It wasn't so much either, the sounds they made as they were dying. It was the ones they made well after they were dead. He used to eat these men – small symbolic bits, understand – just to make a point of who had gained possession. Now he no longer ate them. They reverberated inside him when he knew they didn't reverberate inside any of the others who were also eating them. Last time he'd eaten one, he had to leave the shack, tiptoe round the back, and vomit the man back out.

I hope that rationally explains to you why so many TVs, radios, extractor fans, vacuum cleaners and spinners of washing machines were all sounding concurrently in the Doe household. According to Doe, because he had to block out the Noises of his neighbours, his own place was cracking up. All windows, all doors had to be closed and all light coming in from outside covered with dark hangings. Hence it was chaos. At any moment now, there might be a Doe-house-collapse.

As for Janet, Doe's wife, she had to be included. Doe was affected by Noises. That meant she had to be affected as well.

But she wasn't. That particular madness didn't run in her family of origin. So her way of being affected was to buy earplugs for her husband every time she went out. She had to scour Tiptoe Floorboard's chemist shops for every box of earplugs, even if she herself couldn't grasp why it was that John had to play music, washing machines, fridges, hairdryers and everything mechanical so loud. The Doe children, Julie and Judas, had inherited the Noises, and in their desperation, they'd steal and stock up on the very earplugs Janet would be procuring. Neither husband nor wife knew about this siphoning-off.

So Doe went to the cupboard in the kitchen and you know that cupboard in the kitchen? It's the cupboard that everybody has that they don't know what to do with. What should they put into it? they wonder, we all wonder. We don't know. But how come we don't know when all other cupboards in the house have got sorted? Are we mentally deficient that we can't deal with this one as well? So, in confusion, it becomes a mixture-of-everything-in-the-house cupboard. First it's First Aid, but all that gets put in there is something smelly and old and of the colour brown in a bottle. So then the First Aid gets taken out and chucked through the window to be gotten rid of, and cleaning stuff gets put in, but that confuses, for the cleaning stuff officially is kept under the sink. So then it's eggcups. Eggcups get put in to make it an eggcup cupboard. But hold on. You've only got three eggcups, maybe two, which doesn't warrant giving a whole cupboard to them. So then it becomes a pending haphazard cupboard holding all sorts of things instead. Back comes some new First Aid, or maybe the old First Aid that hadn't been thrown out the window, but instead had been placed on top of the TV to be thrown out some time in the future, then scraps of paper, three eggcups, chipped ornamental plates, a few oranges made of plastic, the odd hammer of varying sizes and an accidental bit of bread. Nothing in there is mentally sorted. That cupboard at the end is left stamped with 'No Definition'. It craves an identity and because you won't give it, it becomes – and it serves you right – the enemy within.

It seeps discontent.

And neglect.

And depression.

And, finally, murderousness every time you enter the kitchen. You begin to feel queasy and unwell. A teacher psychologist might say, 'The problem here, students, is that the cupboard is carrying the shadow. It is the bad child, whom the rest of the furniture, at its peril, ignores.' That's not the point I'm making, though, about the Doe Family Cupboard. This Doe cupboard had long been tagged and sorted. It was for earplugs. So thank goodness – no shadows or hidden trauma there.

Naturally, any talk of the kitchen cupboard would lead one to talk about the space at the end of the space and to spaces chopped up into smaller disturbed abutting angled places and about the sort of people who need to abide in those split-off nook and cranny upside-down corners or in places of transit, like staircases, for some strange, fragmented, demented reasons of their own. I haven't time to get into that now for I must tell you that John Doe had gone into the kitchen and down to the cupboard, thinking he was going to open it and extract one box from millions of boxes of earplugs he thought currently were in there. Thanks to his teenage children, though, and to his wife who had mislaid the latest shopping, he opened the cupboard and there were none.

And that's what brought on the headstaggers. For her part, Mrs Doe had gone out a day earlier to replace the earplugs, for she'd noticed the numbers in the cupboard were getting thin. But she forgot to return with the new stock because she'd left them in a gunshop after being distracted by a plainclothes policewoman, who had been lying in wait to waylay her on the sly. This was the first time this undercover business had happened and it came about because the Top Echelons realised that the new spate of killings in Tiptoe Floorboard were different from the usual spates of killings in Tiptoe Floorboard, that the killers were putting their eyeteeth into their victims for a start. Given the number and the mystery and the news coverage they were engendering, everyone was in agreement that something had to be done. Hence this policewoman latching on to Janet, with Janet not cottoning to her identity or to her motivation. Indeed, Ms Detective Underplain had proved so good at her job that Janet thought she'd made a spontaneous friend she could go to bingo with from now on.

'It's usually easier with men,' said this policewoman, when she was interviewed years later for the history programme *Garden Shed Gang: Heroes or Villains?*, being made for posterity by the TV. By then she had been promoted to Her Royalhighnessship Local Authority Team Co-ordinating Area Flying Commander of the Gold and Silver Battalion Divisions, but nonetheless was good sport enough to speak of her days on the humble plainclothes detection beat.

'Certain kinds of men ignore a certain kind of woman,' she said. 'No. I tell a lie. It's not even that. It's that they don't credit them enough visibility even to see them standing there in order to ignore them. For example, I might be right beside them, or behind them, or in front of them, say at a bus-stop, and they wouldn't see me – no lipstick, no makeup, hair a mess, generally a bit mousy, a bit scraggly – and I'd be holding my shopping bags and rocking my pram. In one bag would be my Glock Extra Sensory 47, which as you know in its day was of the best time-saving, up-to-the-minute brighter and richer colour treble-lamp technology version, and in the other would be my old trusty standby semi-automatic affair. In the pram would be my recording equipment disguised as a big baby, just in case they got suspicious and had a look in. But no. Practically they'd be shouting to each other – about the day, the time, the place and the victim for their next kill. I could have turned to them, shoved the plastic fake infant in their faces and said, "Excuse me. Would you mind repeating that? I think my special secret services law enforcement microphone disguised as this here giant baby didn't quite pick it all up," and you know, still they wouldn't notice, still they'd continue detailing as before.

' "Who's acting as judge this time?" would shout one to the other.

' "Johnjoe," would shout the other back to the first.

' "Who's acting as jury?"

' "Big Chief, John Doe."

' "Who's acting as executioner, and is Jetty still taking the minutes or is she on her break this time?" So you see, as long as you don't look like Marilyn Monroe, as long as you haven't put on lippy, as long as you haven't done your hair or taken yourself out of your dowdy, part-of-the-damaged, can't-be-bothered trauma costumes, then you'll do fine, then you'll do more than okay.

'Not with women, though.' And here she sighed. 'With women, you have to be adaptably careful. With women you have to watch where you put every single one of your little Size Three Cinderella feet. Also, mostly it helps if you look slightly more on the groomed side with women, unless you're dealing with an exceptionally untidy highly traumatised woman, other-wise they'll feel freaked that something psychically contagious and disadvantageous might leap over from your aura and latch on to theirs.

'Not too glamorous, though,' she went on, 'for that would be construed as inverse criticism which wouldn't do either. So you see,' she shrugged, 'it's a tightrope of constant adjustments whenever you're dealing with women. It's almost never clearcut or wee buttons with them.'

Fortunately for this policewoman, Janet Doe turned out to be from the wee buttons category.

'Oh yes! What luck!' she said. 'I didn't have to undergo months of stringent, prolonged "Disguised Authenticity Training" for her. All I had to do was stand outside the chemist on the High Street, look as if I were truly interested in a ridiculous plaque displayed in its window and then, as she struggled out with her enormous shopping, I'd turn, point to the plaque and exclaim, "Yes, but what does it mean – '*Almost* Winner of the Chemist of the Year'?" '

I can't tell you how much Janet Doe loved that question, though she doesn't love it so much now, given all these years have passed, and she's still in the jail section of the mental hospital as an accomplice to everything, whilst the men who did the everything are now famous and iconic and will certainly be hailed as heroes upon their early release. But in those days, at that point, she said proudly to the policewoman, 'I can tell you what it means! It nearly won the award that's awarded every year to the world's best chemist. I actually have a sister who's an employee in there!'

Well, of course this undercover person already knew that, as well as a lot of other things about Janet and her sister, but she said, 'No! Do you really?' plus further praiseworthy comments like 'How great to be a finalist, and to be an employee of a finalist, and to be related to an employee of a finalist! With success like that, it's only a matter of time.' Janet was so pleased with this response that she no longer felt the stranger to be a stranger. Immediately a little friendship bond was struck up. They went for tea and profiteroles – Betty, for that was her name, insisting upon paying – and they had a good natter in one of the café-stationery-launderette-gunshops further along. Janet did most of the talking. She told Betty about how she'd been shopping for years at her sister's employer's and how there were some really good bargains to be had if you just knew what days and times to go in and how to pick the right person, as well as knowing what shelves to look for those best value-for-monies upon.

According to Betty, who reported to her superiors later, Janet also revealed some unexpected high-grade shit about the chief suspect, whilst all the time thinking she was chatting innocuously about bingo, being married, and naked men.

Janet told Betty about him being naked, although later she could hardly credit she'd done so, given the thought even of saying 'naked' would send her plumb blotchy red. But she and Betty had been getting along famously, developing rapidly in their exchanges of soul business that her latest worry about John naturally had come out. She revealed what she did because Betty had said something uncanny that had made Janet think that she and Betty must be twin souls or something. Betty had said, 'Do you know what I hate, Janet, and I hate my boyfriend doing it? I hate it when he puts his hand on my abdomen when we're in bed together, then leaves it there, all heavy on top.'

Janet jumped as Betty had known she would. She opened her mouth and stared at this greatest friend in astonishment.

'Guess what, Betty? I can't believe you said that, because that's exactly what I hate too!'

'And something else I hate, Janet, is when my boyfriend

looks over and watches me from the bed to see what my behind looks like as I'm walking with no clothes on out of the bedroom into the bathroom.'

'Oh me too! Me too!' Janet let go of her cup and broke it on the table because she could have sworn the table was higher up. 'I walk out backwards but with my hands casually over the front of me, for I don't like the way John's eyes go when he looks over and down there as well!'

'I also hate,' confided Betty, 'when we go out and he buys me a drink, saying "Back in a minute, love," then goes away and sits with his mates, and doesn't come back the rest of the night at all.'

Good God, thought Janet. And she nearly fell off the gun-shop's profiterole pouffe. Bits of startled milles-feuilles fluttered to the floor. What identification! When John took her to the Cracked Cup Drinking Club it seemed he behaved just exactly as Betty's boyfriend. Who would have thought to hear anybody else say things that Janet felt, but had never been able to think properly, never mind utter before? She and Betty were so close, she decided, that anyone would think there must have been a microphone or a video-camera planted secretly in the Doe bedroom. And so, because of the uncanniness of revelations, the bit about John being naked came out.

It didn't come out truthfully. First Janet said it was probably nothing, then she apologised for being silly, then she began to cry. 'Oh, that's okay, that's okay,' said Betty. She handed Janet a hankie. It was just that she was worrying, said Janet, because she'd come home one day and John – 'that's my husband, Betty' – was naked with his secret box out. He had his things from his secret box and they were spread around him—'

'Secret box?' interrupted Betty, and that was remiss of her. Didn't she learn that at moments like this you never interrupt people? 'What sort of secrets – if you don't mind me wanting to know?'

'Oh, just secrets,' replied Janet, pulling back a little. 'Normal ones, the type everybody has.'

And here Janet paused and looked at Betty and Betty paused too, thinking, where's she's going with this? But Janet then seemed to realise she couldn't cope with an integration of a 'knowing and a not-knowing' situation, so she veered off and told Betty something else instead. She knew, really, that her husband was sleeping with her sister and that at that particular moment when she'd walked in on him, with him doing whatever he did with those little private packets of his, that Jetty was most likely upstairs waiting for him in his and Janet's marital bed. Janet herself would often be ordered to wait there while he went downstairs to do his little business, but instead of admitting this to herself, she said that John was naked because that was a standard precaution to take whilst making bombs. This time it was Betty's turn to fall off her pouffe and to break her cup on the furniture and to bang her breast accidentally against the table. Betty, in fact, was so prone to table-banging, door-framing and walking into walls that, along with many of the enemy, she now had permanent bruises all down her right side. A spark from your clothing, Janet was explaining, was all it would take to set off the explosives. This she had heard on TV during a programme about international dynamites, so it felt legitimate to relay it to Betty here now. It wasn't as if she was lying. It was just that she preferred dynamite as an explanation than to have Betty think less of John for being a rat for cheating on her – and with her sister too, whom they'd just been praising lavishly for working at the brilliant Almost Chemist of the Year.

Eager beaver Betty, perhaps not being as clever as she thought she was, or else suffering herself from a 'knowing and a not-knowing', foolishly was keen to believe this unlikely bit of information, unlikely because everybody knew John Doe's interests had never lain in making bombs. Perhaps the murders might, she fantasised – now seeing herself elevated to High Commanderdom of All Commanderdoms – be tied in with some bigger transatlantic or international picture. After all, there's no separation. Even God said that.

But as to Janet, when she left the policewoman, her mind was so full of flusterations, and of what she knew and yet didn't know, and about Betty and their new unexpected friendship, that she forgot to bring home the earplugs, leaving them in the gunshop instead. The consequence of this was that John Doe was now going bananas with twenty phantom dead men 'tweak-tweaking, slit-slitting, scream-screaming, fine-tuning' at him; phantom Jetty was glocking big bubble gum bubbles at him; his daughter and her beau were unceasingly murmuring and moving more left hands than either possessed between them, and he had his own hands squashed tightly into his own ears. Continually he kept going back to check and recheck that kitchen cupboard saying, 'Where? Why? Where?' Then he'd pace back to the living room thinking, and where is *she*? Where is that dirty girl?

He meant Julie, and as I said, this teenager did have the Noises but what she didn't have was money, and by money, I'm not talking massive ching-ching. I mean a few bits of coin in her pocket, clicking up and down. Money didn't happen to Julie. She didn't have a speck of it wrapped up in a handkerchief. That was why, when JesseJudges asked her if she wanted to have a coffee, immediately she said no, then yes, then no, then yes again. Confusion. What would it mean to get off the windowsill and have coffee with this boy when she herself didn't own anything? Would she owe anything? And what would her father say if he ever got to hear? She berated herself for panicking herself and for not knowing how to be if someone, especially a non-female someone, asks you for a coffee, and she continued to walk up the street with JayJay whilst giving the impression on every step of stopping and turning around.

Then she did stop. It had become too much. JesseJudges stopped also. He, too, was nervous, for all along he had felt something like reluctance coming from this girl. Then he dropped his nervousness, for it was easier to be aggressive. Then a whole lot aggressive. On the edge of being rejected, hostility rushed to his aid.

'If you're just gonna stand there ...' he said. Then he shrugged. Then finally, fully, he insulted. 'Who are you holding out for? You're not that big you know, Julie. Not that important. Who are you holding out for?' And so he rejected first and walked away.

His words travelled across the tiny bit of air between them and entered her mind and stung her. Further confused, she now felt how bad a person, how disgusting a person, how trashy a person, she was.

And this is where I'm glad I didn't get a summons to go to court to testify, like all those others who got summonses to go to court to testify. How can you piece anything together when everybody remembers everything differently from everybody else?

According to Judas, who did give evidence, his sister Julie came back down the road and, unsuspecting that she and JayJay had been spied upon whilst doing nothing on the windowsill, she went into the living room and her father got her against the wall by the throat.

Judas himself hadn't gone out of the house. He had been

quietly spying upon his father in the parlour whilst his father had been spying upon Julie out the window. Indeed Judas himself had been spying upon Julie out the window up until the point he'd heard his father coming down the stairs. He'd then jumped behind that suit of armour, the one that had been stolen from that museum in Moscow after Moscow had stolen it from Venice who had stolen it from those Flemish people, and he jumped behind it because there's a time for climbing into things and a time when there just isn't time. He waited, breathless, shadowless, as insubstantial as he could muster, while his father did his own noseying out the window upon Julie himself.

Now don't be thinking Judas had been spying on JayJay and Julie because he was a teenage pervert. It was just that he was checking there were no kissing Noises going on. The brain of Judas discriminated kissing Noises as the worst Noise in his repertoire. According to the Judas brain, kissing wasn't linked pleasurably to what most brains would consider kissing was for. Here it was the opposite. It was as if someone had tied Judas up, and had left him a while, then come back, then gone away, then come back, then gone away, then come back, when by now Judas would be screaming, and this time they'd stay and do some kissing of him when he didn't have full words because he hadn't reached the age of even being child yet. He was in-fant. He was infant of infants. And they played with him, this infant, exploring him, tongues forking as they persisted in him, and this, even after he'd struggled and wailed and eventually gone dead and given up. This perhaps was what the kissing would feel like to Judas in his later years of teenage-hood, but that wasn't the point of what was going on in the parlour now. What he did know was not the infant and the forked tongue and the lips of that adult, for how could he remember a supposing? It was that the sound of kissing caused sensations to erupt in a network of torture inside his body, and that was why the situation on the windowsill had to be monitored non-stop. 'Oh for goodness sake!' you might cry. 'Why didn't he just leave the room if he didn't want to feel kissing Noises?' Well, I forgot to mention – a Noises person will be driven constantly to reassure himself that the sound which his body can't bear more than anything isn't, and still isn't, and still isn't, going on.

So, Judas was in the parlour. He was exhausted from vigilance and from the emotional impact upon his lower body of the sound of a kissing that wasn't happening, and from the horror he experienced whilst standing inches from his father, whose naked back bristled as it watched his daughter having a raucous time. And now that he was alone, the boy unwittingly picked up his father's Glock as he tried to work out what next step should be taken in this scenario, knowing all the time really, as he later told the court, he'd have to go down to the back to placate his papa, in order to get those hands away from his sister's throat.

'Ready steady,' he commanded himself. Then 'Ready steady,' again he commanded himself. After a few breaths, he was preparing himself once more. He had set the ornament down, and had tiptoed to the back living room. After a last count-in, he opened the door and there, inches from himself again, was his father.

'Ah, come in, son,' said Daddy. 'Let me tell you something, Judas, about us men.'

Chapter Six

What's a potentially dangerous situation? That's one thing. And the other thing is – I forgot to tell you how John Doe goes on dates.

He goes to a bus-stop. At least, that's what he did first time. I mean first time he had a proper adult date. And there was a woman at it. At the bus-stop. She was a bit older than himself. What he didn't realise was that this woman was more than a bit older. She was one year older than double his own age. He was seventeen. She was thirty-five. Some might say, 'Tut, old enough to be his mother.' Coincidentally, his mother was practically the first thing he spoke about when he started chatting to this woman at this bus-stop. Recently, he'd been to his mother's funeral, for Mamma – tragically, horrifyingly – had been found up some entry after being mutilated by person or persons unknown and was dead.

This woman at the bus-stop didn't believe this boy when he did tell about the mother – but we don't need to get really deep into her having come across many liars in her life before. And I mean best of liars, worst of liars, those who told obvious lies, convoluted lies, stupendous lies, stupid lies, baffling lies, lies with seemingly no rhyme or reason to them. She'd been hoping that, with all the therapeutic help she was now receiving, she'd be cured of her past and wouldn't keep attracting that shit into her life any more. But we're not going to go deep because, you see, we don't need to bother with this woman. She wasn't anybody. I mean she was nobody. Don't be thinking this person was somebody and so we'll have to go back and uncover things and do a detective story on her. No, no and no. Rest yourselves. She wasn't important and, after this current jaunt with her, we won't be needing her again forevermore. I think she may even have been a foreigner – someone from some town other than the splendid Tiptoe Floorboard. Indeed, she responded so unforthcomingly to John Doe's lovely overtures of friendship that in the end – when he had to drag her along the street and up on to the wasteground to give her that beating – a foreigner was the only conclusion he could arrive at to explain her to himself.

So his mother dying was sad. It was very sad. As I said, it was almost the initial thing he spoke about but first, there were the preliminaries to be gotten through. I mean the breaking-the-ice stuff, the 'Where's the bus? Is the bus due? What one are you waiting on?' – all that business, all to be said in a concerned, friendly, nice-guy tone of voice. He had that voice. Indeed, he'd meant that voice. So don't be thinking he'd started out with the aim of doing what he'd been provoked into doing later. He had just come out of the drinking club, into the bright May lunchtime sunlight and he saw her and he liked what he saw. She was wearing red and pink and, unknown to him – but why would it be known to him? – these were her favourite colours. She hadn't worn them in a very long time. So here she was, giving the appearance of feminine, of floaty, of having a body, of liking this body, of winter now being over. That was the top of her. Below, winter was still a bit going on. She had on heavier green material there, flared trousers, and to tell the truth, they could have been less loose and fitted her better. All

the same, she did have contours. There was some flirty definition. From the looks of things, for example, she had a great ass.

Even she liked her ass but, as I say, this wasn't her story. He
took her to be early or mid-twenties and, yeah, she did seem
young. This was because she suffered from Emotionally
Arrested Development. Years ago, due to her family of origin,
she had got stuck at the emotional age of five. If you were to
come upon this woman you'd think, something too little-girl-
like in this person's demeanour. You might decide this was cute.
You might decide this was irritating. She found it irritating.
That was why she sought out a therapist. 'Listen,' she said to this
therapist, 'I'm sick and tired of being five. Do something. Can't
you help me? Isn't there some fast-track way you can bloody
grow me up?'

So she looked about twenty-four to Doe, but if he'd known
she was really thirty-five he would have fallen over horrified
and dead. 'God, that old? Get off! Get off! I said get off!' But no.
He was spared having to have such a reaction – because he was
eager, because he was a liar, and because she was close, so close
he could have put his hands out and laid them on her. And don't
forget – his poor mamma was dead. 'Dead,' he told her. 'Just
come from the funeral.' And he nodded to indicate that up the
road was where the funeral had taken place. By now, of course,
he had walked over and was beside her and was pretending to
be waiting for the Number Six also. But no, he wasn't. He wasn't
drunk either, in spite of the afternoon drinking club. Not even
tipsy. He hadn't been drinking. He'd been collecting money for
he was an apprentice extortionist – I mean apprenticed to himself. When he'd come out, it had been with the intention of
meeting up with his mate, Johnjoe Harrison. Together, they
were going to do the weekly rounds and collect all cash from
every available source.

But first, her.

After the indication of where the funeral had been, he performed 'Funeral Upset That Just Might Be Consolable', but he noticed yer woman wasn't looking distressed for him. Neither was she looking even vaguely upset or annoyed at the way fate had dealt such a hand to him. On getting this unsatisfactory response, he frowned and put his second negative mark against her in his mental retaliatory book.

Yes, second mark. Before the dead mother chat-up line which fell flat, leading to that second mark against her, came the Chit-Chat. Chit-Chat comes after Preliminaries and Preliminaries, as you know, is the friendly talk of the bus and 'Excuse me, hasn't it turned up yet?' Preliminaries could be acceptable as harmless to most people in bus-stop situations. There is a mild give-and-take, so it doesn't seem abnormal, particularly to abnormal people, to slip easily then into the Chit-Chat phase. Chit-Chat consists of a bombardment of personal questions, asked inappropriately by strangers of other strangers. Hugely insulting. Horrifically tactless. In the main, they go like this:

'What's your name? Where are you from? Where are you going? Do you work? Are you a foreigner? Is it that you're on holiday? Are you married? Do you have a boyfriend? Do you want a boyfriend? Are you going to meet somebody? Can I come with you? Can I see your vagina?' – all said as the questioner moves strategically and very physically up close.

Now, a defending barrister person, if such Chit-Chat and rebuffing of Chit-Chat had led to a later court case, might have shrugged at this point and said, 'Is this not simply an example of not very socially practised youth being clumpy and impertinent, but all the same harmless – even if he did go over the line slightly in making that unfortunate vagina remark?'

But the defence and court bit don't matter because they didn't happen, but if they had, don't you think also that this woman should be forced to accept her part in encouraging the Chit-Chat along? After all, she did answer the friendly preliminary questions – 'Yes. I am waiting for a bus,' she said. 'Yes. It is a nice day,' she said. 'No. I haven't been waiting long,' and she even continued by responding to the Chit-Chat initially. Quickly, though, she became reluctant and by the end, when they were just about to reach the questions of the vagina, she turned her back on John Doe and looked quickly down the road. Bus still wasn't coming, so she looked at the bags at her feet as if she were going to reach for them, and that's how she got the first bad mark against her. That was also when he brought up the mother, which, as you know, led to the second bad mark as well.

I use the term 'rape' loosely because, technically, he didn't rape her. Someone else had raped her. But he did physically beat her after dragging her on to the wasteground. This put her very much into that old memory of invasion and annihilation and of grabbing and of despairing, and of the impossibility of connecting to anyone, except through violence, forevermore. By the time they got to the wasteground – and we're talking a matter of minutes – she was no longer sure who she was, who he was, what year it was, what age she was, where she was and couldn't tell if what appeared to be currently happening was happening, or if it was a ghostly re-enactment of one of the traumas from her past. It all became jumbled, just like that Jumbled Time Syndrome I was telling you about earlier. And at this point, before the Mothers, I myself was incapacitated from unravelling things further. This was because, temporarily and accidentally, I fell into her head.

What I could see from inside it was that she had her own

take on age and identity. She had been standing at the busstop, unaware the boy was heading towards her from the drinking club across the way. She was feeling pleased at having gotten the bus into town alone that morning, at doing her errands, and at chatting quite a lot to people, mostly to men. One in the post office had said, 'Oh, I'm getting old,' and she'd laughed and said, 'No, you're not,' and he was pleased and she was pleased to compliment him, and the man at the till heard and was delighted and made a joke with the two of them, to link in as well. The three of them enjoyed a banter and it was a tiny thing, but to her it was a big thing, that there she was – given the tip of the iceberg of her history – making peace, though they didn't know it, with some men. And now she was ready to go home, waiting for her bus and chatting now with some elderly people. Elderly women. These elderly women kept appearing and disappearing with their weights of abundance called shopping. They'd chat and then get on various buses, which would pull up periodically to collect them. Happily, this woman continued to wait for hers.

From his first words about the bus and 'Oh dear, where is it?' she recognised something that hinted of a distant person, that hinted of a memory. She knew violence, and especially she knew the preliminaries of violence – Edgy. Safe. Edgy. Safe. No, edgy again. No, safe again. No, edgy edgy! Get the hell out! Then she'd think, oh for goodness sake, he's just a kid. You're old enough to be his mother. Then came the revelation – maybe being old enough to be his mother was the very thing about her that had drawn him forth.

Behave, she then chided herself for reading too much into situations and for giving herself a hard time always. Fact was she had to be sensible for she had all this shopping and she had to get home. So she answered his maybe harmless questions

113

about the bus – when it should be due, what was keeping it – unlikely topics for a youth to get so worked up about, but when the Chit-Chat started, she felt herself fall into a tailspin. The molecules changed. She felt drained of energy. He had moved up closer. The questions came faster. Any moment now he'd be bringing up the vagina or calling her 'amazing and pretty, and oh, but wasn't she pretty' one minute, only to follow minutes later with 'ugly whore and cunt'.

There was so much she knew already, see. And she really had to get that sorted. I mean the sex and violence. Wasn't it a disgrace to get to her age and not know the difference between both of them yet? Oh, and that he'd hit, and then deny he'd hit, or else start crying, and saying he was a mad man, but that he was sorry for hitting, that he didn't mean to hurt, that he was her father and had only wanted to nap with her, that he loves her, and that he'll give her all his money, he'll give her all the money in his pockets, and his cough-mixture sweets as well. He'll make her chips then, he promises, loads of chips, and he'll give her anything she wants, just so long as she stops that crying. If she doesn't stop that crying, he'll take back the chips and the sweets and his money, and when he'd retrieved everything he'd given her by way of apology, he'd retrieve her from herself and smash her up again as well.

Because Papa was standing beside her at this bus-stop, on the cusp of going one way or the other, she couldn't break out of freeze-mode to lean over and pick her bags up. She couldn't move off, go to a café perhaps, and catch another bus later. Meanwhile, whilst she was in her motionless struggle, he'd moved on to the Mother of God. As you know, the Mother of God is the greatest of all mothers, but by the Mother of God, John Doe didn't mean the mamma of that man Jesus. He didn't mean the mamma of any of those other Masters. He didn't mean Jesus' da's ma or the mother of the oldest god that had ever existed. He meant, of course, his own.

He was telling her he loved his ma, that there was no mamma like his mamma. 'Look at these,' he said, to forestall her, as well as to show off.

He meant tattoos. And there they were – 'Mother of All Virgins', 'Mamma Most Chaste', 'Mamma, Happy Christmas' and so on – all devotion, all running the length of his young upper and lower arms.

Now, you know how, if a man starts going on about his mother in words of virginal, divine, most pure, most undefiled, most inviolate, most singular vessel of vessels, sole conceived without original sin, that perhaps he's got some problems? 'Bats! He's bloody bats!' is what you'd probably cry. I'd say you're right, and further, that this man has just started. He's going to continue with big guns out in fulsome praise of the mother and, what's more bizarre, he's gonna tell himself you're thinking exactly the same about his mother as him. It doesn't occur to him that you're developing an urge to stick pins in this woman and to shout, 'For God's sake! Enough of the mother! We've all had mothers! What age are you? You're not three. Can't you move on to another topic by now?' To help you in this situation, I can say that all you need to know is that this man hates his mother. Unknown to him, he longs to burst and deflate the swollenness of this woman inside him, and of those other female relatives also squashed inside him – all so he can make room for whom he does want in there.

John Doe loved his mother. And guess what – she was dead.

'Just dead,' he says. 'Just buried an hour ago,' and he carried on, having her dead by pretending she was. But the woman he was talking to knew he was lying. She knew his mother was probably at home, eating jellies or lunchtime muesli and watching easy programmes on the TV. But this chewing gum business? she wondered. Why?

'I notice you're eating chewing gum,' Doe had mentioned earlier, and that had surprised her. It had completely thrown her, because at that point she'd been expecting something along the lines of the vagina. 'What?' was all she could say. But it started her thinking, and now, with shame, she wondered if all that sense of threat, if all that sense of menace, was in truth nothing but her own transference of aggression. What does it say about *her* mental state, she now thought, that here she was – and not this innocent boy – imagining the words cunt and whore of herself?

At that moment more old ladies, plus shopping, turned up.

She saw them and thought, good, although I don't know why she thought this – first, because of her history, where witnesses to violence suddenly go blind and deaf and completely insensate and never notice anything and, second, because in Tiptoe Floorboard the belief 'If it's happening to you then, thank God, it's not happening to me' is prevalent in its existence. But she did think, good, although after what happened I don't think she'll think, good, should ever she come across old ladies again.

From John Doe's perspective, this woman hadn't been suitably friendly to his overtures of taking an interest and she had been unmoved, too, in responding to his newly bereaved son-of-a-dead-mother state. He had wanted to invite her. To something. He didn't know what to. He had wanted to tell her she was amazing and pretty. He wanted to carry on being gentlemanly, the good guy noble, which was what you're supposed to be whenever you're with the females. But they're not always grateful, the females, and when they're not, you're allowed to do whatever you want, for they don't deserve to be nice to any more.

So that was what he did.

He stepped over and, boy, when he stepped over, did he allow himself fully to step over. And at this point – the point of his initiation into the adult ritual of the wasteground – he grabbed her, a giant grab, after a whack across the head with one hand, and a simultaneous grabbing of the hair and a pulling of her over to waist-height with the other, then a dragging, a pulling, a walking of her up to that wasteground. This hadn't been deliberate. He hadn't planned it. It had happened like magic. It was just that he'd reached a certain age, and with certain people when they reach that age in the town of Tiptoe Floorboard, hormones take over where you suddenly realise that everybody owes you everything and that handing over everything they owe is the very least they can do. This could be an apology, or their body, or all of their money. And you can take it, and those others, them auld dolls with their wrinkles and their white hair and their mad shopping, or this foreign woman herself, or that unfit, fat, middle-aged bus-driver who had just pulled up and who was looking at you horrified – he didn't matter, none of them mattered. You were the one who mattered. They could go do whatever they liked.

Instinctively Doe headed with her to where his body was propelling him to take her. A few minutes and he'd dragged her along the crowded, sunny High Street on to the wasteground. Sometimes this wasteground was chockful of couples, for it was a popular venue. So far, because it was early, no one but themselves had arrived upon it yet.

He was now initiating his first beating of a proper adult woman. Historically, anthropologically and sociologically this was a valuable moment, a major turning point in his young romantic career. He forgot everyone, and that includes the main group of witnesses – those old ladies who, after the initial shock of witnessing that whack and grab, quickly cohesed into a tight huddle. They started talking. This was their automatic way of not having to admit to any horror going on.

'Mary went a bit mad,' said one. The others latched at once on to this comment.

'Oh, did you see Mary, then?' they said.

'Yes,' said the first. 'She went a bit mad.' They were referring to someone called Mary, as you've probably gathered, but in reality they didn't know who this Mary was. Completely improvised she was. And they were colluding, expertly, in this improvising of her. I suspect that although they'd never met each other until that moment, nevertheless these old ladies had gone through the Mary scenario many times before.

And now, as the screams of the woman on the wasteground reached them, these female elders of Tiptoe Floorboard were growing indignantly heated. This was because the other woman, Mary, had apparently been foolish enough to go up some dark, narrow, isolated entry, after midnight, on her own.

'And at her age!' they cried, as if this was meant to convey something. It did convey something but it seemed contradictory, so I'm not sure what it was. Was it that Mary was too young and so should have waited to go up the dark, narrow, isolated entry on her own after midnight when she was older? Or was it that she was now old and so, at her age, should have known better than to go up the entry after what happened to her when she'd gone up it years ago when she'd been young?

She got attacked, you see, Mary. A savage, bloody attack. It had ended in her hospitalisation. Hit over the back of the head and didn't remember, stabbed repeatedly in the body, intensive care unit in a cot and wondering what she was doing there, all her hair shaved off, with flashes going through her mind of wondering why he'd kept hitting her and why she couldn't get up.

'Well, for goodness sake!' said one of the ladies in a loud voice, and the others anxiously egged her on in it. Already they were nodding their agreement even though they didn't know what else this person was going to say. In a sense they did, though, and anyway, the nodding was compulsory. None of them wanted to acknowledge that godawful screeching reaching down to them from up the road.

They carried on, louder and louder, with clucks of disapproval and intensifying persistence. As you know, the expression 'Pigs before swine' applies to someone who throws rubbish in the path in front of you, with you not noticing and throwing more rubbish down on top of it. Those Tiptoe Ladies with their elaborate Mary story – I think maybe they were an example of that.

As he assaulted her, suddenly there was a memory. She remembered someone had told her that once, years ago, when they were young, twenty or twenty-one, they fought with the person they called their beloved in a car in a foreign country, and the beloved stopped the car and said, 'Get out.' And she got out. She walked along in the dust, this person, and a car drew up after having gone to a funeral. The man driving it was with his elderly stepmamma. They had been to Stepmamma's sister's funeral and had left after the lowering of the coffin. Stepmamma hadn't wanted to see the filling-in of the grave. Turned out this dead stepmamma's sister had, in reality, been this man's blood mother, and that he hadn't known about this for thirty-seven years. Until that day. That was the day of the funeral, his mother's funeral. And that was the day this person walking in the pink dust fought with her lover. And that was the day the car slowed down and stopped.

119

'You can give this girl a lift and drop me here.'

Stepmamma-Aunty said this in that country's language, and she got out of the car, as if in a drama, as if on cue, in the middle of nowhere, in the centre of this pink dustiness. And she was full of anger, this woman, which was why she'd given this information. 'Her,' she'd said, pointing to the coffin. 'Her there. She's your mother.' Sudden and sharp. And this someone told this woman, who was now being kicked by John Doe on the wasteground, this story. She said she got into the car because the older woman who got out told her that that was what she was to do. The man drove away, and drove, and drove, and then stopped, and forced himself upon this girl he was giving a lift to. 'There was something,' the girl said. 'Some sort of something,' and that was as specific about rape as she was ever going to be. But this someone, this person the woman knew later, who then was just a girl, she stayed a girl, and she told this story years later with a little girly laugh in between bits of it. She always told everything afterwards with little girly laughs whether or not anything was funny, and he did this to her just after the funeral of his mamma, she said. She said that he'd said that he didn't know what he'd do as a way of processing this new information just given him. What should he do as a way of moving on? Well, he'd found a way, it seemed, and this someone hadn't been the same since his finding. She just laughed at the end of sentences an awful lot more now. So this woman who had been standing at the bus-stop and who was now lying curled up on her front in the dust of the wasteground, covering her head with her arms, with her torso being hit with something, was remembering all this in the flash of time that John Doe was dealing with her. And isn't that amazing? Imagine remembering someone else's rape memory in the middle of your own battering. It wasn't as if her historical records were empty and she had to grab at anything. It wasn't as if she hadn't a portfolio of memories to call upon of her own.

John's mate Johnjoe appeared. He looked at the scene before him in astonishment.

'What are you doin', Johnny?' he managed to shout.

He was incredulous. He was dismayed. 'Are you serious?' he said, but he said that because he could see, even if John couldn't, that of all the girls his own age Johnny could have picked for his first great wasteground beating, Doe had to go and do it with someone his ma's age. It seemed weird. It seemed disgusting. It was definitely embarrassing. Johnjoe glanced around, relieved nobody else had arrived to see this shameful act taking place upon the wasteground.

'Come on, John,' he shouted. 'We have to get goin'.'

Doe was finished and he felt justified and he felt better. He couldn't stand that screaming, so if it was worse for her, then she made it worse for her herself. He broke away and was already walking off, with Johnjoe throwing back to the woman, 'Don't mind him. He's okay really, wouldn't hit you really.' And that was when he noticed she wasn't an auld doll after all. In her twenties, he now reckoned, and she had a little waist, a little curve, and she was wearing a fancy lacy bra underneath her red and pink thing. 'What's your name anyway?' he stalled and couldn't help asking in the end.

'Where are you from?' he persisted. He leaned over. He touched her shoulder. 'Where are you going? Do you live here? Is it that you're on holiday? Are you with anybody, I mean a boyfriend? Have you got a boyfriend?' But she wasn't answering. A bit rude, and John was now shouting for him to hurry up. 'If ever you're in a pinch or anything,' Johnjoe said, generously too, given her rudeness, 'you'll find me or him at one of the

Community Centres. Just come and ask. Remember now.' And he walked off.

And she remembered.

He'd grabbed her and hugged her, and sobbing and crying, he'd kissed her. 'Your auld da wouldn't hurt you,' he said over and over. He loved her. She must always remember that he loved her, and he reached for her, and don't forget, he winked, 'when we're finished', the pancake pan will be put on. And it was that grabbing. It was that crying. His slobbery waterfall crying, the wet tears of remorse coming out of him and on to her, that in the end had her again breaking down and sobbing. 'Oh, Daddy!' she cried, and that 'Oh, Daddy!' was her defeat, it was her undoing. It again had her trapped and again unable to escape the sequence. She could never get away from that sequence. It was always worse than the rape – the enforced making-up.

By the time they left the dancefloor, it had four couples on it already. Men in their twenties, men in their thirties. Women in their twenties, women in their thirties. Proper men, proper women. All proper grown up.

And that was that. The teenagers had just walked away and were about to go about their money business, Johnny's sense of outrage now soothed by a sympathetic exhilaration, when there she was, rushing over from the other side of the road. This was Mamma, Mrs Doe I mean, John Doe's mother I mean. Now have a look, please. Does this woman look dead and horrifically-ly mutilated to you? I'm not speaking metaphorically. I'm speaking literally and, yes, of course we can see she's not dead and further we can see that here before us is a stunner of a woman. A beauty, still a beauty, even after eleven children, though don't forget – maternity in this town is very difficult to prove. So here she was, late thirties, early forties, and one other thing – she was Pissed-Off Angry Woman. She had been Pissed-Off Angry Woman for so long that she was now no longer aware of it. There was no doubt about it, though. This beauty was in a rage.

She grabbed her son, that good-for-nothing, fucking lazy bastard. Ask him to do a thing, and he can't even do that. She whacked him hard, about the head, about the body, and then she regrabbed him and pulled him over by the hair and dragged him down the High Street. 'I'll show you,' she said, but she was already showing for, continuing in Vein of Curse, she went on dragging him, passing many old ladies at many bus-stops. Immediately they launched into Reprehensible Adolescent – Sore Trial to His Poor Mother. Mary's brother? Her cousin? Her mother's bad, undutiful son perhaps?

And so it went.

'I told you not to leave Hesit!' shrieked his mother. Hesit, if you remember, was the youngest sister of Doe, the one who initiated that tragic shooting incident that involved many people at a séance when she was in her twenties. Well, she wasn't in her twenties yet. Turned out mother was spitting feathers because son hadn't babysat his sister as he'd been instructed to. Hesit had been left alone and God knows what would have become of her if nice Mr McCotter – the neighbour with the crotch and the scary hair and the moving fingers – hadn't shown up and taken her over to his place to look after her there. 'Anything could have happened!' screeched Mrs Doe. 'Any pervert could have taken her!' Apparently, according to Mrs Doe, any pervert wouldn't do.

But I won't elaborate on that, in case I get into legal difficulties, but I will say that daring to grow up and break away from Mamma was the real reason mother was dragging son home. He kept trying to go adult, and she kept trying to child him. She had sat up till four in the morning with a baseball bat and had laid in with it, to great shoutings of 'Get out! Get out! Get out!' when Benedict, her eldest, her softest, her most treasured, had started withdrawing from her as a teenager. He had begun to say less, go out more, come home late until, in the end, she couldn't take it any more. She'd thrown him out that Morning of the Baseball Bat before he'd even entered. Best get it over, to stop him leaving first. After he'd gone, she got all her other sons out of bed, except John, who was already out of bed and on the stairs crying, and she set them everyday arduous tasks to do from that moment on. These were never-ending, designed to be never-ending. Babysitting Hesit had been only one in a host of instructions given to Doe that day.

Hesit had been the presenting reason. She'd never been the real reason. Besides, nice Uncle McCotter had often babysat Hesit when she'd needed babysitting, had often babysat Hale when she'd needed babysitting, had often babysat the twins when they'd needed babysitting but, excuse me, there were many children in this Doe family, and Mr McCotter, he'd babysat all of them. Can we just take the others, and what happened to them, as read?

By the way, where were the fathers here? Is it that John Doe was right in his fulsome praise of these mothers being sinless virgins? And were these children, in fact, genuine virginal conceptions? What of the fathers? What of Doe Senior? Where did he hang out for a start?

Peninsula asylum. No. That is the wrong answer, although I can patently see why your instinct led you to it. What happened was that Doe Senior had a lover. This lover turned out to be his wife's sister – yeah, so very 'John and Jetty and Janet' of the succeeding generation. Doe Senior's lover too, was the mother of Jetty and Janet – Jetty of the Kalashnikov, Janet of the Almost Chemist of the Year.

With all this loving then, Doe Senior had no time to get directly involved in the rearing of his children, although when required, he did attend defence meetings in the town. '*How many clumsily concealed vehicles can you spot in this picture,*' went a lecture, '*compared with how many expertly camouflaged vehicles you might strive fruitlessly to discern in this other picture over here?*' That sort of thing. Enemies existed, and as to who they were, or how to recognise them, unfortunately you couldn't. Vigilance was called for, unauthorised persons were vetted, and codewords like 'This tape will self-destruct in five seconds' were thought up then changed a week later into something else.

It was busy busy busy for Doe's da all those years ago but what about all those years forward? What about her? I mean the foreigner? The one on the wasteground? Will her hair fall out, for example? Is she going to get fat from eating butter? Or bony-skinny from eating nothing? Are her periods going to stop, not because she got pregnant from the beating but because she's so powerful she's going to stop them with her mind? Is she going to wear the same clothes, back to front, day in, day out, baggy baggy, never never never never never never washing them? Is she going to patch them when they go threadbare, and what about when they eventually fall apart? Will she patch and repatch the patches then, spend meticulous hours in artificial light in a particular spot of the same room, in a corner of the same room, with the curtains closed doing all that mending, pretending to herself this is normal activity she's engaging in? Grimy. Dirty. Totally disgusting. That's the way her patches will go, but she'll scrub her body six times a day every day for two years. She won't care, by the way, if her hair does fall out. It'll be on the pillow, perhaps, in the mornings. It'll be in the plughole by the millions. And in the hairbrush. So what? She'll stop wearing brassières too and this brings me to the teeshirt. I'd forgotten to mention the teeshirt. This person, she bought a teeshirt, as practice, that day.

Yes. Practice. It wasn't a trauma teeshirt for that would have been easy. It was a snug-fitting teeshirt and now it was down at the bus-stop, still in its plastic bag. She had bought it that morning, for she'd felt different that morning. And not only did she buy it, she'd been reading certain books as well. Books about pleasure, about nourishment – of the type that wasn't food – and books about trying to get connected, and one of those books, pink with a laughing woman on the cover, had told her to go and get that teeshirt. 'Go buy it, girl,' the book had said. 'Buy some lipstick too,' it added and it told her not to come back with butter, or with something black, or with anything resembling rosary beads. But it was a liar. Perhaps she hates that book as much as she hates that teeshirt and busstops and little old ladies in general now too.

It's so much bad memory anyway so she'll get under her duvet and give up grooming completely. She'll stop going to work and then she'll get the sack. 'Tell her not to come back,' her boss will instruct, and she won't care because she'll be at home sleeping. She'll stay in bed and stop talking. 'Oh, she's hard work. Get rid of her,' pretty soon afterwards will say everybody else.

Eventually, a few years, perhaps a hundred years later, she'll wake up and do versions of what happened to her. This she'll do as a way of resurfacing to the top. 'I met this boy once,' she'll say, 'and he was a tiny bit young and very, very rude to me.' Then she'll deny she said this, not that anybody was listening to her mumbles and secret codewords in the first place.

Later, she'll also deny her next statement, something about something disgraceful having happened to someone in some country that she'd heard about. Then it'll be,

'This cheeky boy – he spat and flicked water at me' – that'll come out after two hundred years.

'This teenager cursed and grabbed at me' – let's say after three hundred years.

'People rushed to help me. The wonderful town I was living in at the time rushed immediately to help me' – on her death-bed, an old woman, with no years left, perhaps?

Or she could go the other way. And the other is immaculate grooming. It's total spectacular dressed-up perfection. It's *haute couture* and *haute* everything. It's where every single hair is impeccably in place.

And so, to suffering, for what about this thing, suffering? Some people would kill themselves over that hair being out of place because that hair being in place has to stand for everything. Others might find this funny and laugh, then be amazed to find yer woman really had gone and killed herself. 'What? But she only had a hair out of place, for God's sake!' they'd cry. They don't believe it. They're baffled. They try to laugh still, but something has frightened them. They think there must have been something other, that only something other could have called for a solution so drastic as suicide. Well, of course there was something other. What's wrong with these people? But no, they don't believe that either. 'Look,' they point. 'It can't have been something other. Her note states clearly, "Can't take it any more. One hair fell out of place." '

But this is Johnny's story. So we don't have to bother with this woman Johnny did a bit of growing-up with. Within days, his wasteground initiation had taken off. This meant that, by the Law of Rite of Passage, even his mother knew better than to continue to drag him by the hair about the area. He became his own property and, two decades later, in his back parlour, here he was with two other of his properties – daughter Julie by the wall, son Judas at the door.

Chapter Seven

'Ah, come in, son,' said Daddy. 'Let me tell you something, Judas, about us men.'

Apart from that Martini fridge, another thing Doe did, along the lines of those men in the bar and how men have to be men because men are men, was to talk about the bookcase. He had this notion about a bookcase that he'd trot out at moments of great insight to his son.

'Us men have to be bookcases,' Father would say. 'I'm a bookcase. You'll be a bookcase too, one day, son.'

Poor Judas. The boy would nod. He'd heard this bookcase talk so many times since childhood that it was almost beginning to make sense, which was mad. What Doe meant by 'bookcase' was 'bookending'. Men were bookendings, the things at the end of shelves to prop books up. Also mad. This belief was based on a TV documentary drama that had been blasting away one day in his house on the difference between the sexes. Through the earplugs and the mechanical raucous, Doe managed to pick bits of it up.

Apparently it had been about that difference, which turned out not to be guns, as I'd thought, but about books and small furniture. Women were the books and men were the bookends, according to this documentary. They were also the shelves and

129

the little delft rabbits at the end of the shelves that physically held the books up.

Complicated. Dodgy. That was why Doe was sure it must have been thought up by someone qualified like Freud or something – someone so deep into his armchair that he got stuck in it and so, through circumstance, was forced to stay in it and psychoanalyse himself.

But Doe got it muddled. What he hadn't done was pay attention, and of course how could he, what with vacuum cleaners, extractor fans, stereos, washing machines, his own manic humming, the volume of the fridge high, plus a session of earplugs going on? The person who looked like Doe's idea of what Freud looked like – some sort of brain surgery Alfred Hitchcock – had made some throwaway comment without realising it was going to be picked up by everybody. It was along the lines of women productively not being very strong. 'They were books,' he said. 'No. Not even books. They were attractive ideas for books,' he said. 'But very weakly constructed in terms of three-dimensional manifestation. They can't get themselves into the world without some strong container to transform and develop them. And that's where men come in.' So you see, men were the pages, perhaps even the text, as well as the varied book covers. They were closures. Turns out he hadn't said they were bunny rabbits after all.

More than this. Some men didn't like the analogy. And some women didn't like it either. The thing degenerated into confusion, and then into fights. First the men complained that they wanted to be the ideas as well as the pages and the texts and the covers. 'No,' said the man. 'Out of the question. You have to be the action and the production side of things. But why be upset?' he went on. 'The production and action and result are not nothing, you know. And besides,' he smiled, 'I'm not talking about males and females as in actual men and—' 'Mister,' interrupted the women. 'What do you mean we're not very strong?' They had bunched around his armchair and were bunching up even closer. They knocked his table lamp over. His smoking pipe fell to the ground. 'Perhaps that was the wrong word,' he began. 'Bloody right it was the wrong word,' said the women. 'Well, you know, everybody,' said the man, holding up his hands in a gesture of surrender, 'I'm trying to tell you, if only you'd listen. What I'm really referring to are psychological constructs. Male in the female, female in the—' 'Why can't we be both?' said the men again.

Next, there was a press conference with the men pointing and saying, 'He says we can't be both.' And the women smirking and, like smirkers everywhere, who pretend they're amused rather than fearful and impotently angry, saying, 'Who digests a bookend? Who walks around quoting and remembering bookends? Whose life is transformed by a rabbit?' So the women reduced the men into being lightweight fixtures and ornamental fittings. Then outsiders, who weren't even present during the initial nineteenth-century disquieting – like John Doe here – unconsciously demoted them into wieldy cumbersome bookcases even more. I think, by the end, yer man in the armchair was backtracking and changing his story. I bet he was sorry he ever opened his mouth.

So,

'I'm a bookcase,' said Doe. 'We, son, are bookcases. We two are the bookcases. Women can't do without us.'

'I know, Da. We are the bookcases. You're dead right there. But listen, do you wanna let go?'

This was a reference to John Doe's grip on his daughter's neck with his right hand. I don't want to tell you where his left hand was. The thing was, Judas tried to keep panic out of his voice, for he knew his father had disappeared into 'I'm Misunderstood and Nobody Understands Me', which meant he wouldn't be fully aware he was strangling anybody at all. Which didn't mean he'd stop doing it or that he wasn't responsible. If startled, which meant accused, he'd strangle even more. So, agreeing with his father, or enquiring after his father's health – which his father loved and which Judas was about to do in a minute – or showing great interest in what an amazing, wondrous 'Your Majesty' his father was, would be the only ways in which Judas could get Papa to relax and relinquish – equally without awareness – those two very deadly holds.

'Never hit any of you,' went on Doe. 'I've never been violent. Never hit any of you.' Gosh, what a whopper. But I think, given the circumstances, Judas was wise to let that one go.

'We know, Daddy. But, Daddy,' said Judas, 'I can see you're holding, and someone like you doesn't need to do that holding. Somebody else can do it. You have a rest and I'll take over now.'

'Bookcases. We're bookcases.'

'Absolutely.'

'And they – they …' Doe's grips tightened about his ragdoll daughter. Julie almost *almost* – did but then didn't respond. Total stillness was the only response ever possible from her, especially at these times, when Papa got into his 'I could strangle you if I want. It's all up to me, you know.'

'I always worked for my living!' Doe's mind suddenly shot off. Just to go with him for a minute – he didn't always work for his living. When he was fourteen he was apprenticed to a bridle-cutter and harness-maker but, after going the first morning and expressing a desire to skin a horse alive to see what its blood was doing underneath the tiny film he'd leave on top of it, and then, in justified rage – for he'd only been daydreaming – trying to kill his employer for sacking him, he never again showed up. Since then, and apart from a brief stint as a carbonator lemonader in the drinks factory beside the haunted egg factory, he'd made all his money from other businesses – not his own. Although still known as a Master Bridler, Chief Cutter and Harness Maker, he knew nothing about horses or things to put on horses. He'll never get the opportunity either, for horses, like ducks, have become extinct in this town now.

'That's right, Daddy,' said Judas. 'I want to ask you about your awful cold ailment and those possible flu symptoms to see if you're feeling better yet.' Doe frequently said he had flu, but it wasn't real flu. It was the flu people say they have when they don't have it. It's a little cough, some sniffs, some spittings on to the carpet. That's not flu. That's annoying – and I mean for the listener. Sometimes when these people yawn and get sleepy at bedtime, they think that's having the flu too. But Judas went on, 'What about your stress levels, Daddy? And I was wondering, how's that little finger, the one that got nipped the other day in the vice hold?' It always worked. As long as you sounded soft, as long as you sounded non-critical, as long as you didn't come out with witticisms such as 'Ach, Da, don't you be worrying. We'll soon have you back on your four feet before long.'

Doe's grip loosened with the lushness of the pampering and his headstaggers mellowed, enough to allow Judas to plead with him to rest and sit himself down. He offered to fetch his father a nice mug of Kaolin & Morphine and, whilst offering, he proceeded obliquely to extract his sister from the stranglehold. It took longer, more compliments and endless comforting of Papa for the boy to gain control over what that left hand was doing. And Julie was silent. She was silent. Her eyes were cast down and how could she be silent? Or was she counting? I think now she was counting. Brain going 'One Two Three Four. One Two Three Four.'

Did you ever notice how people blend into wallpapers? And drainpipes? Or how they hang, in anticipation – usually horrified – from twelve-storey buildings by the tips of their fingers? And just to be on the safe side, they do this from sometime around midnight up until midday the next day or more? That's the sort of thing I notice. That girl was amazing. It must be a skill of many years standing to be able to mix yourself into all sorts of immiscible substances. I'd like to go on about Julie and her powers of disappearance but I think we should return, for it seemed Judas had things relatively under control.

'Thanks a million, Da,' he was saying. 'Now you sit down and relax and tell me about your dreams for you know we love to hear them. Hold on and I'll get paper and pencil and write them down like before.'

Da was shattered. Judas knew he now had about one minute before making another huge fuss of Papa. If he didn't, by the time Doe got to the end of his ramblings, the encore of encores of headstaggers would blast off.

Ramblings began.

'Had a grand day the day before yesterday, Judas,' said Doe, now crestfallen. 'But I haven't felt great, to tell the truth, since six o'clock on Sunday, although I did have a nice sleep, apart from that bat with the wings open, looking at my face when I woke up, sitting itself on my bedclothes.

'And I want amends, Judas.' He made a fist. 'From them! Those bastards! They owe me amends. I want there to be phone calls. And it isn't that they have to ring once and make the first move and say sorry. It's that they have to ring and make the first move and say sorry as many times until I tell them they're forgiven and can stop.

'… had a wee pup there. Did you see that wee pup? Blasted wee pup. Had it in my hand a minute ago.

'Yeah, my finger, son. It's nipped bad. I might have to go to the doctor's or even the hospital with it. Do you wanna see it? It's really sore.

'Want her to be quiet. Murmuring. Next there'll be screaming. I know what I'm talking about – that daughter won't retain its integrity for long.'

During this, the predictable ramble stage, brother quickly propped sister against wall just outside back living room. Then he nipped back into room, closed the door and just in time. Father was coming to the end of 'I said to them, "Guess who's in and guess who's out. Guess who's playin' and guess who's not playin,"' and, looking up, he was already frowning, for the soothing background sympathy of his son had faltered. In spite of 'I know, Da, yeah, Da, gosh, Da, that must have been awful for ye', the poor boy was torn. Time was of the essence and he couldn't get everything done at once.

Rambles were over. Father sat down.

It was a case of 'Phew!' It was a case of 'Whoosh!' It was a case of a look on his face of sheer unadulterated trauma. It was as if it had been him and not her being percentagely raped and strangled against a wall. He plumped, dazedly, tragically, self-sorrowfully, into his armchair, and squashed his wife who was sitting underneath. Yes, I don't think I mentioned. Janet had come in during her son and daughter's débâcle with their father and, because of the headaches she was prone to, once again she had one of her husband's trouser belts buckled tightly round her forehead.

When first she'd come in, Janet had sat down in the armchair and, despite the dreadful headache, had tried to acclimatise herself to just one bit of media. She turned to the TV. Now, what was this? A Jesus programme! Well, she wasn't going to watch that. She flicked over and *Somebody's Got To Do It* was on the other side. Sometimes she liked these episodes and sometimes she didn't. *Tense Isolated Ambition:* the helpful caption in the corner told her what that day's subject matter was.

'*And what about their wives?*' a young man was saying. He was shouting. He was shaking. He appeared to be beside himself. '*Does the wife care that her mad crumpled obsessive laboratory husband's been eating flies and fly larva as a way of trying to identify with them? Does she eat them also? Or does she eat something else – cockroaches? – which at least would put the flies into perspective if nothing else. "Is it about purity or perversion?" you ask me. "Is this a case of great brains and self-sacrifice?" you ask me. "Fanatics to their cause. Martyrs to their mission. We need these people! The world needs these people! Inventors. Discoverers. Innovators. Pioneers. Somebody's got to do it!" That's what you say. Well, I say, "Rubbish!" What's the point in having all that knowledge, having all that expertise, being the best in your year, the best in the country, the best in the world, if you don't know how to say hello to somebody? If you don't know what a human being is, you may as well keep it simple and be a thug in a murder gang.*'

A gasp went up.

'*I say, steady on,*' said the man in the middle. '*This is, after all, a live television programme. Politesse please! We don't want—*'

Janet decided to concentrate on the radios or the washing machines or the hairdryers or the vacuum cleaners. Goodness, she thought. Wasn't there anything but Jesus and strange people on today?

What? What's that you're saying? You'll have to speak up. I can't hear you. I'm trying to identify with these Doe people by trying out some earplugs. I've a pair of the Flakjacket 200 Strength stuck currently in my ears. Could it be you're asking how come Mrs Janet Doe was in the same room and yet didn't notice her husband was assaulting and attempting possibly to kill their daughter, while their son gently, coaxingly, was trying to intervene? This was not unusual. Janet often was busy doing something in one corner of the room while her husband was busy doing something in another. Usually she'd be watching TV, or eating blancmange, or reading one of her *True Detective* magazines. This was in complete contrast to what the behaviour of her sister would have been. Jetty, who never read anything, or listened to radio, or watched TV, except for the great 'Cathy and Heathcliff' film, would have interjected occasionally with 'Don't hit her on the head, John,' or 'That's better. Keep it to his torso,' or 'Not so much now, Johnny, or they'll hate you for sure, when they grow up.'

Poor Judas. Poor only son. Poor, brave, misjudged little human being person. Here was me, thinking he did nothing but climb into suits of armour and snoop about murmuring 'habitable' and 'uninhabitable' and 'inhabitable' all day. And look, here he was, going through angst and fear and confrontation with his very forbidding father, all to save poor sister Julie. How protective. How potential. How fictional. How made-up.

Yes. I'm sorry to give a negation of Judas's version but I have to, in order to give the honest and authentic version. I'll also give a little mitigating analysis, though, as to why Judas might be fibbing at such a phenomenal rate as that. The only bit that was true was the bit where he was spying out upon Julie and JayJay to make sure they weren't kissing, although he *was* in the suit of armour, for that was the only place he could hide whenever his father was looking for him, where it hadn't occurred to his father to look for him yet. That bit about the bookcase might have been true, for Doe certainly did trot it out every opportunity he had a father-to-son confidential but, as Judas didn't go down to the back room to confront Pops and save sister, that bit about the bookcase wasn't true this time.

So there he was in the armour – that one in the parlour, mind, not the one in the master bedroom that was semi-affixed to the wall with a false back and a passage running through it, nor the *trompe l'oeil* one in the bathroom that was really a door, also leading to the tunnels, then the ante-chambers, then the chambers underneath. Both ran underground eventually, although the *trompe* took in the scenic route, going round all the myriad intestines of the town of Tiptoe Floorboard. Judas was in the downstairs armour – the one that had been stolen from the Kremlin that time.

Inside this armour, he was having a little muse on the sounds he liked best to hear. One was telephone boxes. He liked going into them, picking up the receiver and hearing the little 'burr-burr' in his ear. He also liked the sound of cats cleaning their feet. And the clipclop of horses, he liked, except in film music when battles were about to happen and, like his father, he liked the sound of washing machines, fridges, vacuum cleaners, dryers, buzz saws, pneumatic drills and the echoing sound of any type of mechanical bit. Old buildings left for birds he liked the sound of, and yachts rattling their sails against sailpoles. And that wee girl mascot in the miniskirt's giggle as she said, 'Your daddy! Your greatest daddy! Oh, I love your daddy my uncle. Oh, you're such a lucky duck, Judas, to live in the same house as your daddy! I wish I could marry my uncle your daddy, for he really, really, really makes me laugh.'

And here was Daddy now, coming into the parlour. He was

naked and had all his mementos about him. He spread them over the settee and was just about to get going when the sound of murmuring from outside the window intervened.

Murmuring wasn't a Noise for Judas. He could take murmuring or he could leave murmuring. Not so his father. Judas watched through the visor as Doe, now hyper-aroused before he was ready even to be ordinarily aroused, peeped out the window then reached in reaction for his Glock No 5.

Then he put Glock down. Then he left the parlour. Julie and JesseJudges then appeared to leave the windowsill. Judas heard them going. Then all murmuring stopped.

Father came back, this time with his clothes on. He had another spy out, cursed, then was away again, down to the back parlour. Judas could hear him humming in his urgent way as he put TVs and many other noisy mechanicals on. He knew his father was going to wait for Julie, and that meant danger. That meant too, that he, Judas, was staying where he was.

Aunt Jetty went out and Mamma came in. Judas recognised the latter by her footstep. It was a tread of plonk-plank, clack-clunk, clop-clunk-plonk, plonk-plank-flop, platt-splatt, heavy-right, clumsy-left, head-bang, head-bang, doorframe door-frame. Then over the threshold. That sort of tread. As she opened the back room out came the sound of media: '... *One Hundred Favourite Clichés as voted on by the nation!*' Then the clichés returned to mumbles as the door was reclosed.

This brings me to my confusion. Was Judas, at the last minute, going to change his mind and rush down and save his sister? Or even position himself in his armour outside the front of the house and warn her as she arrived? No, no and no. Later, when he did all that false delineation in court on what he said had happened, that set me thinking. Could it be that, rather than the boy having noble, honourable thoughts of placating father to save sister, and maybe also mother, that perhaps he had a little anger towards the whole three of them instead?

A Judasian creation pure and simple. And now, back in the shack, just after the Ouija had accused him, he was muttering his usual 'habitable-uninhabitable-inhabitable' mantra, putting ten circles and triangles of sugar into his tea. He stirred and tasted it and was just thinking one more sugar really ought to do it when he became aware of the silence, and the hearth shovel he'd been manoeuvring in lieu of a teaspoon fell from his arm as he glanced up.

Mr J, and Mr J, and Mr J – I'm sorry, but I have to do those 'Js' for legal reasons as those particular 'Js' weren't later charged with murder – and Mr J and Mr J and Justin and Jude and Jameson and Joel and Jake and Johnny and Johnny were all looking at him. And then his father, also Johnny, was intensely looking at him as he approached him sinuously via the circumference of the room. The boy JesseJudges, nicknamed JayJay by his parents and siblings for, you know, he had had parents and siblings, was now lying dead on the dancefloor with the mascot down beside him. She was rattling her rattle, shaking her resonator and her face was up close and smelling him. Don't get me wrong, but I honestly think there was something wrong with that girl.

They had killed JayJay. Twenty-one years later they admitted that, yes, he hadn't been the informer, but what else were they to do when Messire had given the word? 'It didn't matter, though,' they went on to explain, 'for by then he was near a building for the birds anyway' – clothing in a heap on a space on a dancefloor, semi-clumped semi-slumped semi-arched, a real good battering, and going blue underneath all that stitched-up postal cloth. Although it wasn't cloth. It was paper. It looked like cloth because it was thick and sodden –

something left rotting to take on a smell. I'm telling you, you get to a certain age and it's an age when your hormones go a bit mad on you. You'll join anything, get sucked into anything. 'Hey, I'll join! I'm willing!' and you thrust up your hand. 'Good lad,' says the older man. 'That's a good lad. Sign him up – that one, down there, near the exit, the one that's waving.' And so you do get signed up, and you do get into anything, and later, although you find the exit's open and they're shrugging and turning their backs and saying you can leave if you want to, your mind's saying, too late. You made your decision. You can never leave now.

Unanswered questions. Like, for instance, that famous 'Why?' But the why, and its answer, or lack of answer, will have to wait twenty-one years until the interview on 'Guilt and Remorse', which the gang, in a bemused fashion, all agreed from their prison cells to take part in. But for now, they killed him halfheartedly. No, it was that they killed him absent-heartedly. They said that it was as if they knew that the ending of the teenager, JayJay, spelt the ending for them too.

So Judas was at an impasse and the Ouija was 'SHOUTING OUT THE ANSWERS'. That's what it was actually spelling as the police broke into the room.

Chapter Eight

From early morning these police had been spying on the shack from round the corner of the popular Leprechaun Museum. 'Right, boys,' said the Deputy Commander. 'It's time. Get ready. Get steady—' Johnjoe took off. In the opposite direction. After recovering from his double bout of 'Grandma Getting Nasty', Johnjoe was now peeping down on the police from on top of the roof of an adjacent building. What I don't understand, though, is why did he then clamber down the fire escape at the back and disappear? Why not dash immediately to the garden shed – totally heroically – to warn all his buddies? Or take out his walkie-talkie and warn them from where he was? Because Johnjoe had just made a big stack of money, that was why. Think of what happened that time between those two men in the Garden of Gethsemane and – as long as you don't mix Johnjoe's boss up with that other, rather earnest fellow – I think you'll get an impression of what I'm talking about here. And speaking of kisses, someone had run up to Doe earlier to tell him to 'Watch out, Johnny – your Jetty's after you with a big hammer or something!' And guess who that someone was? Right again. Left-hand man, Johnjoe Doe.

'Ach, is she, Johnjoe?' said Doe. 'Well, I'm a bit pushed. Would you mind dealing with it for me? But don't be killing her because I like her. I've got to go to the shack now and deal with that Romeo, JerryJudges Doe.'

'Ach, no bother, John. You go ahead and I'll take care of it. So will the entire executive be at the shack then, or what?'

Get the picture? I think you do.

I had circumstantial inklings it was him who was the traitor, which were borne out by later circumstantial material circumstances. And these days, of course, now that he's rich and living in that big house in the country, with the security gates and the jewellery dripping off him and that chauffeur-bodyguard chap he pays a fortune to to drive him about, he's giving interviews saying he'll sue the gang if any of them in their jail interviews said it wasn't fair that they got arrested when he didn't get arrested and that when they got out they were going to sue him. I was reluctant to tell you of my suspicions about Johnjoe in case any of you men or women out there were starting to fall in love with him. It's always dispiriting when idols get dashed to the ground.

So he ran away, eventually to get married to that beautiful woman whom he hadn't met yet and who would be after him solely for his money and, in the meantime, right here, the police did a swoop on the shack. They broke in, this police, and eventually – for at first they were nervous – they dove on top of everybody. At that point a high scruff broke out and so did a psychic one as well.

Under normal Community Centre rules, when you visit the shack, unless you're being taken in there to be murdered, first thing you have to do is give the password at the door. The latest password was long-winded: '*I said yer woman said yer man was talking about me and she said that yer other man was also talking about me but to not let on she told me but I don't think he was although I'm not sure, but anyway, I don't think yer woman –*

out of sheer spite perhaps? – was telling the truth about the second man at all' That *was* the password. You get your money's worth in this town. But guess what. The police didn't use it. They just swung their sledgehammers. But then, after this impressive start, they hesitated at the threshold on tippy-toes. In the name of God, us in the crowd looked at each other. What sort of police were they? Were they not going to move down into the tunnels and do their official duty? So me and the Ordinary Decent Folk – a mixture of Pro-Shed, Anti-Shed, and the average Abstention-Shed ghost-hunter who hadn't time to care about the shed or take a stance either way on it – became more and more puzzled at the way the police were carrying on. Instead of rushing in and banging heads and breaking bones and being totally legally violent, after banging and breaking *themselves* ten or eleven times each on the fortified doorframes, they stopped and looked at their deputy appealingly and we could have sworn some of them started to cry. *'Please don't make us go down there!'* some mocking Pro-Gang, anti-arrest newspapers later said the police were blubbering. The Sovereign Commander, the big chief of chiefs, the deputy's boss, got out of his car at this point to deal with the insurgents. With his loudhailer and purple angry alcoholic face we heard him shout,

'You fuckers!' he bawled. 'Giddy-up! Giddy-up! Go down there and get those bastards! Go down there and get them! Are you hearing me? You'll be sorry if I have to order this three times.'

Golly. So it was serious, then. But who did he mean by the bastards? Tiptoe Floorboard is situated, you see, in quaintly subjective territory. Was it the Doe gang he meant, or the ghosts, or anybody perhaps half-tortured but not yet fully dead down there?

Do you know that mocking expression – 'Oh, she jumps

at her own shadow, ha ha, ha ha ha' – that certain irritating stupid people come out with who aren't funny and with whom you find yourself getting exhausted just having your ears in the same room as themselves? Well, sometimes, in certain places, people should jump at their own shadows, and not just at their own, at other shadows as well. Take a place such as this. Even after a helpful 'One two three go!' that that nice Deputy Commander – the one who does salsa in the evenings, with all that bracing and exact and primed elegant movement – well, even after he'd counted down for them and they'd swung their sledgehammers, his boys were startled by the number of shadows running about the place. There appeared to be too many of these ghostly things for the live bodies scientifically to be able to account for them, and that was with being generous and giving every human being – as sometimes happens – three whole shadows each. As soon as natural light fell in, all these shapes at the entrance seemed to go haywire. They screamed and shrieked and that was at the top of the steps that led to the tunnels. What would they find, these police wondered, these police feared, when they got down underneath?

Later, nobody wanted to fill in a report about the psychic phenomena in case they were discreetly put forward for 'mentally deficient dismissal'. Nobody, not even the most anal-retentive, wanted to go by the book. Even the Commander himself, though cross at the reluctance shown by his Gold 'A' Team Swat Team, decided, for the sake of clarity, to leave irrelevant minor details, such as the ghosts, out. 'I've taken the liberty of changing the facts,' he explained, 'but I can tell you now, it was a successful operation.' He told this to a press conference with TV cameras and those little Dictaphone things being thrust up at his fury for him to smile upon. 'We took into account not only the entire street but every street in the

Tenterhook district. Every possible tunnel exit of every possible makeshift tunnel was covered, including everybody's house and their coal shed as well. We used the reconstituted box formation method,' he told the world helpfully, 'with Plan A through to Plan G back-ups. The conductions of my Swat Team were highly commendable. I can assure residents of Tippy-Toe-Under-Tippy-Toe-Ette that we can all now sleep roundly and soundly in our beds.'

So down they went, this police. They were heading for the inner sanctum – the most customised of the gang's spy-proof gloryholes, deep under the very wombs of the bellies of the buildings – 'Sleechy Sleech' Johnjoe had informed them, a plaque upon the door of this torture chamber would say it was called. But the police went haphazardly. They were a dreadful pack of crasher-walkers, and this was because their Combined Spatial Fragmentation Hallucination Syndrome had taken off. They stumbled, tumbled, ducked from real and unreal projectiles and flappy things speeding at them. Luckily for them, though, the Doe gang also suffered from Combined Spatial Fragmentation Hallucination Syndrome so, far from the condition proving a hindrance, the disadvantage of it was cancelled out for both sides.

That didn't stop the Doe gang resisting. Scuffles, to put it ladylikely, broke out and so did some shooting. Everybody in the gang reached for their Plan D ankle holsters because their Plan A Kalashnikovs, Plan B Russian RPG rocket launchers and Plan C Heckler & Koch & Sons & Sons were not that moment to hand. John Doe, the main target, was floored physically by several policemen jumping on top of him, and this, just as he took a shot at his own son. Son was standing, stupefied by the sugarjug, and he ended up still standing, stupefied by the sugarjug, long after everyone – bar him and the mascot – was gone. They left him. 'Leave him,' they mumbled, drawing back. 'He's scary. If we need him, we'll send a stupid beginner for him.' The mascot also wasn't arrested, although they took her rattle-resonators, her rituals, her symbols, scrapes, shakes and battalier status, leaving her crying for her uncle – this abandoned, traumatised, fancy trim of a murder gang. As for the ghost experience, in efforts not to be sent out of their wits by the invisible marching, disembodied singing and clapping, both police and gang threw themselves into a proper third-dimensional brawl.

'Don't believe the police,' said the gang years later, during the series of interviews taking place to mark the twenty-first anniversary of Tiptoe's most famous arrest. 'Them's all lies. All mud in the head they're talking when they say there was nothing supernatural. They didn't want to let on. "Don't be letting on," they even said to us.'

But that day, 'black swirly things', according to the gang, fought other 'black swirly things', at the same time as the police fought with the gang members. Both the real and the unreal were having a go at each other on the dancefloor.

'The ghosts were copying us,' said one gang member. 'They would punch each other when we punched each other, and shoot each other when we shot each other, and stop when we stopped and start again when we started. Us and the police noticed this going on.'

'Could they have been your own shadows?' the interviewer asked, and this may have been a tongue-in-cheek question but I don't think so. In her career, this woman sometimes felt uneasy around certain individuals she was required to interview. That was why, beforehand, at home, she'd carry out aura-protection exercises, using citrine crystals and other spiritual stones. Something about this lot, though, had been so disorienting from the moment she'd met them that already her morning's protection was wearing off. She felt queasy. She felt dizzy. It seemed to her there was something too much of the child about them. As for them, considering her, they were astonished. This was because of her questions – 'Sorry, are you sorry?', 'Do you condemn your actions?', 'Excuse me, but have you any idea yet of what it is you have done?'

'We don't have shadows,' they said, in answer to her earlier question. And instead of 'Pardon? What did you say?' she had a look, and it was true. They didn't have shadows. She did and they didn't. She looked again. And again, she did and they didn't. They seemed proud, just as you might be proud if you were one of those people who had the famous six fingers, or the third nipple, or an extra set of eyes that really did exist in the back of your head. They didn't seem fazed by this lack of shadow and neither did the shadowless, depressed police wardens, she noticed, as she glanced at them when they opened the airlocks to lead her out after the interview. Indeed, she seemed to be the only one with a visible shadow in the whole place.

Now this interviewer was not some giggle out of an expensive 'for-you-to-cut-out-and-keep' journalist comic-book factory, but at first when the gang swanked into the prison gym for this, their fifty-fifth famous international interview, they saw her, a woman, and they were upset and annoyed. 'No harm to her or anything,' they complained to the governor, 'but she's only a woman, so she can't be a big cheese and we're only giving interviews to big cheeses nowadays.' The governor assured them that not only was she a cheese but times had changed so much that often women now were cheeses. This was news to them, although it was still not of their era to have a female supposedly on the same level, especially one who couldn't grasp the rudiments of wee white women and of chisels going into walls by themselves.

'Honestly,' they said to me later. 'You heard us. We tried, but there's just so much you can do if you don't have the material. There's something wrong with her. Did you notice as well?'

They looked anxious, so I nodded, and that seemed to calm them. A temporary lull descended, and I mean over the few who had followed me out of the gym into the prison yard. They approached as I was playing with the raven – that same one Doe had brought back all those years earlier as a souvenir from the Tower in the Big London. It had, over the years, grown very attached. When he had been arrested, it drooped, trailed its wings, then had thrown itself wholeheartedly into missing him. After that, it gave up and had been dying of a broken heart over the next twenty-one years. So Doe had broken hearts. But sure, hadn't all the gang been heartbreakers? 'What's that one minute's silence thing?' they interrupted my thoughts to ask.

When the disciples were charged with all their counts of kidnapping and murder, they got variations on four hundred and ten years each. So off they went to jail, on a squally day, a portentous day – for they were aware, every one of them, that it was the start of a new era, and that they had been instrumental in bringing this new era about. 'You could smell the transition,' they said. And not just for them – but for the whole of the community. They felt responsible, they said, even for the weather. 'Weird!' said one, and 'I know what you mean and fuck me!' said another. They had no words, it seemed, with which to describe the atmosphere that had surrounded them, and 'With poor expectations of being forgiven, I am sorry,' was something else they had no words, or any understanding, from any part of themselves, to say.

149

They joined me and already the little cushion of peaceful-ness I had bestowed upon them by agreeing with them was evaporating. Yer woman hadn't passed her exams for nothing. It seems in spite of their much-cultivated Working Memory Defi-cit, she had rattled their unconscious registers to the core.

'Don't know really,' they said, as if I'd asked them something. 'Maybe it was because of the government. Don't know other-wise, why we killed them men.'

'So-and-So,' went on one, speaking now of their first victim. 'That one going home from work by himself in the dark. Well, he used to let me park my motor in his drive. I didn't have a drive. He had a drive. I didn't have a garden. He had a garden. I forgot I used to sit in the bar with him sometimes. I forgot I used to play handball with him. He lived in his own house with his wife and a baby. He acted kingly. I lived with my ma. She acted kingly. Sometimes he'd let me borrow his motorbike. I don't know why I killed him really. He was all right really. In fact, I think he was dead on.'

'It's just that sometimes it's time,' said another. 'You find that things on the radio, and things on the TV, and things you think, and things you hear other people saying, and things that come in signs and symbols and opportunities and in drink are all clues that maybe you ought to do it. You take a stick out of your pocket, and it's so sturdy, that stick, that it's like a knife. And so it is a knife. It doesn't matter how such thoughts get put into your head or that, before them, you hadn't thought of killing anybody. They're a sort of permission. They say, "It's okay. Don't you be worrying. Go ahead and kill him. That'll teach him not to be a show-off." '

Ah, I thought. It was a case of 'Knock the Nose Off' and do you know 'Knock the Nose'? It's the opposite to being really excited and civilised and good-sportsman-like when you hear about people who have brought about great inventions, or who even have had some modest success and are feeling really good about themselves. 'What a chap! Good for him!' you say. But that's only if you don't know the person. If it's someone you do know, I mean someone who went to the same school as you, someone who lived in the same street as you, well then, it's not 'Genius! Marvellous! What a fellow!' Instead, it's 'What? You mean yer man? – who went to the same school as us, who lived in the same street as us? Well, who the fuck does he think he is?'

Naturally, in this case, what you must do is knock the nose off. When you experience envy, knocking the nose is the only thing you can do. So get in there and have a good bash at it. There are no witnesses. All witnesses are bashing also. Nobody's going to believe him. The police won't believe him. If he lives, the police will believe you.

'Ach, not really,' said a few of the gang at this point, thinking perhaps again I'd asked them another question. 'Who'd be jealous of a funeral?'

Ah, I thought, knowing what was coming next.

'Those flowers,' they said. 'And the salutes,' they said. 'And the prayers. And people coming. And people crying. A whole fence of observers paying respect and holding that one minute's silence. *So, what is that one minute's silence?* Because of that, we stopped dumping them. Because of that, we kept them. That's why we ate them. But they carried on having funerals for them anyhow.'

She never got any of that. I mean the interviewer. She did try. She really did try. I mean not to be hypnotised. She did try not to be nibbled at, not to have blood taken from her. But they bewitched her. In the end she was in slivers when the police were carrying her out.

She'd been sitting at the long table, positioned especially in the gym for these iconic interviews. The men were sitting there too: arms folded, seemingly straitjacketed folded, all wearing zippered-up padded bodywarmers, all in favourite colours of black, brown, green-brown or mud. She didn't know how it happened for, although her questions of grief, guilt, remorse, forgiveness and 'Did they condemn?' caused much fidgeting, scraping, attempts to swivel on chairs that were never meant for swivelling, pretence at pulling each other's bra straps for a laugh when none of these men had ever worn bras, not a single one moved or touched her even once.

She felt teeth on her neck, going into her neck, a gentle tugging, a gentle sucking. Very creamy, very floaty. She liked it. She felt she ought not to like it. She closed her eyes and leaned her head to one side to experience the seeping teeth some more.

Apparently the interview had taken place. It really had happened. Afterwards, when she woke – perniciously anaemic, listless, strangely tearful as if some death had occurred to her – she couldn't remember what any of this interview had been about. Time had elapsed too. The men were gone. They were out in the yard, and I was out there also, shaking my head as I looked back in the window at her. They came to lead her out, those stealthy silent shadowless police wardens. Her own shadow too, by the way, was fainter than it had ever been in its life before.

She was not permitted to re-interview. Besides, she had no energy, and now no inclination. Therefore, with no way of being able to account for it – the Dictaphone having gone blank, the white pages written upon having erased themselves of writing – she left the place with no idea of what it was they'd been talking about at all.

How it destroyed her. In the end, she had to crawl home feeling the worst she'd ever felt. She got into bed, then couldn't or wouldn't get out of it. She didn't file her copy and her boss, now of the opinion that brinkmanship of cheese and supercheese was nothing but a sham and a lottery, told her in short terms that she was never to come back.

So Gunshop Tom Spaders, 'The True Story', never became public knowledge. He was to have been the topic of this interviewer's 'thinking-out-of-the-box' original lead-in. After she'd got them settled, 'That man Spaders?' she'd been going to ask.

Chapter Nine

Tom Spaders. In the gang's eyes, yer man, who had gone mad since being set upon by the babies, had always been of the calibre of the Guardian of the Filing Cabinet. Therefore they ignored him on the inside just as they had ignored him on the outside, which didn't seem to bother him, keeping himself to himself as he was.

Initially, whilst in prison, Spaders withdrew and had refused to interact with anybody. He refused also to see visitors, ie Jotty, who came expressly seven times a week, fighting her own demons, to see him. Why should I see her? he thought. This is like Samson and Delilah and women's guiles and manipulations. Well, she can stop all that 'Tell me your secret! Tell unto me the answer to the riddle! Put forth your riddle for I won't tell it to the Philistines,' for look – she's got me with my eyes out! Got me with my strength gone! Got me where she wants me! So of course it stands to reason, from her point of view, she can afford to be nice to me now. Well, I know her game. I got her number. Sometimes Tom knew he wasn't being dignified in his trauma, but it was early days. He hadn't got through his bitternesses yet. To be precise, he had only started in on his bitternesses and, as you know, it's not until you've been through that one really Big Bitterness that the other bitternesses people think are huge, and who feel sorry for you because you've got them, you know don't count a hoot at all. Tom hadn't got there yet. It was still the time of the Big One, so he was bitter and broken and angry at Jotty, and angry at everybody, and disbelieving in his horror that, actually, he had killed somebody. Jotty, for her part however, and encouraged by the Salsa Dancing Policeman, continued to come to the prison to try to meet with him, with him continuing to pretend, in his pain and grief, to be far too busy in executive meetings to grant any favour to her.

To get it exact, though, when first he'd been arrested, on the same day the gang had been arrested, Tom had been sent to the hospital because of new physical injuries that had been done upon him. Then, when he was recovered, he left hospital and went to court to get sentenced and then was put imme-diately in jail. When he was in jail it was decided, fairly quickly, to transfer him – because of his bitternesses – to the mental asylum, but then they moved him back to the prison after deciding he was a bit on the bitter broken shocked side, but apparently wasn't mad after all. This, by the way, was the opposite to what happened to Janet. They didn't arrest her at first, so she was up at the chemist, giving herself some hefty staff discount. She was arrested later, around the same time her husband and sister were released. John Doe was released on a 'technicality', and 'technicalities', if you can get them, are worth shed-loads of money. Jetty was released not long before him, with a warning to pay proper legal tender for her guns next time. As for Janet, when finally they did get round to her, first they put her in jail, then decided, after some apparitional episodes followed by psychiatric testings and interpretations of watercolours, to remove her to the mental hospital. She's still in the mental hospital. So is her sister, only, as you'll see later, Jetty Doe being in hospital wasn't really the case at all.

As I said, Jetty got released on the same day she got arrested, and this happened just a few hours before John got released, also on the same day he got arrested but, because she didn't know he was going to be released, she had to get herself another lover, the way you do. Yeah, 'cos life goes on like, doesn't it? She took up with an ex-prisoner right away from another gang, and when Doe came back in the late afternoon, walking through the door, all thoughts on setting up a new Community Centre Team, she was in the hall and looking surprised to see him. She stopped what she was doing, twisted her torso round the banisters, called to yer man up the stairs to stop unpacking, and to start packing, and to get out.

John was annoyed and upset. First, that she could forget him, wipe the slate clean of him, just like that, all in a jiffy, even though there existed the fact that, due to concern with his own furtherance, he hadn't gotten round to giving a single thought to her yet. Also, he was annoyed and upset at her moving so rapidly into the Doe premises. I'm referring to her moving in in the *energetic* sense, understand, as the house's new proprietor, and not in the literal sense, for you already know she was already living there. It was a case of spreading yourself out, having big breaths, kicking things out of the way, throwing things on the floor, breaking a window if you wanted to, moving all your stuff from the poky wee back room up to the front majestic front room, as well as holding most deliciously every key of every tunnel, of every secret passage, of every single backstairs intrigue chamber in your hand. And she did that because, you see, it wouldn't occur to Jetty that the house didn't belong to her. Who else would it belong to, given she was a grown woman who was related to Janet and John, who were now going to be gone for years and that might be an understatement? Not Cousins Jotty and Mad Janine, who were John's sisters, because they had their own house and so it would be greedy of them to try to take another also. And not teenagers Julie and Judas, for they were kids, far too irresponsible to own any kind of property. So of course it was Jetty's. What more was there to be said in the way of ownership than that?

John said, 'Who was yer man? What was that man you had living with ye? Who were ye shacking up with during all that time today I was gone?'

'Wha'd'ye mean?' asked Jetty, playing for time. And you know how people do that? They say, 'Pardon me?' 'Excuse me?' 'Come again?' 'Sorry?' – putting their hands exaggeratedly to their ears as if you hadn't spoken loud enough. Dirty liars. You know they've heard you. Or they say, 'What man?' – even though he's walking by you right this minute, shame-faced, head lowered, with coat and suitcase in his hand. Or they go on the defensive: 'Oh, but you're possessive!' Well, I hate that. Lying like that might not be worse than thieving, although I don't know. Maybe it is worse than thieving. I think the 'worse-than' scenario was the viewpoint John took here.

He killed her. And I don't know why that would be surprising to her. After all, he did kill those men, and a certain contingent believe he did kill an older daughter for, let's face it, is it likely a school-age teenager would be allowed to emigrate, all of a sudden, with no money, and was now writing, as they said she was, successful cookery books on the other side of the world? And also, look at what he did to those girlfriends he had dates with. Then there was the younger daughter he had made attempts on. Then there was that shot we all witnessed he'd taken that very afternoon at his son, Judas, himself. Jetty knew this. Oh yeah she knew. So how on earth could she be astonished at Doe proceeding now to strangle her? Stands to reason. The mistress, or the wife, who defiantly holds the conviction 'He's okay, my man's okay. Not violent to me. He said to me, "I promise you, honey, *you*'ve nothing to worry about," ' will, at some point in the reckonings, most certainly have to be next.

Minutes after the strangulation of Jetty, and unaware of what had happened regarding the Doe arrests, and what would happen regarding the Ordinary Decent Folk's knee-jerk lynch reaction – which you don't know about, but don't worry, I'll tell you – Tom Spaders, like John Doe, was *en route* to where his angels and guides were meaning him to be. He believed himself out for a walk after all that débâcle with Jetty, Jennifer, Julie, Johnjoe and then Customer Tom at the gunshop and, as he walked along, he was experiencing that feeling of the dragging out of the anxiety – although come to think of it, maybe that's what anxiety is, all that constant dragging out. As he turned a corner, wondering what had become of Cusack, and wondering what he was going to do about that bit inside him that kept urging him to kill everybody, he heard three screams coming from the Doe house. Immediately there was hesitation. As with everyone in Tiptoe Floorboard, when it came to reality rather than fantasy, and especially when it came to any reality involving the Doe family, it would be a case of 'If it's not happening to you, then don't invite it happen to you'. He wished to God – the one he didn't believe in – that on top of everything, he hadn't just witnessed those three female screams. He should walk on, he told himself, not get involved, for who would thank him for it anyway? Doe would shoot him. The Doe Sisters would rip him apart down his middle and take half each to wipe the floor and windows with him. And the Ordinary Decent Folk would say, 'Hell, slap it into him. He's nobody to blame but himself.'

Another scream.

Now, there was something Spaders couldn't get out of his head and it had happened years earlier. It seemed to be binding him to the Doe family whether he liked it or not. It wasn't Jotty, whom he was insisting to himself he had not started rethinking about. Her lack of experience, given her age, and the feeling that she might accuse him of rape, even though he hadn't raped, or else that she might go into one – he meant the Doe Family Headstaggers – or even worse, stick a knife in him just because he put his arm around her so he wouldn't put his arm around her, was a bit too much for his well-honed, clued-in switch for mentalness to take. Here was him, struggling along, making an effort not to kill anybody, and here was them, that Doe family, not bothering their arses to struggle not to kill anybody. The thing, though, that he couldn't let go of was a certain feeling he'd had around Doe regarding an older daughter who Jotty one day had told him had disappeared. At the time, he hadn't been long back in town after being out of it for ages. When she told him about the daughter, he assumed that in reality this girl must have gone off on holiday – a euphemism, of course, for being transported to the town's grim mental asylum on the hill. He assumed *that* based upon the fact that that's what periodically seemed to happen to so many of the Doe family. There had been a funeral of one of them from the asylum around the time it was said the girl had disappeared. At this funeral – of John Doe's aunt, though some rumoured it was really of his actual birth-mother – the Doe boy and girl, Judas and Julie, had stood by the graveside and cried their eyes out. It was phenomenal crying and Tom, passing on the cemetery periphery, noticed it and felt the amount of grief displayed couldn't possibly be for a person they had never met. So was it a nervous thing? he wondered. Were they crying from the sheer emotion of contemplating death in the abstract? Or – and this was the dread – could the tears be for the loss of something or someone – such as a sister – much closer to themselves?

Tom stopped himself – both thoughts and actual walking – and held on to the railings surrounding the graveyard. He didn't like his mind to be going this way. He was a comfortable guy, he told himself. He was an average guy. And he was happy to be average and comfortable. Certainly he didn't want to find himself pondering whether John Doe had murdered his daughter or not. He cut his thinking short, however, because the children, still sobbing, stepped too close over on to the false grass and do you know that false grass, that pretend greengrocer grass, that gravediggers use at funerals? They cover the open grave with it once the coffin has been lowered, and then leave it, without filling it in until all the relatives have said last prayers and gone away. Well, those children, who hadn't gone away, though all the other mourners had crossed the road and were on their second drinks already in the drinking club, went too close to the edge, not realising that soon there would be no earth to support them. Indeed, the fabric was already giving as Tom rushed up from the side.

They screamed and clutched at the crinkles, shocked out of crying. When Tom made a grab, they saw his hands and frantically grabbed back. He got a hold, lifted them, high above the earth, one arm for each, and then it was back to the earth, where he set them down, but still went on holding. They, too, held, clutching fistfuls of shirt, sobbing into it. He was down on the muck by this time beside them, and all those hearts beating. All those hearts beating. 'There,' he said. 'It's all right. You didn't fall in. You're okay.'

The gravediggers came over. They'd been standing by the digger further down, oblivious to what was happening. They were having a fag and a gossip as to which of the asylum women had been John Doe's real ma. It was then they realised that something was up and they looked towards the grave and saw the Doe batch being handled by yer man, Tom Spaders. 'What's he doin' with those childs?' they asked. 'He doesn't own those childs. Look how tight he's holding the Doe childs. Will we tell John?' And, although they didn't tell John, they did tell others, and that was how the pervert rumour got started up.

They watched in silence, with Spaders unaware of their scrutiny. It was only when they came up and one flicked his cigarette butt into the now uncovered grave – keeping Tiptoe Cemetery tidy, as it were – that Tom noticed they were there and straightened up.

He got fully to his feet then, dirty and sticky from the nether-clay-earth, as also were the children. Nodding to the men, but giving no explanation, he held the girl's hand and carried the suddenly sleepy, angular eight-year-old boy across the road to the club.

In the club, Janet was with her vodka and blackcurrant and seven other gangster girlfriend-wife companions. Tom had intentioned passing her children over, with – if he could muster it – a light-to-moderate telling-off. Had she forgotten them? he'd say. Just like maybe she'd forgotten the other one? Was it that she was wanting rid of them? he'd say. Just like maybe she'd wanted rid of the other one? In that case, why not send them up on to Greystone Cliffs and tell them to have the play of their lives up there? Of course he'd never say that. And when he got to the bar, the place was so Doe-heavy that he lost his nerve to say anything and instead passed them rapidly to their mother. Bundled them, he did, and it seemed dismissively, and then he turned away. This was so he could pretend he hadn't heard and therefore wouldn't have to respond when one of them shouted, 'Hey! What's-your-name! Thingy! Gunman! Hey, you! Gunman!' Also, he forgot to say goodbye. I mean to the children. But in the middle of this scenario, with all these adults, all drinking, all looking at him, it would be amazing if such a thing as saying goodbye to a batch were ever to occur to him at all.

As for the gang, also now watching, it was puzzling. It was outside their philosophy that Tom Spaders should come in here. This was one of their haunts and he was one of those people who would wear white and go barefoot and not carry a gun and wouldn't even rate as important enough to speak English or to be a member of the other side's gang if this were a spaghetti film. It didn't matter that they got their weapons from him more than they got their weapons from anybody else. It was outside their philosophy too and, indeed, outside Tom's own philosophy, that he should be carrying children. And not just any children. The Doe children. Didn't the kids have all these uncles, with all these arms, who could carry them themselves? So yer man here had some explanations to give, and the gang members who were sitting down stood up, to get themselves ready to hear them. Tom saw this, and so walked, casually as possible, towards John Doe at the bar.

Tom knew that the only way he'd get out of the club in a fairly okay state would be if he acknowledged and got the blessing of the gang leader. It was the right decision. Doe was facing outwards and Tom positioned himself beside him and passed off some easygoing humour about the Doe children having got lost. He'd found them, he said. And that was why he'd come in, to hand them over to their mother. And could he buy John a drink, for he'd heard about John's tragedy? He was awful sorry to hear of John's momentous sad loss.

Doe's loss was the person in the coffin and Spaders could have stopped there but, because of anxiety, he went further and spoke also about the children seeming sad over having lost their granny. It was then he realised that it mightn't have been Granny. Perhaps he should have said Great-Aunty instead.

Doe was silent. Oh God, thought Tom. Was he gonna go ballistic? Was he gonna throw the headstaggers? Why had Tom been stupid to come out with illegitimate and incestuous connotations like that?

God would forgive him for being a coward, he decided, but quick as he could, he said, 'Your aunt was a lovely and a great woman, Johnny. And so was your mother. I always thought they were brilliant – towers of the feminine, queens assumed into Heaven, blessed, revered, wise and merciful. Everybody said that most of all they were merciful. Your mothers were the most total virgins of all.' Had he overdone that last bit? he wondered. In truth, too, he couldn't have distinguished the Doe creatures he was referring to from almost any Doe female except Jotty. For all he knew, they could be the women sitting across the room from him right now.

Instead of the headstaggers, Doe sighed. His body relaxed. He put his hand heavily upon Spaders's shoulder. 'Here. Have a drink, Tom,' and he passed him over his own. Doe was giving off an air of sadness, of grief, of heartbreak, and it was a demeanour that demanded you'd better be full of compassion for him. 'You're right,' he said. 'Those two women were perfections of the universe.'

Ice broken. Not Tom's head broken. Things were looking up. The ominous silence that had been thickening in the room turned and retreated to the sidelines. Somebody handed Tom another drink and so he had two drinks in his two hands. He stepped back in relief and as he did so it was on to the toe of a serial murderer – just one serial murderer, though, out of the many serial murderers he could have trodden upon currently in the room. It had an ingrowing toenail on it, however, this toe, which meant for the owner, excruciation. Tom didn't know the ingrowing nail existed but, even without this knowledge, he knew that under normal circumstances a simple step-upon would be enough to get him killed. He turned to apologise anyway, but the toe-owner was already patting his other shoulder. The man said in a strangulated voice, 'Don't worry about it, mate. Just a toe. Totally expendable. Let me get you a drink. What'll you have there?'

So Doe and Spaders were best friends for the minute. Doe was getting drunk and had moved into intimacies in his talk about the mother.

'It was my ma, Tom,' he confided. 'She was my ma all the time and not my Aunty Jacky I buried today.'

At this point JanineJoshuatine burst in. I guess that meant she was back from one of her holidays. Jotty came in behind her. She saw Tom standing with her brother in an embrace of fraternity – Doe's hand upon Tom's shoulder, other hands upon other of Tom's shoulders, and many, many drinks in all of Tom Spaders's hands. That was how it looked to her anyway. Her mouth fell open. I don't believe it, she thought. I don't want it to be true. And yet it is true, for look, the proof's here in front of me. He *is* a gang member! The bastard. I hate him. I wish I hadn't slept with him. I wish I hadn't let him go down on me. I wish I hadn't enjoyed him going down on me – although I'm glad, especially now I'm seeing this, I didn't let him get inside. Now, don't get her wrong, Jotty wanted somebody inside. Although don't get her further wrong, she didn't want just anybody. This was not a case of 'any man will do'. But let's be thorough, for it wasn't either that she had contracted that pernicious disease: the terminal, the disastrous, the 'Mr One and Only', where the poor thing has to be the Soulmate, the Right Man, the Proper Man, the one who will suffice in every and any circumstance, that it will have to be him and only him in the whole wide male-filled world. If it is, and if it isn't, God help him, for he'll have to carry everything – just like that poor hair on the groomed suicide's head. He'll be responsible for all her sexual and romantic baggage, for all her female relatives' sexual and romantic baggage, not just for the current generation but for all the female generations past and in future to come. And that's not all. There'll also be his own sexual and romantic baggage, plus all those relatives of his squashed explosively inside him. So carry everything? What man could do that? Further, what man should do it? Nobody should have to do it. The hair on the head shouldn't have had to do it. And it didn't. Remember – at the last moment – it did fall out of place.

It was just that she didn't want to be like her sisters – more of them in a minute – grabbing the knife from under their pillows, stabbing everybody – I mean their husbands – after they'd been inside. But oh, this womb business. How are we to deal with it? Are there any cosy adult evening education classes started up on it yet? But see what's happened? She's gone off the point and is dragging me, then you, with her. That's what happens when you have multiple thoughts. To get back to the bar and to Jotty, looking over in horror at her ex-almost-lover, and having such thoughts as those running through her mind – all you need to know is that I speak her language, that I am fluent in honours and distinctions and 'most esteemed' in the fluency of this language. So trust me when I tell you that all that 'men and baggage and womb' business was the exact translation of the expression of devastation upon her face.

After the stare of devastation she refused to acknowledge Tom and went quickly towards her sister. JanineJoshuatine had already reached her brother. She was determined to stab her brother, believing in her mind, as usual, that he was somebody else.

But first to a sad story:

Beautiful women, with blood on their hands.

Chapter Ten

Your stunningly beautiful sister says to you,

'You know how, Jotty, when you come to and you look down and you've got all this blood on your hands?' She shows her hands across your kitchen table and yep, there sure is a lot of blood on them.

'No, Unity,' you say. 'That doesn't happen to me.' Resignedly, you get up to fill the basin and to get the soap and the towels and all the hygienic stuff with which to clean her up.

Unity doesn't hear.

'And you know how, after you've been sitting in a daze, Jotty, and you come to in the armchair and you just know you've been fighting with somebody?' She frowns at the ghost-memory of recently fighting with somebody. And that's right, that doesn't happen to you either. You say this too. Again, Unity doesn't hear.

'And you're just calming down,' she continues. 'You're right on the tip of the sword of revelation' – here, as she's talking, you gently raise her hands and place them into the water. As you're doing so, you notice gashes, initially hidden by her hair, down the side of her skull.

'Just as it's coming,' Unity persists, 'all that delicate and fragile memory, the last thing you'd want is for the bloody knocker to get knocked, the bloody bell to get rung and for five of those police people to be standing at your door.'

'Unity,' you interject but, as usual, you do this softly. You are patient with your sister, with all of your sisters, even though you've heard variations on this story from all of them, many times before.

'I know this happens to you,' you say. 'And I know it happens to our JanineJoshuatine, and to our Hale, and to our Gussie, and to our Hesit, and probably it happens to some or all of our brothers but—'

'You're right,' says Unity, thinking you've said something other. 'I agree. Sometimes the police don't come right away. That's best, isn't it? That gives you time to get out of the armchair, to get washed and changed, do your hair, put on lipstick, then to sit down and think a good story up.'

You are silent. Unity doesn't know she has interrupted you. Unity hasn't yet come to the awareness that you are in the room. She doesn't know she's in your house. This happens. She thinks she's in her own house, in her own armchair, having come to and now in the process of pulling herself together. She begins this process by practising telling everything to an imaginary you. When she's calmed down and recovered, she thinks, she'll get washed and change her clothes, do her hair and put on lipstick. Then she'll come round and really visit you. You're her baby sister, and while she's visiting, she might, as usual, tease you about your appearance, taunt you about your seriousness. 'How do you expect ever to get a man, Jotty love, if you keep going about looking like that?' All jests at your expense will be done in light-heart, however, and at the end she'll offer, as often she does, sisterly advice on how you could groom yourself up. Thing is, all your sisters do this. In their bloodied state, they feel comforted by you in a way they don't feel comforted by anybody. They feel soothed by you when they have no idea they are in need of soothing. They can be remonstrated with by you when ordinarily they'd be outraged at any interfering remonstrator. It's just that they patronise you. Can't help it – for look at you. Your hair used to be thick but now it's thin and you're not even bothered. Further, you stopped going to work and then you got the sack. Worst of all, you are odd in your appearance. Patched clothes is your appearance. Rumours are spreading about some sort of mental breakdown and, they're horrified to say, they're spreading about you.

But they are you sisters. They would not accuse you. They are your sisters. They would not harm you. They are your sisters. For now, they'll be light-heart. Today, it's Unity's turn. Still she thinks she's at home practising. I don't think she's come to yet. Do you?

'Yes,' she says, as you, now dizzy yourself, ease her head towards one side to start cleaning out that head wound, 'it's better to tidy up and remember first, in order to do preparation. That way, when the police bang the door and I open it, they're shocked and that gives me the edge. They've just spoken to the big bulldozer down the road, you see, that woman who thought that just because I was beautiful I wouldn't know how to kill her. Well, after speaking with her, the police were expecting to find another bulldozer, but when I open the door, Jot, instead they find me. Know what I mean?'

Yes. You know what she means.

You're not as beautiful as your sisters. In fact, you're not beautiful. You're okay, I'm not saying you're ugly. It's just that compared to them – in the stakes of astounding beauty – I'd advise you to keep the day job and not to get your hopes up.

One good thing, though, in your favour – they're insane and you're not.

One bad thing, though. If a line-up were held and you and your sisters were in it and people were told, 'Fifty pounds if you pick out the mad one', they'd look along this row of beauties, then point urgently when they got to you.

'So I deny it,' said Unity, 'and they have to believe me, because look at me – I don't mean now,' she dismissed her present been-in-a-fight condition. 'I mean when I don't have this blood on me. So I give them a denial on the doorstep and of course they're embarrassed and apologise, not just on behalf of themselves and of the entire Tiptoe Floorboard police force, but also on behalf of the bulldozer and do I want to press charges for jealousy? they ask. "That's okay, I won't," I say. But if *that* doesn't happen and I have to admit, because of the blood, I get upset and say, "It was awful. I don't know how such a thing – *to me* – could have come to pass." The police don't know either, and they are soothing. They go away, saying some befuddlement must have occurred and that they would unfuddle it. I say goodbye and go up to the bathroom to deal with my memory and with the blood. But you see, Jotty,' she leaned forward, 'the police coming to the door must have been proof, mustn't it, that I *had* been fighting with somebody? And I know this is silly, but if they don't tell me who it was, somehow I don't feel I can ask.'

One day you have all your sisters round at the same time. I don't mean they've all got into fights and simultaneously turned up on your doorstep. I mean they've turned up, *en masse,* for the first time *ever* on your doorstep. And guess what. Not a single one has blood on her hands.

But to take a jump back for a minute to when Unity said she sometimes says, 'I don't know how such a thing – *to me* – could have come to pass', she wasn't completely lying. In one respect this was more truth than not.

When your sisters are not having the headstaggers, they really are the loveliest of people. They try and try and try and try. To all intents and purposes they look like they have succeeded. They've done all the normal, conforming things of growing up. They have proper jobs. They are all married. They are all spectacularly groomed and spectacularly beautiful. They have houses, children, cars, good credit references, department-store bonus points awarded for outstanding good-buyer behaviour. Undoubtedly, they are of the community. There appears to be nothing rough or odd-angled about how they fit in.

Every so often, though, the psychic cracks they put their makeup over crack a bit more and out come these seepages. Strange rage attacks burst from them and that's how come they get that blood on their hands. Someone does something – sucks on takeaway bones in a public waiting room, for example, drinking the marrow, gnawing their fingers after, all in a manner of suggesting they would devour everything and anything that got in their path. Or someone flosses her teeth, using the edge of a plastic bag, looking at her bared-teeth reflection in a dark night window, not caring where the bits of the flossed get flung to, and a Sister, watching and hating, feels a bout of retaliatory violence coming on. Or else someone fiddles with her hair – twists it, eats it, twirls it out with sinewy, snoop-like fingers a whole rope's length and again, just inches from a Sister, and again, huge overwhelming revenge attacks come on. Or perhaps someone sniffs, hoiks catarrh, swallows mucus, or extracts her finger out of her nose with a slurp just as that nose is passing the ear of a Sister. Well, that finger may as well have been *in* Sister, given the entire sexual disturbance repertoire that has now been set off. Any general sort of tapping therefore, or drumming, or scratching, or clicking, or fiddling would also count as

171

examples. All are standard for what – sexually abusively speaking – could set the Sisters off.

So much for torture – I mean the Noises. And so much for torment – I mean the fighting. These are issues that are delicate points. After they get into their fights, believing 'I was perfectly within my rights – that person was attacking me', the Sisters find them impossible, initially, to shrug off. When they come to later, alone, scrabbling for breath, trying to regain their memory whilst sitting bloody in their armchairs, these women dread the secret, uncontrollable side of their nature that once again took possession of them, and know that somewhere, sometime in their past, something unspeakable must have gone on.

But this would be temporary. They'd do a fantasy of visiting their sister. They'd rehearse offloading this rubbish on to their sister and thus feel better all over again. After that, they'd decide to go round and *really* visit Jotty. God help her, they'd think. If only she'd make an effort. It wasn't as if she was ugly – though if there were a competition for 'Doing Your Best To Look Ugly', let's face it, she'd be up there with the greats. The Sisters could help her. She could be like them. Get her hair done, get a funky wig – a few wigs – wear proper sensual classy gear or even gear that just fitted her. The Sisters would help her. There was hope. They would help her. She could still, if she tried, get a man and kids before long.

And this is what I don't understand. Although they were keen for Jotty to come and join the party, they themselves, in spite of appearances, weren't really at this party themselves. They had husbands. That is correct. But guess what? They didn't accept they really had these husbands. Their husbands merely helped them present to the world how perfectly these Sisters had joined. They had children too. Also correct. But guess what? They didn't accept they really had these children. And they were women of the community – nine-to-five jobs, school-runs, communal committees for the benefit of the parish, 'Hello. Good morning. Good night. Congratulations. Well done. Happy birthday,' they'd say to people – but yes, that's right. They didn't consider they were really of the community. They wouldn't touch this community – not from their essence, not from their true spirit-soul connection – but in case there is any misunderstanding, these women had no conscious awareness of the true state of their unbelonging. This is hard to imagine too, given how long they've been wives and mothers and human beings in this world.

As for the husband situation, instead of their real ones, they preferred their imaginary ones. They'd married these perfect men from their imaginings long before any real husbands had come along. All these years on, the Sisters still persisted in involved daydreams about themselves and these ideal partners. Their fantasy husbands adored their wives, constantly observed their wives, spoke admiringly of their wives, were always on the point of crossing the room to come and join their wives but crucially, at the last moment, Sisters would press 'Rewind' and husbands would have to return to admiring wives from way across the room once more. Most important of all, these husbands never had any bodily problems and do you know those bodily problems? One only, really. What the Sisters meant was that their fantasy men never, ever, ever wanted to have sex. Understand, please, the men of their imaginings were happy *not* to have sex. Don't be thinking that, treacherously, they said to Gussie, or to Hale, or to Hesit, or to Unity, or to JanineJoshuatine, 'Bye-bye, darling. See you later. I'm just off up the road to peruse a good map or something', and then went off and had sex with somebody else. No! Gosh! Dreadful! Please! Don't be thinking that. The Sisters wouldn't have brooked any such bodily problems taking place in any of their made-up husbands. No imaginary women were ever going to sneak off with their steadfast, adoring, imaginary men.

As for the real husbands, well, first thing, they've got to be felt sorry for. Really, though, you'd have thought they could have researched this better before they got involved. 'Just like Hollywood,' they boasted, and they did this to other men to make the other men jealous, although the other men were already jealous for they could see for themselves how just like Hollywood these amazing-looking Doe women were. 'Very filmstar, *very* glamorous, *very* supermodel,' cried the husbands, 'and guess what, *we*'re getting married to them!' And they did, believing themselves to be getting stunners of the 'I do! I do! I do! I do!' category, whereas later – when they were stuck in the mud and too afraid to get out of it in case those other fellows jeered at them – it dawned on them that what they'd really conjoined with were women of the 'Don't! Don't! I'm warning you! Get off!' type instead.

Baffled. A bit unhappy. A bit emotionally shaken. Not much articulate. Maybe about half of articulate. That was the husbands. What about the children?

Little visitors. That's what the Sisters called them.

Absolutely extraordinary but I don't know how to explain this. The children did exist, as I said, but the question was, were they virginal conceptions? And as well as the matter of the actual conceiving of them, did any physical births, even Caesareans – I'd settle for Caesareans – ever take place? The Doe women shrugged. This was not a question that interested them. As far as they were concerned, it had been a case of some *really really really really, really really really really, really really really really* bad period happening to them, and at the end of it, yeah, well, okay, a baby had appeared. Then there'd been another *really really really really, really really really really, really really really really* bad period again happening to them and, yeah, okay, once more some other baby had appeared. And so on. These particular bouts of menstruation that kept happening to these women were of a duration that no period in the world had ever enjoyed previously. Nine-month sessions. That, ladies and gentlemen, should have been a *Guinness Book of Records* Number One Hit for the town of Tiptoe Floorboard. But it wasn't. Quirky legacies, sinister bequests, diabolical hand-me-downs – they were all pretty much the normal practice here.

And now these five impeccably groomed females were calling to visit their mess of a sister. As I say, Jotty opened the door and first thing was, God Almighty! All of them! Second thing was, is this a Spatial Fragmentation moment I'm experiencing, or is it a fact there really is no blood on the hands?

Now this blood thing. That should have been a clue to Jotty. I mean a warning. To call with no blood meant something was wrong. I won't get into the theme of ironic dangerous unconscious collusion at this point – and I mean on Jotty's part – until I tell you what she was doing at the moment of them knocking. She was alone at her kitchen table, looking at an old newspaper photograph.

This was of Tom Spaders. You remember Tom? The one from the gunshop? The one she had visited? The one who had undressed her? The one who had started kissing her? The one who'd asked her, as he leaned her back on his bed during the kissing of her, 'Can I do this? Do you want me to do that?' He loved her arching, he said. He wondered if she'd mind screaming, he said. He was astonished by her white nun skin. He kissed it. Then he kissed her hipbone. Said he loved her hipbone. Kissed it again. Then again. To her surprise, at the continuance of this bone-kissing, she raised her head from the bed to have a look on. Then it was he, too, after their row, who'd got out of bed, saying, 'Okay, does this mean you want me to sleep on the settee or something?' She hadn't wanted him to sleep on the settee. And he was the one – even though he'd wonderfully touched her – to whom she hadn't been able to give a single touch back. So she was in confusion, I mean about him. But I think we've established him. Yeah, Tom Spaders. The one from the gunshop. He was also the one in the photograph.

She was looking, scrutinising, staring fixedly at this photo, urging every so often, 'Back. Turn back. Please, please – change!' Mysterious. Puzzling. To what do we owe this behaviour? As to the glass she was sipping water from – bangs, splashes, a very bad arm-to-mouth-to-furniture co-ordination – there was no puzzlement. We can safely say the old Spatial was up and running here.

So what about that urging? Thing was, Jotty Doe had sex hardly ever because she had to be careful. I mean extra-special-super-careful. If she wasn't, the man she was with would turn into her da. He turned into the Fathers, not just the one father. I mean *the* Fathers, as in 'We're here! We're here! No room for any other person! We told you, daughter. We warned you, daughter. We are many, many, many and you will never make us leave.' Bit nasty. Bit spooky. Good news, though. This father business only happened whenever it came to the penis. Bad news, though. You kinda want the penis. That means, at least for Jotty, Conflict Impasse Syndrome always gets started up.

Now this is not dramatic. Don't be thinking this is sudden. It is not like it is on 'Get Your High Melodrama Television Here!' Nor is it conscious. At least, not while sex is happening. She's not in bed with one man, then post-penis – clash of cymbals! – suddenly she's in bed with another. No, no. Maybe so with some women, but with Jotty it never happens like that. The transformation takes place quietly, sneakily, even rather unpleasantly ordinarily. It's as if it's minding its own business. Very clever. And it's always *after* sex too. Not right after, later after, after they'd got up, got washed, got dressed, kissed good-bye and both gone out on their separate businesses. She'd be off on hers, remembering with a smile the wonderful 'this' and 'this' that Tom Spaders had done for her. Then *that* face, that other face, would slide over without her awareness. Next time she'd think of Tom, his features would be gone, with the other's imposed in their place.

At first she'd continue to think it was Tom and not make a big deal of it. Then she'd start to feel she wasn't enjoying thinking about him any more. Then there'd be a sensation of being followed and she'd look behind, and always at first, she couldn't understand why. Must be Tom, she'd continue to think, but by now did she mean the face in her mind, or the sense that it was he who was following her? Some sort of danger? Some sort of panic? Some sort of terrible 'Can-I-borrow-you-for-a-moment?' sneaking-up?

Well, no one was following her. I'm sure you've already guessed that. And as for the face in her mind – both you and I know Tom Spaders looks nothing like that. She herself still wasn't questioning, still wasn't registering, but she continued to get more and more uneasy until –

Sudden Reality Shock.

And now for the melodrama. It's not very melodramatic. She falters in her walking. She halts dead in the street and people tut and cry, 'Hey!' and 'Watch out!' as they manoeuvre around her. She's no longer happy. Something is mocking and it is very close by. Now, she doesn't like that he undressed her, doesn't like that he kissed her, that he'd looked up the bed towards her when he was down on her and said, 'You keep trying to say sentences,' which, at the time, had made both of them laugh.

She wasn't laughing now. She wasn't screaming either. He said he'd love her to scream, 'to make as much scream as possible'. No screaming, the Fathers said. '*If you scream ... If you scream ...*'

She blamed Tom Spaders now for that.

Hence the photo. She must look at it. It was proof he really was someone. She meant someone other than the Fathers. She must separate the right man from the wrong men. '*Once Again Tiptoe's Best Gunshop Owner*,' said the caption. As further evidence, his name was printed underneath.

'Tom Spaders,' she said. 'Tom Spaders,' she repeated. 'Tom Spaders,' she kept on, but let's face it, even she knew she wasn't fooling anybody. Before her was not the man she had originally cut from the newspaper. She turned the clipping face down and, as she did so, the Fathers in her womb began to laugh.

Now, this is where, had she not felt an aversion for them, she could have rung some Well-Meaning people. You wouldn't class Jotty Doe, not really, as disgraceful. But sometimes, you know, she was.

She used to have these books, Self-Help books, Human Potential books, Recovery books, most of them borrowed. But she woke up one day and knew it was time to get rid of her own and to give the others back. They were on incest and sexuality and on recovering from child sexual abuse and on adult children of child sexual abuse and on love and lust and greed and grabbing and on giving and receiving and on trust and sharing and on co-operation not domination and on aggression during sex with or without consideration for the other person and on partners of rape victims and on 'No, get back. Stay back. Don't! Don't! I said I'm not ready yet.' Those sort of books. She decided to get rid of them because, in the years since acquiring them – and rather furtively acquiring them, if you ask me, and initially from far-flung distant Self-Help bookstores where nobody knew her, as if she were ashamed or something – Jotty hadn't gotten round to reading even one of them, even once.

She had tried.

'Must read them, oh, I must read them, simply must read them. I might get cured.' So she'd pick the latest book up. But the moment of 'is-ness', of ripeness, of propitious occasion, never, ever, came upon her. An instant heaviness, a ponderous drugginess, a self-protective lassitude would come over Jotty whenever she tried to read one of them. 'If only I would read them,' she yawned, 'I might find out stuff.'

She'd attempt. I mean she'd attempt to open one. But she'd get overwhelmed by the tyranny of having to do so and instead would set the book back down. Then she'd lie down herself and fall asleep. She'd do this on her kitchen cushions for, like most people in Tiptoe Floorboard, Jotty never slept in her bedroom. Forty years she reckoned the nap would be, but it would go on seventy, threatening another seventy should she, when she awoke, again try to pick that book up.

They were constantly being lent to her too – by people she didn't like but to whom she couldn't say, 'You come too close, you talk too loud, you ask too many questions, you overstep, please go away and stand over there.' These people would say, though not to her, 'That's Jotty Doe, poor thing, the sister of those beautiful Doe women. Well, there for the Grace of God most certainly goes us.' They were terribly well-meaning, these people, self-appointed saints of the apparently inarticulate, people who banged the table on your behalf because they didn't believe you knew how to bang the table on your behalf, people who – Holy Jesus save you – you could well do without.

So duty-bound, she'd look at the latest loan: *Sex and Spirituality and Sex and Sexuality and Sex and the Ordinary and Sex Which is Supposed to be Love but Which Leaves You Feeling Shame and Pain and Lonely So That Means It's Not Love It's Just Bloody Awful Although That Might Be All Right If That's the Sort of Thing You Want But Do Victims of Child Sexual Abuse Really Want That?* God, she thought, even some of the titles took ages to read.

Jotty had about two hundred of these books that belonged to her outright, bought by herself for herself – for she really had tried to help her expansion on. She secreted these books around various parts of her house and that meant, of course, the bedroom. Best, she thought. That way, she'd never have to see them as she never went in there. The remaining hundred or so had been lent to her by all those indignant 'nothing funny about incest' people. Since having them thrust upon her, she'd tried, without success, to give all of them back.

'Absolutely not!' boomed a Well-Meaning. 'I simply won't hear of it. You need those books and remember, Jotty, you don't need to be ashamed of being a victim, of not being normal, of never getting beyond the management of it, of knowing that for the rest of your—' Oh! Loud confident stupid person! thought Jotty. Kill her for me, God. Kill her. Will you kill her? Failing that, at least turn her into a tree.

But God wouldn't. That meant yer woman was able to force another two or three volumes deftly over on to Jotty, with Jotty going, 'No-yes-no-yes-no-oh, all right then, yes. How long am I to have them before you want them back?' Of course she wouldn't read these either. They'd go among the things that she didn't want and that didn't belong to her and that were piling up in her house and smothering her. In truth, Jotty didn't know how many of these borrowed books there now were.

She gave them to charity. She made sure first her name wasn't on hers. Well, of course it wasn't. Tough titties for the Well-Meanings. Names or no names, they should have taken them back. Before leaving the house, Jotty dispersed the books amongst many different carrier bags. Outside the house, she dispersed them amongst many different charity shops, disguising them first with hats, scarves, socks and a few innocent Shakespeares. Before long, all of them were gone.

Except one.

This book she had bought by mistake but had then kept back deliberately. She had thought on buying it that it was another of the usual, but when she'd taken it out of the wardrobe to get rid of it, she found that it was not. It had been written for teenagers – normal teenagers – awakening to the joy of their budding adult sexuality. It had only a short mention – plus tiny list of helpful addresses – for those condemned teenagers who were not. Jotty wouldn't have bought this book had she known of its exclusive trajectory. Instead she would have been enraged, for it would have reminded her of all the grief of all the loss of everything she'd never had. But now, a bit on from the purchase, years on, too, from when she'd been a teenager, she stood in her bedroom with it, finding it a light, blessed, joyful thing to hold.

And so she had gotten rid of them. How did that feel? Did she *really* feel okay at not having read even one of them? Jotty had a think and said she felt fine. She was definitely not too bad, she told herself. Not annoyed or upset or anything. It was just that every so often there was this little niggle. There was this little something. It said, 'Pity you didn't manage to read even one.

'It might have revealed something to you.

'It might have unlocked something for you.

'You could have tried, Jotty girl, that waterfall exercise even once.'

Ah, yes. The waterfall. That had featured in one of the chapters from one of the very early books Jotty had attempted fragmentedly to get cured by. In it, the author, an expert in her field, had been interviewing women about their sexual fantasies. She wanted to know how they got aroused, especially to orgasm, given their child histories of incest and sexual abuse.

'Are you stupid?' they shouted. 'It's obvious. Torture fantasies! Something on TV, or a word let drop, an innocent word, a deliberate word, or an expression that conjures up a whole range of torment. Case histories of abuse, written by experts of abuse. You should know this. Are you an expert or what?

'Well, of course we're ashamed,' they then cried, believing this woman had the cheek to be accusing them. 'But hey! Have you tricked us? You said you were giving us pseudonyms. Are you still giving us pseudonyms? If you're not giving us pseudonyms, we'll be abused as we were as children, only by you in the guise of Recovery this time.'

'Of course I'm keeping my promise,' said the expert. 'Of course I'm giving you pseudonyms. What I'd like to suggest—' But they wouldn't let her suggest. They were distraught. Her insinuations had touched into their shame core.

'It's what we learned!' they shouted. 'It's our theme tune, our song, our story, our something we haven't been able to get out of us. These are our triggers. So don't you dare, specialist, to look at us like that!'

'You think I'm judging you. I'm not judging you. It's just that I want to make a suggestion,' the expert tried again. 'Instead of torture fantasies, how about practising getting turned on by the cycles of nature? Getting aroused by the pink and the red and the orange and the peach and the apricot of sunsets? By the rhythms of life and natural green leafy things and then, when it's time – having orgasms to the thought of waterfalls?'

There was silence on the page, a palpable silence, a silence you could have fallen or been pushed to your death from – five or six whole paragraphs of astonished bated breath. Who is this specialist? scrabbled the thoughts. Who sent her? What are her credentials? Is this an idjit, a child sexual abuse virgin, a day-release intellect, sent by some older armchair intellectual specialist, to advise and patronise us?

Ridiculous, thought Jotty, setting the book down at this point. She had been so in sympathy with the abused child-women, and astonished at the naïveté of the expert's suggestion, that in her annoyance she forgot she was actually reading instead of nodding off. Those books, she thought. *Oh, those books, those books.* They go too far sometimes. They start off saying it's easy, promising you things, saying if only you do all the written exercises. Then they spring the impossible – to move from darkness and torture and repetition and stuckness to having orgasms to leaves falling off trees beside pretty waterfalls!

Someone from rape couldn't do that.

She couldn't imagine someone from rape doing that.

Could someone from rape do that?

Well, said her mind, you'll never know. You didn't read on.

After her initial relief about the books being gone – with all their 'musts' and 'shoulds' and 'better-hads' which she couldn't prevent herself seeing in them – Jotty now felt scared, guilty, and alone. Oh, not to be alone, she thought. But she was wrong. I mean – *she was wrong*. I mean, *always* she felt such a dreadfully wrong person. Could it be, she thought, that someone could start something off, and so long ago that you, who experienced it, couldn't remember the starting of it? Yet you carry on the legacy – the self-rubbishing, the negating, the sabotaging, the breaking of your own heart with your thoughts?

Obviously, given that the borrowed-book situation was now 'Thank you very much, how lovely, I'll return them soon, goodbye' and then straight off to the charity shop with them, approaching the Well-Meanings – had she been inclined – to find out how normal was this waterfall business, would be well out of the question now. The books were gone. She couldn't look up any index. She couldn't consult any paragraph. So, when the Fathers started up after her encounter with Tom Spaders, she did the unthinkable and sought psychotherapeutic help for herself.

I'll tell you about Jotty and her therapy when I get on to the Death Threat but, for now, the newspaper cutting was still face down on the table. Afraid to look at it, Jotty slumped over the table and covered her eyes with her hands. In her mind she was still trying to separate Tom's features from the Fathers' features but definitely she was not succeeding. And it was during one of these failed attempts and repeated attempts that the five Sisters, currently bloodless, came knocking on her door.

She let them in. They came in. They went into the kitchen. Two sat at her table whilst three leaned gracefully against various worktops and walls. Jotty, puzzled by the absence of the blood-sequence-blueprint, went over and put the kettle on.

It started as usual.

'You could get your hair done.'

'We could help you get your hair dyed.'

'We could help you get your hair styled.'

'Or a wig – it would look better, Jot, thicker, not thin, not so as if it's falling out all the time.'

There was an edge. Not the usual cajoling, controlled banter each of the Sisters would come out with after Jotty had cleaned up the blood for them. Perhaps the only true question to have asked at this point would have been 'Come on, girls. What's the reason you've really come to see me?' but Jotty didn't ask it, and I think it's time we had our talk about collusion now.

Collusion's tricky. It's a bit like those gangster wives and girlfriends – and just for the record, none of these Sisters was a gangster wife or girlfriend, although I can't speak as to the professions of their fantasy husbands, of course. Well, we look at these gangster wives and girlfriends and we say, 'Oh, those gangster wives and girlfriends! They're crazy. How can they reconcile to themselves all those violent things they must know their men go out and do or have done?' Is this a case of memory loss? we wonder. Is this a case of amorality or immorality? Is this a case of certain men coming home at night and certain women forgetting propriety and going, 'Hot damn! Warrior undressing!' – thus overlooking in their excitement that they ought to be frowning and disapproving, just as we ourselves would have been?

Who'd be them? we think. 'Not us,' we say, but hold on a minute. I've just heard a rumour that would make the way of the gangsters seem as babies. It's a spooky rumour and, I'm sorry to say, it's circulating about you.

You people, you women there, who were just this minute running down the wives and girlfriends to me, what sort of men do you get mixed up with yourselves?

Women who pooh-pooh the gangster girlfriends, believing

themselves vastly above the morals and intellects of somesuch-likes, who would never dream of getting into such obvious dysfunctional relationships – they get into not so obvious ones themselves. Their men might not swagger about being boss, being self-appointed judges and juries, jabbing guns into people, setting up illegal enterprises, hanging people by their ankles out of top-storey buildings or having their girlfriends tailed whether their girlfriends got highly sexually charged by being tailed or not.

Instead, these men, these non-gangsters, these law-abiding civilised people, might walk out the door before you, with you pleading, 'Don't walk away from me, don't shout at me, please don't slam the door on me, don't hurry me, don't walk so much in front of me. We've been married twelve years so why do you still get my name wrong?' Or it might be that they're too important to take time to let you know that they cancelled any arrangements they made with you. Or they might say, 'Don't mind me if I snap at you and seem truly as if I hate you. It's just me being me – nothing personal at all.' They are not softies, these men. These are not the men who say, 'Hiya love,' or who put requests into the radio: 'For my person, from her person. Tell her I'm busy in my office working, thinking of her in her office, also working. My heart desires the pleasure of having her name nationally called.' No. Not softies. Not warm lovers. They won't be kind, and I'm giving you the toned-down version here, which is that the man who belittles, reduces, downgrades, shames and envies his woman – 'Yes, please! Oh yes, please!' – that's the sort of non-gangster men these women will have.

They'll reconcile this by saying, 'Oh, all men are like that! That's the way all men are!' Well, I've noticed that expression 'all men' and the women who say it. They're the ones in the abandoning, uncelebrated relationships, who must, at all costs, have these abandoning, uncelebrated relationships, which is why they'll shrug and say, 'What can I do? You're naive. All men are like this. That's the way all men are.' When they start, I want to shout, 'Stop! Oh shut! Shut! Shut!' which is not exactly cursing but also not exactly not-cursing. 'Look around you,' I want to say. 'It isn't all men. It's *your* man does this. It's *your* man does that.'

And in that vein – the vein of collusion – Jotty was well alert to the type of relationship between a man and a woman where violence, inside or outside the relationship, was the fulcrum. Most certainly, she kept away from that. She was also alert though, to that other, non-violent, but elusively shaming, subtly discounting, joyless form of a relationship, where the man has to leave in the end anyway because, after bringing her down to the level where he believed he could now let himself have her, he has realised that, with her down there on the mat crying, he no longer wants such an unexpected inferiority to himself. Jotty, always the analytical technician, was also alert against taking up with someone she didn't want as a way of preventing her desires for whom she might want overwhelming her, perhaps ending up in a relationship, even a marriage, hating the make-do, stand-in man.

Jotty had it mapped out. Everything was sussed. She hardly dated. On one level this was to keep her safe from the Mothers and the Fathers, and I'll tell you of the Mothers later on. It was also to keep her safe from what she didn't want in a relationship. As for what she did want – well, she'll need another hundred years into Recovery before she can move on to that. So, she had all vulnerabilities guarded, thinking nothing in the way of danger was ever again going to get at her, but oops. I said oops. What's this? I don't mean Tom Spaders. I mean this thing called irony. The point I'm making is that one thing Jotty didn't take into account as part of her vigilance against danger, were her sisters. Her sisters, at present, constituted her biggest threat.

If you were to be on the receiving end of one of these sibling visits you might – given their proneness to headstaggers – get a bit nervous and not let them in. Not Jotty. This was because the Sisters together made up her blind spot. Including this blind spot, Jotty had four Achilles' Heels. Tom got her on three of them. One was with '*When I fuck you*' which, no matter how much of a turn-on it might be to some people, just kept seeming to her like some shocking big slap. Another was his angry '*You snore*', which stripped her, in her moment of near nakedness in the bed beside him, of any shaky sense of femininity she might have had. Third was the sexually crushing '*Have you any idea how childish you are?*' Her fourth Achilles' Heel was the blind spot, and here I mean her collusion with her sisters. These were women who, under threat, or perceived threat, could quite possibly kill anybody – their husbands, their children, all of the community, even themselves and their fantasy husbands if need be – to keep their defences from coming unstuck. So, given the situation, did Jotty honestly think that just because she was a Doe herself these other Does wouldn't attack her? I wonder what her therapist would have to say about that.

An academic question, I'm afraid. We won't know what her therapist would have to say about it, because in well over a year since she'd started going to therapy, Jotty hadn't spoken to her therapist even once.

She was going three times a week. Did you know that? I bet you didn't know that. Three times a week, mind – 'Psychoanalysis Divided by Five and Multiplied by Three' officially was what it was called. She'd rush there every time. 'Oh, hurry-hurry, puff-pant, pant-puff, can't-be-late, can't-be-late,' and so she was always early. That meant she'd have to pace up and down for a while on the street. Not the therapist's street, of course. I hope by now you'd know that she'd be thinking her therapist might be spying out on her. Another street. She'd rush round to it and do all this pacing up and down. She'd count the seconds, count her alarm clock, wait for the big hand to go to the hour then, seconds before the dot of nine, she'd push clock away, run round to the right street, rush up the garden path and, dot reached, press the therapist's bell. She'd get buzzed in. She'd go in, sit down, fold her arms and refuse to speak for the whole of the session. I mean she refused to speak. I mean she did not talk.

At nine fifty, end of session, her therapist would tap her watch and say, 'Time to let you out of jail now, Jotty Doe.' Jotty wouldn't laugh, even though she knew that was meant as a joke. When first she'd made the momentous decision to get herself into therapy, she wanted to, longed to, but wouldn't let herself speak to her therapist. She couldn't – not until her therapist had said sorry until Jotty was satisfied and told her she could stop. Jotty wasn't sure what the therapist was to be sorry for, or even when this 'wanting an apology' business had crept up on her. All she knew was that it ran in the family. Apparently all her siblings, all the Mothers, all the Fathers, all of them, wanted all of these 'sorries' too. She hadn't briefed her therapist about this because, as I say, Jotty Doe wasn't speaking to her therapist. Funny little thing, therapy, isn't it now?

Anyway, Jotty would leave therapy after all this angry non-speaking, and head somewhere, usually her kitchen-cushion floor bed. She wouldn't remember getting home, wouldn't re-member undressing, would wake up hours later in the night, thankfully back in her repressions. Jotty liked her repressions. She loved them, for it was only when she was in them that she could manage to get anything else done. When she was out of them, I mean like now, when they were breaking down, frightening her with their fragmentations and unmistakable disintegrations, it was like she was going mad and watching herself go mad at the same time. The repressions had been in this state of 'collapse-and-cobble-back-together-quick' ever since that last sexual encounter she'd had with Tom Spaders. So it was anger at him – for interfering with her repression, for that Achilles' Heel business, for that photograph that no longer looked like him, and for issues in her childhood and young adulthood for which she knew he couldn't possibly be responsible – that drove her eventually to her therapist's door. But in this day of therapy, with all her broken reality returning in jigsaw pieces to reassemble itself painfully inside her, whenever moments of repression returned, when once more she was unable feel anything – not madness, not murderousness, not terror, not violated – they were, to her, blessings ever to be thankful for.

But back to the Sisters and their ostensible reason for calling.

'You've got to make an effort,' urged Unity. 'We make efforts. You're part of society, Jotty. You simply have to join.'

Excuse me? thought Jotty. Was she hearing right? Might this be the moment to bring up blackings-out, comings-to and you-know-what on the hands?

She tried.

'Don't you care you could have killed someone?'

That was one effort she came out with, after explaining a few of the blood, police, bulldozer and coming-to examples.

'Or been killed?' she went on.

'Or gone to jail?

'Or lost your mind?

'One day, girls, if you don't get help with this problem, you'll freak – just like poor Mamma and Aunty and all those others in the asylum and jailhouse we're related to, and you might not come back from blacking-out by that time at all.'

So, she tried. The Sisters didn't believe her. The Sisters stared at her. What was she talking about? They looked at their hands. *There was no blood on their hands.*

It was a lost battle anyway because, you see, there was this thing of your father having done it. And your mother having done it. And your brothers having done it. And your sisters having done it and, who knows, maybe at some point you yourself having done it, not to mention the generations way back, and the not-so-way-back generations too – they probably all did it as well. So we're stuck in that sequence. 'Who smashed those windows?' said Father. 'What happened to that wall?' 'You took a sledgehammer to it, Daddy. You knocked that wall down yesterday when you were in a temper.' 'For God's sake! Listen to those children! Stop that lying, you children,' said Mammy. 'We hate liars. We never want it to get to the point where it's a case of "What's going on? What's that?" and the answer is "Oh nothing. Just a little liar" – meaning you. If it gets to that point, children, we'll be very cross. So. You're being asked one more time. Who broke those windows? Who owns that blood? Who spilt that blood? That's the last time of asking. Tell the truth or Daddy'll take his belt off.'

The Sisters didn't know what to say to their poor Jotty. It was becoming apparent she might indeed be in need of therapy. And yes. Maybe you've guessed. Therapy was the real reason the girls had come to the door.

Before I get on to the Death Threat, I'll just say the Sisters had all been accompanied to Jotty's by their loving fantasy husbands. Not exactly accompanied. As usual, each wife had her husband not quite alongside her. He was positioned at a distance, admiring her, mostly from against Jotty's farthest kitchen walls.

Now, the Sisters didn't split off their fantasies. They were not conditions from Tom Cusack's wife's stolen medical dictionary. These women literally didn't see or hear imaginary people conversing and interacting with them. What they did, though, was mentally play out their super-intense, highly enclosed daydreams from the moment they awoke in the morning until they were placing their knives back under their pillows in whatever nook or cranny they happened to be sleeping in that night. They were so skilled at this formidable fantasising that, even though they had come round to tackle Jotty about this therapy business, they could use a small percentage of mental energy for doing so, whilst keeping ninety-eight per cent bulk time for having their dream husbands on the go.

At present, and as usual, these husbands were observing their beloveds, commenting favourably on every single thing their wives did. Hesit would gracefully open a drawer to take out a teaspoon. Janine would elegantly pick up her cup to take a sip from it even if – spatial fragmentationally speaking – she didn't quite so elegantly set it back down. Hale would approach one of the cupboards – not the psychopath one we're all desperate to get rid of – and she'd do this as if indeed she were a supermodel on the catwalk. And so on. The husbands watched all this, saying, 'Look at the superb manner in which my wife lifted that teaspoon,' or 'That cupboard was so lucky to have had my love's fingers upon it.' These men were speaking to their friends – also conjured up by the Sisters. Unity, meanwhile, was one hundred per cent somewhere else.

She was in the supermarket, going round the aisles, picking

up baby food, nappies, feeding bottles, dummytits, compound solutions – for she was a brilliant mother – and putting them in her fantasy trolley, just as any normal mother would have done. Her imaginary husband, standing to the side, was overcome by the sweet perfection of the way in which his wife stretched for those nappies. 'Hardly past being a child herself,' he remarked. Unity was pleased. Like the others, bar Jotty, she welcomed reference to her woman-child status, but regarding the children who had worn those nappies their mother Unity had been so admired for reaching for so childlikely, they knew their ma would be upset and annoyed to be reminded there had been days when, in reality, she had had to go nappy-shopping for them and, while we're here – I mean at actuality – let's carry on a bit more. The Sisters' husbands were having affairs. I mean their real husbands. And I don't mean they were having them with Ordnance Survey maps, or with conjured-up fantasy women. Hale, Unity and Gussie's husbands had all taken up with real skin, bone, blood, muscle and private-parts women. JanineJoshuatine's husband was at home at that moment, packing to leave her. He was taking their baby daughter with him, knowing it would be madness to leave Lisa – not because she wouldn't be physically provided for, but because in every other respect she'd be ignored. Hesit's husband was already suspicious about the marriage – and I don't mean her first husband, who'd already gone away, not caring a damn whether or not the townsmen laughed at him, but the second husband she married immediately after, in order to keep the 'being joined' sequence up. Don't you think this is creepy? I think this is creepy. Thanks for being here with me, by the way. I'd hate to be bystanding this on my own.

So eleven people were in that room and five of them were invisible – that's not counting the husbands' friends –

indistinct, variable and not that important. Nor was it counting the Mothers – vastly important but countless in their generational lineage – but before I get on to the Mothers, I'd better tell you about something else.

Jotty Doe was seeing a therapist.

Yes, I know *you* know, but the Sisters had only just got wind of it. Thing was, it was causing serious repercussion stigma on the street.

The five had been warned by some friendly reliabilities that their sibling had been seen pacing up and down the street that was next to Therapy Street. She had been consulting her clock in the manner of people who go to therapy, and did the Sisters know she'd also been buying, borrowing and giving away to charity 'recovery from incest and rape' books by the score? 'Pacing up and down three times a week mind,' concluded the reliabilities. 'And for a considerably long time now. Just thought you girls might want to know about that.'

Well!

The physical appearance of Jotty, doubtless, had been offensive enough to the Sisters but add on this new therapy dimension and they're sorry, they're really sorry. Try as they might, the situation was now beyond a joke.

They couldn't discuss it with each other, of course, for that would be acknowledging that something needed to be acknowledged. Instead they met up and combustibly began to talk Jotty's hair. They decided unanimously, and subconsciously, to go round and see her, just in case this was going to go the way it had gone years before. The way it had gone years before was 'Strict Emotional Policy'. That meant 'Top Secret'. That meant you kept the lid on.

Years ago, oh, way before Jotty had had that sexual encounter with Tom Spaders, and way before the pound pound! jackrabbit encounters she'd had as an adult with various others, there had been another encounter. This one had been with the Fathers. It hadn't been welcome. And it had been forced.

Afterwards, it was said Jotty Doe had started eating mounds of butter. She kept on eating butter until she got fat. Then she'd gotten fatter. She got so fat, so big, so swollen, to the point where the Sisters were afraid to look at her. Must be one of those big long endurances called periods, the young Doe girls nervously, dismayingly, thought. Eventually Jotty had to be taken to Tiptoe Hospital to have the period extracted. This was when the Mothers slapped a nurse, kicked another nurse and threatened some doctor with some glass instrument, all because something had been said, but it doesn't matter, don't worry, because after that, Jotty – young woman? teenager? child? – was taken home. As for the menstrual period, it stayed at the hospital. Everything went back to normal and everybody shut up.

As for Jotty, well, hard to remember. She stopped being fat and she developed a hankering for knitting. She knitted little Leprechaun things. This made no sense. She continued the tiny garment knitting, in a corner, not talking. I mean not talking. I mean not talking to anyone. In the end it all came happy, though. The titchy garments disappeared or were taken away and memory blanks ensued although, for some reason, Jotty, in the years after, wouldn't follow her sisters down the path of grooming and of clothes-shopping. Instead of fitting into society, she refused to fit into society, remaining forever stubborn and stony-faced, on its rim.

As for clothes – oh, the precariousness, the paradox, of wearing something that's baggy and so is supposed to hide you and yet, because of this threadbareness and bagginess, could fall off you at any time. It could fall down over your waist, could fall apart in its stitching, collapsing in a heap of unsightly patches and leaving you naked underneath. Like abuse again. Like concealing and revealing again. It's like when people say, 'I was on the toilet when you rang,' and you think, why is it important for that person to tell me that? The thing is, clothes and clothes falling – is that trauma? Is that normal? Is it important for a person to recreate bad times over and over for themselves like that?

And now, all these years on, she was threatening again to do it. She was affronting them with her patent lack of groom. This time, though, she wasn't eating butter. She wasn't distorting herself on distended, extended nine-month cycles. She wasn't knitting either. The Sisters suspected, perhaps rightly, that this new therapy was standing in for all that.

So what were the girls up against? Were we talking Dirty Linen in public? Were we talking Noises? Were we talking families of origin? Were we talking Mamma Doe and Papa Doe and Mamma and Papa's friends and other relatives? Were we talking Mr McCotter? Or impacts, consequences, earplugs, rolling legacies, headstaggers, four brothers in war factions, another brother not in war factions but hardly normal given his Community Centre leanings? Were we talking mental asylums, sex, no sex, or sex where you concentrate on the wallpaper? If she's saying she wants to sleep in her bedroom, would that be casting aspersions on them because none of them slept in their bedrooms? If she's saying, 'There's something wrong and I'm going to the doctor', would that mean she's implying there's something wrong and that they should be going to the doctor too?

Of course we know that Jotty, so far in therapy, hadn't been saying anything. But I think that information would have freaked the Sisters even more. To sit in a room, facing a person, a few feet from a real person, and not open your mouth for hours and hours, over days and days, weeks and weeks, over a year and still not opening it – the Sisters would not be able to comprehend the ultimate in being listened to so completely like that.

'A greedy and superficial practice,' said Hale.

'Selfish,' said Hesit. 'It's self-indulgent, Jotty. Empty-headed, anti-social.'

'It's spending the state's money. After all, you're on sickness benefit,' said JanineJoshuatine, 'and you're buying therapy, when you should just get another job and credit cards and not get sacked this time and get on with life and have kids and husbands just like us.'

And, of course, there was always the unspoken: Who – and where – was the man?

And that was it. It was about him. Where was he? Why hadn't he appeared and why hadn't she gotten married to him? Being married to him would have stopped all this 'being-on-the-rim' long ago. As far as Jotty was concerned, this was Total Exclusion and Explosion Territory. Being carefully non-committal, she applied brush-off crumbs absentmindedness to it. She had to stay defended with her sisters, keeping all openings – when it came to her and men – closed.

She hadn't told, most especially she hadn't told about the last one, Tom Spaders – that she'd had that brief involvement with him, that she'd had that night of Going Under and losing control with him, instead of keeping alert or else moving sideways into the wallpaper, which had always been her child-woman experience with sex before. The reason she didn't tell was because she'd learnt from the past that any man attracted to was going to be put through the computer. That would be the Mother Computer. Like Jotty, the Sisters had ingested the

Mothers, and so questions would be asked – who, what, where, when, how?

Yes. Those Mothers.

There had been a famous lecture at the Leprechaun Museum one day in Tiptoe Floorboard. The museum held fortnightly lectures, not all of them on the Little People. Some were community action-based and to do with humans too. This one had been entitled '*If You're a Woman and Your Mother was Mentally Ill – You're Fucked*', and the reason I'm mentioning it is because of those women, I mean the Mothers, I mean the ones who *were* mentally ill and who *had* managed to get themselves inside their daughters. It was different for the Sisters than it was for Jotty. Different because, first, the Sisters' actual husbands were men none of them wanted. That meant the Mothers didn't deconstruct them for, as I said, they only deconstructed at any spark of attraction. Luckily for the Sisters, so far, this didn't include attraction to fantasy men. Second difference was that, because the Sisters could have their fantasy husbands without the Mothers dissecting and shredding them with: '*Hmmm, bit of a devouring baby, isn't he?*', '*Hmmm, rather a sex addict, isn't he?*' – this meant the Sisters could super-heighten the fantasy of themselves being adored and admired in the supermarket, whilst blocking out any real sexual contact that was going on at that moment between them and their actual men. Hence the real husbands tending to feel not quite satisfied, as if they'd just made love to an apparition, to a ghostling, to something bordering on a straightforward occultation of the sinister. Hence also a poor little infant, who transpired not to be a virgin birth, coming into the world every now and then. The Fathers never put in an appearance either with the Sisters, as they did with Jotty and the penis. This was again because of the non-attraction aspect, and also because the Sisters didn't appear themselves. They were off in that supermarket, I mean the wallpaper super-market. They were intensely interested in the types, textures and superabundance of foliage right inside those wallpapers. They had developed this escape route to expert level way back in their little girlhood pasts.

Wallpapers. I don't want to get into the Wallpaper Story and, anyway, given all the Recovery books that now exist most defin-itively covering it, where have you been if you don't already know? Nowadays, you don't even have to have been sexually abused to know off by heart the Wallpaper Story. So, taking it as looked at, this brings us to an already touched-upon subject: Going Sideways or Going Under. Which would you prefer?

Disappearing into wallpaper is Going Sideways. That's cutting-out and slipping-out – I mean out of your body – until it's done and over with. Just count your numbers, recite your alphabet, examine that leaf on that tree beside that waterfall inside that wallpaper, until Daddy or Daddy Substitute falls asleep or crawls off. Going Under, therefore, can be very con-fusing, I mean for an adult who has, since childhood, always been used to Going Sideways. Going Under is slipping *into* your body, it's *giving it up* to your body, it's acknowledging that your body knows more about everything – most especially sexual – than anything your little head of super-intellectual control believes it can think up.

First time Jotty went under, first time, mind, was with Tom Spaders. First time ever. So Going Under was good. Definitely it was progress. It was also why she had her breakdown, by the way.

And until those Achilles' Heels, and until the Fathers came with the penis, she had experienced Going Under brilliantly. With Going Under, you sort of lose it. Just before that, though, you've got your head keeping control as usual, monitoring, caution, caution, careful now, caution, mapping out how this sexual encounter, no – this procedure, this clinical procedure – was going to proceed. Therefore, clinical and more clinical for, remember, what's required from you is to be as objective as possible. You don't want some emotional factor coming in and jeopardising everything you could well do without. Under no circumstances must you lose your head so, with these instructions reverberating, you keep forgetting that you're going to go under, and that when you do go under, all head control goes. Then? Why, he could do anything. Then? Why, you, too, you could do anything. It's like reaching your hands out while you're dreaming and wondering why ...? Why ...? Is this abuse legacy or is this the body doing what it's wired to do? You want, theoretically, to ask yourself that question, but you can't think that question, even though you'll wonder why later you couldn't get your teeth into that question, why there was no point to it, why it would have been ridiculous even to think it, but it's because, you see, you've already been swept away. Another thing. This Going Under takes place without any substance ingested so, of course, you've nothing but your body, your desires, and him to pin it to. Sounds scary. I mean why wouldn't it sound scary? I mean to someone who'd only ever gone numb and sideways. Yet Jotty liked it. She was amazed by it. She felt she'd read three hundred and ten Recovery books to make up for the equivalent of it. And more good news! She still hadn't killed anybody. And I mean a man.

I mean in mistaking him for the Fathers. He'd surfaced in her haze to say something to her and she heard them saying, 'Fuck you', 'When we fuck you', as she was lying in her 'out-of-the-head' experience in his arms. And that was when her head control whizzed back and her body snapped and she recoiled from him. And that was when he got angry with 'Just an expression. It's just an expression. I'm just ... I'm just ...' It was no wonder the fight after. How could I? she thought. How could *I* have let *him* make *me* – lose control like that?

What had he given her? That feeling of play. Incredible. New. Even at her age. The experience of Going Under. Incredible. New. Okay, definitely she'd liked that. Her body had trusted him for that. But also shame. And, of course, her new femininity complex. 'Here, darlin', he said. 'Here's two presents' – one was the childishness of her 'fuck you' reaction. The other, the backlash to a very masculine snore.

No way, though, would she let him go through the computer. She might blame him. She was in the mood to blame him. Certainly, with the Mothers inside her, she was going to blame him. But those Mothers inside her sisters were not going to blame him as well. She shrugged as they asked the 'man' question, then she looked at her watch and wondered when they would go.

So Jotty had had it once – the true, authentic Going Under experience. The Sisters had had it never. They thought they were safe not having it, not knowing about it, and instead holding fast to wallpaper patterns and to the love story with their shadow husbands going, in formulistic grooves, in their heads. But do you remember when I told you about the Noises and how they returned to John Doe and caused all his bafflement as to why they were returning to him? It was similar with the Sisters and their fantasy husbands. Life's like that. Little connecting patterns. Here was the pattern of how the Sisters went mad.

They couldn't keep it up. The faceless adoring men in their minds became not so faceless. That was within a year of this visit to Jotty, and I know you know whose faces they became.

With the Fathers now starting to appear regularly – both through fantasy husbands and real husbands – the Sisters' defences started to break down. As they experienced more consciously the blood on the hands, the ratcheting of the Noises, the police, the denials, the comings-to, the blackings-out then, finally, the wallpaper collapsing, one by one each sister did her vanishing act. Soon there was only Jotty and half of Janine left. But before the moment when Jotty and Janine burst into the bar to confront their brother, who was getting drunk with his new pal, Tom Spaders, we're back in Jotty's kitchen, with her sisters issuing the definitive Death Threat.

It was that suicide thing.

I'm sure at least some of you must have experienced this.

It's when your loved ones unexpectedly say to you, 'If you commit suicide, Jotty – and very soon – do you mind if we don't do the sorting? We don't wanna do the sorting. Is it okay if someone else, some stranger, comes in and does it instead of us?' And, either because you really do understand the not wanting to do the sorting, or else, in the moment of them springing this upon you – for, after all, you're not suicidal – you're startled into replying, 'Yeah, okay, that's okay. Just leave it to the authorities. The police or whoever will come and sort it out.'

However this may hit you, soon you start to feel pinpricks of upset and annoyance. What a thing to come out with. So what if you understand? How weak of them, you're now thinking. What cowards. Why – even on a standard, basic, societal level – anyone would agree they were being discourteous female bastards. Aren't they supposed to be your loved ones? Who but your loved ones should come and do the sorting? No wonder you're suicidal if that's the best of love you can get.

So the Sisters harped on a bit more about Jotty being suicidal and about them not wanting to do the sorting. But hey, to make up for it, they said, they'd be perfectly willing to make sure she got the third grave.

'Third grave?' Jotty asked, now not sure she wanted the answer. That was when the second part of this Death Threat came up.

It was that Third Grave thing.

Years earlier Doe Father had been killed by accident by a big cooking pot of cast iron coming down on top of him. His wife killed him but she had changed her mind about killing him in the split-second before doing so and that was what made it an accident – gravity and momentum, no longer will and despair – had brought that pot down. But it was too late. He was dead. However, regardless of how many mother funerals John Doe, full of grief, went to, Mamma Doe was not dead. She was very much alive. Of course she was in the mental hospital, but after Father's death, a particular grave plot had been purchased with spaces for three coffins. Papa was in one. Mamma, naturally at some point, would go in another. But look, there's an extra space, and Jotty, according to the Sisters – given she was the only unmarried daughter with no family of her own to speak of – should legitimately be awarded the eternal place of that. If she committed suicide any day now – they paused but got no confirmation – she'd go on top of Papa. Or, they continued, for they had it worked out so Jotty wouldn't have to worry her suicidal head about it, if Mamma died before her, she'd go on top of both.

Jotty was freaked. Freaked even more than she had been by the sorting. This was a bullseye counterattack to her freaking them by going to therapy. 'Okay, then. If you're going to keep up this therapy,' implied the Sisters, 'we're going to bury you smack bang in between.' The Sisters, on a deluded level, believed Jotty would be reassured by this, just as they had been reassured by her not blaming them for not wanting to do the sorting. Passive aggressively – unusual for them – they carried on.

'Besides,' they said, 'you know Mamma would be furious at the thought of Aunty Jacky going in it.' This was a direct reference to *you-know-what* which took place years ago in these older women's pasts.

But hold on. You don't know what. I don't think anyone's told you. I know you know that Papa Doe had been having a long-standing affair with Aunty Jacky, who, as I say, was Mamma's sister. But as for the next bit, I'll put you in the know right away.

There was a fight and this is tricky – Aunty Jacky had got into it with their mother, who turned out years later to be their aunt and not their mother. This fight was ostensibly over teenager Jetty, Aunty Jacky's daughter, who was dating her cousin, the Sisters' teenage brother, John. You know Jetty and John. Well, John's mother – I mean impostor mother for, as I say, she turned out years later to be his aunt – told her son that she had had enough of this impossible dating. On two counts. One was that this son, like all her other sons, ought not to be going down the route of getting married while she was still living. It was bad manners. Out of respect for his mother, he could at least wait until she was dead. The second count was that Jetty was his cousin, possibly his sister, and that information, out of temper, burst forth from her that day.

Now, if you want to get married in Tiptoe Floorboard, you have to go to the Town Hall and consult a big list that's hanging there to see if your name's on it. If it is, then you look to see if the name of the person you're wanting to marry is on this list as well. If it is, then you're not allowed to marry that person. This is because you're in some close blood familial relationship already with that person. For example, you and that person had given birth to each other at some point long ago in the past. It's an inconvenience but you have to do this checking. If you don't, and get married when you shouldn't have, you have to pay a fine which stands currently at three pounds.

Mamma Doe mentioned this to John, who told Jetty, who told her sister Janet and that's how Aunty Jacky got to hear. She was furious. If anyone was going to forbid this marriage, most certainly it would be her. She had told Jetty and Janet anyway, time and again, not to play with their cousins, not to use their toothbrushes, not to use their hairbrushes, not to sleep in their beds, wear any of their underwear, try on their socks, try on their shoes, mix their spittle with their cousins' spittle or even touch them if they could avoid it. 'Keep out of that house,' she warned. 'The Devil, full of tricks, lies awaiting in there.'

Jetty and John had not been thinking of getting married, and Jetty still wasn't, but now John was musing that such an occurrence might strengthen the kudos he'd already gained from beating up that bus-stop woman. Being married might increase his irreversible adult standing even more. It was just that he was in a terrible muddle. He had heard his mother crying, her heart breaking, after her temper tantrum that day long ago when she'd thrown out Benedict. As a boy, John too, had cried for the loss of his brother, whilst down on his hunkers at the top of the stairs. So you can see his predicament. John Doe loved his mother. He loved her even more than he loved his brothers. And Mamma Doe wasn't dead. She was very much angry and very much alive.

So the two sisters got into a fight over the slandering of each other's family – perhaps the one family. But don't be thinking this was a case of the women having to get down and go dirty, and the men going off to plot important secretive plottings underground.

Doe Senior, when he announced he was leaving his wife, Jessie, experienced one of those milkbottle moments, I mean similar to the one his son escaped experiencing all those years later in the Community Centre. Here, though, milkbottles were more cast iron than that.

He was so trusting. What was wrong with him that he was so trusting? Was he stupid? After telling his wife in the kitchen that he was sorry but that he was leaving her, he looked away and bent over and got down on his hunkers to search in the cupboard for some inessential thing. And he was so trusting. It was as if he was asking for it. Why be so trusting to turn his back on her like that? It hurt her to see it. She could easily run a knife into him from this position, using one of the knives from the stack over there. She could hit him over the head with the white enamel waterbottle, or the grey and white marble pastry-roller. Or she could very easily lift that cast-iron pot from the stove. And then kill him. Just kill him. She wasn't frightened thinking these thoughts for it was human to have thoughts, all sorts of thoughts, and so she was human having them. But the thing is, can someone really be trusted when they're standing over you with a funny look on their face, having thoughts about you like that? And so, because nothing was happening – as in third-dimensionally happening – yer man continued to stay bent over, rootling away in the cupboard for that ridiculous inessential, and she continued to stand over him, her mind making imaginative little story pictures like that.

Before they came to take her away, Mamma, already heightened by what had just taken place in the kitchen, went out to have a terrific long-term roiling love-affair fight with her sister. During this fight, teenage Jetty produced a twig of a stick from her pocket. But if it was any consolation, and she should have said this in court as defence against stabbing her mamma, she thought – and how could she have known otherwise? – that she was stabbing her Aunty Jessie instead. Both women, Jessie and Jacky, and for the usual Tiptoe Floorboard unfathomable reasons, had switched mamma and aunty roles and we, as outsiders, will just have to accept this. I myself cannot explain it. I can only proffer that one man's surrealism is another man's reality here.

The Doe girls, however, never accepted it. They insisted their mother was who their mother had always been, and that their Aunty Jacky, when they jumped her, couldn't possibly be their actual mamma. As for their brothers, the males in the family, their braincells never deigned to compute the maternal question. They were busy in their Factions, busy in their Junior Scout Factions, busy in their Community Centres, being stoical and so on, with no personal lives to speak of at all.

Years later, back in Jotty's house, she had just been delivered of the sisterly Death Threat. 'Thanks for understanding the not-sorting,' said her sisters. 'And don't worry, we'll keep an eye on that bugger John, to make sure he doesn't steal your grave.'

''Bye,' they then said, this time hyper-cheerfully, with Jotty thinking, boy, they're so angry they can't even get violent. She walked out to the hall with them where, in the mirror, they were adding last preening touches before rejoining society – a touch of powder, a reapplication of lipstick, then a pat-pat, tweak-tweak, as they made sure every single hair was magnificently in place.

Chapter Eleven

And now, a year later, here was Jotty and a much transformed JanineJoshuatine in the bar, with Janine heading straight towards her brother. At this point Doe was telling Spaders, and us, that he'd just found out that his Aunty Jacky was his mother and that she was dead. Another surprise for Doe was when this information about his Aunty Jacky penetrated. First thing was it confused him, for he'd already decided it was the first mother who was going in the grave. When I say 'decided', I really mean that. He thought he'd been doing another 'beloved mother just dead' fantasy, I mean with the first mother, the usual mother, whereas in reality – which normally he didn't much bother with – he could have sworn on all his mammas' graves that neither of those women was actually dead at all. Nobody had told him they were dead, and it would be a disgrace and a laxity of the authorities, he reckoned, if they were dead and no official word had reached him of it, especially as official word had reached him of the true maternal identity affair. Well, as you know, both women were not dead. And that was why Jotty, who had just seen them at the asylum after going there to pick up Janine, was now wanting to gauge whether her brother had flipped completely and was this time orchestrating an over-the-top singing and dancing funeral – with costumes, setting, speeches, mourners plus, as usual, a corpse that was imaginary – or whether some real person, her niece who had gone missing, for example, was in the coffin that had gone so ceremoniously into the ground.

Yes. I completely agree with you. It *was* childish of Doe still to be doing that construct, and at an age of thirtysomething-adult-almost-responsibility, but to be fair, perhaps we all reach for the aspirin when things get a bit tough. Don't forget, he was under stress. Vengeance – and I mean of the type of the Lord – was on its way to get him, there was a traitor in his midst whom he still hadn't been able to murder, his domestic, sexual, romantic and business lives were all reaching total crisis and his compartmentalised mind was busting all its boxes because he was still trying to compartmentalise it, even though clearly there was no room for any further divisions to take place.

As I said, when she went into the dinge of the drinking club to deal with her mad brother, Jotty was thrown by Tom being there. By now, given that two and a half years had passed since she'd last seen his penis, he was back to being Tom and was no longer the Fathers, though that didn't stop her jumping from suspicion to suspicion that he was a secret member of the Doe Community Centre Gang. Even now, though, in spite of herself, she still found him attractive, which just goes to show, she thought bitterly, how sick she still was. She was also still in therapy, still not speaking to her therapist. After two and a half years, though, the apology thing didn't seem to matter much any more. Now the sessions had less of the quality of 'I'm not speaking to her! Why should I speak to her?' 'Here's my bill,' she said, 'for October.' 'Thanks,' said Jotty – for those words were allowed. Those words weren't caving-in. They were words that didn't lord it over Jotty. They were civilisation, administration, as when she delivered her holiday dates. 'Here are my dates,' she'd say, and Jotty would say, 'Okay,' and that had been the state of affairs when Jotty had first gone along to have her head examined. Now there was more a quality to the sessions of 'I don't quite hate her, though I hate her a bit, so perhaps I can just sit quiet for more years and make up my mind as to whether or not I do hate her'. All the same, because of the not-talking, she hadn't been able to tell her therapist about not wanting to be a gangster girlfriend and, also, about her heart.

In psychotherapeutic terms this heart business would translate as 'unforgiving qualities', but I think her therapist had already guessed about that. It seems Jotty felt unforgiving in spite of not wanting to feel unforgiving and, because she wasn't into half-measures, she didn't just feel unforgiving – as the ordinary man in the omnibus might – towards the odd psychopathic serial murderer, but instead she felt unforgiving towards everybody in the whole world. But how do you forgive? The spiritual leaders of the world snack on their halva and say, 'You gotta forgive, baby. Listen, honey, if you don't forgive ...' but they never finish that sentence. They leave it hanging, implying, obviously, that if you don't forgive, then you go to Hell. But how do you forgive? How, mechanically speaking, do you do it? It seems to me – though I can't speak for Jotty – that if you forgive before the quality of really being able to forgive has come and settled itself powerfully about you, you'll only end up having to go back and hating the forgiven all over again.

Puzzling. And the heart. Another puzzle. Jotty's was sore, particularly whenever she caught sight of Tom Spaders. This annoyed her. In fact it annoyed her multiplied by a million. How dare he stir up particles when she'd been trying, forever, to keep them covered up.

So you open your heart and it hurt. You stand up straight

and hold your shoulders back to let your heart out, and it hurt. You take big breaths to get those breaths into your heart to make it feel something for it was time it felt something. And it hurt. No wonder – most rigorously, most violently, most murderously – none of your married, mothering sisters had wanted anything to do with that. 'Practise!' say the books and I don't mean the books Jotty had gotten rid off. I mean new books, books she'd recently bought – this time about abundance, about expansion, about letting yourself have the knowledge of your desires whether or not you can ever fulfil them, about going through the 'middle' to reap the fruits of the other side. 'Practise!' they say. 'That'll help the hurt heart situation.' But when you're in the hurt heart situation, you don't want to practise. You want to take those books, get on the floor with those books, and rip those books up.

Most definitely, therefore, she was thrown by Tom being there, and another thing she was thrown by was the sorry state of her sister. Although JanineJoshuatine had a reputation for going around stabbing people, in actuality she'd never stabbed anybody at all. Ever since she'd fallen apart physically, she no longer even did the elementary *'My God! Whose blood is this I have on my hands?'* scenario. Following on from her husband and child leaving, her perfect sisters collapsing, her fantasy husband transforming himself into Papa, she herself had dwindled so rapidly that she almost now never crossed her threshold. Soon, Jotty felt – next holiday perhaps, or maybe the holiday after – her sister, given her deterioration, was going to go away and, like the others, never come back at all.

As for the police, her latest interaction with them over the niece situation had also thrown Jotty. When she had entered the Police House earlier, a group of them, in their shiny uniforms with their shiny holsters and shiny guns, was at the front desk swinging a pendulum over some big pieces of white paper. They were trying to divine whether the food in the canteen fridge had gone off. It was swinging maniacally, this pendulum. First it pulled one way on its cord, then changed direction and pulled the other. Then it circled furiously and that meant 'Yes, of course the food has gone off!' They asked another question. Was it off to the point they'd be sick if they ate it, or could it possibly be a case of mild diarrhoea or, even better, slight stomach discomfort that would wear away within, say, twenty minutes to an hour? Jotty went up to the desk and waited timidly, waited politely. She felt a gentle scream working up inside her. Being ignored, finally she banged the desk and shouted, 'Hallo! Where's my lipstick? Am I invisible standing here?'

They looked at her. The vibration of the bang had shocked them but, worse, it had shocked the pendulum also. The latter withdrew into psychic petulance, refusing to be drawn further, leaving the degree of the fridge's bad food unclear.

'We can't speculate,' they said when, ignoring their sulks, she told them of her suspicions. 'Yes you can,' she answered. 'You're detectives. That's what you're supposed to do. To say you can't speculate is like saying, "We can't solve who killed the body be-cause we don't know who killed the body." There's a time to get out of people's heads' – she banged the desk again – 'and a time to get in there.' They told her she was to stop banging the desk and that she was not to talk to them like that.

She asked then to speak to the new Interfering Outside Police Officer. This new officer was known generally as the Interfering Outside Police Officer because that was easier to say than his correct name, Derwent Ligge. 'Deer With Twixt Legs' or 'Dear Wift Twixt Legg' was not a mock as some might suspect, given few people liked this officer. Rather, it was a variable offshoot of the town's combined Spatial Fragmentation Syndrome, expressing itself this time in words. Mr Ligge was a high-ranker of the law from abroad, who had been sent recently by the International Community to investigate the new Tiptoe murders. In the course of his interfering, it had become apparent – and the police didn't like this – that he had been sent to investigate them too. They wouldn't let her see him.

'He's busy,' they said. 'Extremely busy – going to the toilet. If you want, you can write a letter and we'll see he gets it instead.'

They guffawed at this, like animals that guffaw, if you know of any. And speaking of toilets – given that little interaction she'd just witnessed with this particular batch of policemen, if she were to write that letter, she knew exactly where it would end up.

'Just address it,' they sneered, 'to "The Man Who Takes No Shit".' That was it. They were off guffawing again and I was shocked, not just at the dreadful sound – much worse than seeing the word printed – but at their open partiality. Jotty leaned over to me, saying, 'That's peanuts. You've seen nothing of partiality yet.'

She tried to get them to help. They hindered all her trying. Constantly, they were attempting to be funny at her expense. In the past, when Jotty had experienced this with others, she had learned to respond by pretending not to understand them. 'Pardon?' she'd say, looking puzzled, taking them literally. Also looking politely interested, looking as if she truly wanted to comprehend this person's meaning, if only he or she could coherently get their point across. So she would force them to repeat their butts, their puns, their derisive jokes and, during the repeating, they'd lose, of course, the impetus. Wilfully misunderstand. Don't understand. And don't let them know you're doing it. Do it so well, the worst they can say is 'Oh, her? She's dim,' or 'Oh, her? She's no sense of humour.' And tell me – not being thought to have a sense of humour – who but a stand-up would lose sleep over that?

Finally, after explaining and deconstructing all their jokes at her expense a thousand times and her still being too dim and humourless to get even one of them, they were exhausted and so pulled the authority card. They said she was in danger of wasting police time and precious police resources. The undertakers from the confectionery morgue would not have buried a coffin, they said, either empty or with the wrongly identified body inside. She knew this to be rubbish and knew further that the police themselves knew it to be rubbish. Everybody knew the morguers, notorious for cutting corners and doing favours for Doe because they had to, often buried bodies either with no names or with the wrong names on top. The confectionery morgue, by the way, was familiar-speak for one of Tiptoe's joint morgue and funeral parlours. It was situated abundantly close to the town's famous three-storey sweetshop. This was the sweetshop that had four gunshops, a tanning shop, a betting shop, a booking-your-holidays – I mean real holidays – shop, all inside. Of course Jotty knew her brother had complete control of the morgue confectionery, the confectionery morgue and almost all commercial properties. Indeed, of all the town's businesses, only the Almost Chemist of the Year was still defiantly and valiantly holding out.

When she refused to leave and instead tried to coerce the police into declaring who they thought, then, was in the coffin, without a blush they announced they were sorry, but that she had to face facts. It was her ma. So quickly had the rumour spread of one of the women being dead and of the dead one not having been the aunt but the mother, that it had already been entered officially in Births, Deaths and Rumours

That Are Probably True at the Town Hall. So ingrained by now, too, was this belief in the heads of the policemen that it took Jotty a while to get them to understand that it was the niece she was referring to, and that her worry was that her brother had taken his daughter and done something to her, and so – given it would be a feasible search in a good disposal point – why didn't they dig it up and have a look? They shook their heads and refused to accept this. For starters, they said, even if both those poor women were alive – for now they had them both dead – it didn't alter the situation. Everybody knew her brother had been doing harmless dead-mother funerals ever since puberty. So why didn't she run along and have a chat with him instead?

Later, when they did manage to get rid of her and were back to being cosy by themselves, toasting the fridge's food over the police hearthside, they got involved in a detection-provoking discussion. It was entirely about her.

'Isn't she the repressed one?'

'You mean is her repression the reason she's having these passive-aggressive morbid fantasies about an attractive, younger female being dead – who, by the way, I've never heard of? Have you heard of? Could she be in a syndrome from *Snow White*, or from *Cinderella*, or *Rose Red*, or *Annushka Petrovna*, with her playing the part of the wicked stepmother from the 'Scary Older Woman' side of such fairytales?'

'Yes. That's exactly what I mean. Do you think there could be something there?'

'Could be. But not married, you know.'

'I know.'

'Never been married.'

'What? You mean never?'

''Course not. Why else do you think she's on our Spinster List in the hall?'

'I thought she was married at least once.'

'No, no. That was the Sisters – before they had their crack-ups. She wouldn't marry. Not even to make a point of it. Not even if she had to divorce the guy straight after the ceremony because she didn't love him. At least she could have waved the certificate. "Look, everybody. I'm all right. I've joined." '

'Good Bats and Holy Godfathers! That puts a different slant on it.'

'How so? Are you thinking we should be harbouring suspicions about her, then, within the next three days?'

The more they pooled their hearsay, the more it looked that way.

Next, given they were thorough, they looked up a reference book to check the word 'repression'. It said – no, wait a minute, that was something else. Here it is – it said 'repress, to constrain, to put down, to banish to the unconscious, to have a tendency to repress unacceptable thoughts and feelings etc'. It doesn't explain the 'etc' but there was 'repressor – a protein which binds to an operator site and prevents transcription of the associated gene'. Well, okay, we don't need that one, not unless we're determined to get into some extended, meta-physical conceit here. And I'm not particularly determined. Are you?

Next, for they were following through, they had a wee mock at her. Couldn't help it. Come on, they said, this was probably all because she hasn't had sex in yonks. Sure, everybody has to do something with their sexual energy if they don't have sex with it. Yeah, like sending anonymous letters to distress law-abiding, sex-having ordinary decent people. Yeah, or like making sweets and putting poison in them to give to children and unsuspecting vulnerable adults at religious fairs. Yeah, or like doing your citizen duty and sending people to the guillotine to have their heads cut off. 'Yeah, so let's face it,' they said, 'all she's doing is her sexual anorectic version of that.'

So, as objective law enforcers, they concluded that this was her problem, not their problem, although they did agree that, coming from a family of jails, graves and mental asylums, there was no question but that she would have to have suspicions harboured against her within the next three days.

From Jotty's disturbed but well-meaning perspective of trying to get someone to help her, I hope you can understand the police were pretty useless here. Worse than useless. They issued a written warning, stating that if she wanted to bring the matter up again, she'd have to keep a daily log with proper CAD reference numbers to back it. And she'd have to do that for at least four years. In the meantime, they thanked her for any future letter she might take the trouble to write, but what she had to appreciate was that this letter they were sending her was not to be considered in any way an idle threat. They didn't sign the letter. They didn't date it, and they ended with the usual 'If there's any problem, please don't worry about hesitating to call.'

But look. I've gone too far from what it was Spaders thought linked him to the Doe clan. There he was, standing at the bar with Doe and a whole bunch of other murderers, with the gangster wives and girlfriends sitting with their drinks around the sides. Jotty and Janine came in. Doe sighed heavily when he saw his sisters, especially his half-portion sister. Mostly, he found her funny. Other times, like now, she just made him upset and annoyed.

'Here we go,' he said. 'This is a sequence me and her can't get out of, Tom.' And Janine, cutting straight across the dancefloor to get at him, picked up speed, knocking against everybody *en route*. Halfway into her sprint, and just as Doe was

217

setting down his glass to get himself ready for her, she lifted her arm as if there were a knife in it, then, moments before contact, threw herself over the last table and stabbed her brother through the heart.

He tutted.

'For God's sake!' he shouted to Jotty, for Jotty had rushed up behind. 'She's only out,' he cried, 'and already she's spilling the drinks again. I'm warning you, Jotty, if you don't get a handle on that woman, I'll have her committed for good next time.'

None of the gang made a move to intervene in this fantasy-stabbing of John by his eldest sister. First, it was embarrassing and people like to give wide berths to embarrassment whenever they could. Second, this was just another of those Family of Origin facts that outsiders of the family in question have to turn a blind eye to. Thing was, regardless of how many times her mistake had been pointed out to her – 'He's your brother, your brother, Janine! Your brother!' – JanineJoshuatine kept thinking he was somebody else. Not long after her husband and baby had left, and following on from the dismantling of the Sister Orbit, Janine's own fantasy husband had broken frame. He'd developed a laugh that felt like a finger, and unpleasant facial features that hinted of a distant memory and, in spite of how urgently she pressed 'Rewind! Rewind!', he would carry on, with impetus, in crossing the room to her. Naturally she had to cross the room herself to get him off before he got on her. So, even if Doe didn't look like the Fathers – which he did – and even if he had never approached her from across the room – which he hadn't – it was irrelevant. New settings in Janine's mind had already been switched on.

After the stabbing, Janine was helped up from the ground by Jotty and Tom, with Jotty shouting, 'Leave her alone! I can manage! I said I can manage!' – even though clearly she could not. Janine's head, just by itself, now weighed a complete ton. She had gone 'flop' and, as 'the flop' do, her body had added on extra thousands of psychic stone to her usual seven stone something. But even if Jotty could manage, how's managing all the time supposed to be a good thing? All this managing by Jotty Doe, all this martyring, all this goodie-good, squeaky-clean, this trying to locate her missing niece when nobody else seemed to be giving a damn about her, all those 'Psychoanalysis Divided by Five and Multiplied by Three' sessions – I'm starting not to believe it. Forgive me for doubting her, but come with me. I think we should tiptoe into the shadow side of Jot now.

Total confusion around sex, I'm afraid. And I mean when all other adults in the world have got it all sorted. And also, it's those books, I'm afraid – those recovery from incest books she'd earlier gotten rid off. I think – given her history, and the sexual confusion she's still carrying around with her – she's wishing she'd read at least some of them now. Specifically, it's that waterfall business, and do you remember that waterfall? It had been recommended by the sex psychology expert to the Pseudonyms, as a way of helping them shift their ingrained historic sexual abuse patterns. In this case, however, I'm talking about the *shadow* side of the waterfall, I mean the sadomasochistic fantasies Jotty gets into now and then for swift, orgasmic release.

Ah. I knew there was something.

Question is, if you've been abused, 'What's normal?' And if you haven't been abused, 'What's normal?' And are both 'normals' meant to be the same thing? What's supposed to turn a person on *normally*, before it gets to the point where others think, *hell, that's not normal. That's replay of old trauma. That's recreation of past painful circumstance. Come away from that person. There's something funny going on here?* Also, is there a difference between 'What's common?' and 'What's normal?' Jotty didn't know. Sitting under a dryer at the hairdresser's, she was perplexed about these issues. She was becoming more perplexed as she read a women's magazine – *Director of Indulgence*, it was called.

Yes, Jotty now ventured into hairdressers. This was part of a practice of grooming she had embarked upon recently, similar to her other practices of venturing into beauty parlours, of going into clothes shops, even of buying the occasional garment that wasn't just a fit, but a *perfect* fit. And now, here she was, in the hairdresser's, flicking through a women's magazine as if 'flicking through' had always been her forte. In reality, those magazines, with their 'what to do' and 'what not to do' in order to be a proper woman – '20 Per Cent More Adultery and 15 Per Cent More Marvellous Mums!' for example – had always made her feel even more wrong. This one she had picked up to see if she could practise reading it without getting dizzy, but it threw her immediately in at the deep end. The magazine had carried out a sex census in the previous issue. This issue was carrying the results.

'Do you have sex more than fifty times a day?' *What?* Jotty reeled. That had been the first question. 'Do you have sex more than twenty times a day?' 'Do you have sex at least ten times a day?' 'Do you have sex less than once a day?' 'Do you have sex less than three times a week?' 'Do you have sex less than once a week?' 'Do have sex less than once a month?' And that was it. The categories of the first question stopped there.

The highest percentage of score – to both Jotty and perhaps *Director of Indulgence*'s astonishment – was in the latter category. Seventy-seven per cent of the women respondents hadn't had sex in one month or more. That was a lot of days and, according to the number of respondents, an awful lot of women. Too high a percentage of its readers for the sheer sexual sophistication of the magazine to know what to do with. It mentioned it briefly as a way of demonstrating its accuracy in relaying unpleasant information, then immediately ignored the statistic, and shot on to the twenty-three per cent of women having sex, thank goodness, all the time.

Just a moment, Jotty thought. Hold on, hold on. Seventy-seven per cent! That seems important. Especially as fifty-four per cent of this seventy-seven per cent turned out to be married or in long-term relationships. Were her sisters, in their marriages, not that unusual then, after all? Also, even though the 'tickbox' question had asked 'less than once a month', did the 'tickbox' answers mean 'less than once a month'? Or did they mean 'less than half a year'? 'Less than once a year'? 'Less than once in five years'? 'Less than once in ten years'? 'Less than ever' – unless you're supposed to count rape, for example, in childhood? How long was it really since that seventy-seven per cent last pushed the envelope out and had proper 'yes' tick-box sex?

Well, what was wrong with her? Didn't the magazine already make its position clear on that subject? To repeat – it had sliced off the seventy-seven per cent as if it had never existed. Then it had made the remaining twenty-three per cent into the new one hundred per cent instead. And now for the next question. It too, caused Jotty alarm.

'Are you on the Advanced Sophisticated Sex Agenda because you're into total experimentation and explicit sex entertainment, or do you and your partner stick to the old basic routines?'

Unsurprisingly, being one of the seventy-seven per cent who no longer existed, Jotty was not *au fait* with this Advanced Sex Agenda. Such advanced sex as 'playing at torture', or versions of 'I'm your father and your uncle's

221

downstairs waiting' is what you and your partner aim for if you're contemporary, up-to-date, and sexually with-it. If you're not with-it, as in you're sexually boring, then I'm sorry, but you'll have to form your attachments and your emotional connections in the old-fashioned, time-consuming, basic routine way.

And that's the thing. I mean Jotty's confusion. What's the difference between sadomasochism, bondage, fetishes, pornography, hard porn, soft porn, porn everyone's supposed to laugh about and be at ease with and talk about and engage in, and that can feature in sitcoms before the watershed without any sense of humiliation or disturbance of children who might just be watching, also without any bodily discomfort – meaning unpleasant arousal rather than welcome arousal – for anybody of any age in the room? Are things meant to be private or are they not meant to be private? Or are they meant to be private if you're on the basic routine because the basic routine of looking in a man's eyes and taking in his whole face, and enjoying his whole body as he's making love to you is not worth making serious violent crime dramas over, whereas if you're on the Advanced Sophisticated Sex Agenda, you'll be on a par with Hollywood for sure? But then confusion again, for take a look at incest. You can't get anything more private than incest. See? Total perplexity. And this was Jotty's perplexity – though, to be honest, it was my perplexity too. And what is eroticism? That's another thing. And what is consensual sex if what started out as consensual sex then turns into 'No, this doesn't feel right. It feels wrong. I've changed my mind. I don't want to any more'? And what about role play? Sex toys? Props? Paying lots of money out of your dole or out of your high-powered job to have yourself raped and abducted? Is all that *cheating* – as in not knowing *really* how to have sex at all?

The magazine laughed and said, 'Have you any idea how childish you are? Of course it's not cheating! Sex isn't an exam. If it works, do it!' But in that case, what about that man who was jailed and is now on Death Row but who was convinced of his rightness when he said, 'If they say yes, then that's great, we can go back to my place because that's where I keep the equipment. But sometimes they say no after they've said yes or don't say yes after I thought they were going to say yes and I'd spent all that time counting on them saying yes and so couldn't hold back to find someone else to say yes at such short notice so I took them. But I always promised, and I kept my word – except for those two times when I didn't before you arrested me – that whatever was done to them, they'd still be all right when I untied them at the end'?

So then, thought Jotty, what about killing someone during it, or after it? Does that come under 'tick-box' murder, or is that simply having sex under the category 'If it works, do it!' as well?

'I'll just adjust this,' said the hairdresser, and Jotty jumped at the suddenness of this person. She dropped the magazine in a flood of shame. The hairdresser touched her hair, adjusted the dryer, then bent over and picked the magazine up for her. 'Sorry,' she laughed, and Jotty, right or wrong – probably wrong, but even if she was right, so what? – thought this woman was laughing at her.

And that's the thing too. Apparently Jotty's ashamed but doesn't know if she's supposed to be ashamed, or ashamed of being ashamed because she should be proud about not giving a damn where damns maybe don't need to be given, or because if something's a fantasy then that means it's not real and doesn't matter, so you can do what you want in it – and *this*, imagine, coming from Jotty Doe, who places more emphasis and significance and spiritual perambulations on the non-material aspect of the Fourth and Higher Dimensions than anybody *ever* but, to get back to her shame, should she be ashamed, she wondered, about feeling stimulated, as she had been programmed to feel stimulated, by unloving, uncaring images when, according to this recent poll in this magazine, such arousal appears to be the goal for everybody on the Advanced Sophisticated Sex Agenda as well?

Didn't know. She didn't know. And this magazine wasn't helping. It said, 'More and more women are super-confident and proactive in their sexual habits today and taking the initiative more than ever in the bedroom,' even though it also said, 'Drunken sex and sex where you can't remember having it because you had to get so drunk before you'd let anybody near you and if you hadn't been drunk you wouldn't have dreamt of going to bed with that particular person' was, apparently, at an all-time high. Also, a huge proportion placed absolute conviction in being monogamous in their relationships, even though an even huger proportion of the same proportion weren't monogamous – 'Yes, but we're only being unfaithful in case he's being unfaithful as well.'

Jotty was shaken. The magazine appeared to be suggesting that this was a world of no sex no sex no sex no sex no sex no sex, or else it was one of instant highs and addiction. They didn't want to write about middle-of-the-road basics. Extremes were better: one, appetite and grab; the other, deprivation and death.

Well, I feel better. Now that we've cleared that up about Jotty and her shame and shadow underneath all that concern and niceness, let's get back to what was happening in the bar. Tom was picking Janine up and was being shouted at by Jotty, who was also picking Janine up. In the end, they both got her from the floor and into a chair. Meanwhile, knocked-over tables and other chairs were being picked up by various gangster wives and girlfriends and Doe, observing this, rolled his eyes and shook his head and sighed a big frustration. Jotty, hearing it, looked over and rashly shouted,

'Who's really in that coffin? You're not going to get away with this. Who's really in that coffin, John Doe?'

Chapter Twelve

John Doe's ominous non-answer to that question was what finally propelled Tom, years later, to enter the Doe household. He was half-deterred and half-urged on by hearing those female screams. At the end of trying to pluck up his courage, he plucked it up by the sight of a suit of armour. It had appeared on the threshold, banging against one doorframe, banging against the other, then it came fully crashing out of the door. Visor down, the whole suit then missed its footing. It toppled and fell flat on its back on the path. With effort, it rolled over, tried to roll over, third attempt successfully it rolled over. Then it climbed to its cranky knees on the grass.

Who? What? thought Tom, as he ran towards it. Reaching it, he touched the arm but the suit of armour wasn't having any of it. Immediately it rattled his touch off. Then up it clambered and, visor still down, off it went. Clank, it sort of went. Clank-clank, for we cannot describe this as elegance. This was not catwalk, or any of those astounding supermodel walk examples we make fun of, but could we do it? I don't think we could do it. Anyway, this was not that. Tom watched as the racket went down the road, then he turned and found himself on the Doe porch with the front door wide open. So, without thought for the future – which was probably the only way to have done this – Spaders crossed over and went inside.

There was a dead man in the hall. He was lying over a suitcase. Later, the police, standing around it, confidently asserted, 'Probably money or drugs in that.' When they opened it, however, all they found was toothpaste, a toothbrush, a razor, some wee shaving cream, some underarm deodorant, a teeshirt, three sports books: one about a boxer, another about a footballer, the third, a ghosted autobiography by some opinionated racehorse, now dead.

So the poor man was in the hall, but all Tom could think of on first coming across him was – nothing. Absolutely nothing. He half-stepped over and half-walked around. Instinctively he followed the silence down the hall until he reached the back living room. Whatever was happening, it would be happening in there. He opened the door without a second to prepare and there, immediately before him, was John Doe strangling his daughter. Next thing Tom saw, in a cut-to-pieces visual flasharound, was one of those Doe women – the one who had come into his shop for the Kalashnikov that morning. She was dead, part-sitting, part-sprawling – one shoe off, the other shoe on – in and out of the armchair.

Dead. Quite dead. Really and truly dead. This was no fantasy. But Julie Doe was living. Half her father's height, a quarter his size, none of his girth and her hands were pulling on his anyway. I was surprised. Could only mean even *she* was able to realise that, in certain situations, there really wasn't a second to spare. Her leg was up too, the sole of one flexible foot positioned between herself and her father's abdomen. She appeared to be pushing on his navel, practically sitting on the mantelpiece and pushing on his navel. All the same, she was losing. Those hands at her throat weren't messing about.

Pity she'd walked in when she had.

'Cept my mistake. She hadn't. She'd been there already, in that back room, even when Jetty had returned after being arrested. At first, Julie had been remonstrating with Judas, who'd got himself into the front room's armour and was refusing to get out. She was telling him to get out for, given what had just happened to their parents, they really, really, really had to talk. Judas, rattling and tin-canning, delved totally into the tactic of deafness with his sister. He pulled down his visor, stood still as a statue and gave no acknowledgement that she – or even he – was there. So down the hall to the back room she went, to look for clues, to talk to God, to cast around for guidance. It was at that moment Jetty and her new boyfriend came in.

'This is your Uncle JimmyJesus,' said Jetty, and the man looked at her, embarrassed, shocked, then horrified. He hadn't been told of a niece. There'd been no mention of any niece in this lover-transaction business. Or of any commitment to children. He looked around. How many children? Someone should have consulted him about this. Julie looked back at him, defeated, despondent, and he continued looking at her, knowing he didn't want to be related. Then the mature adults turned away and headed up the stairs.

Father came in.

Just before that, though, poor Jetty had to come back down to throw out some art dealers. Some 'gallerists' – as now they termed themselves – had sneaked in and were upstairs rummaging about. They had heard rumours of precious works of art – most casually stolen from around the world if you could believe it – and supposedly secreted on these here premises. Naturally, as soon as the gang had been safely arrested, they had snuck round in droves, to unravel this rumour and find out. They set to immediately, foraging, pillaging, raping and looting. They ransacked the place and in their sheer excitable happiness – because the art *was* there – they weren't even abashed when Jetty came in and caught them in the act. They thought she, too, would be thrilled by the extraordinaries they had come across but, for some reason, she was not.

'Ouch!' cried one. 'Listen, Miss, I mean Ma'am, I mean Missus – ouch! We could do a deal. I could sell this for you. This could be worth – ow! Ow!' She threw him and the framed original of *Dead Girl with Dead Bird* – still-life of a version – out. She turned to another gallerist. He, too, was intensely blabbering. Something about percentages as he clutched the world-famous *Rifle Post*. This was the original, mind you – forget the cheap copy you have hanging in your bedroom. I mean here was the hand-painted prophetic effort, made to look like a computerised diagram before computers had been invented: *[TMH] front – locking pin, magazine, catch, cheekpiece. [TMH] rear – locking pin, trigger mechanism housing [TMH] sight base, dust cover, ejection opening, cocking handle, holding open catch, safety catch, handguard, flash eliminator* – 'The Rifle'. Wow. This was culture. You couldn't deny this was culture. It even had the Van Gogh signature underneath.

Jetty grabbed it off him. He screamed for mercy – he meant for the picture. Too late, too irrelevant. She broke it over his head. He, too, was then kicked out, followed by the shreds of the picture. Shrewdly he took this as a sign he could have it. Gathering up the masterpiece, he skipped happily with it down the path. She continued to throw out all pests and rodents and works of art, not realising that a further brand of anoraks – ghost-hunters, fraud-busters, arch-sceptics, which is not to say they were not deeply committed to the genuine supernatural article whenever they came across it – with their psychic-detecting cameras, paranormal sound equipment and talcum-powdered bags of flour to catch out pranksters, were ensconced and already carrying out experiments in the tunnels underground.

So she was downstairs, having swatted out into the universe the last of the dealers when Doe walked in and, boy, was she surprised. To cover her guilt she launched into that brief 'What man? Oh, but you're jealous!' conversation, then Uncle JimmyJesus came down and he'd been the first to be killed. Julie didn't see him being killed, for she was still standing in the back room, by the once-beautiful Versailles walnut and purplewood secretaire cabinet. Although stolen in pristine condition, with Marie Antoinette's list of to-dos for the Petit Trianon still hanging out of it, the Doe family's petrol cans, garden implements and First Aid from that inconclusive mentally ill kitchen cupboard had caused it to become rather on the lopsided front now. So Julie didn't see the killing, but she heard the killing. Then she saw her father kill her aunt. They had come into the back room to have their final 'till death do us part' chat in there.

Doe lowered his lover into the armchair just when he was at the very end of strangling her. Then he took his hands away and looked up.

And so, to Julie, and her fate.

And so, to Tom, and his fate.

And John, too. Let's not forget John Doe's fate as well.

You know how, when you're ready for something, when time is ripe, something inside you finalises itself without even having the decency to consult you about it? It seems to take ownership completely – without ambivalence or ambiguity – into its own hands. Isn't it further the case that when this happens, everything else is commanded to fall into place also? Could go either direction. Could be things lovely, things perfect, things most joyous and wonderful. Or could be things terrible, the most evil, things you'll definitely have long-term Lady Macbeth sleepwalking episodes about.

The latter type was what happened here.

Tom slipped a dimension as he went for the Chief Harness and Bridle Maker and strangely, as he did so, he glanced around as if one hundred per cent expecting something to appear in the way of assisting him and, needless to say, given the hundred per cent, something did. A knife was handed to him. It came from out of nowhere, from no place earthbound. Believe me, though, this was definitely an earthbound knife. Tom took it and stuck it in Doe's back.

Doe turned around. He pivoted. He looked at Spaders in surprise in the tiny space of meditation that now existed between them. Everything extraneous fell away that was not of that moment, then Doe fell backwards, with widening eyes, widening arms, into his own armchair. He fell on top of Jetty, as if she was not there.

But she was. Remember – she was.

So, who passed the knife? I can tell you it wasn't Julie, for she was gagging on the floor, lying half on the hearth, half on the carpet. And it wasn't Judas, who hadn't yet slipped back, although he would slip back later in his armour around the time the police again showed, so he could take in the latest of what was happening. Tom himself didn't come in with a knife, for he'd never been a knife-carrying person. And as for guns, he hadn't been a gun-carrying person for quite a while now as well. So was it a ghost? Did a ghost hand over that weapon? Or did the knife materialise itself out of strong desire and an unshake-able conviction that it bloody well was going to? Or was it Ja-nine who handed it? Or Jotty? For yes. Janine and Jotty appeared at this point.

All so fast. And all so incredible. One moment the room was empty, except for two dead people and two live people. Then the next moment it was full. Jotty was there first. She was before Tom, clinging, crying – as if it hadn't been a whole seven and a half years since she'd last put her arms around him. Anyone would have thought by the way she was shouting, 'Tom! Oh, Tom! Why him? Why throw everything for him?', that they'd breakfasted together, read the daily paper's 'Comment and Analysis' together, then temporarily parted from each other with their habitual pecks on the cheek that very day.

But there was something else happening, so much so that Tom couldn't respond to Jotty. It seemed his heart was intervening, that it was trying to say something. Not to him. And not to her. Instead it was trying to appeal to something or someone approaching from behind. He tried to turn, to catch a glimpse of whoever could be this phenomenon, but a dullness, a heaviness, a feeling of a pile of furniture suddenly piled on top of him, anchored him rigidly to the spot. At that moment, the tip of a long sword appeared.

Then this happened. He looked down – and he himself was on the floor and hadn't realised he was on it. From that position he saw his chest had completely opened itself out. Was this a heart attack? he wondered. Was this how heart attacks happened? There were sharp jerks, little darts, feeling sick, but there was no left arm stuff that you hear about, and no hands suddenly going tingly, though just as he was thinking this, pins and needles of a high gravity began to press upon him, pinning his chest to the floor.

A woman in a headscarf and a housecoat stepped through him at that moment. Just that. Straight through him. Then she stepped through Jotty, who was also down on the ground. Continuing over the room with her big sword out, this woman reached the armchair and in it were two babies. Here, she put her sword away, leaned over and picked the babies up.

Always babies. There are always babies. At first, though, all Tom could hear was heart. Distressed, inconsolable, he felt his heart was pleading silently with this person. Then, after a time lag, some of Jotty's words, uttered earlier, came down a tunnel and broke upon him at last.

'Janine! No! No, Janine!'

So Tom had fallen. This was because of Jotty's sister. Janine-Joshuatine had followed Jotty in. Turns out Jotty had also been on her way to the house because she wanted to check out the kitchen cupboard situation. In her deteriorating state of paranoia about what might have happened to her niece who had gone missing, she was battling her conviction that this cupboard held the key. She didn't know it had been turned into an earplug cupboard. She had only known it when it had been an eggcup cupboard. And who puts padlocks on eggcup cupboards? That was suspicious in itself. We know already, of course – grotesque and impossible as it sounded – that Jane, the niece, couldn't have been squashed, disseminated, distributed either into the cupboard or into the eggcups that were supposed to be in that cupboard. The cupboard had been robbed of all its contents before the recent era of the padlock and at that moment was empty of anything at all.

Jotty didn't know that. So she was on her way, like the gallerists, taking advantage of the fact that everybody had been arrested. That was when she saw Tom and a suit of armour on the grass. Why are they rolling on the grass? she wondered. With growing alarm, she rushed over and reached the house from one direction just as her nephew got up and clanked off in another. Tom was up too, and was stepping over the threshold when Jotty, full of dread, shouted to him, in vain, to stop.

Ah, thought Tom, now noticing Janine hovering behind Jotty. Still up and running, that JanineJoshuatine. He could see, though, that as with her other sisters, she was now no beauty and had turned into some sort of mad biscuit. Probably harmless, though, he continued, not realising that Janine had taken another knife – for certainly they were being handed out that evening – and had stuck it, with a great grunt, into his side. She had made two mistakes – I mean apart from the one of actually stabbing anybody. One was, she mistook Tom for John Doe, her brother, and two was, she mistook her brother – as usual – for somebody else.

That's why Tom had been downed, and he was currently instructing himself not to breathe, for normal breathing hurt, whereas little sips of breath were much, much better. And he needed silence. He needed stillness. He needed Jotty not to clutch or fuss over him. As long as nobody fussed or touched or clutched or tried to get him to interact by screaming, 'Hello! Tom! Tom! Tom! Can you hear me?' at him – as long as none of that happened, he'd gather himself together in a second and be fine.

Jotty, not a Florence Nightingale at the best of times, was weeping and screaming. She was definitely down, clutching, fussing and shouting, 'Tom! Tom! Speak to me, Tom!' with the woman with the sword and the babies in the housecoat continuing, in total dispassion, to walk through them on her way – ironically – out the material world door.

I said to her, 'Are you taking him?'

Now, you know me. You've been with me a while and you can see that nothing gets me angry. You can vouch for that, can't you? Have you seen me angry? Well, I'm sorry to say yer woman, Sworden, she gets me angry. Only you're not allowed to say 'gets me angry'. Nowadays you have to say, 'I feel angry when Sworden does this.'

That's her name. Sworden. Though she has other names. I mean her with the sword, her with the babies, her of the *sang froid* and very sniffy attitude – very clear, very sharp, very delineated she was. I said again,

'Are you taking him?' – meaning Spaders. For look – he was stabbed, he was on the floor there, dying. It seemed a clear case of taking him to me. But do you know something? What she does is ignore me. Although, to be easier on myself, she ignores everybody. She even ignored a whole stack of police who, for the second time that day, turned up at the door.

They were back. And they were thinking they were apprehending everybody, but most of the everybody in the room by this time wasn't in the material world at all. Tom Spaders was also gone. He had been worrying about his heart. And Jotty had been unnerving him also. She was stopping his breath and preventing him from attaining the 'dying-down-from-hurting' sensation he was longing for. He tried to tell her this, but rather than 'Jotty', the name 'John' came out instead.

Then Cusack appeared.

'John!' cried Spaders. 'Thank God, John! Do us a favour. Help me get up here.'

Cusack didn't answer and Spaders realised that that was because his friend was unconscious and lying in a hospital. He still had feathers, crumbs, spiders' webs, long threads stuck all over him. Spaders appeared to be the one in the visitor's chair, visiting him.

Why?

Then he wondered why he'd called his friend 'John'.

Oh! he thought. Oh no! he then thought. Is it that I shot

him? Is it that I did something to him? He began to think he had done something. Then he was certain he had done something. Was it that he'd killed his friend, John?

'John!' he shouted again, and then he shook Tom and continued to hold him by the shoulders. Getting no response, and now thoroughly frightened, he cast around the hospital ward.

It was high in height, and long, and narrow. And there seemed to be an immense level of activity going on in it. High-level energy. Couldn't have got higher. A large number of babies and adults were making themselves heard. These adults were saying, 'Hi there. Hi, mate. Awright?' – with lots of questions, mainly 'Did you see John?' Everybody seemed to be calling to somebody or asking for somebody and everybody seemed to be called John. Even the women, he noticed. They were John as well. He felt himself grow more anxious as to why there was this commotion and mystery. The main thing, though, was how could he find out whether or not he'd killed John?

'Oh, that's just a phase, that John thing,' said someone. It was a woman's voice and she was talking close to him. 'That's the name that always gets used here. Trust me,' she said, and he did, for he felt at that moment that that was the easiest option. I mean, what were his choices? What else was he gonna do at this point?

'Don't!' said the woman. 'Oh, don't! Don't!' And she laughed. 'Don't call me that,' for he had suddenly called her 'Mother'. She laughed again. 'I'm not your mother now.'

Then she reassured him. She said she'd stay for a bit and that he wasn't to be afraid when she was there, and then when she wasn't there. So that was it. He was the one in the hospital now. He wished she'd speak of this place for it didn't have a floor. Or walls. Or ceiling. But because of the confidence, which seemed to consist of colour, everyone seemed buoyed up all the same. It had boundaries of some sort too, but they weren't of any recognised substance. They weren't even properly visible. It was then, as he was looking around, that nurses, a whole phalanx, marched in.

'Oh, *excuse me*,' said one, stepping right up to him. 'You certainly can be discharged, right away this minute.' In spite of his anxiety, he didn't want to be discharged. He tried to tell her he'd only just arrived.

'She didn't take him on,' said another nurse. She was referring to the emergency room intake person. She herself, a learner-nurse, was reading from his chart and ticking something off.

'That decides it then,' said the first. 'You can have sustenance, a bit of nourishment, but after that, Angel of Beginnings instructs you're to be off.'

He wanted to protest and put in a complaint about Angel of Beginnings but then Cusack was there, visiting him. 'Hi, Tom,' Cusack said. Tom Spaders registered he hadn't called him 'John'. He didn't have time to feel sad that that might have something to do with him soon leaving, because a buzzing, one he'd heard earlier, was sounding again in his ears.

It was Life – a woman, not unlike Sworden in her formidable dispassion, but without the sword – and she was coming to get him. He looked at her fearfully for he didn't want to go. He held on. First to a pillow but that didn't work. Life just took him and the pillow also. So he held on to the bottom bedpost, but Life took him and the pillow and the bed with a trolley attached to it. So he dropped the bed and all that clatter and grabbed on to some people instead. His hands went through them. They went on chatting, never realising they'd been clutched on to. Then the nurses chided, 'Now, behave. Behave. You're acting like a baby when really you're an outpatient' – so he knew it would be fruitless to grab on to them. Soon, though, he grew less afraid, for he had forgotten until that moment that everything was sheer colour. It was a spirit colour and it was blue. He tried again.

'Everything's blue,' he said. 'Heaven's blue,' he said, as if this were a password. Then he grabbed on to a jacket, felt bones under this jacket.

'This isn't Heaven, mate,' said a voice. Then it shouted, 'We don't need that extra bag, Raphael. Call another ambulance' – and from that point a policeman took over and hauled Tom back into the room.

'Hmmm. Two new knife-ins,' said the police. 'This sure is some family.'

So the police were in and yet no one had called them. What I want to know is, how come they came? An incident between Betty and Jetty – which ended with Betty's decision that Jetty would have to be re-arrested, was the disguised personal grudge reason the police came back that day.

You remember Betty, the great policewoman soulmate buddy of Janet? She tried a similar move on Jetty, not realising that just because two women were sisters, and had names that began with the same letter, and worked together at the same chemist, and lived together in the same house, and had sex with the same gang leader, didn't mean their minds were exactly the same as well.

I think Betty knows that now.

It was a case of 'Success of Jetty'. My God, her brilliant success. But we don't have an awful lot of time for this. I'll go quick. They don't beat about the bush, women. 'Who the fuck are you?' they say. 'Are you that fucky police? You're that fucky police! Police! Police! Hey, everybody! This is a fucky police I have here!' Betty thought it best to call it a day. Before she did,

238

though, she attempted to laugh at the idea of being mistaken for a fucky police person. But it didn't work. Jetty didn't believe the timbre, which is fair dues to Jetty. That timbre, you see, it was false. Luckily for Betty, there were no other women present. Just men. And you know what men are like. They didn't believe Jetty because Betty had on lipstick.

It was red lipstick, you've got to know that, but know also that it was not just any red. It was that particular genius shade of red that, on rare skins during times of conflict, was definitely more to icy blue. It was blue. And I don't mean Heaven blue. I mean the shadow side of Heaven blue. Ask anybody. I mean a woman. Blue-red, which is really blue, doesn't promise but indefinably holds out something. And what it's holding out is a little corpse in its little coffin – a dead nothing, back from the grave and waiting just for you. You'll have mystery, followed by unattainable, followed by what is definitely never to be attainable, then a nice big long chill, without mercy, if that's what you're after, right through to your heart. Orange-red on the other hand, of the type that is really orange, promises warmth, and who the fuck wants that in these very cold, freeze your soul, 'I'm going to kill you after I've had sex with you' situations? Orange-red that is orange? I'm telling you. Sane-Girl-Next-Door – that's what you'll get.

So thingy, Betty, who had on blue-red, which was really blue, had a stroke of genius – what with her hair and that skin that would stop any man in his tracks of conviction. She was able to escape, thank you, with only that spectacular hair pulled and a kick where her balls would have been from Jetty, if Betty had been a man. She didn't retaliate to this physical attack with all her training in arm-to-arm combat, because in some situations to have displayed her military prowess over a trifle would have given much bigger fish than sore feelings away. Luckily for Betty too, that day Jetty had been preoccupied with thoughts of John, her lover, and which new twenty-year-old nubile, connubial, nuptial, nymph or nymphet he might now be bedding, or would have been bedding if – thank-God-to-sweet-Jesus – he hadn't been arrested before he'd got his dick out that day. So she hadn't time, or the temperament, for contemplation upon underground plainclothes policewomen detective agents, other than to kick Betty cursorily, as I said, in the balls. Bet, therefore, was able to get away with an acceptable level of intactness. Just a bit of humiliation and it was having the hair pulled in public that did it. The kick in the balls was nothing. That rolled off her back. But hey, what of the bafflement of the policewoman saying in her later famous interview that, 'As long as you dress down, you can hoodwink even the most intelligent of locals', yet what about Jetty's assertion about 'grooming-up to fool those shaggers, the police'? I'm confused. Betty had been dressed up. Jetty had been dressed down, so why weren't they doing those things if that was their conviction about them? More and more I'm thinking humans, even to God, can't make much sense.

I hope you followed that for I had to sweep along yet try to combine my rapidity with some sort of reason and succinctness. Generally speaking, the gang, and of course Janet, had long been under surveillance, so that was why they sent Betty to intercept Jetty, not realising, as I say, that Jetty wasn't a clone of her sister, and so Betty's manoeuvres through Operation Bus-Stop Chit-Chat had proved a big failure that day.

Betty went back to the barracks and the more she thought about it, the more that attack upon her balls did sting and did matter. It wasn't nothing. Turns out it had penetrated the old sense of sexual humiliation after all. Jetty Doe had been arrested, she'd heard. Jetty Doe had then been released. Right then, she decided, I'm detective here and I say Jetty Doe must now be re-arrested. This time Bet intended giving Jet the worst grilling of her life. She'll be sorry, thought Betty. She'll be shamed too, because I'm going to shame her. Then I'll make her cry, make her realise that I'm of top crucial cheese status in this police army, whereas all she does is take gang minutes and work at a shop that doesn't even rate First Prize of the Year. Poor Betty. I feel sorry for her. As far as her understanding of certain women went, she really wasn't much better than a flesh and blood man.

So that was how the police turned up. Only too late for Jetty. And for Betty. Betty will have to swallow her indignation at having been bested by Jetty – even a Jetty who was no longer living. She'll have to speak to a counsellor if things get too psychological for her, bury her pique, go on a few dates, send a few Valentines, then get back to work and emotionally move on.

Incidentally, are men more visually influenced than women? Does this matter? Do we need to talk about this now? Or ever? I don't think so. Let us also walk on.

Judas was back. Spying again, I suppose. I'm telling you, that boy can be so silent unless having bouts of his magical mutterings – 'habitable', 'uninhabitable', that sort of thing. He's oiled castors. You open a door, he's there. You close the door, turn round, there he is again. You open a wall cupboard, he's squashed into the top shelf of it. In the name of God! And look – there he is again. He was back in the house from wherever he'd disappeared to out of it, and he wouldn't speak, wouldn't declare himself. He was still in that armour and had sidled in, inch by inch, little movement by little movement, pretending he was part of the chaos of the ornaments. And all so the police wouldn't notice he was there.

He had had another fantasy. At least, I'm assuming it was a

fantasy. It was that it wasn't his father but he who had killed Jetty Doe. According to the brain of Judas, Doe Senior thought he'd killed her, but hadn't because, before closure, he'd looked up and seen his daughter hovering by that Versailles thing. So he'd run to get at her and that was when Judas, who'd gone down to the parlour to save his sister as usual, realised that, despite the bloodstains about the nose and mouth, his Aunty Jetty wasn't dead after all. Now, if this really was a fantasy, at least Judas was getting closer to some sort of true desire in it. Here, instead of fantasising he had come in to be saviour, this time he clanked over, lifted a cushion and held it over Aunty Jetty's unforgiven face.

She'd laughed at him, you see. She'd tormented him. All those years he'd kept watch on that mouth because she made those 'crack-crack', 'clack-clack' Noises. Then bubbles. Big bubbles. Smack! All over her face. As a child, he'd covered his ears, closed his eyes, and every so often peeped through them to see if she'd stopped yet. Whenever he'd peep, she'd be covering her eyes, and her ears, and would continue to crack the bubble gum bubbles whilst peeping back over at him. Now, it's entirely open to interpretation as to whether or not this woman thought she'd been imitating the child in order to amuse him. Some children perhaps like to play in patently distressed states like that. But we don't need to interpret because it went down in history that Doe, not his son, had murdered his sister-in-law. I can say with assurance, though, that regardless of what went on in that room during that little window of opportunity, in Judas's opinion, nobody possessed a forked tongue like his Aunty Jetty in the whole, wide, psychologically conflicted world.

So you wouldn't have thought the boy had it in him, would you? As for Julie, his sister, I think we should talk about therapy again now.

Chapter Thirteen

I like therapy, but I mean good therapy. Crap therapy? Hell, you can send your ambassador for a cardboard cut-out of that for you at the corner shop. Don't be thinking you go along and therapist says, 'Ah, *guten morgen*, analysand. Please to come in and to lie down and to make comfortable. *Gut? Ja? Gut.* Today's suggestion, which I sense through intuitive transference, is that we progress immediately to "Archetype" unless you have strong utility preference – owing to nightmare of previous evening – for "Transpersonal Imago", "Insane Projection" or something else?' 'Sure thing, whatever you say, Doc,' you say. No. Even bad therapy doesn't happen as badly as that. What it is, is you – *yes, you* – rushing to be there on time even though you know you're ridiculously early, and even then you're not going to speak until that fucker says sorry first. Or else it's you arriving minutes before the end of the session so you won't have time to get into anything difficult, or else it's some ornament on the bookcase freaking you, because it's been moved a fraction since the last time you were there. The rest of us watching could hardly credit that this therapy business you've engaged in is, in fact, voluntary, what with all the apparent self-sabotage that's involved.

For example, one day Julie Doe – to get her off that hearthrug

and away from that strangulation scene and to jump her forward twenty years for a moment – in the thirty-sixth year of her
life, left Tiptoe Floorboard's only feminine bra shop feeling
happy and tremendously female. She was on her way to the bus-
stop with a magnificent luxury carrier bag over her arm. Just as
she got to this bus-stop she was clutched on to by a woman.
This was an acquaintance, rushing over from the other side of
the road.

'Julie!' acquaintance cried. 'Can I speak to you for a moment?
It's urgent. Sorry too—' This was said to someone else, who had
also magnetically appeared and simultaneously had grabbed
hold of Julie. This person was jealous – I mean that was her
name. Character-wise, she was possessed of no great sense of
propriety, tended on salivation as a way of facial expression,
wasn't – unlike Julie and acquaintance – in any sort of Recovery
and, to top everything, had never even heard of a Self-Help recovery book.

'I know I'm being inappropriate in barging up like this,' went
on acquaintance, 'and, believe me,' she said to jealous, 'it's not
like me to crash – in an immature, irresponsible fashion –
through other people's boundaries. But this is of the utmost. I
must speak to Julie. Do you mind? Do you understand?'

Of course jealous minded. Of course she didn't understand.
She herself had rushed over specifically because she wanted to
know what was in that fancy carrier bag Julie Doe was holding.
What was she doin' – this maid of all work, this necessary woman, this emptier of chamberpots – coming out of the ultra-
feminine brassière shop, when the rest of us are happy to get by
on the basics of underwear? After all, if black or white – with
full-on functional cups and proper woolly long-john knickers
to match – were good enough for our grannies then, jealous
thought, they ought to be good enough for us as well.

Now, however, it was 'Forget grannies. Grannies are dead.' Jealous wanted to know who was this other person, what was all her personal business, how did Julie Doe know her, was she happy, was she married, how much money did she have? Did she live in a detached house also, and did she have children, and were they Opposition Defiant Disordered children, and what were her problems generally – and specifically – and did her partner ever cheat on her if she had one – did she have one? Did she have tragedies? Did she have illnesses? Were they mental illnesses? And certainly, certainly, jealous didn't want to feel left out of any of this urgent talk. Julie, however, was relieved at the opportunity of de-latching jealous, so she de-latched with 'Goodbye, see you again some other time.' She shouldn't have said that last bit, for it was surely bringing the 'next time' upon her, but it couldn't be helped. It had been said in haste and out of habit, the way people part from each other with 'I'll say a prayer for you', when both parties know they won't bother their arse doing anything of the kind. Julie and this new person walked many good and quick steps away from jealous and away from the bus-stop, but by the time they'd reached the junction that used to be near that old wasteground which now had an excellent two-storey Giving-Birth Hospital built on top of it, the acquaintance couldn't keep the delay in talking up.

'Julie,' she said, and by now she was beside herself. 'I've just come from therapy. Just found out at therapy. My therapist says that even though I say I'm upset and annoyed – she says that in reality I'm much, much more than that!'

Julie started. Her acquaintance nodded and hurried on.

' "*Merely upset and annoyed?*" she said, and she seemed to be gloating as she said it. "*No, my dear. No, my poppet. No, my ignorant, forty-year-old childling*" – and I'm not forty! Do I look forty, Julie? – *"Upset and annoyed?"* she said. *"Oh no no no. It's time you knew – you're so much more than that."* '

Julie was stunned. Both of them were stunned. By this time they had stopped walking and were staring fixedly into each other's eyes on the High Street.

'How'd you mean?' said Julie. 'I don't understand. Where is the evidence for your therapist to be saying this? How is it possible anyway, to be *more than* upset and annoyed?'

'I walked right into it,' said acquaintance. She was shaking, her whole body was quaking. 'And I believe, Julie,' she continued, 'my therapist set a trap for me. You're lucky to be in Not Speaking Therapy. I wish I'd done Not Speaking. Mine tricked me into talking before I realised I had a choice.'

Julie felt a cold fear – a grabbing, clutching, 'got-you!' fear. She'd always suspected there was trickery in therapy. Whatever trick this woman's therapist had played upon her – no matter different therapies, different streets, different fifty-minute hours, different patients, and even though Julie and her therapist were definitely on the Not Speaking agenda – would Julie's one day break frame, jump agendas, and try that same trick on her? She shuddered and urged her fellow therapee on.

'I was late as usual,' said this woman – and I'm afraid I can't give her name because I don't know it. I think it was Mary, or Ann, something spectacular like that. All I know is that she and Julie used to meet and speak the programme of Recovery in the Self-Help bookshop until one day, unaccountably, Julie didn't want to talk 'Recovery' any more. She started wanting. That was it. Just wanting. Then she went further and started buying things as well. First she bought toiletries when she never used to buy toiletries. Then she bought a bangle. Then a lipstick. Then she went to the beauty salon and came out *an hour later* with a list of treatments in her hand. Before we know where we are, she'll have gone and done that homework she received just now on leaving the bra shop. I mean she'll be bringing that suit of armour to a charity shop before long.

I'd better explain. As I said, Julie – like her Aunt Jotty years before her – was in this Not Speaking Therapy. In this type of therapy, over time, someone possessed of the rare experience in the art of keeping quiet would facilitate Julie in moving from the silence of 'Fuck you, I hate you!' to the more subtle silence of no words being necessary because 'There's nothing to be afraid of – we are all one'. Her Aunt Jotty assured her that, even if she didn't make it to the gold medal of 'We are all one' and thus got head-hunted into Heaven because of super-fast-track-enlightenment, Julie wasn't to get downhearted. Jotty, even after her three-times-a-week sessions for twelve years during which nothing was said except the civilisations, never managed to attain 'We Are All One' herself. 'But things improved,' she said. 'The fact of going into the room, Julie. Just the fact of getting to the point where you can sit down and face, then hate, then stop hating, then feel rather okay in the presence of another person will change a lot internally. Then, of course, externally. Most certainly, you will have started to come in from that awful, terrible, freezing, damaging cold.'

So, there wasn't much to report, really, about what went on in those early sessions of Julie's, apart from – as with Jotty – 'Time's up', 'Here's my bill for October' and 'I'll be going on holiday during these dates'. Gradually after most sessions, though, Julie would feel better without realising why she was feeling better. She hadn't grasped the concept that her therapist might be holding all her hatred for her, thus enabling her, meantime, to venture out into new territory and to be half-decent – at least some of the time – to everybody else.

Hence the bra shop.

During one of those, now more frequent, lulls in the radius of her negativity and suicidal tendencies, Julie surprised herself one day by going straight to Tiptoe Floorboard's only feminine bra shop. Of course, as often happened in the town, years ago it had been trebled up with a tool shed shop, a motor maintenance shop, and with a 'man with van' business begging to be allowed to tag on also. But even then, more businesses soon wanted to join as well. In the end, meetings were held, deals were struck, percentages worked out, shareholders invited and an arcade of shops was opened all along that side of the High Street. The bra shop was now part of it. In it, Julie bought herself this totally beautiful bra. I'd love to tell you about the bra because of everybody I know, you, personally, deserve to be the one told about it, but I can't because it would be notches down from undergoing the consequences of looking into the very face of God. It was awesome. It was super-incredible elegant. Perhaps I'd better tell you about the packaging instead.

It had been tastefully packaged, in layers upon layers of pastel-coloured wrapping paper. After that, it had been placed, along with flower petals, a few fat chocolates, a tiny bottle of special aura ruby red magic protection Fourth Dimension potion, into a pink and black, King and Queen, luxury carrier bag. This bag had long satin-shiny cord handles for slipping over one shoulder and, I'm telling you, if there was any way you could swing this, you'd wear that carrier bag as well. It had black satin slips of tiny ties also, I mean on the inside, to hold both edges of the top tantalisingly together. And the whole of the inside was wallpapered in strips of pink and cream. The inside rim of the bag had little gleaming black polka dots on a soft pink background and the outside rim had little pink polkas rearranged on cream.

What Julie now had in her possession, if not yet on her

body, was in contrast to what usually she had on her body, and by 'usually' I don't mean something from the average 'plain bread and butter', 'middle of the road', objective masculine bra territory. I mean one of her 'Actionman', 'Ruthless Aggression Assortment', 'Pesticide Application' ultra-masculine bras. She hadn't bought any silk thong, cami, shortie, string, brief or any other kind of ethereal delicate knicker to match the total feminine she had just purchased. *They* were still too much of the lower territory for Julie's fragile Recovery to be able to engage with yet. But she had bought this ultra-feminine, and that can only mean inroads were being made into Julie Doe's relinquishment of trauma clothes. And I know you know trauma clothes.

'Ach, these auld things?' you say.

'Don't make me laugh,' you continue. But you know you're not going to laugh because you don't think this is funny. Too close to the bone. I've gone too close to your bone and what a cheek, for you don't even know me. 'Not trauma clothes!' or 'What are you talking about, trauma clothes?' or 'Trauma clothes! My clothes aren't trauma! I'm not in trauma! This is a case of One Size Fits All!'

You give a terse smile and you brush off my remark and you make a rude gesture of dismissing me also, along with my preposterous trauma clothes claim. These are just clothes you put on when you're cleaning, you say. These are just clothes you wear about the house. These are just clothes you pop to the garage in at midnight to pick up your icecream and fags before the garage closes for the evening. These are just clothes you wear to hold and comfort yourself.

'Yes, but why do you need comforted?' I persist. 'And are you sure, friend, they're not trauma clothes you're wearing?'

'Yes. Am sure! Not trauma clothes!' And now, thoroughly cross, you turn and walk away.

Did you know it was Jotty Doe's sister, JanineJoshuatine who, indirectly, twenty years earlier, had got Jotty interested in taking over the management of Tom Spaders's old gunshop? He had been imprisoned and she said she'd look after it for him and she did. She turned it into a bra shop. This happened by accident. One day she found herself down on the floor scrubbing out the old energy. Then it turned into a bra shop magically by itself. Full of guilt – for she could see how this looked – she had been working up to coming clean and telling Tom about this slight swap-over in merchandise. She meant to do so during every single time she visited him over the next five years he was inside. He had been sentenced to eight for 'Slaughter of Man' but had been released early. Even so, right up until the day she met him and they were walking back into town where he could see for himself the extent of her 'renovations', Jotty still hadn't been able to own up even then.

For his part, though, whilst in prison, and once over his bitternesses, Tom had begun to suspect something like this was happening – not that he knew it was a bra shop. His powers of intuition had not become as fine-honed as all that. It was that his rather enforced period of reflection and reassessment upon himself and of his values during the time he was in prison had detached him somewhat from the need for his shop to be Tiptoe's Best Gunshop. In fact, it no longer seemed to matter that it should be a gunshop – though don't be thinking that meant he was okay with it being a bra shop instead. 'But, my love,' Jotty would say, taking his arm and squeezing it, 'don't be thinking it has to be just women's underwear. I wouldn't be averse to selling men's underwear too.' But that wouldn't work. Let's face it. Heterosexual men are strange. Apart from the town's gay-men percentage catchment coming in and having fully fledged happy discussions with each other about the material, the style, the texture, the colour and should they buy it?, or else coming in singly and having fully fledged happy discussions in their heads with somebody about the material, the style, the texture, the colour and should they buy it?, you'd only have the wives, or the mothers, or the odd monosyllabic hetero-orphan bachelor hurrying in, with no interest, to buy the average, sensible, practical stuff instead.

It was not that sort of bra shop. It was the opposite to that sort of bra shop. You had to take an interest in the merchandise or face the consequences of being barred from the place.

Anyway, this 'to be or not to be' a bra shop is something me and you will have to get into before we part company. For now, just know that Jotty had taken on the invaluable Superdeluxe Director-Facilitator role. This was a job somebody with the right spirit simply has to take on during women's vulnerable bra-transition shocks in the Recovery business. I'm talking about when a client tries on a bra and finds she is wearing something where, for the first time, the physical fit is perfect but the emotional discomfort and grief engendered by the physical fit is terrifying. Jotty, now fifty-five years old, a golden, groomed, womanly woman, who read her clientele expertly and who was unafraid of any colour, of any texture, of any design, of any line, was eminently qualified to implement the feminine. She would soothe, reassure and encourage these women not to give up. She herself had had lots of practice and the town knew she'd had lots of practice. She used to coax herself – then later her sister – down from ceilings, prise herself and her sister out of trauma clothes, many times over, many years before.

Not an easy thing to do. Look how touchy you got just now when I suggested – merely as an experiment – that those clothes you're wearing might, oh, just might, be trauma. You hated me as an emotional terrorist. How much harder, then, to approach someone unmistakably deep in the wearing of trauma, and to persuade that person into the changing room to take that trauma off.

That's what Jotty did. She was really terrifically good at this. Not only did she get Julie as well as many other women out of the numerous ranges of super-ultra-masculine bras and into ultra-feminine bras for the first time in their female existence. She also, through personal example, got them to do homework. The homework centred on what to do in order to welcome your beautiful new feminine bra home.

Basically, to break this down, know there are three things to remember. First, don't disrespect yourself by undercutting and attacking yourself if you can't manage to do your homework. Second, if you do disrespect yourself by attacking yourself, then simply remember that, automatically when you do this, you will also be disrespecting and feeling hostility towards everybody else as well. Can't explain the science. Don't ask me for the science. Third, there are some nasty cruel bastards in the world, but hold to the thought that there are many less nasty cruel bastards than currently you think there are. And that knowledge I've just given you – via Jotty and her homework – is Step One in getting the lovely new bra home.

Step Two is running the gauntlet. This happens automatically and it's as if the Devil himself has been keeping an eye from the Leprechaun corner to plant little bomblets to happen to you as soon as you've left that bra shop. The gauntlet, in contradiction to what you think, could be just one negative or hostile person, who keeps appearing and reappearing, with you simply unable to get rid of her, or it could be one person after another person, or it could be whole groups of people. It's extremely unpredictable and again, don't ask for the science. All I can say is, it has something to do with Post-Purchase Trauma

Syndrome, and with you thinking you're the only person in the world who can get excited about something and not know what to do about it, when truth is, in reality, you are not.

After you've run the gauntlet, chances are, when you get in through your door, you might want to kill yourself. That's perfectly normal. At this stage you take out the envelope with the instructions that the Superdeluxe Director had the foresight previously to write down and slip into your luxury bra bag. These instructions make up Step Three. They consist of an easy bit and a hard bit. Do the hard bit first. Are you ready? It's to make up your bed, *in your bedroom*, as if you were going to sleep in it. Yes – I mean spend the night in it. Then do spend the night in it. Jotty glosses over this bit in her instructions as she doesn't want to give you time to protest. Next day – easy. All you've got to do is get rid of something, or even just to entertain the thought of getting rid of something. It could be from your person, it could be from your house and Jotty suggests the scraggliest of one of your numerous masculine bras. If you can't manage that, how about closing a few drawers properly or, if you're really up to it, go for that suit of armour. Why have you got such an ugly disturbing stolen heirloom in your house in the first place? As for that feminine bra, you'll be relieved to know you don't have to, for now, put it on your body. I know you're dreading this and so have slipped on a few 'somebody's got to do it', 'masculine managerial brio' bras all at the same time instead. That's fine. Do that, but hold to the thought that the feminine is now on your premises – infusing the place from deep within its luxury wrappings – and that it will be on your body, believe me, before long.

That explains the suit of armour and how it might end

up in a charity shop. On leaving the bra shop Julie, with a marked softening of her features, had been confident of being able to do all of her homework but now, standing beside Mary, who was continuing to detail her therapist's onslaught into the 'upset and annoyed' position, Julie was less confident, less sure of herself.

Mary always went late to therapy, very late – five minutes before the end of each session she'd turn up. She did this as a way of putting her fingers up at her therapist and also as a way of controlling the therapy session itself.

'So I went in the door and went over to sit in the chair as usual,' said Ann, 'because as you know, Julie, I won't lie on that couch thing.' Julie nodded. There was a couch thing in Julie's therapist's also, and she too, would never lie on it lest, her therapist – taking advantage of a moment of trust which would never happen anyway – leant a over and tried to strangle her for sure. So far, so understandable. Everything was making normal therapy sense to Julie. 'But then,' said Ann, 'it happened. I saw.'

'What? What did you see?'

'Oh, Julie!' cried Ann. 'The chair! The therapy chair – *my chair!* – it had been moved! It had been moved three to four centimetres! I know, because I always measure it on entering by the lines on the floorboard.'

The women were clutching each other, Mary unwittingly holding tight to the cord handles of Julie's new luxury lingerie bag and Julie, in the build-up of tension, reverting to the comfort of clinging to Mary's shabby trauma clothes.

'My God,' Julie whispered. 'What did you do?'

' *"Too close! You're too close! You moved your chair closer since the last session!"* That's what I shouted at first,' said Ann, 'for, in my upset, I made a mistake in thinking the moved chair to be hers and not mine. And she said, *"I haven't moved my chair,*

Mary." And I said, *"You have moved your chair"* And she said, *"No. I haven't moved my chair."* And I said, *"Moved the chair and being dishonest! Disgraceful in a therapist! Did move the chair! Did move the chair!"* And that's when I realised my mistake and that she hadn't moved the chair. Meanwhile she said nothing but just sat there observing me. I know she hates me. All those therapists all those times, they've hated me.'

'I agree,' said Julie. 'So what happened then?'

'So I said to her, *"You misunderstand me, therapist. This is what's been moved. This chair! This chair here's been moved,"* and I stood by the door, pointing over to my chair, and I pretended I'd meant that one all along.'

Apparently, though, according to Mary, her therapist didn't stop there.

' *"Okay,"* she said. *"So you think the chair's been—" "Has been! Three to four centimetres!" "Well, what does it mean, Ann? What have you lost, that this chair's been moved from the position you normally find it in? We've got thirty seconds left of the session. Do you feel strong enough to begin to explore that?"* '

Totally horrific. No wonder Ann or Mary or whoever she was crashed through other people's boundaries. If something like that had been said to me, I'd be crashing through everybody's boundaries as well.

Mary couldn't let the matter drop, but also she could hardly say, 'Someone's been sitting in my chair.' She didn't want to give her therapist the power to say, 'Yes, Mary. Other people come to see me. Many, many other people. You're not special. It's not you I love.'

So Mary was still stirred up, and Julie, grasping her predicament, was unable to stop herself transferring it to a potential one of her own. As she did so, all her happiness and sense of achievement at having bought that bra dwindled. All sense of good transformation, of anything lovely ever being possible, all the firing up of excitement, instantly was gone.

'Mary!' she interrupted, now very panicked. 'I think this is bad therapy. Very bad therapy. Bad psychobabble, bab-bab-I mean bad—'

'Exactly,' interrupted Mary. 'Only she's not a bad therapist, Julie, don't be saying that about my therapist. How would you like it if I said your therapist was a bad therapist?' Mary was allowed to slag off her therapist, in fact slagging off her therapist was a requirement, was part of her healing process, the thing to remember though, was this was *her* therapist, *Mary's* therapist, just like the chair was *her* chair, *Mary's* chair, and that meant it wasn't the ticket for anybody else to go having a sit-down or a slag-off as well. 'So I said, "*Stop!*" ' said Mary. 'I said, "*Stop! You're not helping me. You're making me upset—*" '
'*Oh, so you're upset?*' interrupted this therapist. And here, the therapist raised her right eyebrow, the way Ann said she always did when she wanted to indicate she could say more than she was choosing. What this eyebrow said, according to Mary, was '*No, poppet. No, my dear. No, my middle-aged helpling. It's not merely that you're upset and annoyed. The reality is, for years, for your whole life maybe, you've been much, much more than that.*'

By then there were only six-five-four, oh God, three seconds left of the therapy and the session ended by running over. Mary hated running over because she knew it was her therapist's way of putting her fingers back up at her. Also, she didn't like to meet the next patient coming in, for who's this? she'd think. How dare this person be here and how dysfunctional was *he* in comparison with her own dysfunction? How long had he been coming? Who, between them, had more right to be coming, because they'd been coming first?

'Hold on,' said Julie. 'Are you saying that your therapist didn't actually say "*more than*" upset and annoyed, and didn't say either, all that "*poppet*" business? That it was just the look on her eyebrow that told you she said that?'

Julie was relieved – greatly and selfishly – for while Ann had been splurging, she had automatically begun her own process of imagining what her own therapist might one day spring on her.

'*Well, Julie,*' she'd say, '*what about that rape? Those rapes? And what about your mother – or is it your aunt – still up there in that madhouse? What about all those relatives up there also? How come you don't visit, and as for the Doe gang – what do you feel about their imminent early release?*

'*As for Tom Spaders*' – and here the therapist would put her finger on it – '*why do you still believe the rumours? Why won't you acknowledge that your Aunt Jotty's husband killed your father probably in order to save you from being strangled? Why do you still pretend twenty years on that Tom Spaders is either still in hospital, recovering from some long ago mugging and stabbing, or else that he's a mass murderer, or else that he never existed at all?*'

The hearsay that had been circulating at the time of the arrests and which for a long time afterwards had gone down in 'Births, Deaths and Rumours That Are Probably True' was that Tom Spaders who, on the whole, except for the odd time, hadn't killed anybody, was in fact a serial murderer. It was he, they said, who had been the leader of the gang. Julie, on the whole, accepted this, simply because she couldn't bear the direct chaos of knowing it was her father. That meant she had to believe – through a huge manipulation of her brain – that someone else, not Spaders, was married to her Aunt Jotty instead. She ignored this person, either by not going where he was, or by instantly removing herself from wherever he was if she turned up and found him there, or by instructing him, by the use of powerful telepathy, not to approach her, or by having her aunt never refer to him, on pain of shunning and never seeing her aunt again.

Other rumours that had circulated at the time also were that John Doe, Julie's father, had in truth been Tiptoe Floorboard's Great Messiah, thus totally innocent of killing anybody – except Jetty Doe. He was still viewed as having killed Jetty. Indeed, the Ordinary Decent Folk had always known he would kill her. Some said he killed her over chewing gum, some said he killed her over a cough, and some said he killed her over a sneeze. As for Jotty Doe, his sister, the woman went mad, they said. Just like the other sisters, she had broken down and had had to go into the mental hospital. When they let her out, however, she was even madder than before. She closed down the town's best gunshop, for example, then reopened it as something unrecognisable and, although it did sell masculines, you had to plead a strong case if you were a woman and wanted one of those. As for the First Daughter, Jane, there had never been any First Daughter. The daughters had started with the Second Daughter. That daughter had been called Julie and, went the rumour, Julie Doe was dead.

Well, that should've given the game away for Julie knew she wasn't dead, but here we have an example of the strength of denial in the face of absolutely anything. However, just as Mary or Ann, in her therapy, was currently being brought to the realisation about her skeletal wardrobe of two words business, Julie was being brought to the realisation that she couldn't buy a bangle or a bra or close drawers in her house or take a suit of armour to a recycling centre – all in the context of going to therapy – without expecting other parameters to shift inwardly and outwardly as well. So, it's no wonder – when faced with the 'Fingers on the buzzer: "Who was the real perpetrator?" ' – people prefer to focus on chairs being moved, people cracking chewing gum or the hidden meaning of eyebrows moving up and down instead.

Well, thought Julie, her therapist could try to shift her from the Not Talking position to the Talking position but it wouldn't work, for Julie had her protection. This was her amnesia and her constant passings-out. I don't mean faints. I mean disappearings into other dimensions. At that moment on the High Street, for example, a passing-out cut in to stop Julie receiving any more transmissions from deep-struggling Mary. She had a merciful split-off moment, during which she, deep-struggling Julie, disappeared. She came back quickly, only to be conscious of standing on the High Street, speaking with that woman she'd met a few times in the town's Self-Help bookshop. Maryanne or Annemarie – she believed she was called.

At this point Annemarie realised she was clutching Julie's luxury carrier bag and the effect upon her was as if she'd just realised her hands had been stuck in a rancid bag of dead blow-flies, and she pulled them away shrieking, looking at Julie as if betrayed. On Julie's part, she had just come to the realisation that she had been clutching Maryanne's trauma clothes but, before she could wallow in them – for at that moment she was needy – Maryanne callously yanked the old familiars away. The two women parted then, with Maryanne thinking, she did say it, my therapist did say it, and with Julie thinking that as soon as she got home she'd take her practice clothes off and fall asleep in her kitchen with her trauma clothes on.

On the way home, however, the Superdeluxe Director note decided prematurely to jump out at her. It reminded her that she was never going to do it, that is, give up her old ways, except through the chaos, that only through the turmoil itself would she, in fact, change. She must resolve in small chunks, it said. She must develop a whole new lateral outlook. And why not? it added, given she had developed such a momentous fragmented outlook in order not to have to deal with it for so long? Yes, she was back in the old groove, in that old sequence, but that didn't mean the sequence was all there'd ever be. Putting her key in the lock therefore, she entered her house and, instead of stuffing her luxury bag into the first cupboard she came to, she set it prominently on the table then, ignoring a midday-nap pull towards the safety of her haphazard kitchen cushions, she went into her bedroom, crawled into her bed and fell asleep.

Chapter Fourteen

In the Doe house twenty years earlier, the police, after they had re-entered, bent over and picked Julie up from the hearth. Jotty, Julie's aunt, still clutching Tom Spaders, was having her fingers prised off Tom by the police and by the ambulance crew also. She was holding on because she wanted to make him alive because she thought he was dead.

Of course, the Ordinary Decent Folk were back outside amassing. Now the point was, were they amassing out of approbation or out of disapprobation? One can never tell with amassments, not until someone starts the applause off or else throws that first stone.

This particular group of Ordinary Decent, this general public, this great curious commonality, was by now a big pushing shove. It was a whole pile of grabbing pulses that everyone was plugging into, one insatiable wave upon wave of mounting excitement. Folk were dashing over from everywhere, some carrying babies, some shouting, 'Here's half a coin. Mind this baby!', some abandoning their positions in long-established queues outside phoneboxes, all because everybody wanted to know what was going on. 'Were the Does being arrested?' they asked. 'You mean they're *actually* being arrested? So, it *was* the case then that someone had tipped that Interfering Foreign Policeman off.'

The composition of the Folk too, had split further. Until this second, there had been the Pro-Gang, Anti-Gang, ghost-hunting and the art dealer contingents. Now there was a fifth faction. I call it the Fifth Faction because I don't want to confuse you. It really consisted of members of the six war factions rolled into one. I contend, and hold my contention, that they weren't part of this story because – in terms of logistics and the time component we're dealing with, as in 'We have to finish soon' – I don't know how to fit them all in. 'Well, they must be fitted in,' I hear you pipe up. 'If they hail from this town, then they're part of society. Society's made up of everybody!' 'Well,' I say, 'go change your trauma clothes and leave my methods alone.'

They turned up, this Fifth Faction, to have a chat with Doe. Unlike their attitude towards the other town gangs, they had let him carry on his Empire without any interference or taking of it off him. This was unusual, but it was because Doe's four brothers had been committed members of the Fifth Faction, up until the point they'd been caught in an ambush and slain. So, out of respect for the dead martyrs, they were leaving Doe alone and were only coming now to pay him a visit. A problem had arisen and they had to check him out, along with everybody else. So these steely, detached, emotionally unmovable insusceptibles – if you believe that – were going to put a few words to him. These words were, 'Do you have our stuff?' Further words were, 'If you have our stuff, Doe, regardless of Benedict and Samuel and Abel and Abel – God rest their souls, your brothers, for they were great soldiers – we're going to kill you.' All of the factionists' bombing stuff, you see, had disappeared.

But back to the house and the Ordinary Decent Folk, and don't get the Ordinary Decent Folk wrong. Nobody wanted the house to be set fire to, except perhaps the children. Children of the town tended to like things like that. They were not insensate, these young ones. They had picked up the adrenaline that was spinning round the area, and naturally they wanted their little crumble of something too. So there they were, six-, seven-, eight-year-olds, with their high and tight GI haircuts, strapped up, kitted out, made to look like armed men and armed women any postage stamp would be proud to carry a picture of but, instead of guns, they were carrying bundles of sticks and matches whilst trying to conceal what were obviously petrol cans in their hands. But no. The house would not be set fire to. The Fifth Faction had no opinion on it. The ghost hunters, however, needed it intact because they had to carry out their paranormal investigations. The dealers wanted it intact because of all the art objects in there they were planning future fests with. The Pro-Gang supporters wanted it intact because it had to be made into a Miss Havisham Museum in honour of their beloved Community Centre members, and the Anti-Gang wanted it intact because the more evidence gathered from within the bowels of that evil building, the more chance those perpetrators would get sentenced for far more than their already estimated five hundred years each.

Similar to when the police had led the gang out during their arrests earlier, again we craned our necks to get a good ghoul. It was definitely exciting but in that rather nauseous, stomach-heaving way. I mean the way you might feel if you were a three-year-old and hadn't yet got addicted to horse-racing or to boxing. It's on the telly, this boxing, this horse-racing, and although you want to, because you feel sick, you simply cannot pull your little three-year-old self away. I guess this is where parents could come in handy.

Anyway, due to the excitement, I was on the verge of throwing up over the person standing in front of me when all exigencies of vomit vanished because it was Tom Cusack standing in front. He was intact too – not a single gunshot wound was available on him. We recognised each other immediately and greeted each other more heartily – given we were practically strangers – than was meet. But you know how it is. When communal energy is heightened owing to something unbelievable, you'd take a hold of anybody. You'd take a hold of some bellboy from some hotel on the other side of the world, who just so happened to be rushing by on an errand at that moment, and you'd splurge your whole incest history to him, regardless of whether he wanted to hear it or not.

'What's going on?' Cusack said, for he had just arrived and hadn't realised the current Doe versus Police situation. I couldn't answer initially because 'Didn't Tom Spaders shoot you?' I was trying my best to be polite not to ask.

Turns out he wasn't a ghost, for I know you're tutting and thinking, oh, move on, move on! for that must be the plausible explanation. No. Turns out that, despite the sound of that lone gunshot we all heard in Spaders's place that morning, Spaders hadn't shot him. They had had one of those partings that hadn't ended in a shooting instead.

'Ach, he's a hard man to talk to,' said Tom suddenly of the other Tom. 'And he's getting harder every time I meet him. I've exhausted advice and even Anti-Blueprinting as ways of getting through to him. I myself am exhausted, and now I won't be able to reconsult the dictionary, because Angelus has decided to bring it back to the library because she doesn't like the way I'm being affected by it any more.'

I nodded and clucked sympathetically.

'Yeah. Poor Tom,' he said. 'But don't be telling anybody I told you …' He paused and looked at me and that was when I gave my word that I was as the grave and that I wouldn't tell anybody, but it's okay – he didn't say anything about not drop-ping big hints.

Supposing you have this torn-out page from a stolen medical dictionary and you want someone to read about a mental con-dition in it that you think that person's suffering from. What do you do? You take it out of your pocket in a gunshop and you spread it right out between you and yer man over the counter, pushing the loaded guns a bit out of the way. You point to the relevant section. But him, the unstable one, who might have this syndrome you're indicating, is not listening and instead is picking up these guns and starting to try them, to see how they handle. He's adopting his firing position. And in every one of these positions, he's aiming these guns at you.

'So I said … then he said … then I said …' went on Cusack. And apparently, whilst he had been pointing to the torn page from the book in order to educate Spaders, that shot was fired that we ourselves heard. Turns out, though, it wasn't the third-dimensional Spaders who'd pulled the trigger. Instead it was his psycho-spatial part. I mean the part that was annoyed because Spaders hadn't gone out yet and killed anybody. It had got itself into such a temper that, in the end, its only recourse was to go and get an immaterial essence gun and fire it off itself.

So it did.

It shot that little human being construction, Tom Cusack, shot him in the solar plexus. What a dirty bastard Psycho-Spatial! And it was over in a jiffy, and there was the poor plexus – disrupted, shocked, gaping and ever so creepily silent. A huge hole was visible in poor Cusack's non-third-dimensional front.

So you see, all easy of understanding, if only one goes back and unravels from the beginning. The annoyed Psycho-Spatial Spaders was able to shoot the Psycho-Spatial Cusack, with the physical Cusack feeling not so much that something had winded him but that something, out of nowhere, had busted him apart. That was why he was unable to continue reasoning with Spaders and had to give up on the Anti-Blueprinting. That was why, slightly staggering, feeling ill, mumbling something about having to get home, to get to his wife, he had left the shop.

I must say, he was looking bad, and no wonder, given what had happened to him. And don't you realise that if Spaders had been a bit more ratcheted-on in his psycho-spatial condition, that murderous part might have stepped outside its psychic dimension and picked up one of those loaded guns for real? So luckily for both Toms, one wasn't killed and the other didn't do the killing of him. 'He keeps mixing people up,' Cusack concluded. 'I honestly think he thought I was somebody else.'

He said goodbye then, for he wasn't interested in what was happening at the Doe house, and this completely astounded me. 'Maybe later,' he said. For now, his digestion wanted him to go home. So off he went, and I watched as he walked along the pavement, under the grey-darkness of the shop canopies, with the sun blazing beyond him just a little upfront.

Now the thing to tell which I should have told earlier when we were talking about rumours is that a rumour is 'a type of fish'. That's according to one dictionary. It is 'the shifting five minutes before dusk', according to another. It is 'false words on the air', according to a third. It is a 'calumniator for pouring treacle' according to a fourth. The main thing a rumour is, though, according to the one true source of definition, is a world people enter after they've fallen into, and can't be bothered climbing out of, some really big, man-made hole.

Gravediggers, two of them, had initiated a rumour a while back about the gunshop man, Tom Spaders. They hinted he was a child molester. Well, Ordinary Decent Folk only have to get a whiff of the word 'molester' to be entitled to open up their china cabinets and to get their lynch ropes out. Molesting is different from incest. Incest is a subject, as I've intimated, that automatically closes Tiptoe's mental curtains. Molester, on the other hand, is a subject that opens them wide up. It's somebody out there, see. Not you, for you're my friend. And not me, for I'm your friend. Nor is it our spouses – for they're upstairs babysitting whilst we're down here, reading and writing to each other. The thing is, though, you don't actually have to have a molester. Context is everything. The gravediggers' hint was the context here.

The Ordinary Decent Folk were edgy. Apart from the ghost-hunting, the gallerist antique dealer and the Fifth Faction contingents – none of whom were interested in the topic of the molester – everybody else was feeling upset and annoyed. The Anti-Gang section, though, glad of the arrests, had already gone home to have their 'justice has been served or better have been served' dinners. The Pro-Gang, on the other hand, already cheated out of offensively slanging the police, which people naturally incline to out of some deep inherent constitutional hatred principle, hung around, for they felt there must be something else in the way of destructive protest they could do.

'This is a warrior culture,' one of them asserted to the press during a street interview. 'And them!' – meaning the police – 'Those iconoclast busters! They're trying to take away our Greek Myth Syndrome.' 'Yeah,' said another. 'And if they think we're gonna hold some peaceful demonstration on some little grassy knoll ...' While that was going on, the journalists came over to me for the official spokesperson quote on the supernatural aspect. I must have one of those faces. 'How should I know?' I replied. I was astonished. 'I don't know any supernatural aspect.' And I demonstrated my denial with a rather huffy shrug.

So here, right now, after the latest murders and arrests and ambulance transportings, the crowd was being told to disperse because everything was back to normal and there was nothing more to see. This made the Folk bristle. It certainly was not going to disperse, it muttered, just because it had been ordered to. 'Oh, leave them then,' said the police. 'We're understaffed and overstretched. They'll go home soon enough when it rains.'

The police went away with all the things they had come for and, immediately, the antique dealers orgasmically ran back in to ransack the house. The thing to know, though, was that it wasn't raining, and because it wasn't, the last of the Ordinary Decent – for the Fifth had gone also, given Doe was dead and so wouldn't be helping them with their enquiries – was at a loss as to what to do next. Normally they'd set fire to something but, as I said, the most obvious thing was sacrosanct. They could fight the gallerists, they supposed, to stop them taking out the Havisham furniture. But that was ordinary, rather predictable. There must be something. Something more dramatic. They cast around for a lead.

It was a case of bored-bored-bored, but not really bored. It was more like shock-shock-shock after all that excitement. That's an extreme cocktail. It's always hard to get emotionally grounded after any upheaval, and it would be even harder for this lot for, remember, they only had two words.

They found one. A lead, I mean. And it was Tom Cusack. It was a rampage and, yes, all right, I'll admit it was a rampage. But from their point of view, it was akin to hanging out the bunting, to avenging their rights, to taking the law justifiably into their own hands.

'Look!' cried one. 'He's over there! Just passing the morgue confectionery. Quick! Quick! Let's head him off at the sweet-shop!'

So there you are. As far as the Ordinary Decent Folk and that lynch reaction were concerned, all it was really was that they had to get somebody. So they got Cusack. They got him as a child molester, even though they knew he wasn't a child molester. And it wasn't a lynch reaction either. That was the rumour played up about it later on. In reality, it was a tar and feathering and it took place against a lamp-post right outside the sweetshop. As usual, it happened like lightning. And it wasn't fatal. Was that easier than a lynching? Should Tom Cusack be grateful for that?

Apparently, as I discovered later, the Folk had seen Tom talking to me over on the sidewalk, just up from the morgue confectionery. The morgue confectionery, as you know, was beside the confectionery morgue. They closed in on him just as he passed the last of the sweetshop's gunshops, unaware anyone was bearing down on him. He was thinking how well his day had started, but then how it had gone astray and in the end had run away from him. He was glad he would soon be home, running things by his wife.

The Ordinary Decent Folk, for their part, were remembering how the gravediggers long ago had said they'd seen Tom messing about with some children in the graveyard. Even though they knew it had been the other Tom, and even though, anyway, the other Tom hadn't been molesting either, one Tom was as good as another. So they rushed over to get this one instead.

Now, the thing about tar and featherings is, if you're not there when they begin, but say you stroll up just after, I'm telling you, you won't know at first what you've come upon. That happened to some passers-by. Strangers. Two girls. Maybe eighteen or nineteen. They strolled into the tail end of this almighty tar and feathering and they were chatting – on whether to buy tights or stockings or those new hosieries called hold-ups which, apparently, were the latest beauty things in the shops. The girls were taking into account that these new lovely items might be better than the usual, because tights can pull at the groin and suspender belts for stockings can be uncomfortable at the waist sometimes but, on the other hand, what if they were to buy those hold-ups and they didn't stay up but fell down? This was what the poor girls were discussing when they came to the realisation that they were in the middle of a silence. No sound at all was suddenly coming their way. Until that moment, they could have sworn there had been some sort of noisy commotion going on just around the corner from them. Yet, now they were round this corner, there was only silence, with a huge group of people at the bottom looking up their way.

Why were they looking? Why were they staring? The teenagers nervously moved closer, one to the other. Then they looked at the conglomeration of rubbish all around them on the ground. There were sweet packets, cigarette packets, cigarette butts, dirty sticky stuff and tufts of hair that had been shaved or cut off and black stringy tufty things. Pieces of bread and pieces of dead pigeon. Just the odd fluffy feather – and that's because, you see, you can always get tar, but feathers aren't always easy to come by. Would you hand over your pillow? Why should you hand over your pillow when them others taking part aren't rushing to their houses to donate their pillows? Don't be a fool. Hold on. Like everybody else, just stick on rubbish and whatever else comes to hand instead. So, what a mess, the girls were thinking. Has some party just happened in this spot where they were standing? Was someone getting married? And that was when they registered the lamp-post. And that was when they let out those two big screams.

Well, I was about to sidle away myself but Jotty appeared,

eyes red, face a mess, every hair out of place – I mean *every* hair – and all from that earlier crying. Blind to everything, she headed straight over and took a hold of my arm.

'Ow! That hurt!' I said.

'Want you to do me something. Need a big favour.' Didn't sound like a favour. Sounded like an order. And my arm was getting nipped terrible, she was gripping it that hard.

'Don't do favours,' I said. 'Can't.' I made things up on the spot as to why I couldn't do favours. I even took topics from her own favourite filing system – Fourth Dimension, spirit realms, Upper, Lower and Middle Earth territory examples – then finally, 'Let me go, you're hurting me and, anyway, I'm leaving town about now.'

I knew what she was after, see, and I wanted none of it.

'No,' she said. 'You're gonna do it. You're gonna help me dig up that coffin. Maybe even all his fantasy coffins.' Then her mouth fell open and she forgot about me and the digging up of the coffins. The grip on my arm got tighter, though. I noticed that.

'Who?' she whispered. 'Who's that? Tied to the lamp-post?'

Through her own disturbed urgent perceptions, the screaming of the girls had at last penetrated. Puzzled, she looked over their way. What was the matter? Then she, too, noticed the silence. She saw the crowd, which had pulled back to the sidelines. Some appeared nervous, some with arms crossed, still defiant, all of them looking up our way. She looked back towards the girls, and that's when she, too, noticed the lamp-post. She squinted at the lamp-post.

'Tom Cusack,' I said.

She let go. No more nipping. No more demanding. Over the road she was running, bolting, falling over herself – and that meant, of course, I had to continue bystanding. All the same,

I was dreadfully shaken. *Do her something!* And to me – when I don't do things! *Help her dig up coffins!* Was she out of her mind?

She had taken charge. I mean sort of. In some kind of hysterical fashion, she yelled to a group of children to go and get Mrs Cusack, or any of the Mr Cusacks – that was Angelus and Tom's four brothers. I hadn't met any of the brothers and was just thinking this was the time I was going to meet them when I realised it wasn't the children she was yelling instructions to. With another frisson of horror, I realised it was myself.

'*Me?*' I squeaked. 'You want *me* to do something?'

'Do it!' she yelled. 'Go and get them now!'

Well, of course I couldn't. I just couldn't. What was she thinking, to involve me in these matters? Hurriedly – for I could see she was worked up and might explode at any moment – I whispered to nearby children, possibly foot soldiers, possibly baby-faced street robbers, possibly innocent kiddies who might run errands in exchange for instant pots of money. I gave them instant pots of money and they dropped their petrol cans and, straightaway, ran off.

And there went Jotty's plans completely for the day. But then, what were her plans? Initially they had been to accompany her friend, Angelus Cusack, to the library to drop off some dictionary, then to talk with her of urgent worries about the kitchen cupboard contents at her brother's house. But her plans spontaneously changed, the way plans do. Brand new plans moved in and these were to make the man she could have loved alive, yet not being able to make him alive – although he was alive, but she was too much in shock yet to be aware of that. And that's the thing with shock. It operates at the surprise level. It's like you've had a shock and half an hour later you're telling your friends about having had this shock and then an hour after that you realise you'd still been in shock during the telling of your friends. Naturally, you're astonished at how shock works. So now, thinking you're out of it, you ring up another friend to tell them about this shock business, only to discover another four hours later that four hours earlier you'd still been in shock all the time. Are you out of it yet? you wonder. An alternative to that is, some people get to the point where they have fleeting moments in their lives when they're out of shock rather than in it. But they don't want to be out of it. Everybody else is still in it. *So why them, God, why them?*

It was a whole lifestyle. Besides that, though, Jotty Doe was not someone you'd ever want about in any type of emergency. She'd be the one crying and dropping and unravelling all the bandages and getting germs from cross-contamination all over the place. Then she'd faint – just your luck too – from the sight of the blood, or of the wound, or of her emotions, and she'd faint over the person you're trying, *in extremis,* to give CPR to. After that, when she came to, she'd be completely in child mode. Five years old she'd be, wandering in the woods, crying, still unravelling the bandages, still contaminating, but now searching for the corpse of some little household pet the family had ordered to be taken into the wood to be shot for practice that day. Daddy had come home turtleless. He came home turtleless. 'The turtle ran away,' he said, yawning and setting his gun down.

So she was untying Tom, trying to untie Tom, who had slumped down to the bottom of the lamp-post. In the process of trying, she'd stop and drop the messy, fraying knots of impossible sticky twine. All around was rubbish, loads of rubbish, and the thought became impressed upon her that she should sort through this rubbish to see if some of Tom's contents had got spilt out of him and were there amongst it. But then the thought was gone and she'd be thinking she had to check to see that he had a pulse and heart still beating first. That was wrong too, she'd then think. Oh, how she was wasting time! she now thought, for of course she should go back to untying all those knots again. So one moment she was untying. Next, she was trying to work out if he was living. She was terrible. 'Oh God! No pulse! No heartbeat!' But come on, Jotty. You should know that no pulse, no heartbeat meant absolutely nothing. Often the people of Tiptoe had neither – it was the best way of keeping the safest, lowest profile in town.

What a mess. Tom, tied to the lamp-post – half-unconscious, unconscious, even dead – probably could have managed his own rescue better himself. But she did take that first step, so in the realm of goodwill – and we can't measure goodwill with a tape measure – and perhaps, regardless of her scatterment, she took exactly the right action. Why should someone know everything? A person could step in and shout, 'Stop this! Stop this outrageous behaviour!' even though if it doesn't stop, they don't know how to stop it but, by their stepping in, they might have temporarily shocked everybody and critically changed the molecules around. People who do know what to do, who might not have known how to shout, 'Stop this outrageous behaviour!' can then step in and manage things as the best of First Aiders, rescuers and saviours can. Luckily for Jotty, in her flustered state, she looked up and saw Angelus running up at this point.

As for Angelus. All those days of authenticity paid off. All that being in touch with herself and with her deepest intuition. I don't mean the silly intuition. I mean the real intuition. You know, washing the dishes before going to the library, for example, and knowing that something momentous has just happened somewhere involving your man. She left the dishes, didn't dry her hands, rushed out the door, shouted to her brothers-in-law, who had just come back from work and who were having a relaxing pre-dinner game of fast handball by the gable wall together, to leave what they were doing and to come and follow her. She headed to the corner of Bock Street off the High Street, knowing that whatever was happening would be happening to Tom there. Was it something to do with Spaders? she thought. Had Tommy Spaders, in his illness, harmed her husband? Meanwhile, it seemed those children I had newly made rich in return for bringing back the relatives hadn't delivered their message. Three of them had run away, the dishonourables, immediately to spend their gold in the town's second best sweetshop, the first best sweetshop being inaccessible because of the tarred and feathered person outside. The other two had headed to the Cusack house as commissioned but, *en route,* passed the wife and the brothers coming towards them from that direction. 'Misters! Missus! Misters? Missus?' they tried but, as the adults looked grim and in such a ferocious hurry, the children also headed to the second best sweetshop, assuming news of the tar and feathering had penetrated by now.

Yes. Angelus and the brothers had picked up speed and were running to get to Bock Street. Before they arrived, however, some of the Well-Meanings of the 'You gave our books away!' were also running to assist Jotty and Tom. Well done, I thought. How damned decent of them not to hold the borrowed Recovery book bad behaviour against her. Before they reached her, though, certain Ordinary Decent Folk, still on the sidelines, were beginning to whisper and move forward again. They were saying something about Jotty's hair being too long, and uh oh! I thought, for I knew, then, another tar and feathering was coming. This was despite Jotty – ever since long ago when her hair had fallen out after a happening – having hardly any hair growing on her head now at all.

They sidled up. I glanced around. Where were those rich children? Where were the relatives? By the time the multitude reached her, Jotty still hadn't managed, in all her fumbles, to untie even a little scrap of Tom. As for himself, to this day, I couldn't get a gist as to whether he was aware of anything. Was he unconscious, or was he in that state where you can perfectly hear the bones cracking and perfectly feel the blows landing, and perfectly pick up every and all sensation and hear animals guffawing above you, but to anybody looking on, you're stone cold dead and gone.

They grabbed her and I hovered. One-foot-to-the-other-foot. Then back, one-foot-to-the-other-foot. I hopped and hopped and glanced and hesitated. Then I don't know what came over me for it hadn't come over me earlier but –

'Deer With Twixt Legs! Watch out!' I yelled.

That did it. They scattered. Me and Jotty and Tom Cusack and the hosiery girls were the only ones still present. Then the Well-Meanings arrived. Then the Cusacks arrived. Instead of guns, these men had fighting sticks. Oh, I beg your pardon. They had guns as well. They ran up and Angelus reached Tom and fell upon him and, between them, all the women managed to get him up and away from that lamp-post. The Well-Meanings then saw to Jotty, who was totally hysterical because of one Tom being dead and the second Tom maybe being dead, plus other people she was related to recently being dead, and all whilst the Cusack brothers crouched and scoured and pointed their guns and wouldn't turn their backs on anything. Cusack didn't die. I thought maybe you might want to know that. Turns out he wasn't even unconscious but, not to get too deep into conse-quences, it was said that afterwards he would jump at his own shadow and also at other shadows, and wouldn't let anybody, bar his wife and four brothers, near him for a long time.

I thought with all this distraction and with the Well-Meanings blocking her from me, and with her being in shock anyway, I'd be safe. I mean from Jotty. I mean from that thing she was wanting me to do. She stood up. She thanked the Well-Meanings, said she was grateful to the bitches for not holding the book disgrace against her. She seemed like she was growing sleepy. Then, seeing me, the wits snapped back and she dove over and took a hold once more.

Before I tell you about the coffin and her making of me to get involved in it, there's something else I need to reveal as well. It's about Jotty and another of those shadows. This one, so far, she hasn't got to grips with. If she doesn't get to grips with it soon it's going to destroy her. If it doesn't destroy her, she'll end up half-destroyed, along with her poor relatives in that place on the Hill.

Chapter Fifteen

For all her worry and hysteria about her missing niece and 'Where's Jane? Where's Jane?', with her disturbed mind taking over and making coffins out of everything – fridge? kitchen cupboard? washing machine? stereo? vacuum cleaner? egg-cups? thimbles? – I say hold on. How come Jotty hadn't been able to take on board that this teenager had been in danger when clearly, even before it was said she disappeared five years earlier, she had? Knowing Jane had such a man as Jotty's brother for a father, and knowing Jane had such a family of origin as descended from Jotty and John's and even Janet's family of origin, how come Jotty hadn't been taking protective action way before the 'missing' stage at all? Also, she had this other niece and nephew, Julie and Judas. You may have met them. She acts as if she hasn't. And she acts, too, as if she's never met her other nieces and nephews – the virginally conceived, mysteriously birthed, physically provided for but emotionally neglected children of her poor sisters. What was going on? How come that less than an hour earlier, during all that arresting and carrying out of dead bodies, Jotty hadn't noticed Jane's sister, Julie, on the hearth, half-strangled by her father, even though the girl was only inches from herself?

Are we back to this 'Not Knowing But Knowing' business?

278

For seven and a half years now Jotty had been in therapy and doing her best to pull herself to consciousness, whilst simultaneously trying her best to keep those mental curtains closed. This is normal. It takes as long as it takes. You might say, 'Heck, it didn't take me that long in therapy,' but someone else might counter with 'Yes, but patently you're not cured yet.' Anyway, how do you start something? And, anyway, how do you stop something? Residues of bits just keep clinging on. Your super-proneness to distort, to distrust, to dissociate, maybe even to multiple personality disorder if you're creative enough to do so, isn't really, in the long run, going to help matters. You can't throw out the baby with the bathwater and, by the way, 'baby with the bathwater' is a virulent little clue to the past spilling into the present right here.

But am I being unkind to Jotty specifically? After all, she wasn't the only one storing things in the space at the end of the space, stuffing unpleasant what-nots into mental kitchen cupboards. When it was first intimated Jane had disappeared, Jotty seemed to do what others did as well. She didn't notice. When she did notice, because the not-noticing was reaching red-alert proportions, she continued to do what most did even then. This was now to believe that her niece had gone off to live with relatives in some place so far away she may as well not have existed. But then, when some in the town started the rumour that perhaps Jane Doe hadn't left Tiptoe Floorboard, Jotty at first couldn't grapple with that piece of consciousness as well.

Until now.

Now she had started to question. First Janet. But Janet was impossible. Her answers struck Jotty as sinister jigsaw-puzzle parts.

'It was just blood,' she said. And she seemed to parrot this expression as if rehearsed, even though Jotty hadn't brought up the subject of blood with her. That was what she said when Jotty waylaid her with her Big Shopping coming out of the Almost Chemist of the Year. Waiting on the corner, Jotty got a hold and manoeuvred her sister-in-law-cum-cousin into one of the stationery-launderette-gunshops by way of imparting crucial newsreel information about a new virus that was circulating. Janet was startled but Jotty said John wouldn't catch it just so long as Janet took the proper precautions, which Jotty would give her as soon as she came along this way. So, luring the woman with promises of precautions, she got her into the gunshop and, once inside, pinned her into a corner and put it to her straight.

The effect upon Janet was similar to the effect of 'having it put to her straight' not that long afterwards. This was in court, when she was charged with being an accomplice, with conspiracy, with aiding and abetting, with accessory before, during and after, and with murder as well. It had been a highprofile case and the court had been packed, and outside the court had been packed also. Tension was high although, as far as Janet was concerned, the only odd thing about it was her sensation of feeling accused.

She frowned at the man. And was it that he was accusing her of omitting to admit to something? Charged with not preventing? All proven by way of false authenticity meetings, camera footage, evidence painstakingly collected via covert chitchat operations, tea and buns in gunshops and complicated wiretaps?

'Well, yes,' she said, rather exasperatedly. 'I already told you. Of course he came in with blood on his hands. But I thought he just had blood on his hands. I didn't know. I thought it was just blood, y'know, just blood, y'know. Blood.'

'Weren't you concerned when you saw this blood?'

Janet Doe shrugged. Her sister, Jetty, who had been having an affair with John, was at that moment glimpsed by Janet. She was sitting in the jury. Good God! Janet's mouth fell open. The cheek of the woman! To be sitting in judgement when look at the morals upon her! Janet was so overwhelmed by the unfairness of this discovery that she could only point in astonishment. There were moments of alarmed murmuring, bodyrustling, as counsel, press, guardsmen, guardswomen, gallery, everybody, even the jury tried to work out Janet's indications and dumbstruckness. Jetty Doe, however, remained poised and motionless. She sat in her chair – which seemed to encompass half of the jurist Mrs McGonigle's chair and half of the chair of the jurist Mr Strain beside it. She had been grinning at her sister and she continued to grin at her sister until, finally, the judge banged his gavel and warned everybody they'd better sit down at once. Janet was asked the question again. I mean about the blood. This time, both sisters shrugged.

But he was talking again. He was saying something now about the laundry, to which her sister, now up in the gallery, was making some very pronounced chuckling. How come the judge wasn't banging his wee stickie now?

'Wasn't like that,' Janet cried. 'It was ordinary. The lamps were on. It was cosy. The TV and the fridge and washing machines and vacuum cleaners and hairdryers and tick-tocks were on. It was all nice, apart from that entire racket, but that's the way he likes it, and when John's calm, I'm calm, and he was calm, until the murmurs of the neighbours next door.'

'You felt no inclination, no instinct? Female? Maternal? Human?' The man paused. He looked incredulous. He spread his hands, glanced at his jury, at his gallery. Jetty, still in the gallery, leaned forward and, when her body rose into the air until it was spread prone just above the heads of the people in the gallery, Janet saw her give this whippersnapper the fingers. She noticed, also, the whippersnapper pretended not to see that.

'The police, Janet Doe? The neighbours? For your own safety? For the safety of your children? You did not think to act as a mother, a citizen, a member of the ordinary decent human community? You informed nobody of your husband's activities over a period of—'

Janet shook her head.

One reason she shook it was her befuddlement as to why he was changing the picture. Second thing, she realised Jetty had been giving her the fingers and not him all along.

'Janet Doe,' the man persisted, 'your children—'

'They were losing their integrity,' she cried. 'They were starting not to come home.'

At this, Jetty Doe's body, which had sunk partially beneath the floorboards of the gallery, now rose, much more swiftly this time, again into the air. Janet, perching on her own chair, squinted as she watched this rapid phenomenon. 'What's she's doin' …?' she muttered. 'Why's she …?'

Jetty swooped down on her sister and Janet forgot the court, forgot the Martini fridge boy cross-examining her, forgot everybody who wasn't her sister. She let out a screech as she tried to back through her chair.

After much gavel-banging and 'Shut up! Shut up! Everybody shut up!' and guardspeople running over and Janet being ordered to sit down for she'd jumped up and was pointing to Mrs Asmoday, then Mr Cleave, then Mrs Fearon, no, Mr Legion, no, no, hold on. Just a minute. Where? Oh! She's gone! Janet did begin to sit down. But – *Guess who! Guess what! Guess who!* – that's right. She sat on top of Jetty. She saw the arms then come up and around from each side to envelop her, and that was when she screamed and spectacularly passed out.

But all that was in front. For now, she was upset and annoyed. This was at Jotty, not Jetty, because her sister-in-law was hemming her into this gunshop corner, and on false pretences. Turned out there was no dangerous virus going around after all.

She bulldozed her way out, shouting, 'Almost Chemist of the Year! Almost Chemist of the Year!' as her credentials for further protections and also as her final parting shot to the air.

As to Jane's sibling brother and sister, their Aunt Jotty couldn't, or wouldn't, go anywhere near them. One reason was because it was physically impossible. Julie and Judas didn't get their reputations for slip-sliding even the most determined person for nothing. Second reason was that, unconsciously, it was easier to ignore them. After all, might one of them be next to disappear?

Then there was Doe himself. She tried flattery. As you know, the man was pathologically susceptible to those who took an interest. His dicky stomach was your passport to anything you desired. Efforts had to be oblique, however. Patience had to be relied upon. 'Heard you were feeling poorly, John. I've got all day, so tell me about your bowel movements.' That was the tack utterly required here.

But it ended up as a disturbed state of conversation. Jotty, in going to the edge of obliquity – which was taking a risk of coming full circle and falling into directness – asked her brother in a sharp tone if it was stress he was feeling at all. John didn't notice she had just walked into his house when she hadn't walked into his house for many years previously. But he was delighted, most appreciative of her question. Yes, absolutely yes. Stress, Jotty, was what it was.

And off he went. Ramblings. You know ramblings. So did Jotty. Even before he started, she felt Early Onset Compassion Fatigue Syndrome set in. At great cost to her already not very integrated person, she listened as he launched into his neck being stiff with an incredible stiffness from a Dark Age cemetery – 'one of them stiffnesses, Jotty' – with Jotty thinking, who cares? Everybody hates you. Even your gang hates you. *Rub my belly with a lump of jelly, Mickey Mouse is dead!*

Her revulsion at his self-indulgence was threatening to prevent her keeping up the solicitude, which was why she had to slip into her childhood Mickey Mouse mantra. In the end, no matter how much she padded with incurable diseases and terminal illnesses, she didn't know how to broach Jane with John except by doing so full-on. The first few times of trying she went away, dizzy, without managing to get him to admit even to having an elder daughter. When she did confront directly, that had been in the bar, as you know, and if it hadn't been for Spaders rushing between them with 'I'll look after your sisters. I'll take your sisters home for you, Johnny,' she might have had it confirmed definitively – if at cost. So, something else to blame Tom Spaders for.

Since then, over the next five years, there had been her official attempts to get help from the authorities. Going through the proper channels – the hospitals, the hostels, the missing persons, the 'have there been accidents, have there been blackouts, has there been amnesia?', the circumstantial evidence and the anecdotal rumours, the listening at doors, the police, Citizens Advice, solicitors, Town Hall, the International Community, then back to Citizens Advice, back to solicitors, back to police, back to listening at doors – was undoubtedly taking its toll on her. Then there were the letters – 'Dear Your Township', 'Dear Your Lordshipnesses', 'Dear Your Ostensible

Figures of Sanity'. These were the ones she was sending. The red-taped, nicely packaged, vacuous 'Dear Madam, At the present time' letters she received in response were knocking her, by the end, to the floor.

It was only after she'd exhausted all the proper channels, with her mental state now impressing upon her how someone could easily be hidden behind a cushion, squashed into a teapot, put in ridiculously small boxes, spaces getting tighter and tighter, that her head felt about to explode with all the hypotheticals she was doing on herself. It got to the point of her lying in bed at night, feeling there was nothing for it but that she herself should go and dig up that coffin. And that was when the idea came to be seen as a viable option. That was when, too, she decided to see me.

At first I tried to reason. If she goes and digs up a coffin, I said, it would only put her down in history as the last of the Great Mad Does. By now her sisters, and indeed all her brothers and even her parents, were in jail, in graves, or in that mental asylum. She had turned into a half-portion, and soon, similarly to poor Janine, would be going to Greystone Cliff for top-ups herself. That was slightly in the future and I felt it best not to frighten her, on top of her already fear, by revealing such a truth to her. But to try to prevent the half-portion from developing into a full portion – I mean in the wrong direction – I suggested she send another strictly worded letter to the Town Hall. She looked tired, unconvinced, like maybe I was being tactless. Ignoring my advice, she harped on again about me coming that evening to help dig it up.

Now, we all like to think we'd have done it differently. We'd have done it morally. We'd have done it sensibly. We are the people who say, 'It's simple, really. All you need to do is this, this, this, this and this.' Well, that's your call. That's entirely your life you're living. I did help her. So I suppose that means you'll be sitting in your armchairs passing judgement upon me now.

When I met her that evening by the plot of the three graves, I was still protesting that it was outside my jurisdiction. But then one of those situations took over where you say, 'Oh, I can't give up tea. I can't give up coffee. I can't give up alcohol. I can't give up cigarettes. I can't give up violence. I can't give up delicious nasty gossip. I can't give up making lists, saying prayers, short-handing the prayers so I can fit in more prayers. I can't give up Noises. Can't give up fantasy relationships. Can't give up having no sex. Can't give up sadomasochistic sex. Can't give up torturing and killing little animals.' It seems you think you can't give up anything but – in paradox to all that knotted and tangled wool – guess what? Miraculously, one day you do. It's that part of you again. I mean the part that does what it likes, that presumes to act on its own initiative without informing you of it, the bit that doesn't believe in interactive goodwill or in mutual co-operation. Instead it goes unannounced into the Blueprint in the dead of night while you're snoring, and it breaks open all the 'Do Not Tamper' boxes and changes all the rules around.

I thought I was immune to that.

I can't understand why I'm not immune to that.

We didn't do it, by the way – dig it up, I mean.

I used my powers instead.

Thing is, I didn't have to use them because there's this other shadow side to Jotty as I was saying but haven't told you about yet. It's that there is no Jane. Jotty Doe made Jane up.

I think you must have guessed that. And I mean in spite of Janet being charged with the murder of a daughter who had never existed, and of the Ordinary Decent Folk spreading rumours, first about a girl going to Australia, and then about a girl who had never left town at all. 'Contrary to appearances …' was what they whispered but, you see, there weren't any appearances. As I've tried to impress from the beginning, rumours and only rumours were the *lingua franca* of this town. Julie and Judas crying at the graves you might muster as an attempt at proving the substantiality of the death of their elder sister. Well, for all we know, maybe those children were developing their own psychoses. After all, how do you think you'd start behaving if your daddy kept burying your granny, once a month, over and over, in different places, for years?

So it was all rumour. All conjecture. All anecdotal. There was no Jane Doe. That doesn't mean, though, there hadn't ever been anybody. Remember. Cast your mind back. Do you recall Jotty had that long menstruation once?

If that little visitor whom she'd conceived hadn't been taken away, he – for it had been a 'he' – would have been nineteen now. Five years earlier he would have been the same age as fictitious Jane when it was put about that she had disappeared. More crucially, he'd also have been the same age as Jotty, I mean when she'd been taken up to that master bedroom – believing, as she had been taken, that Mamma and Aunty, just in the kitchen there, would never let this happen. Mamma and Aunty, however, had got into such an animated conversation all of a sudden about some very engrossing interesting thing that, still talking, one put on the teapot, while the other quickly crossed the kitchen and shut the kitchen door.

I looked in anyway, I mean the coffin, 'cos I was feeling, well, I'm not the one to be revealing this truth to her, so I humoured her, thinking that when she got to a certain level in the silence of her therapy, her unconscious would probably reveal the truth to her itself. That could be now – what with the domino effect of the Sisters, and with Janine being taken away, then the batches of nieces and nephews running about the area whom she didn't feel adult enough to round up and take care of, then those murders being solved with her own brother being responsible for them, then with Tom Cusack suffering that lynch reaction, then John being dead, Jetty being dead, Tom Spaders being dead – so, yes, maybe the time had come when the truth would crack open upon her now.

Of course there would be nothing in it. The coffin. Just another mother fantasy. I closed my eyes, imaged the circle – and there was something in it. I was wrong.

'Well?' said Jotty. 'Is she there or not?'

I was hoping it would be nothing. Or else some irrelevant thing. Or maybe, if it had to be relevant – as in painful – it would be one of those poor pet dogs or stolen turtles or giant Madagascar poodle beetles he'd dragged out of the house and up the hill with his rifle for their final walks. When I saw what it was, however, the expression came to me that you always come across in those gripping 'Business Management Skills' books – 'Whenever possible,' they state, 'kill two birds with one stone.'

Although, as you know, he didn't make bombs, John Doe had buried a coffin full of bomb material. And not only *that* coffin. As far as I could gauge, other flamboyantly buried fantasy funerals had things warlike stuffed in every nook and cranny as well. We're talking booster charges, fuses, gun cotton, plastic bottles, nails, bolts, brass nuts, control knobs, empty fire extinguishers, magnets, watch primers, Co-op mixes, receivers, transmitters, carbon fibre aerials, Superglue, easy-take-apart two-wheeler shopping trolleys, timers, detonators, remotecontrolled devices, cluster bomblets, pieces of paper with 'Go', 'Stop' and 'Get Ready, Get Steady' written on in pen, old rags, milkbottles, beerbottles, consignments of empty coffee jars, sugar hooks, salt hooks, black tape, bell wire, pink rubber gloves, something primed in a glove compartment, other spare glove compartments, nylon masks, black leather gloves, stacks of beautifully ironed black trousers and stacks of pretty trimmed black skirts, well-shiny shoes, six-inch stilettos, black berets, lipstick, wigs, dark glasses, makeup compacts, red nail polish – *looking good, oh, looking good!* – baseball bats when nobody ever played baseball, a few rounds of ammunition and – why ever not? – a handgun in each and every coffin as well.

What had been going on?

For the simple reason of wanting to make an impression – something we might all like – Doe had taken a very high-handed route to fulfilling this desire. He had intercepted all those covert deliveries, not because he wanted them. 'Course not. Hardly art. Load of junk, he thought. Best to take them, though, he decided, so the Fifth Faction, the war faction, couldn't have them, and he did, straight to his own house. He disseminated them in and around various cabinets, cupboards, settees, armchairs, under dressing tables, inside suits of armour, and when he ran out of space in his house, naturally they went into the tunnels underneath. After the tunnels were packed, he took to burying them elsewhere. First place that occurred was the graveyard east of the town. It was more or less his anyway for, after all, his father and countless of his mothers were buried in it. That's how come the materials were in a fair majority of the graves. Of course, he didn't actually reveal to Group Faction Number Five that he was the one lording it over them. He was undoubtedly compulsive, delusional and self-sabotaging but, so far, he hadn't been as suicidal as all that. After a while it occurred to him that, to save time and to make sure he remained centre stage – even if clandestinely – why didn't he combine his grief days with burying all the coveted material in the coffins at the same time?

Poor Doe. He had been throwing a spanner in his own works, into his own empire, one that he had set up and been lovingly cultivating for years. He had started to destroy it, and all on account of his growing manic obsessive uncontrollable behaviour. Could he not have got a simple prescription from the doctor to stem the likes of that? Pointless, too, the whole exercise. So what if he out-bested the Fifth by getting himself killed before any of them were able to kill him? There's no doubt about it. The man had been possessed of the hugest capacity for cutting off his nose to spite his face that ever was.

'You're not lying to me, are you?' said Jotty. This was after I told her there was nobody in it. 'Tell me you're not lying to me.'

'I'm not lying to you,' I said, and Jotty exhaled her relief.

'She isn't there!' she cried. 'Oh, Jane's run away! She really isn't there!'

She let herself have that respite, before the other, the usual, the one where he had killed her, came back.

'You must go to the Interfering Outside Foreign Policeman,' I urged.

'Can't,' she said. 'Those other police won't let me. Besides, I don't think he exists.'

''Course he exists.' I was shocked. 'He's here – straightening rumours, arresting groupings, ordering police officer suspensions and calling for deep-seated enquiries. He's instigated – haven't you noticed? – those dedicated teams of community gang specialists, experts on gang strategy, eminences on gang idolatry. He has Behaviour Support Teams on every corner. The man's so into precision, Jotty, you could cut cookies with him. Go to him. He's the only show in town.

'As a tip,' I then said, 'you might find it easier to approach him via the Salsa Dancing Policeman, who is more the human, as opposed to the guffawing, side of the police in this town.

'Go see him first,' I persisted. 'How about this morning, at a quarter past six on the dot?'

I recommended she do this because he was so contemporary, this Salsa, so 'of-the-minute', that he liked to try out new things and at present was into breakfasting *alfresco* at one or other of the town's eating places. This morning, I told her, he'd be having croissants and espressos on the patio of that new café – solely a café – opposite the Leprechaun Museum.

'So, Jot,' I said, 'go home. Get washed, get changed and, if you can, do your hair and put on lipstick.' I held up my hand for I could see the bristles coming out on her at once.

'There's such a thing as having the form without having the substance, Jot,' I continued. 'And then there's the form along with the substance. All I'm doing is suggesting you honour your body while you're in it. It doesn't mean you're betraying it. It means, in fact, the opposite, so don't shout at me when I tell you that your body knows: *When you get it right down there'* – I pointed to her groin – *'it'll come right'* – I pointed to her head – *'up there'.*

I left her then, in bristling mode because of the hair suggestion and the lipstick suggestion and the putting on of fresh clothes suggestion and, most especially, her 'all you need is a good fuck' misinterpretation of my 'fixing it down there' remark.

That's because she can't remember. She doesn't know any of it, doesn't remember any of it. I mean about the baby. All she knows is that she's having these mounting anxieties about this girl – *oh, very important, but why won't anyone listen to her?* – about this girl having gone missing, and about herself feeling desire when she doesn't, in all truth, actually know what desire is. How could he love her and want her? How could she let him, any of them, love her and want her? How could she imagine that he could desire her, that she could be his person, that he could be her person, with all those ravenous Fathers getting in the way? That was why she was in the Blueprint, stuck in that Blueprint – worried, so worried, terribly worried, that Jane, poor niece, had been raped and battered, brutally murdered, with nobody giving a damn or caring as to her whereabouts. Further distress was that she herself was remembering less of what this girl looked like. Oh, suddenly thought Jotty. Might Jane – because of the genes in the family – have looked something like Jotty herself?

'Besides,' I remembered, calling back to her, 'it's not just yourself you'll be helping.' And that was when I told her Tom Spaders was still alive.

And that was it. I could hardly get out my final 'Goodbye, I'm going now – look, I'm really going now', for there she was, rushing off herself. She was going to groom up – in a hurried, panicked, falling-over-her-feet fashion as usual – to go and see the Salsa Dancing Policemen, all on the tail of this resurrection of Tom. I said, 'Goodbye,' to the air and the surrounding molecules anyway, and headed towards the town's pedestrian exit. Almost immediately, I passed the new café where, in an hour and a bit, Jotty would be treated to breakfast by the Salsa. He would be standing on the steps telepathically waiting for her. And they would help her, those two, and they'd help with two things. One was that they were not going to find Jane Doe, as in the dead or alive niece of Jotty Doe, and reunite her with her family. But they would help in the removal of the sequence, for Jotty would have it brought to her consciousness after they had instigated enquiries that there was not, and never had been, any Jane Doe. Further, they'd let her know that the girl she was yearning to mourn was an ethereal construction made up of at least two people. One was herself and the other was her son.

The doubt would be removed then, and that was the big thing – whether or not she ever met this son – for it's the knowing and the not-knowing that really prolongs the damage. Along with her acceptance that there was no niece, and greatly helped, of course, by the silence of her therapy, these two policemen, via their many conversations with her, were going to lift her out of her half-portion state.

Then they'd help with Tom. As you know, poor Tom Spaders, because of the cast-iron rumours in the town, had already been labelled as the worst of the world's mass murderers. This 'fact' had been entered in the Town Hall register of 'Births, Deaths and Rumours That Are Probably True'. Once something like that gets a hold, the person on the receiving end is in a lot of trouble. In Tom's case – unless someone of the right power challenged all this falsity – he was going to be charged with the rumour versions and not with reality at all.

Fortunately for Tom, the Interfering Policeman was already suspicious of this Town Hall register. To prove the truth against it, he had had top Anti-Rumour Advisers flown in to dissect it minutely. So Tom's sentencing would, in the end, reflect that his Psycho-Spatial had not generally been out and about, doing damage, hatching and plotting, murdering and kidnapping, unaccompanied or not by the rest of his dimensional bodies, which was more than could be said for many Psycho-Spatials currently operating in the town.

I passed by the museum then, and came to Tom's gunshop. The door had been busted, courtesy of Johnjoe, with makeshift planks now nailed hurriedly over the top. Tom had intended fixing it properly, after he'd taken what turned out to be that fateful walk in order to have his head showered. That meant, of course, it would be Jotty, and not Tom, dealing with the door now.

'But, my love,' I heard her say, for most certainly, and most importantly, she and Tom would help each other also, 'don't be thinking it has to be just women's underwear. I wouldn't be averse to selling …' and I looked, and there they were, outside the shop, her squeezing his arm, and it was now five years later. The gunshop, as you know, had been transformed into the bra shop and they were now in their forties, with Tom just released from prison. He seemed acquiescent, or at least not resistant, but what was he going to do, I wondered, to express his side of his own enterprise now?

And now there was everybody – Tom and Jot, and the Cusacks, and a few of the Cusack brothers, and a couple of Jotty's nieces and nephews, I mean the denied children of her poor sisters. One of them, a teenage boy, was trying to change the 'ding!' on the door to something a bit catchy, and a teenage girl, an apprentice to her Aunt Jotty, was learning rapidly that a job is never just about the job, 'And when it is, Lisa darling, you must leave'. There were also a few Well-Meanings, and even that taxi man. Do you remember that taxi man? He had a lot of money now because of Napoleon. 'Napoleon's balls would be worth a lot of money,' some antique ammunitions man had gone up to him not long after his 'witness who didn't know guns' court appearance and said. JimmyJesus had turned up too, and what a cheek, and at his age, for he had done so in order to extort money. John Doe hadn't killed him, as you see, and besides, the Angel of Death hadn't left with three babies. She'd left with two babies, leaving him lying wounded over his suitcase in the hall.

So now, all these years on, he had turned up unexpectedly. He had heard Tom and the others were planning to conjoin and expand their businesses together, so he reckoned there might be a little packet of pickings in it for him. When he appeared, though, and started threatening, he sounded silly and embarrassing and terribly old-fashioned that the others didn't know whether to laugh at him or feel sorry for him. In the end, the Almost Chemist of the Year man, who was now a Tool-Shed-First-Aid-Shop man, offered him a job.

And that's the thing, see. The tables had turned. It was a new social order and no longer about that old aberration 'Give me all your money' – for people always think it's about money when they don't know what it's about. The Interfering Foreign Policeman had done his neutralising work and, by now, had left Tiptoe Floorboard. Even the Fifth Faction, which had made up the six war factions as you know, had now dispersed and disbanded all their units. They had jumped on to the media spokespeople bandwagon and were often to be seen giving syndicated history interviews on the TV.

Julie was there too, though now it was twenty-five years later. She was passing a baby she had been holding over to Jotty and Tom. But no. This was not her baby. And it was not Tom and Jotty's baby. It was the baby of her brother Judas and the mascot. Judas had married the mascot of the Community Centre in spite of neither of them being in love with the other, and also in spite of officially being warned against doing so by that list at the Town Hall. Judas still lived in the family home, which had been diagnosed long ago with Sick Building Syndrome. He had also started following in a few of his father's footsteps, inasmuch as he would take his little dogs, with his gun, for walks of an evening, coming back down the mountain later, all alone. When confronted, which his father had never been, he'd say that each of these pets, one after the other, had run away or met with some fatal accident. So when this baby arrived, everybody – instantly and unofficially – became her mother or her father. 'Another little thing,' they murmured. 'But we'd better, we think, keep our eye on this one.'

I left them. I carried on out to the Tiptoe Floorboard Fourth Dimension Boundary, and stepped over to the sound of them discussing – through various shifting time eras – their future plans. They threw themselves into these meetings – on strategy, on returns, on investments and on one hundred per cent projections then, full of enthusiasm, they began to knock down walls. Some shops naturally slipped into other shops, whilst others, like Jotty's Bra Shop and Tom's Toolmaster-Chuck-Key-Precision-Laser-Oiler Shop preferred a slight adjacency. But guess what. You could have knocked me down with a feather, had I not already been dematerialising, at the rush of 'New Free Trial!' Emotional Word Centres, unashamedly popping up amidst all these multiplications overground.

ACKNOWLEDGEMENTS

Thanks to friends Clare Dimond and James Smith for their support, kindness and generosity. Please know, you two, I couldn't have done this without you.

Thanks to Magdalen Jebb, the best example of grace I know. It meant a lot to me, Magdalen, that you listened to me speak about issues, initially peripheral or even outside my book, which later came deeply to infuse it. Your gentle support and comments – always insightful, always kind – were very much appreciated by me.

Thanks to Sue Gee for letting me finish my book in her beautiful, tranquil house. Putting that last full stop in your little office, Sue, with your books surrounding, and with the tree and the daffodils and even the little washing-line outside, was very satisfying. Thank you for the peacefulness of that.

For their invaluable support I also thank Philip Gwyn Jones, Drue Heinz and all her staff at Hawthornden Castle, the Oppenheim-John Downes Memorial Trust, the British Arts Council (South West), Ian Whitfield at the Scottish Arts Council, Jon Butler, Jyl Fountain, Laetitia Kelly, Jenny and Ron Swash, Deborah White, Margaret Buckley, Dr Georgia Lepper, Dr Sarah North, Astrid Fuhrmeister, Pixie and Richard Greathead, Barbie Lyon, Rachel Hazell. Thanks, everybody. Everything offered was of tremendous help to me.

ANNA BURNS was born in Belfast, Northern Ireland. She is the author of three novels, including *Milkman* and *No Bones*, and of the novella *Mostly Hero*. She has won the Man Booker Prize, the National Book Critics Circle Award, and the Winifred Holtby Memorial Prize, and has been shortlisted for the Women's Prize for Fiction and the Orange Prize. She lives in East Sussex, England.

The text of *Little Constructions* is set in Minion.
Composition by Palimpsest Book Production Limited.
Manufactured by McNaughton & Gunn on acid-free,
30 percent postconsumer wastepaper.